# THROUGH THE
# FIRE

## MKP

THROUGH THE FIRE

ISBN-13: 978-1-61317-192-9 (ebook)

ISBN 13: 978-1-83557-013-5 (print)

Grateful acknowledgement is made for permission to reprint lyrics from "Face It" by Kansas. Courtesy of John Elefante.

Cover Art & Design: Midjourney, Miz Kit Productions, & so much guilt

*How many times do I have to tell you*
*That things just can't go on this way*
*We've tried so many times but things go on the same*
*We've spent one too many years in all this pain*

— KANSAS, "FACE IT"

*For Kate Sheehy*
*(obviously)*

# THROUGH THE
# FIRE

# C.E. MURPHY

a miz kit production

# CHAPTER 1

*DAD'S DEAD. YOU PROBABLY DON'T CARE, BUT THE FUNERAL IS Friday.*

The text carried the same body blow every time Nick read it. Both the news and the sheer assholery of the delivery. Punch to the gut, followed by a groin shot. Enough to make him sick. The phone had fallen out of his cold hands when the message first came in. Tyler, his roommate—wide-shouldered, dark-skinned, with a handful of dreads caught in a band and the rest falling free—picked it up, read it, and handed it back. "So your brother's a dick. Need a lift home?"

"Yeah." Nick hadn't said a whole lot else since. Tyler called Stephanie for him, because he didn't seem to be able to do it himself. She met them at the truck less than an hour later. Ty drove, while Nick and Steph sat in the back, Nick alternating between staring at the message and out the window. Eighteen hours between San Fran and north-east Colorado, a stone's throw away from the Nebraska border.

"There's nothing fucking out here," Ty said at one point. "Like a million miles of nothing."

"Yeah, that's kind of the appeal."

"I thought your dad was a bounty hunter," Ty objected. "Don't you have to be, like, near people to hunt them?"

Stephanie said, "Shut up, Ty," but Nick shrugged.

"You go where the hunt takes you, that's all. It's okay," he said to Steph, more quietly.

"You don't like talking about it."

"Yeah, well, I don't like my dad being dead either, but here we are."

Stephanie inhaled sharply but said nothing. Nick looked out the windows again, tension thinning his lips and flaring his nostrils. It took a minute to say, "Sorry."

"It's all right." Her hand, warm around his, squeezed.

Nick risked a look at her. She hadn't slept much. Shadows marred her dark, concerned eyes and made the gold-brown depths of her skin look sallow. Her loosely curling hair, usually worn down, was back in a severe ponytail that made her look worried. He tried to offer a more apologetic, or reassuring smile, and knew it didn't work. "It's not, but thanks."

She nodded, and Nick turned his attention out the window again, then almost immediately pulled his phone out to stare at it. He'd texted Chris back after he didn't know how many hours. *You okay?*

*Not really,* had come back faster than he'd expected. *You?*
*No.*

No answer since then. No asking if Nick was coming to the funeral. No information on what had happened. Just '*not really*', which—honestly—was more of an admission than he'd expected out of his older brother.

Nick had already been on the road, but if he hadn't been, that would have been enough to bring him home.

"Turn here," he said to Tyler. The north-eastern corner of Colorado didn't have much going for it: wide roads, repetitive views, and a wind that came from every direction at once. Dry snow blew in gusts across the road, although it was surprisingly thin on the ground, for March. They'd passed through Sterling, close to the state border. It had looked like nobody had even needed to bother with snow plows that year.

"This is south," Ty objected. "Didn't we just spend a long time driving north coming the other way?"

Nick chuckled, barely a breath of sound, but still, the first laugh since he'd gotten his brother's text. "Yeah, but you can't get here from there."

"This is a 4x4, my dude. I can get anywhere."

"Tell that to the bison."

Tyler flashed a quick wide-eyed look in the mirror and took the rest of Nick's directions without complaint.

"Hey." Steph smoothed her thumb over the back of Nick's hand. "You're tensing up, babe. Are we almost there?"

Nick tried to loosen the strain in his hands, but it came from his neck and shoulders, coursing through him. As soon as he shook it out, it seeped back in. "Another couple miles."

"You haven't been home since you left for college, have you." Steph knew the answer, but Nick appreciated the effort to distract him, so he nodded.

"Three years. Almost four now, I guess. I left as soon as I graduated high school." His brother had been hurt. Their dad had been furious.

He hadn't seen the old man since.

His stomach clenched and he closed his eyes, jaw rigid to keep tears from coming. Stephanie squeezed his hand more tightly, but she didn't know what to say. Nick didn't know what she should say, either. There wasn't anything *to* say, except, "Left up here," to Ty.

The bumps in the road were still familiar. A pothole that had gotten worse with time; a sharp dip that he'd loved as a kid because it left his stomach behind. Asphalt turned to gravel and Nick swore he knew the exact rock that pinged from beneath the tires to hit the truck's undercarriage. Without opening his eyes, he said, "Left again at the next chance," and felt the back tire sink into a divot that could drag a whole car down, if it had been snowing.

They turned, and a minute later Ty said, "Nick?" uncertainly, which told Nick he was home. He sat there a few seconds, eyes still closed, then unlocked his jaw, forcing himself to speak.

"Just…gimme a minute, okay? Just…stay in the truck a minute?"

"Yeah," Stephanie said quietly. "Yeah, of course, babe." Tyler started to protest, and she kicked the back of his seat as Nick got out of the truck. From the corner of his eye, he saw her crawl into the front seat as he walked past the truck toward a familiar scene, surreal only because this time it was *his* dad who'd died.

A few dozen trucks and other big vehicles were parked in a loose circle on the prairie, half or more of them with their headlights on. About as many people were gathered around the funeral pyre that the headlights illuminated. It stood tall and stark, stacked high with dry wood. Nick could see, but couldn't look at, a body wrapped in white at the top of the pyre. A few people turned his way as he approached, all familiar faces. Mostly older, mostly male, mostly white, all with a rugged or hard edge to them, all with skinny long shadows thrown by the headlights that lit the scene. Some of their faces softened as they recognized him. One or two gazes widened as they looked again, either at Nick, or into the small crowd around the pyre.

Beer and harder alcohol were being passed around, and the tremendous empty night sky swallowed most of the low voices anyway, but as people recognized him, silence was traded like the booze, until the last voice was a familiar one, putting on an air of *hail all and good cheer* that exhausted Nick just to hear. The silence got to even that voice, though, and the crowd made way as the speaker turned to see what was going on.

Nick's big brother had gotten shorter, somehow. Otherwise Chris looked like himself, hair cut brush-short, jaw as

4

tension-lined as Nick's own, a bottle in one hand and a forced cock-of-the-walk grin smeared across his features.

His face crumpled for a heartbeat when he saw Nick, relief and disbelief crushed instantly by the return of the forced smile. "Ayyyyyy, there's my little brother. Jesus, Nicky, you got tall."

"Nah, man." Nick's throat felt thick, like the words couldn't find their way out. "You got short."

"I can still kick your ass. C'mon, bring it in, big guy." Chris gestured and the gathered mourners took another step back as Nick crashed awkwardly into his brother's unfamiliar hug.

For a minute the world vanished. Why Nick had come wasn't real anymore, what had happened before he left disappeared, everything he'd done since then didn't matter. Chris's hug was as tight as iron bands, which all by itself told Nick how bad things were, but it didn't matter. For a whole minute, he held on, and Chris didn't even try to let go. Then, his voice deep and rough, Chris said, "Aight," quietly into Nick's shoulder. "Aight." He released him, pounding on his back, and handed the bottle in his hand over to him. "Drink up, buddy. No way I'm doing this sober." Chris's gaze skittered to the truck behind Nick. "You brought company?"

"They brought me. My, ah, my roommate and my girlfriend, they drove me up. I couldn't get here fast enough otherwise."

That douchebag grin slid across Chris's face again and he punched Nick's shoulder hard enough to hurt. "Seriously, a girlfriend? You? Is she hot?"

"Don't be a dick, Chris."

"So she's hot." Chris lifted his chin toward the truck, and the doors opened, Stephanie and Tyler climbing down from opposite sides. "Damn, she is hot! What's her name?"

"Stephanie. Chris, don't—"

Chris had already walked forward, offering a hand. "Hi,

Stephanie. I don't know what you see in him, but I gotta say, my little brother's got good taste in women. Chris Cassidy. Nice to meet you."

Stephanie glanced at Nick. He could see her reeling back half a dozen sharp comments and choosing to say, "Stephanie Moreno. I'm sorry for your loss."

"Yeah." Chris's voice went rough. "Me too. Chris," he said to Tyler, who shook his hand in return.

"Ty Jones. Sorry about your dad."

"Yeah," Chris said again. "Me too. Thanks for bringing Nicky home."

"No problem." Just like Stephanie had done, Tyler glanced at Nick and just as obviously decided not to say something pointed. "'Nicky', huh?"

"Don't," Nick said. "Just don't."

Tyler's grin, much like Chris's but in a darker face, flashed. "I'll give you tonight."

"We can go," Stephanie said, a little sharply. "We'll go, if you want us to, Nick. We didn't know your dad."

"No, it's okay. I'd like you to stay, if it's not too weird."

"There's a Viking funeral pyre over there," Tyler hissed. "It's super weird and totally cool. We're staying."

Stephanie started, "Tyler, I swear to god," but Chris gave a big hard laugh that interrupted her.

"Cool. Yeah, totally cool. Guess you didn't tell them much about the family business." He took Nick's beer bottle back and walked away, leaving Nick standing between his bewildered friends and enduring the hard, sympathetic looks from his dad's friends.

Tyler's whisper would have made a librarian scold him. "What's that supposed to mean?"

Stephanie elbowed him hard enough to make him grunt as Nick shook his head. "I'll explain it later."

"No, you won't."

Nick turned his head toward Ty, knowing his gaze was

tired and blank with incomprehension. "You never explain anything," Tyler said. "Especially when you say it that way."

"Jesus, Ty, this isn't the time." Stephanie put her hand in Nick's, glancing around at the older men and women who were slowly turning back to their own conversations and drinks. "You don't have any friends here?"

"I've got you." Nick managed a smile that didn't touch his eyes, but Stephanie's answering smile appreciated the effort. "No, we didn't have a lot of fr—*Dayton*." Even he couldn't mistake the relief in his own voice as a young white woman about his age came around from the far side of the pyre. "We didn't have a lot of friends our age," he told Stephanie, truthfully, "but Day is one of them. Dayton," he said again, as the blonde girl shouldered through the gathering and slammed into his arms. "I'm glad you're here, Day."

"I'm glad *you* are." Dayton hadn't shrunk any more than Chris had, but she seemed a lot smaller than the last time Nick had seen her. She'd always been little, though, and wore it like an open wound. "Chris didn't think you'd come. Hi. I'm Dayton, yes, my middle name is Ohio, yes, whatever terrible reason you're thinking for naming a kid that is probably pretty close to right." She stuck her hand out to Stephanie, whose smile brightened again.

"Nick's mentioned you. I'm Stephanie. This is Tyler. I'm sorry for your loss."

"Hell of a family reunion to introduce you to. Shy and Jake are here," she told Nick. "Chris is waiting on Dakota before he lights up." She scowled over her shoulder through the cold night. "Well, before he lights up the pyre, anyway. He's pretty lit himself already." She turned back and punched Tyler's arm. "You guys want a drink? There's beer, there's Jack, there's a goddamn bucket of moonshine if you want it."

"Moonshine?" Tyler's voice cracked with interest. "Seriously?"

"One cup of hooch coming up. Stephanie? Nick?"

Stephanie shook her head and Nick wavered, then bared his teeth. "I think I could use a beer."

"Gimme a minute." Dayton slipped off again, her hair bright in the darkness until she disappeared around the pyre.

"She's...not what I expected," Stephanie said after a moment. "Smaller. Cuter. Angrier? She's mad at your brother, isn't she?"

"Day's been mad at Chris for most of our lives. She used to have a thing for him."

"I can see why that would make somebody mad," Tyler said. "Dayton? Dakota? What, you only know women with place names?"

"It gets worse," Nick said with a faint smile. "Shy's full name is Cheyenne. I don't know, it was a thing around here twenty years ago, I guess."

"You really gonna light that thing on fire?" Tyler asked. "Like, Viking funeral shit? What's that about?"

"Tradition."

"Man, your last name is Cassidy, not, like...Ericson or something. Cassidy isn't Nordic, is it?"

"No, it's just...I don't know, my family's been doing it as long as I can remember. There was a big pyre when my grandpa died. I don't remember my mom's."

*That* left a gap in the conversation wide enough to drive a couple of the idling trucks through. After a few seconds Ty muttered, "Fuck. Shit, man, I'm sorry. I didn't think about this meaning you were, like, an orphan now."

Nick barked a short, hard laugh. "I'm not, as long as Chris is around."

"I thought he was your brother." Tyler, for once, almost shut up before he'd finished speaking, the last words coming out in a mumble as Stephanie gave him another, bug-eyed, hard stare.

"He is. He still pretty much raised me. Lemme tell you, it's great, having your big brother and your de facto dad being the same guy." Nick stopped himself, eyes and teeth both clenched, then said, "Look, can we just...not, right now? I really...can't."

"Yeah." Ty still sounded genuinely apologetic. "Yeah, sorry, man. Want me to, uh..." He glanced around in search of something useful he could do as Dayton came swinging back around the pyre with a couple of bottles and a red plastic cup in hand. Nick took one of the bottles, sniffed it to make sure it was beer, then took a swig. Tyler took a large swallow of the red cup and didn't so much wheeze at the shine's strength as sit like a pole-axed ox. From the ground, he said, "Fuck," and took a more cautious swallow that did make him wheeze. "Jesus fuck."

"Yeah." Nick snickered. "That works. I want you to do that. Sit down and drink."

"My ass is already half froze," Tyler announced. "Also I may be inebriated."

"You said Shy and Jake were here?" Nick asked Dayton. "Do they, uh."

"Want to see you? Yeah, you're not persona non grata to them, regardless of what Chris says. You okay there, big guy?" Dayton said that to Tyler, then frowned up at Nick. "Except I guess you're kind of the big guy now."

"I'm good," Tyler said. "I can definitely stand up on my own. No problem. I just...don't want to."

"Go see your friends," Stephanie said wryly. "I'll keep an eye on Ty for a bit."

Nick whispered, "You're the best," and dipped his head to press his forehead against hers. She stole a kiss, murmured, "I am, and don't you forget it," then shooed him off before putting a hand under Ty's elbow to lever him up from the frozen earth.

Dayton, obviously not concerned with Steph overhearing, said, "She seems pretty cool," no more than two steps away.

"She is. Seriously, though, Day...how's Chris?"

"Fucking awful. He misses you like you're his lungs or something, and he's been holding himself together with baling wire and booze since your dad died. Are you back for good?"

"What? No. I've got school to get back to, Day, I've got mid-terms and I'm starting med school this fall."

Dayton's grunt sounded like a lifetime of judgment wrapped up in one short sound. Nick necked the beer before they got around the far side of the pyre and wished he'd had another one when he rounded its corner. His brother looked drunker than he had two minutes ago, although Nick thought the greeting then had been the performance, and this was Chris's real state.

The Black woman he leaned on was nearly as tall as Chris even without the shit-stomping boots that laced all the way up to just beneath her knees. She also wore her thick curled hair tied up in a poof that added four inches to her height. The harsh lighting sharpened her cheekbones to blades, and her jaw stuck out like she was waiting for somebody to punch it.

She was a paramedic, and intoxicated people tried, not infrequently. They almost never succeeded.

The other one, a broad-shouldered white guy, had shoulder-length hair that looked like a film team was always tending to it. He'd always been shorter than the other two, but he was also a lot smaller than Nick remembered.

Everybody was shorter than he remembered.

Cheyenne said, "Fucking hell, Nick," and let go of Chris to come hug him. "When'd you sprout another three inches?"

"I don't know what everybody's complaining about," he said hoarsely, into her shoulder. She smelled like cloves and wood smoke. "It's not even an inch a year since I've been gone. You look good, Shy."

"I always look good. You look like shit." Cheyenne let him go and gave him an appraising once-over followed by a sharp glance at Chris before her black-eyed gaze came back to Nick.

He got it. If he looked like shit, then Chris looked like the bowels of hell. Shy always had been good at expressing things with a couple of cutting glances.

Dayton took over holding Chris up when Jake released him and came in for a hug, too. "Nick." He wasn't just shorter than Nick remembered. His voice had deepened, an always-rough edge in it turning to a burr. "Glad you're home, man."

"Me too. What—" Nick's voice broke and he stopped the question before it went any farther.

Jake's eyebrows drew down as he pulled back from the hug. "What, what?" Barely a heartbeat passed before he figured it out. "He didn't tell you? *Jesus*, Chris—"

"I didn't think he'd care!" Belligerent intoxication, then sulky defensiveness, filled the words. "I didn't think he'd come home."

Nick, quietly, said, "It's all right," to Jake, whose eyes all but disappeared under the depth of his frown. "Seriously," Nick said, still quietly. "It's okay. C'mere, Day, let me do that, Chris weighs twice as much as you do."

Dayton and Chris, both equally offended, said, "Nuh-*uh*," and earned a soft chuckle from the others. Nick stepped in anyway, taking Dayton's place in supporting Chris.

Chris didn't sober up instantly, but he suddenly was able to take his own weight and keep his own balance. "Forget it, Nicky. I'm good."

"Yeah. I know. Just like always." Leaning on friends came hard enough to Chris. Leaning on Nick, figuratively or literally, went beyond the pale. Some things in the universe were constants. The sun rose, the sun set, and little brothers were for taking care of, not relying on.

Jake, a couple steps away, recognized that and drawled, "Shit," with a quiet intensity just loud enough to be heard.

Nick ignored him, sort of. "Is Dakota coming or are we just waiting for midnight?"

"She'll be here. She said she would." The words carried a

heavily-implied *unlike you* that Nick ignored, too. Dayton heard the implication, too, and drew breath to defend him, but Nick shook his head. They would have plenty of time to fight those battles later. He just wanted as much peace as could be had, right then.

Dayton gave him a deadly look that would have been more alarming from somebody who wasn't a solid thirteen inches shorter than he was, but he appreciated the effort. Jake said, "You must have driven all night," like he'd just figured it out, and Nick nodded.

"Some friends drove me. They're…" He waved toward the other side of the pyre. "Dayton brought them hooch."

"Right." A note of grim amusement came into Jake's voice. "I'll go make sure they're still conscious, or at least in their car and under a blanket so they don't freeze to death."

"Only Tyler had any, but yeah. Thanks."

Jake disappeared around the pyre. Cheyenne eyeballed the brothers, then jerked her chin at Dayton. "C'mere, Day, I got a thing to show you."

"Shy, I've been telling you for years I don't want to look at your thing." Dayton went with her anyway, because she and Nick were both sober enough to understand the point was leaving the brothers together, not showing anybody anything.

Chris, though, stared after them both with continued belligerence, albeit with an appreciative edge. "They'd be a hot couple."

"Cheyenne makes anybody she's standing next to at least twenty percent hotter. Chris, what happened?"

"Dad went out on a hunt, man, and he didn't come back."

Threads of ice, much colder than the winter air, seeped through Nick's belly and wrapped around his spine. "A *hunt*? Not a bounty?"

Chris gave him a disgusted look and started searching for another bottle of beer. "Like a bounty could take Dad out."

"Chris…" Nick looked for somewhere to sit, and, not

finding it, crouched as if he couldn't take any more news standing up. "What was he hunting?"

"Buffalo, Nick, what the hell do you think he was hunting!" Chris had found a bottle, but he threw it against the pyre, glass shattering as it hit the dry logs.

"I thought you guys..." Nick put his fingertips against the frozen earth, balancing himself. "I thought you stopped *hunting* when I left."

"Yeah, sure, right, of course we did. Seriously, no, why would we do that, the money's good—"

"The money's shit."

Nick looked up to see Chris shrug expressively. "The money's shit," he agreed. "At least for the freaks. Somebody's gotta do it, though. Somebody who knows what's out there *to* hunt."

"Dad did. So how...?"

"Well, he obviously didn't know about this one, did he!" Chris obviously would have thrown another bottle if he'd had one to hand. "It was a fucking vamp, Nicky. There's a hundred things it coulda been and Dad got iced by a weak-ass vamp. And I wasn't there to save him."

"It's not your fault." Nick couldn't look up from watching the heat of his fingertips melt spots on the frosty ground. A litany of guilty thoughts, ones he'd tried to excise years ago, ran through his mind like a song. If he hadn't left, if he hadn't wanted something different, if he hadn't been the disappointing son... "It isn't your fault, Chris. Dad would have brought you if he'd known—"

"I should have known!" Chris's explosive anger brought Nick to his feet after all. "I should have known, if I'd been there, if you'd been there, he'd still be alive if—"

A woman's voice said, "Fucking hell, Christopher, shut it before you say something we all regret," and threw a wad of burning cloth onto the pyre.

# CHAPTER 2

"JESUS CHRIST, DAKOTA!" CHRIS JUMPED FORWARD TO KNOCK the cloth off the pyre before the wood went up. "What the hell, you don't get to do that, you don't get—"

"Nicky won't and you're too caught up in your drama to —*oof*." Dakota Martinez grunted as Nick stepped up and hugged her with more ease than Chris could ever do. He heard a muffled, "Nicky," spoken into his brother's shoulder, and Nick's more muted response. It was easy for Nick, so goddamn easy all the time, just out there with his *feelings* and shit. Women liked that. Everybody liked that. Chris rolled his jaw and looked away from the hugging pair.

"Come on. Kody's here now, so let's get this party started."

"What do you think I was trying to do," Dakota asked, exasperated, as Nick released her from the hug. She stalked over and pulled Chris into one, too, roughly, like he'd avoid it if he could. She said, "You okay?" into his shoulder, and to his own surprise, Chris muttered, "No."

"Yeah, didn't think so. Don't be too hard on Nicky, okay?" Kody stepped back half an inch and grabbed Chris's face in her hands, making him look down at her. She was dark-haired and pale-skinned and skinny, like a wraith in the headlights, but she was strong. "Okay?"

"Yeah. Yeah, okay, whatever." He tried to pull away, but Kody held on, scowling at him until he had to put his hands on her wrists and break her grip. "Cut it out, Kode. You don't gotta mother-hen me. I'm glad you came. Now let's do this thing."

"You and me are gonna talk later, Chris."

"Later I'm gonna be too drunk-ass unconscious to talk, but if you wanna crawl into bed with me I'll do my best by you."

Dakota rolled her eyes and swung away from him, grabbing a bottle off the pile by the pyre. "To John Cassidy!"

A shout of agreement went up, mostly from the other side of the pyre. There weren't enough voices, but Chris couldn't do anything about that. Their dad hadn't mixed much with the people in Sterling, and even if he had, inviting people to a funeral was one thing. Inviting them to a body-burning was something else. And most of the old man's friends were bounty hunters, spread all over the country. Getting to the ass end of Colorado, even in a year without much snow, wasn't exactly the fastest or easiest trip to make. He should probably be grateful as many people as were there had come.

Nicky had come.

Nick had barely been his *little* brother anymore when he'd left, and sure as hell wasn't anymore. Younger, maybe, but not littler. Chris had seen a couple pictures of him on social media since he'd left, not that Nicky knew that, but you couldn't tell somebody was six five or something from a photo on the edge of the Grand Canyon. He didn't look like somebody who needed taking care of, anymore. His hair had grown out until it was almost as good as Jake's, and his shoulders had filled out until he looked like an adult.

Their dad had never seen him looking that way, and never would.

Chris finished the beer he was holding, then yelled, "To our old man!" in the wake of Kody's shout. He got a bigger roar from the gathered mourners, and cuffed Nick's shoulder. "C'mon, let's do this thing. I bet Kody brought Molotov cocktails to light it up with."

"We're not blowing him up, Chris." Nicky sounded old and tired, like he couldn't wait to be done with it and out of here. Neither could Chris, not that he had anywhere else to go. He pulled a thin stick from the pyre and stuck it into the ball of rags Dakota had tried throwing on the pyre, letting it come alight with the rags' dying flames. Nicky, silently, did the same, and without talking about it they went around the pyre in opposite directions, like they were torch bearers at an official occasion.

Which he guessed they were, but it didn't feel like it. Somebody else could have arranged pomp and circumstance, but not Chris. Nicky could have. The only thing Chris could do was mutter, "The old man was a bastard, but I guess he was our bastard. I'm gonna miss him," and thrust the flaming stick through the pyre branches toward the kindling and straw within.

Nicky ducked his head, hiding a pained smile, and said nothing as the gathering gave another mournful shout. He added his own flame to the pyre, and, like Chris, stayed within touching distance of the catching wood until the growing fire's heat drove him back, step by step. Chris fought the impulse to fall back in step with him and instead held his place just a moment or two longer, until he couldn't breathe from the heat. They retreated with every step like that, Chris staying just ahead of Nicky, just that much closer to the fire as he stared up through the wavering air at the flames engulfing his dad's white-wrapped body.

He didn't think he cried, but if he did, the heat seared tears off his cheeks before anybody else saw them. Nicky's jaw was bunched like he was trying to fight them, but tears, gleaming orange in the blaze's light, leaked down his face when Chris finally glanced at him.

Nobody else was even close to them. They were too near the fire, for one thing. Nobody else had even tried to stay as close to it as they had, but more to the point, people were obviously given them their space, too. Jake was less than ten feet back, but not much, his green eyes as orange as Nicky's tears in the firelight. The Geography Girls were another couple steps back, their arms wrapped around each other. Dayton's hair looked red, and Cheyenne's dark skin ate the light until she glowed with it. Kody just reflected the light like she was a mirror, her skin flushing with heat.

Nicky's college friends were about the same distance away, but standing closer to Nick than Chris. The guy, darker than Cheyenne, was as warmed by the fire's tones as Shy was, and kept glancing back and forth from the pyre to Nick, like he couldn't quite believe they were really burning a body. The girl watched Nick like she was worried, but not surprised.

Everybody else fanned out behind them in a semi-circle colored yellow and orange from the front, and stark white and black from behind, thanks to the headlights. They mostly held bottles in their hands, but a couple of the men had taken their hats off in respect, and the few women, far enough away from the fire to feel the chill, wrapped their arms around themselves as if warding off the cold.

Nicky looked all alone, against that backdrop. Tall and young and alone, standing too far away from anybody else to be comforted. Chris tried to memorize the image anyway, then fell back another couple of steps to stand beside his brother. After a long time, Nick, hoarsely, said, "My ass is freezing," and Chris gave a hard, unwilling blurt of laughter.

"Mine too. Wanna get another drink?"

"Man, I wanna…" Nick's silence drew out before turning into a sound too ragged to be a sigh. "I wanna fucking scream, man. I wanna throw bottles at that fucking pyre and watch them explode and just fucking *scream*, Chris."

Chris, wordlessly, handed the bottle he held over. Nick

took a long drink from it, then threw it, without screaming, at the fire. It shattered, and his fists clenched like he was holding back a sound. Chris looked over his shoulder, catching Jake's eye, and Jake jerked his chin in acknowledgement.

A couple minutes later engines revved, and a few minutes after that, the only light on the plain was from the fire. Nicky looked back once, and Chris, thick-voiced, said, "Jake'll take your friends back to Dad's place, or to a hotel in town. I'll call him when we're done here."

Nicky nodded. "Why don't you get the rest of the bottles."

Chris hesitated. "You still gonna be here when I get back?"

There he was. The little kid he remembered, there in the lost dark eyes and unhappy set of his brother's mouth. Nicky didn't answer, not out loud, but Chris went around the fire to get the bottles without being afraid Nick would be gone when he came around the other side again. For a while they alternated between drinking and throwing booze, watching bursts of blue flame explode where the raw alcohol hit the searing heat. Chris could hardly himself screaming over the sound of the flames, and didn't know if he said anything or just yelled at the dark and the stars and the fire. Nicky didn't, for sure. Nicky just howled it out, until all of a sudden he stopped, and when Chris looked, he was on the ground, forehead pressed against earth softening with the fire's heat, hands clenched in the icy mud.

Chris sat beside him, clumsy in the cold, and pulled Nicky into his arms. Nick curled muddy fists against Chris's shirt and cried like he was a kid, his whole body shaking with sobs. Quieter tears escaped Chris every once in a while, but mostly he just kept his head bent over Nick's shoulders until the worst of it had passed.

The pyre hadn't exactly burned itself out by then, but it had died down a lot, its heat having made soup of the frozen ground. Chris was pretty sure his butt had turned to solid ice and was wondering if he could convince his brother to stand up when Nick muttered, "I think my shins are frozen in place. Or they will be if we don't get up before the fire dies any more."

"Yeah." Chris levied Nick up, then accepted Nick's hand and let him pull him to his feet. "Can't go until it's burned out, though."

"No, but your truck's warmer than the ground." Nick, looking pained, glanced around. "Your truck is here, isn't it?"

"Other side of the pyre." Chris gestured and Nick started limping around the fire, like his legs hurt from being pressed into the cold ground for so long. Chris felt just about as stiff and clumsy, though, so he didn't give Nick hell. "It won't start getting light for another couple hours, but it should be pretty well burned out by then."

"I know what time sunrise is, Chris." Nick's voice, thin with irritation, came over his shoulder like a knife.

"Jesus, I didn't mean you didn't fuckin'..." Chris, lip curled, climbed into the truck and reached into its skinny back seats to drag a blanket onto the front seats. "Don't get mud everywhere," he warned as Nick got in the other side.

"I'm not the one whose butt is covered in it." Nick unfolded the blanket down the cab anyway, and reached for the sun visor.

Chris knocked his hand away, getting the keys out himself and putting them in the ignition. The huge old engine rumbled and cold air blasted from wide-open vents. Nick said, "Fuck!" and grabbed the blanket, trying to pull it out from under Chris and over his own legs.

"Knock it off, asshole! There's more blankets in the back!"

Nick twisted over the back of the seat, which had been funny enough when he was a kid and not like six four. Chris cackled as elbows and knees went everywhere. "You look like a giant spider, man."

"There's not a blanket back here, there's a frickin'

hundred and seventy pound tool box oh no sorry *you're* the hundred and seventy pound tool—"

"One ninety, and I can still kick your ass."

Nick came back over the seat with a couple more rough wool blankets and wrapped up in them both, one over his legs and the other over his shoulders as he hunched toward the heaters, which were starting to warm up. "Like to see you try. I forgot how cold it gets up here."

"California made you soft, man."

"Yeah. And I liked it." Nick ducked his head, retreating into a woolly ball of silence. Chris put his hands on the steering wheel, which was cold, and flexed his fingers around it until it and they warmed up some. After a while Nick unfolded from his hunch and rubbed the blanket over the shins of his jeans.

"Sun won't be up for another hour," Chris said over the heater's blast. Nick stared sideways at him and he shrugged. "Just saying."

"Thought we needed to stay to watch the fire burn out."

Chris shrugged one shoulder. "Jake's at the house. I can call him to come out and keep an eye on it."

Nicky cracked his knuckles under the warmth of his blanket, gaze fixed forward again, watching the darkening flames of the pyre. "You know where it is?"

"I know where Dad was. Got his GPS tracked."

"Hah!" The sharp sound bounced through the truck's cab. "Did he know you were tracking him?"

A tight smile slid across Chris's face, partially reflected in the windshield. "'Course not. You know he didn't like that kind of crap. He wouldn't even use Bhuntr. Not that you know what that is anyway."

"Bounty hunter app. People track sightings, keep tabs on each other, make sure everybody's safe, probably hook up, I don't know." He hunched defensively again as Chris sent a surprised glance across the cab at him. "Just because I left doesn't mean I stopped paying attention, okay? It's not like I use it. I just know what it is."

"Yeah, okay, whatever. So are you in?"

"Yeah." Nick slid down in the seat, eyes closed. "Yeah, of course I am." Then he sat up again, eyebrows drawn down. "Except I'm driving."

"The hell you are. When was the last time you even drove a truck?"

"About a week before I graduated high school, but I've had a lot less to drink than you have and either I'm driving or we're not going anywhere."

"I haven't had a drink in like two hours!"

"And you were shitfaced when I got here."

"That was last night!"

"I drive or we don't go."

"Fine, you can get the fuck out, then. I'll go by myself."

"And get yourself killed, just like Dad did. Two funerals and no family left, that'll really make my week, Chris, thanks."

"Dad didn't know what he was getting into! I do!"

"What the hell is wrong with just sleeping it off? A vamp's gonna be quieter during the day anyway, so what's the rush?" Nick took a sharp breath and let it out again. "You think I'm gonna leave. You think I'll leave before this is taken care of."

Chris thrust his jaw out and shrugged one stiff shoulder. "You left once already."

For a long time the only sound was the engine and an occasional pop from the dying fire. The horizon started going grey with twilight before Nick finally said, "I spent half the drive here promising myself I wasn't gonna fight about this. You knew I was gonna leave, Chris. You told me to leave."

"Yeah. And then you did anyway." It didn't make any sense, but feelings never did, which was why they were better off stuffed in a box where they couldn't bother anybody. "Forget it."

"I won't leave until this is dealt with, Chris. I'm not gonna leave you to…" Nick shook his head and sighed. "This isn't… this is a lot. This is bad. I'm not gonna just…leave."

"When was it ever good?"

"You could've come with me."

"Right. Me. Out there in California with you and all your brainiac friends. Yeah, no, I don't think so."

"Believe it or not, not everyone in California, or even college, is a super genius. And it's not like you're dumb. You just didn't go to class."

"Well, I couldn't, could I, because Dad was never home and somebody had to feed you and make sure the electricity wasn't gonna go off."

"Jake managed."

"Jake went and lived with his friggin' grandma after he came out, Nick, what was I gonna do, send you to the ass end of Montana with Grandma so I could go read Oliver frickin' Twist in Sunday school? Gran didn't exactly move to the edge of nowhere for the company, and I—" Anything else he could say was too much, so he just stopped, not that Nick noticed.

A grin flashed across Nick's face, although he looked down to hide it. "I don't think anybody was reading Oliver Twist in Sunday school, Chris."

And that was his baby brother, always laughing about getting stupid details wrong. "You know what I mean!"

Nick closed his eyes. "Yeah. Look, text Jake and tell him we're gonna go after this thing once the fire's burned out. I'll keep an eye on it for a while. You get some sleep."

"I don't need—"

"Either that or I *call* Jake and tell him to be ready to drive that pimpmobile of yours into the lake, because I swear to god I will if you think you're driving before you're sober."

Heat flushed Chris's face. "You leave my van alone."

"Man, it's not like you're gonna have a hard time pulling in a booty call without it. Probably be *easier* without it. I'll never understand why any woman would get in a van with that artwork on it."

Chris muttered, "It's been repainted since you saw it," and Nick snorted a laugh.

"Yeah? Does it have *Shagmobile* painted on it now, or is that still just the license plate? Is there still three inch deep orange carpet in it? Do you—"

"Jesus, just shut up already. If taking a nap will shut you up, then fine, I'll sleep, Christ." Chris yanked the blanket off Nick's shoulders and threw it over himself, arms folded beneath it, jaw clenched above its rough hem. It was red with a black stripe, three times Chris's age, and had been in the back of one truck or another as long as he could remember. Using it felt like wrapping up in fiberglass, but it was warm.

"Good." Nick got out of the truck, slamming the door behind him, and Chris glared at him through the windshield for a minute or two.

Problem was, between the blanket and the booze and the warm air roaring from the truck's forty-year-old heating vents, sleep actually started to sound like a good idea, and in another minute, he was out.

————

He woke up when the weak spring sun lined up with his eyes well enough to bleed red through his lids. It took a minute to orient himself, not because he wasn't used to sleeping in the truck, but because he didn't usually sleep sitting up. But Nicky had crawled back in at some point after the fire'd gone out, and was sleeping with the top of his head mashed against the side of Chris's thigh.

He'd done that more times than Chris could count, as kids. But last time, Nick had been about fifteen inches shorter, and they'd both more or less fit. Not comfortably, but kind of, at least.

Now, though, he'd pushed Chris all the way up against the driver side door and was still curled in an uncomfortably small ball, his knees pressed against the dashboard and his feet smushed against the far door. He'd tucked another one of the blankets around himself to keep his knees from freezing off, but his booted feet were probably icy, just like Chris's shoulder was, from being flattened against the door. Especially since he'd cracked the window open half an inch so they wouldn't die of carbon monoxide poisoning. They probably wouldn't have anyway, but Nicky always had to make sure. Chris muttered, "Safety first," and took his phone out of his coat's chest pocket, checking for messages.

There were three from Jake, the last of which said *when the hell are you coming back, Nick's friends are starting to freak out,* and a couple of others from the Geography Girls checking up on them both. He put his phone back without answering any of them and scooted back into the middle of the driver's seat, making Nick curl up even more.

Then he groaned and sat up, still curled like a pill bug, and rested his forehead on the dashboard. "Ow. That was more comfortable last time I did it."

"Yeah." A smile ghosted across Chris's face. "That's what I was just thinking. There's water in the back."

"Of the truck or the cab?" Nick reached back, flailing, to feel around the extended cab.

"Cab. It'd be froze if it was in the bed. Here, it's…" Chris twisted over the back of the bench seat and Nicky cackled, croaking, "Who's Spider-Man now?"

"Man, your arms and legs are even longer than mine, so don't…" Chris grunted, finding the water, and shoved a bottle at Nick as he slid back into his seat. "Ow. See, this is why I have the van—"

"I don't even want to hear it."

"I'm just saying it's more comfortable to sleep in." Chris

drained half a bottle of water, cracked his neck, and glanced at his brother. "*Now* can we go kill this thing?"

"I could use lunch."

"You'll fight better if you're hungry."

"You are completely full of shit."

"Yeah. But your college buddies are wondering where we are, and if you don't want to have to explain it to them, we probably shouldn't take any more time than we have to."

Nick cursed under his breath and took his own phone out, answering messages. "Yeah, okay, fine. We probably need to stop for gas."

"There's five gallons in the spare tank in the back of the truck. S'already got antifreeze in it."

Nick's eyebrows rose. "Never let it be said my brother is not prepared."

If he'd been prepared, their dad wouldn't be dead and Nicky wouldn't be there at all. Chris clenched his teeth on the thought and muttered, "It's about eighty miles north of here, anyway. There'll be somewhere to stop for gas if we need it."

"Eighty…"

Chris could see Nick calculating the time and coming to a number he didn't like, but he didn't say anything. He just used the phone as an actual phone instead of a thing to text with, like a weirdo, as Chris pulled the truck away from the pyre and headed for the main road.

Not that it was much of a road. They had almost three hundred acres covered in lousy farmland and gravel tracks they'd laid down themselves to reach places like the burn site. There was a lake over that way, too far to really be of much use if a burn went out of control, but it wasn't like they spent every weekend building bonfires, even when Nicky had still been home. The gravel they'd laid down could lead them past the house, but the last thing Chris wanted was to have Nick's soft squishy California intellectuals tagging along on a hunt.

Nick was over there making excuses to his girlfriend. 'Stuff to work out' and 'time to catch up' and other totally plausible crap that covered the truth. That they were going to go catch and kill a monster. An actual monster, the kind people didn't think existed, and which mostly didn't. Chris couldn't exactly remember—

"That went well." Nick put his phone down and bounced his head hard against the headrest. "I told them to go home and I'd come back later but Stephanie says they're getting a hotel and will wait. I'd have come home on my own if I'd known…"

"It wasn't like I could tell you in a text."

"You could have friggin' *called*, man."

"Yeah, like I was gonna mention a vampire on the phone, either. Do you even remember when we found out they were real?"

Nick turned his head a couple inches, eyeing him, then scowled and looked away. "I guess…I don't know. I guess I was like eight? When Dad got the one but there was another and it followed him back to the motel. That was vampires, though. I guess I kind of knew about the freaks before that. Did you know before then?"

"Yeah. He told me when I was littler than you. He'd come back from a bounty and hadn't gotten paid, and he told me it was because he didn't take money for the freaks." Chris's hands tightened on the wheel. "I'd forgotten that. I thought I'd always known."

"He shouldn't have told you," Nick said in a low voice. "That was too much to put on a kid. You shouldn't even have known there wasn't any money."

"Well, I could sure as shit tell there wasn't any *dinner*, so why not tell me the truth about why not?"

"I don't know, Chris. He didn't really let you be a kid, that's all."

"No, that was all saved for you." Chris bared his teeth like he could bite back the words, too late. From the corner of his eye he saw Nicky's nostrils flare and his jaw set, ending the conversation. Because that was Chris's particular talent, saying the wrong thing and not being able to find a way to back down from it. He drove a couple miles in silence, then turned the radio on. Old school Garth Brooks blared and he muttered, "Jesus," and rattled through channels until it picked up a Nebraska classic rock station that was at least better than the sullen quiet. Nick didn't object either way, his gaze fixed out the window as the miles slipped away, one bit of landscape mostly indistinguishable from another.

The roads, though wet with melted ice from the thin sunlight and traffic, were clear, and the speed limit in Nebraska was forgiving. It only took a little over an hour of music interspersed with static to reach the GPS location his dad's last fight had been recorded at. The house sat on the edge of a small town, close enough that they could park elsewhere and walk back instead of announcing their presence by driving up through acres of nothing before coming in for the kill. There was a reason their dad had spent every dime he had on wide open spaces with not much to hide behind. Chris parked in front of a diner that he thought they might want to eat at later, and they both climbed out of the truck, stretching without speaking, until Nick said, "I gotta find a john," and went down the street toward a gas station.

Chris stared after him a minute, then went into the diner, bought a cup of coffee, and went to use their bathroom, which was no doubt cleaner and warmer than the gas station's, while the waitress poured the cup for him. Going to the gas station was something their dad would have done. Off the radar, nobody looking twice, uncomfortable but discreet. Chris had stopped doing that as soon as he'd started taking bounties on his own.

Because yeah, that was him, all right. The rebel son, marking his territory by taking a piss at a diner bathroom instead of freezing his balls off in a gas station. He drank his coffee too hot, left the waitress a tip he couldn't afford in exchange for a smile that was worth it, and went back out to the old truck.

Nicky stood in its open door, layered up with a canvas coat that had fit him better four years ago, flannel beneath it, his pretty-boy college student shirt beneath *that*, until there was enough fabric to slow down a knife and stop teeth. Chris's coat was leather and padded for the cold midwestern winter, but the layers built up just the same for him, making a pass at armor that nobody took a second look at. "Nicky?"

His brother stared into the tool box that had been in the back of the truck, the one that was really full of weapons, not hammers and screwdrivers. His expression was blank enough that maybe other people would see it as unreadable. Chris read a whole lot into it, though, all of it summed up when Nick said, "This is exactly what I was trying to get away from, Chris. This is the reason I left. This whole life. Bounty hunting, I mean, it's weird from most people's perspective, but it's a life. This, hunting freaks, this is…"

"I know." Chris went quiet a couple of seconds. "I'm sorry."

Nick looked up, surprised, before giving a stiff, one-shouldered shrug. "Yeah. Okay. Let's get it over with."

# CHAPTER 3

THE PART NICK HATED, THE THING THAT REALLY BOTHERED him, was that the knives strapped to his thighs, the holy water hidden in his coat sleeves, the silver cross worn at his belt...all felt natural. Comfortable. Like he'd been wearing somebody else's clothes for most of four years and he'd finally put his own back on. If he'd forgotten how to walk silently, or how to signal to Chris that the room ahead was clear, or how to stop listening to the raised hairs on his nape that said something intangible was amiss, then he could have believed that Nick Cassidy, pre-med student, boyfriend, roommate, general laid-back dude, was the real him.

But he hadn't forgotten. He still cased a room when he walked in, even his apartment or a classroom. He just hadn't known he was doing it until now, when walking through the low-slatted afternoon light of a killer's house reminded him that he'd never, ever stopped being what his dad had made him.

A hunter.

Mostly a bounty hunter, sure. He didn't even know how his dad had gotten into it, except he'd been good at finding people, and then somebody paid him for it, and then some-body else heard he was good at it, and...that had been most of their childhood, really, driving around in whatever beater their dad had gotten running that month, and staying at cheap motels, or in the car, while he found his quarry and turned them in. Nick thought Chris kept his old Dodge truck —and his slutmobile van that he'd rebuilt the engine on—in working condition as a commentary on their dad's inability to keep any vehicle functioning for more than six weeks. He didn't think Chris did it consciously, probably, but…yeah. Chris had never in his whole life believed he could walk away like Nick had done, but he had his own ways of letting their dad knew what he thought.

Anyway, it would have been harder *not* to learn to track and cross-reference and follow clues, following his dad around like that, than to pick it up along the way. Chris had actually tried to. He'd wanted to be like their dad. Nick just fell into it, because with Chris and their dad, what else was he gonna do.

And like Chris, he'd been good at it. Good enough that now, creeping through a poorly-lit house, looking for a monster to kill, seemed more like coming home than last night's funeral had.

He swept around the last corner, entering a tired-looking kitchen: worn linoleum that had been printed with green and white flowers once upon a time, dirty windows made cloudier by thin brown paper, rust stains in a sink missing its faucet handles, a gas stove with only one knob, and a table surrounded by wobbly-looking chairs. One door led outside, and an inside door led to what was presumably the basement.

Chris stood at that one already, waiting for him, and nodded down its steps. The first vampire Nick had ever seen came at them during the day, which their dad hadn't expected. He hadn't known enough then, but to be fair, there really weren't a lot of *monsters* out there. Not the non-human kind, anyway. There were more freaks, regular-looking people who could do things normal people couldn't. Chris crept down the stairs, knives out—they were quieter than guns—

and Nick followed a few steps behind with a blade in one hand and a fragile vial of holy water in the other.

Vamps caught their prey with glamours, mostly. Made people think they were something they weren't, until they ate them. Knives and guns slowed them down, but the rule was to kill them with something blessed. Holy water did the trick, or a blessed blade, but the blades only worked once if you wanted to save the vampire's soul. Anybody could bless one, too, if they believed, but it took a minute, and spare time didn't come up a lot in fights. Their dad had always figured cheap vials of holy water could be refilled with two minutes at a church font in almost any town anywhere in the country, which made them more reliable than blessed knives.

Chris went still ahead of him and Nick froze automatically, sharpening his hearing. Vampires breathed because people did, like they weren't just animated bodies. Like they were something living inside the human body, still powering it, except the whole body went to liquid goo if they were sprayed with holy water, like the Wicked Witch of the West. Nick didn't think that qualified for any kind of residual humanity.

But they breathed, and when they breathed, they could be heard.

Chris skittered a look back at Nick, who heard his neck bones creak when he gave a fractional nod in return. It wasn't a vampire.

It was *vampires*.

They didn't usually hide together. The one that had come after his dad when Nick was eight had been unusual for being one of a pair. Normally they were solitary, hiding at the edges of society where people wouldn't notice somebody going missing.

Chris lifted his chin, indicating he would press forward. Nick loosened his shoulders and followed one slow step at a time, keeping to the outside edges of the stairs to avoid squeaking. Chris paused again, listening. There were two of them, which made Nick feel both better and worse. At least their dad hadn't died fighting one stupid vampire. On the other hand, Chris really never would forgive himself for letting the old man go out alone, and it would never matter that even Dad hadn't known he was hunting a vamp until it was too late. As far as Nick's big brother was concerned, keeping other people safe was his reason for existing. Regardless of how much or little he knew about the situation beforehand, if anything went wrong, it was somehow his own fault.

So it was obviously Chris's fault when two vampires turned out to be seven.

———

They swarmed from below, the first couple grabbing Chris's legs and yanking them out from under him. Chris went down with a yell, his head bouncing on every step as the vampires hauled him toward them. Nick could only see two, then, and two was enough. He threw himself forward into the darkness, tackling them to give Chris time to regain his feet.

Which would have worked just fine, if there hadn't been five more in the shadows. Their hands were everywhere, pinning Nick down, teeth gleaming in the dim light. He wrestled a hand loose and smashed a vial against one's face. It screamed, rearing back to claw at the wetness while the others howled rage and flung their weight against Nick, trying harder to pin him down. A flash above his eyes warned him that one of them had cut its wrist open to drip blood in his mouth. Nick clamped his lips together and twisted to the side, feeling thick warmth fall against his cheekbone.

Something bludgeoned the one trying to feed him, and it collapsed on top of him. Rage passed through the others like a virus, and two of them were stupid enough to release him. Nick shoved the bleeding one off himself and grabbed the floor for purchase, then roared and ripped his other arm free of the vamps holding him down. For an instant shock was visible in their pale faces. He shook another vial of holy water into his hand and slammed it into an open mouth, palm-thrusted the mouth shut around the vial, and didn't take time to grimace as the thing died horribly all over him.

A hand came out of the dark, seized his, and pulled him to his feet. A heartbeat later he and Chris were back to back and there were only three vampires left, all of them gaping at each other and at the brothers. Then one bolted for the stairs.

Chris's knife caught it between the shoulder blades and it fell without a sound, and without turning to goo. He'd used that knife before, then. Its blessing had saved another vamp's soul, but couldn't do this one any good. Not great, but better than either letting a vampire loose in the town, or—worse— letting a vampire turn one of *them*.

The remaining two exchanged a glance, like they were weighing their odds. Nick's knife remained unbloodied, but he'd taken two out with holy water and had a third vial in his hand already. Chris gave a low cackle and drew another knife. Nick couldn't see it, but he knew Chris had crooked his fingers, a "c'mere, let's you and me fight," gesture that every-body recognized.

And for some dumb-ass reason, the two vamps who were left decided to take him up on the offer.

They came at them together, smart enough not to let the brothers pick them off one at a time, but not smart enough to run. Nick kept his knife out as the vamp rushed him, making sure it kept its attention on the blade. It wasn't afraid of it— vampires weren't—and all it needed to do was avoid a killing blow before it took Nick out.

All it *really* needed to do was stay out of arm's reach, but it was so busy trying to get past the knife it forgot about the holy water in his other hand. He caught it by the throat, crushing the flimsy glass vial there, and the thing went down with a gurgling scream.

By the time he turned around, the final vampire was dead, too. Chris, grinning and panting, said, "That was freaking *awesome*, man!"

Nick threw his knife down. "That was the end of it." He went up the stairs, stepping over the one body they'd left whole, and paused to pour a vial of holy water over it. It dissolved, bubbling, and he continued up the stairs. Vamps were a lot easier to clean up after than freaks. Holy water didn't do anything to the more human monsters that were out there.

"Wait, what the—wait up, Nick! Nicky! Nick!" Chris followed him upstairs, muttering as he stepped in goo, then catching Nick's arm when he got to the kitchen. The sun had almost set, leaving the room dimmer and grungier than before. "What the hell, man?"

"We did it," Nick said. "We got the thing that got Dad. It's over."

"But we were awesome! Come on, don't tell me you didn't miss this!"

"Driving for miles to sneak into an abandoned house and kill things most people don't even believe exist? No, Chris, I didn't. I miss you." Admitting that much nearly silenced Nick, but he plowed ahead. "I even miss Dad, and that's…man, that sucks, because I can't fix that. But I don't miss *this*. I don't miss…"

"Working together? Having my back? Doing something to help people?" The anger in Chris's voice covered the hurt, but not well. "So that's it? You're just gonna go back to your soft Cali life with your babe girlfriend and forget about me again?"

"I never forgot about you, Chris." Nick's shoulders sagged. "But yeah. I'm gonna go back. This isn't home anymore. I'm gonna go home and get my medical degree and I'm going to help people that way. That hasn't changed."

"But Dad's *dead*. You're just gonna leave me out here on my own?"

"Chris." Nick pulled a hand over his face, then dropped it, sighing. "You don't have to do this, you know? This isn't your only choice in life."

"It's the only thing I'm good at."

"Man, it's what I was good at too, before I tried something else."

"I don't want to try something else."

"You're *afraid* to try so—"

Fury flashed across Chris's face. "I'm not afraid. I'm good at this, and so are you. How long is it since we fought together? And it was just like old times."

"Yeah, except there were seven freaking vampires, Chris, that's not normal. That's not cool. And it's not like old times, when there'd be two at most."

"And don't you want to know why?" Chris demanded.

"No!" Nick drew a deep breath, trying to modulate his volume. "No. I want to go get Stephanie and go home. I want a normal life."

"Yeah, the girl and the dog and the white picket fence and two point three kids you're never gonna see because you'll be too busy trying to save the world at the hospital instead of on the ground. That'll be great."

"How is that any worse than the two kids Dad never saw?" Nick demanded. "It's not what I'm planning to do, but even if it is, at least I'll be bringing in a steady paycheck so they don't wonder if they're gonna have dinner tonight! And how's it any better than what I guess you're doing, hooking up with a new girl every time you hit a new city, and never putting down any roots? You're gonna be just like Dad, living in that armpit of a trailer when you're not off trying to get yourself killed by some monster or freak or asshole bounty!"

"I wouldn't have to worry about that if you'd keep hunting with me! But you're too good for this life, aren't you? Nicky, the smart one, high-tailing it out of Dodge as soon as he could—"

Nick, very quietly, said, "You encouraged me to go to college, Chris. I wouldn't have had the nerve without you."

Chris's mouth curled. "Yeah, well, I'm not the smart one, am I. Maybe I figured you wouldn't go. Maybe I figured you'd come back once you realized what you were missing. This is the life, man, seeing the whole country, making your own hours, hunting down bad guys…"

"You knew I was never coming back."

"No." Chris's voice went flat. "No, I didn't. I didn't know you and Dad would stop talking completely. I didn't know you'd only send a text at Christmas."

"Like you do any better! When was the last time you called?"

"I can read the room, can't I? You obviously didn't want any part of us anymore, so why would I call?" Chris's jaw worked, strain in the cords of his throat. "I didn't think you'd come home for Dad's goddamn *funeral*, Nicky. I didn't think—"

"So you texted me in the worst possible way to make sure I probably wouldn't! You *texted* me to tell us our *dad* was dead, Chris! And said I probably didn't care! What the hell did you think I was gonna do, with that?" Nick spun around, looking for something to take his frustration out on. A wall, or the counter, or the papered-over windows, maybe. Not that it would do any good. He forced his hands out of fists and dropped his head, sighing. "I miss him, Chris. I missed him before he died and now I'm never gonna get to tell him. I miss *you*. But I can't stay. This isn't the life I want." He stood there a minute, listening to Chris's frustrated breathing, and sighed again. "You're right, though," he said in a much lower voice.

"The whole...*hive*...of vampires thing, that's not cool. That's..."

"You help me figure that out," Chris said swiftly. "You help me figure out what's going on there, and then, fine, you go home. But help me with that, Nicky. Because one or two, that's one thing, but no wonder they got to Dad, with seven of them. Or more, because I don't know if he took any out before they got him."

Nick's shoulders dropped farther, gaze locked on the faded linoleum floor before he shuffled to the table and sat. The chairs were as rickety as they'd looked, and a plastic-y table cloth, faded from red to an unhealthy orange, had yellowed polka dots and old food stains on it. At least, he chose to believe they were food stains, and not something else. "Fine. All right. You said Dad thought it was just a bounty, right? Not a freak?"

"And definitely not a vamp, never mind a whole pile of them." Chris pulled another chair out, turned it around, and sat on it backward, his arms folded over the back.

"Tell me what happened."

"He came out here to pick up the bounty and next thing I knew somebody was calling me because he'd sent up an SOS on friggin' Bhuntr."

Nick scowled. "You said he didn't use that."

"I didn't even know he had an account. I'm not sure he did before then. But I was in Dodge, there was no way I could get to him if he called, so I guess he used what he could. Anyway, by the time they got here, he was..." Chris's voice went tight. "He was already dead. They hadn't tried to turn him or anything."

A thin smile pulled Nick's mouth. "Takes too long. He'd have killed them all before they got enough blood into him."

Chris chuckled, just as thinly. "Yeah, I guess so. Anyway, he didn't say anything on Bhuntr except he needed help, and the guy who brought him back said there were vamps. That's all I got. So here we are."

"Wait. If the guy knew about vamps, Dad must have posted in the Beowulf board. We should talk to the guy who picked him up and see what else he might know."

Chris lifted his head, staring at Nick. "How'd you know about that?"

A shred of guilt sizzled through Nick. "I told you. Just because I left doesn't mean I don't know about Bhuntr."

"Yeah, but knowing Bhuntr and knowing about the Beowulf board—"

"The thing is, Chris, if Dad posted there, he knew about it too. Maybe he's got more of an account than you know about."

"Maybe *you* do!"

"This isn't about me."

Chris bared his teeth and pointed at Nick, warning him that he wouldn't let it go, but for the moment, he did. "I've got his phone. I guess we can check, if we can figure out his pass code. I already tried our birthdays."

"Did you try Mom's?"

A twitch of anger crossed Chris's face. Nick nodded. "We'll try that, but I guess we can call the provider and see what you do if somebody's dead and you need to get into their phone, too. There must be something." He turned his head toward the stairs, like he could see what was left of the vampires in the basement. "Do you think a freak could have been controlling them somehow?"

The anger faded from Chris's expression as his eyebrows drew down. "Hadn't thought of that. Maybe. Can they do that?"

Nick shrugged. "Have you ever come across two freaks who could do the same thing?"

"I mean, yeah, there are a bunch of them that are just

freakishly strong or kind of bullet proof, but…yeah, I guess not. There's all the others."

"Psychics," Nick said. "Teleporters. Sorcerers. Maybe one of them just vibes with vamps."

"I'd freak too," Chris admitted.

"Yeah, me too." Nick didn't know why some people had powers. He did know most of them went crazy, which was more than half of why they were called freaks. The rest of it was they were just…freaks, as in, highly unusual and abnormal, since people didn't normally have talents that looked supernatural or superheroic. He'd wanted to call them grendels ever since he found out about the Beowulf board, but changing a whole subculture's terminology wasn't easy even if he was actively part of it. Which he wasn't.

Or he hadn't been, not for a long time, not until today. "You still got his number? The guy who called you about Dad?"

"Yeah, you want me to just call and ask?"

Nick lifted one shoulder and let it fall. "Got a better plan?" His own phone buzzed like he'd caught its attention. He took it out to find a worried message from Stephanie, said, "Give him a call," and got up to walk a few steps away before calling her back.

"Nick?" Relief rushed her voice as she picked up. "Are you okay?"

"Yeah." Nick closed his eyes, chin ducked to his chest. "Yeah, Chris and I are just…we're dealing with some…there's a lot to do when somebody dies."

"I know, but…I could help, Nick. You don't have to do it all on your own."

He breathed out, almost a laugh. "I know. If there's anything you can help with, I'll let you, okay? This stuff, it's just…Chris and I have to work it out."

Stephanie's voice lowered. "How much of this is about official paperwork and how much is about you and your brother's relationship? Because you don't owe him anything, Nick. Ty and I saw how he treated you." Her voice sharpened. "How he treated *us*."

Nick closed his mouth on defending his brother. "Yeah, he was kind of an ass to you, and I'm sorry. And I haven't been much better."

"Well, your dad just died." Steph went silent for a heartbeat, then sounded wry. "Which is the same slack I should cut him, I guess, but…"

"But you know me, and you don't know him, and…" And what she did know about Chris from Nick wasn't particularly flattering. Calling out the rough spots had always been easier than acknowledging what had gone right. "I think I'll be back late tonight. You want me to come find you or wait until morning?"

"Text if you'll be later than midnight?"

"Okay. I love you."

"Yeah." Her voice warmed. "I love you too."

Nick hung up to find Chris already off his own phone and staring at him. A flush crawled along Nick's jaw and he felt himself setting it defensively. Chris said, "Seriously? You really love her?"

"Yeah. Yeah, I do."

Chris rolled his own jaw and glanced away. "Good for you, man. Wes says he doesn't know anything about a whole pile of vamps. Dad was dead when he got here and there was goo everywhere."

Nick looked around. "*Here*? This place is dingy, but it doesn't have vamp goo all over everything."

"This is where…" Chris trailed off as he stood, lines appearing between his eyebrows as he frowned. "This is where Dad's GPS said he was. But you're right. The upstairs was clean too. And we weren't wading through week-old goo downstairs."

"So you're saying somebody, what, came back and cleaned up afterward? Who would do that? Why?"

Chris muttered, "Who, what, why. All you need is how, and you'll be a swell little investigator, Nicky."

"Screw you, man."

"There is a long list of reasons why that'll never happen."

"Ew!"

Chris cackled, but it drained away into thoughtfulness again. "Why would you come back and clean up after a bunch of vamps?"

"'Cause you were gonna sell the house."

"Well, that's the most boring explanation I've ever heard."

"Makes the most sense, though."

"Except for the seven vampires in the basement would have eaten you if you just came in to clean."

"Maybe there was only one vampire in the basement before they came in to clean!"

Chris's gaze rolled toward the ceiling, his lips pursed before his eyebrows shrugged a concession. "Yeah, okay, legit. Guess we better call the local cleaning companies and see if anybody's missing. Is that all it is?" He sounded disappointed. "Just…Dad got unlucky and a vampire made lunch of the people who came to clean up afterward? That's it? It's solved, you go home now?"

"Probably." Nick spread his hands as Chris scowled faintly at him. "Seriously, dude, it's more likely than a whole pile of vampires sat around waiting for him in the first place."

"Sometimes I hate this job." Chris turned away as he spoke, the word so quiet Nick didn't think he'd been meant to hear them.

He had, though, and took an awkward step toward his big brother. *Older* brother. Chris being smaller than him kind of didn't make sense, but a lot of things didn't make sense, and he had to live with that anyway. "You don't have to do this job, Chris. Why don't...why don't you come back to California with me? We could get a place and figure some things out."

"Yeah. I bet your hot girlfriend would love that. Her bae's asshole big brother coming to mooch off him."

Nick, dryly, said, "I've met you. Mooching off somebody is not in your repertoire. Seriously, Chris, why not? Will you just—will you just think about it?"

"Yeah. Yeah, sure, fine, whatever. Come on. I guess we found our answers, even if they suck, so let's go. Out the side door, so if anybody saw us come in they won't see us leaving. We can walk around the long way and come up on the other side of town on our way back to the truck."

"We gonna stop at the diner for dinner? I haven't eaten since…I dunno." Nick's voice dropped, grief hitting him. "I don't remember eating since I got your text."

"Well, Jesus, no wonder you wanted lunch earlier. You always ate a lot even before you ended up nine feet tall. Why didn't you say something?"

"I did! I said we should get lunch!"

"Yeah, all right, fine. Come on." Chris yanked the back door open and a monster of wings and fire slammed him to the floor.

# CHAPTER 4

THERE'D BEEN AN INSTANT THERE WHEN TIME SLOWED DOWN, that split second between opening the door and hitting the floor. A half a heartbeat where he'd seen the thing out there and his brain had screamed *run!* or *duck!* or *close the door!*, and his muscles hadn't been able to respond fast enough. A breath of time where he'd *seen* the thing, even if he couldn't make sense of what he saw.

It barreled over him in a wash of heat and claws. Not claws. Hands, but long skinny thin ones with black nails long enough to *be* claws. All of the thing was long and skinny and white. Not people-white, but cadaver-white, with a hollow beneath the ribcage so deep he could almost count the vertebrae. It was made of shadows, shadows cast by wings that pummeled and struck at him, at the walls, at the table, and set them smoldering.

Chris dipped a hand to his waistband, came up with a knife, and dragged it down the thing's thigh as it swept over him.

Turned out that was a good-news-bad-news situation. Good news: it stopped flowing over him, no longer heading deeper into the kitchen. No longer heading toward Nicky.

Bad news: Chris now had its full attention.

He'd seen its face for that time-slowed moment in the doorway and filed it under *terrifying; see also: gross*, but at a second glance it was much, much worse than that.

Stringy black hair caught the light from its fiery wings, and too-sharp features stood out through oily strands. White skin, hatchet nose, cavernous nostrils, a mouth slashed with black and filled with teeth. Its chin and cheekbones looked as if they could cut, and its eyes glowed deep and unforgiving black, like the stars had all burned out of the night sky.

It looked as though it had been inhumanly beautiful once, before someone with only a passing guess at what humanity or beauty meant had bleached it, stretched it, carved it, and left it to bleed out at the side of a road. It rose up, one hand lifted to drive taloned fingers at Chris's throat, and a series of gun shots slammed into its chest, knocking it backward.

Ichor spat from the wounds, hissing as it hit the floor. Chris threw an arm over his face, protecting his eyes, and felt the impact of the hot blood burning holes in his coat sleeve. Another round of shots fired above him as he rolled and scrambled back, putting distance between himself and the thing. Nicky stood between them, tall and confident and stupidly unafraid, like he always was in the middle of a fight. Chris got to his feet, slid his gun from the back of his jeans, and lifted it to fire at the thing on the floor.

Except it wasn't on the floor anymore. Nicky had hit it, no doubt: gaping wounds showed through its torso, and the upper part of one arm was half torn off. But it was up, it was moving, it wasn't even fazed by having been shot five times.

It pounced onto the wall, and crawled around it, igniting the ceiling and counter top with its flaming wings. Six of them, three to a side, one set massive, the other two smaller, moving in such tandem with the big ones that it was difficult to see it wasn't all just one set. Something about the fire looked like eyes, blinking and opening and watching every motion they made, watching every motion *everything* made, like the whole world was under its gaze. Nicky shot a wide-eyed glance over his shoulder at Chris, who shrugged. He didn't know what it was, either, but knives and bullets didn't seem to slow it down, which didn't leave them in a good place.

His voice dropped, like the winged thing couldn't hear him if he spoke quietly. "Get out of here, Nicky. I'll cover you."

"Oh yeah, like hell."

"Nicky—!"

"Chris!"

The word was as much warning as argument. The winged thing threw itself from the wall to the ceiling, craning its neck almost all the way backward to watch them as it crawled above them. They both lifted their weapons and fired, enough bullets this time to at least make it scream. Then Nick was out and reloading while Chris emptied his clip into the monster.

It smiled when he ran out of bullets. Smiled, and leaped for them. Nicky yelled and threw himself at Chris, knocking him out of the way, and the thing landed on Nick's back, slashing through his coat with its clawed fingers. Chris punched upward, hoping he'd hit the monster instead of his brother, and couldn't tell if he'd landed in the thing's mouth or a bullet wound. Whatever it was had hard bits like bone and soft hot squishy parts that sent a shudder through his whole body. He clawed his fingers into the squishiness and hauled it sideways, getting it most of the way off Nicky.

The floor caught fire when it rolled, which didn't seem fair. Nick yelped and fell off Chris, rolling the other way, trying to escape the flames, which at least were only sputtering with the waxy smell of nylon melting instead of blazing. Chris rolled after him like they were all a bunch of goddamn Lincoln Logs spilling across the floor. Then pretty much all at once everybody was on their feet again, and the monster was launching itself toward them again.

Nick grabbed one of its arms and gave a wordless bellow

that meant Chris should do the same. For a heartbeat they had the thing, each of them hauling backward like they could tear it apart down the middle. Then with a flex of impossible strength, it slammed them together like it was doing a butterfly press. Chris bounced off Nick, stunned, and Nick staggered back a couple of steps, his expression changing from the familiar edge of fear and survival to quick-kindled rage.

Nicky didn't get mad, often, when they hunted. Said it clouded his judgment, made him make bad choices, all that kind of sensitive new-age crap. He liked to fight calm and smart. Even when he did get pissed, Chris always thought it was kind of like watching a terrier go ballistic. Little and fierce and not to be messed with, for sure, but also slightly ridiculous because it was like shin-high and fluffy.

Turned out another four or five inches of height and close to that in breadth turned his little brother from a terrier into a frickin' mastiff, or something. Nick grabbed the thing's arm and stepped inside its guard all in one smooth fast angry motion, then clawed his fingers into the thing's throat. It shrieked, but didn't sound angry, only slapped its huge taloned hand against Nick's forehead, like it would pry the top of his head off. Something surged, not quite visibly, but like a sound wave rolling through. In its wake, electricity thrummed like generators were being activated. The hairs on Chris's arms stood and he ducked in, stabbing at the thing's guts while Nicky freaking one-armed it into the air. Then it did scream, and kick, but there was only one of it. It didn't have enough arms to fight them both at the same time.

Too bad the burning, watching wings more than made up for that. They pressed around both Chris and Nick, setting their coats to smoldering. Everything smelled bad: leather burning, canvas burning, nylon burning, old paint burning, everything burning. The whole place was going to be on fire in a minute.

At the back of Chris's mind, something clicked. He grated, "Nick. Run," and met his brother's eyes for half a heartbeat. Nick's gaze held a question. Chris nodded his certainty, Nick's eyebrows twitched in acceptance, and all at once they both let go of the thing, racing in opposite directions. Nick bolted for the front door. Chris ran for the kitchen door, slapping his hand across the stove front on the way past. He careened out the door, threw himself around the corner of the house and yelled, "Run!" again.

About six seconds later the whole fucking place blew as gas from the stove he'd turned on met fire, and ignited.

———

The next couple minutes were kind of hazy and mostly involved failing to push to his hands and knees while his ears rang and he tasted blood somewhere in his throat. There was an awful lot of heat behind him, just far enough away that Chris didn't figure he'd melt. After another minute he could hear himself saying, "Nick? Nicky? *Nicky*?"

It felt like for-fucking-ever before Nick croaked, "Yeah. Yeah, man. Jesus. Ow."

Chris stopped trying to push himself out of the half-frozen earth, relief collapsing his muscles and maybe even his bones. "What the fuck was that?"

Nick's cackle sounded distant and slightly crazy. "It sure as hell wasn't Hope."

Chris lifted his head, staring incredulously across the frozen yard at Nick. "What the fuck does that mean?"

"You know? Hope is the thing with feathers? It's a poem? Emily Dickinson?"

"Man, the only Emily I know is the one who played Mary Poppins, and I'm all over that, but I don't think she's a poet."

Nick lay there for a second in silence. "See, now I'm

thinking you've got a thing for Mary Poppins and I didn't need that living rent-free in my brain."

Chris cackled and got up, shifting his shoulders and hips to see if anything hurt more than it should. "Well, whatever the fuck it was, it sure as fuck had feathers. Or wings, anyway. What the fuck was it?"

"Do you think you could say 'fuck' more times in one sentence?" Nick sat up, knees drawn up, arms looped around them, and head dropped so his hair shadowed his face. "Ow."

"That was two sentences and a question. Are you okay?"

"Sure. I'm just out of the habit of being slammed against walls and blown up." Nick rocked a couple of times, then all at once surged to his feet like he hadn't believed he could do it. The fire was still roaring, but not with the explosiveness of gas. Just a nice ordinary house fire. Totally normal. Nick walked unsteadily to Chris's side and offered him a hand, then pulled him up with an ease that reminded Chris of when they were kids. Except then, he'd been the one helping Nick to *his* feet. "We better get out of here. We're lucky the whole block didn't go."

"I was putting money on the gas being turned off to the house, since it was abandoned. I figured what was left in the pipes would be enough." Chris wobbled a couple of steps, stopped to get control over his legs, and walked on with more certainty, Nick in his wake.

"Pretty smart."

"Pretty lucky."

"Think we killed that thing?"

Chris looked over his shoulder at the burning house. "It hasn't come out after us, so I'm gonna go with yeah. Shit," he said more softly, as lights and sirens lit up the street. "Better move it."

Neither of them had it in them to run. They both did anyway, or at least made a respectable effort that slipped them between houses and across the least-snowy ground they could find, trying not to leave tracks on the cold earth. A few minutes later they circled around to the truck, crawling in like it was a house of refuge. Chris drove out of town sedately while Nick sprawled over his half of the bench seat, eyes closed and his breathing only slowly calming down. "You okay?"

It took a long time for Nick to answer. "No. I'm not hurt, but...no. I'm out of practice for this, Chris."

"You did good, though." He hesitated, waiting to see if the praise was rejected, and added," The way you picked that thing up, Jesus, Nicky. You been working out?" when Nick accepted it.

His brother, eyes still closed, chuckled. "Maybe a little. It didn't weigh that much, though."

"Weighed enough to knock me down."

"It caught you off guard."

"Jesus, Nick, I don't need you to make me feel better for getting knocked on my ass. I'm trying to be nice."

"Yeah, that lasted all of two minutes."

Chris hit the heel of his hand against the steering wheel and shut up, because what was the point in trying to talk if it backfired on him every damn time. They drove in silence till a road sign announced there was food up ahead. He turned into the town and drove up the highway until a blue and white sign on a red brick building said *Grandma Ann's*. "Dinnertime."

Nick opened his eyes as they pulled into the parking lot. His jaw tightened, but he nodded, which was probably as much thanks as Chris was gonna get for thinking to feed him. Some things never changed. "There's baby wipes in the glove compartment. We better get cleaned up before we go in."

"I did not miss this." Nick scrubbed his hands and face with one of the little wipes, though, and came away looking less like he'd been in a fight. Chris did the same and Nick gave him a nod that suggested he was passable, before they went in to a diner that *looked* like it should be called *Grandma Ann's*. Twenty minutes later Nick had a whole semi-circle of food spread around the table and was eating his way through it by folding entire pancakes into his mouth at once, cutting burgers into quarters and apparently swallowing them whole, chewing through fists full of fries, and guzzling soda like he hadn't drunk anything in a month. Chris sat there with his own dinner half forgotten, watching in horrified admiration. Nick eventually said, "What?" defensively, and Chris lifted his hands.

"Nothing, man, I've just never seen anybody eat that much."

"Dude, you and Jake used to eat 20-inch pizzas in like two minutes."

"I know, but…" Chris gestured at the empty plates in front of Nick, and at his own half-eaten salad.

"I was hungry!"

"Yeah. I know." Chris heard his voice soften and grimaced at his plate. "Sorry I didn't feed you earlier."

"It's fine, Chris." Nick pushed the closest plates away and put his elbows on the table, hands hiding his face. From behind them, muffled, he said, "It's what, another forty miles back to Sterling?"

"About that."

Nick stayed silent a long minute behind his hands, then said, "I'll tell Steph we won't be back until tonight." He lifted his face far enough that Chris could see his eyes, bruised with tiredness, above his fingertips. He looked about twelve, that way. "Think that'll give us enough time to figure out what the fuck happened back there?"

"No, but it's a start and…" Chris swallowed. "I appreciate it. I know you…you've got a life to get back to."

"So that's okay now?"

Chris said, "No," way too fast, but it wasn't like it was

gonna surprise Nick, who smiled thinly as he dropped his hands. "But you're leaving anyway, aren't you."

"Yeah."

"So I guess I'll take what I can get." Chris would rather cut his own throat than let his voice crack, but it was a near thing. Near enough that Nicky gave him a sharp look, but Chris covered it with a tight smirk. "You can check Bhuntr on the way home. Maybe somebody's got something about that thing on the Beowulf board."

"Yeah." Nick went quiet, finishing his dinner with a focused, downcast gaze. Chris poked at his own salad, glancing at Nick's tense shoulders and controlled movements, but kept quiet until they'd paid and were back in the truck. Then, finally, he said, "What is it?" and Nicky cast him a guilty look.

"Nothing. What? Why'd you ask?"

"Because I know what you look like when you don't like what you're thinking, Nick. What's going on in that big brain of yours?"

"Do you really think we killed that thing?"

"No." The word came out too fast again.

Nick turned his attention out the window, jaw working with stress before he spoke. "Yeah. Me either. I think we slowed it down. Maybe. Or…"

Chris waited until they were on the highway again, the occasional truck passing them the other direction, before he finished the thought Nicky didn't want to voice. "You don't think it was trying to kill us."

Guilt skittered across Nick's face again, obvious even in profile. "That thing…you know what it looked like, right?"

"I don't have a fucking clue, Nick. Enlighten me."

"An angel."

Laughter barked from Chris's chest before he could stop it. "An *angel*? Man, you and me, we know about different angels."

"That's because you only know about Charlie's. Seriously, though, shut up. Biblically a lot of angels are kind of monstrosities. Lots of wings and eyes and—"

"Fire?"

"Yeah, actually."

Chris shot his brother a hard look. "You can't really believe that thing was an angel."

"Dude, we went there to fight a vampire, so sure, why not? Besides, there's..." Nick pressed the heel of his hand to his forehead, eyes closed. "I feel like I *know* it, somehow."

"From those Sunday school lessons I never went to." Not that Nick had either. Church hadn't exactly been a big part of their upbringing. The first time Chris could remember even being in one, he'd snuck in to grab some wafers because he thought they might make a decent snack for Nick, after school. He'd been wrong, but that wasn't the point.

Nick, sounding tired, said, "I guess." He fell silent again until they crossed the state border, sparse snow whisking around the truck in devils. "Chris, do you...do you think there's a chance it wasn't a vampire that killed Dad?"

Chris said, "Fuck," under his breath, and aloud, said, "I'd kind of feel better if it was that thing, but what would be the point? And there were vamps there."

"What if the point was...us?" Nick's mouth worked as if the words were hard to get out.

Chris gave him a sharp look, then shook his head. "That doesn't make any sense. We'll figure it out when we get home."

"It does make sense," Nick protested. "How would you get both of us in one place, after all this time?"

A knot tied in Chris's gut and wouldn't loosen, but he shook his head again. "Let's just get home, Nicky. We can't figure anything out on the road. It's only another few minutes anyway."

Nick put his head against the window, eyes closed again, and after a long minute, said, "I'm tired," very quietly.

The knot in Chris's belly tightened dangerously, like it wanted to squeeze tears out of him. He reached over and put his hand on Nick's shoulder, cautiously. "Yeah. Me too, Nicky. Me too. Hang in there, buddy. We'll be home soon."

Nick nodded, and Chris drove a little faster.

————

The double-wide they'd grown up in when they weren't on the road hadn't changed much in four years, except it was cleaner than Nick expected. He stopped in the kitchen door, honestly confused by recently-vacuumed carpets and windows that had obviously been washed within the last week or two. It smelled decent, like somebody had cooked something worth eating in the not-so-distant past. The living room couch, visible around the end of the kitchen wall, had the same frame he remembered, but the pillows no longer caved in at sprung, crushed corners.

Chris, a few steps ahead of him, said, "Close the damn door, you're letting all the heat out." Nick did so with a guilty twitch, then glared at his brother's shoulders.

"I'm not four, you know."

"Yeah? Then why didn't you close the door behind you?" Chris threw his ichor-covered coat over the back of a kitchen chair and started stripping off his clothes on the way through a door that hid the laundry room. "You've still got some clothes here from when you left. The sleeves are probably short but it's gonna be better than what you're wearing now. You wanna shower first while I get the laundry going?"

"You do laundry now?"

Chris gave him a peculiar look from just inside the laundry room. "I always did laundry, dude. Who do you think kept your clothes clean for school?"

Nick opened his mouth and shut it again on the obvious answer, which was 'Dad', because if he thought about it at all, he could only remember their dad washing his own clothes, not theirs. "…thanks."

"'swhat big brothers are for." Chris came out of the laundry room in his underwear, which was more—or more accurately, less—than Nick could handle right then. He made a sound of dismay and put his hand up, blocking his view, then grunted as Chris smacked his shoulder on the way by. "Man, get over yourself, you've seen me more naked than this. Fine, I'm taking a shower first. You do the laundry. Detergent's on the shelf. Make sure you use the yellow box. The other stuff gives me hives."

"Then why do we even have it?"

"'cause Dad."

For a second Nick thought there was going to be more to that sentence, but 'because Dad' was actually reason enough. He went to do the laundry, using the stuff in the yellow box, then took the blue one off the shelf and held it to his nose, inhaling.

Chris found him sitting against the washing machine in his underwear twenty minutes later, the blue box spilled by his side, his head buried against his knees, and the body-wracking sobs all but abated. "Shit, Nicky." He slid down to sitting, put an arm around Nick's shoulders, and pulled him sideways into a silent hug.

"I haven't even talked to him in years," Nick said hoarsely. "You'd think it wouldn't matter."

"Nah, man." Chris sighed. "He's your dad. It doesn't just go away. I couldn't throw that stuff out. Smelled too much like him. Couldn't do it. It's okay, Nick."

"It's not. He died mad at me."

"He died stubborn," Chris said quietly. "I don't think he's been mad at you for ages. He might have even been proud."

"Bullshit."

"No. I don't think so." Chris fell silent a few seconds. "You need a shower, man."

"Yeah, yeah, whatever." Nick climbed to his feet and this time Chris blocked his eyes.

"Jesus, Nick."

"What was all that talk about me having seen you more naked than that, then?"

"Man, you were *smaller* last time I saw you this naked! Go! Jesus! Go take a shower and cover yourself!" Chris threw a handful of laundry detergent at Nick and he gave a small rough laugh, more than he'd thought he could a minute ago, and went to shower.

The bathroom was a *lot* cleaner than he remembered it, and he stood in the hot water a while, the backs of his eyelids flashing between images of the funeral pyre and the burning angel. Saboac. The heat from the pyre had been worse, but purer. Burning away—not sins, but maybe lies. The kinds of lies people told themselves to get by. That it didn't matter if his dad wasn't supportive. That it was okay to have cut Chris off as well as their old man. Burning it all away so uncomplicated heartbreak could do its thing. He was pretty sure it wasn't just hot shower water sluicing down his cheeks, but no one else was there to judge him.

Just himself, and that, Nick figured, was enough.

Saboac's fire had smoldered, clogging the air, thickening in Nick's lungs. Killing, instead of purifying. As if its slow burn had intended to sink into his skin, melting it like it had the old house's carpets. He couldn't scrub the sensation off, regardless of how hard he tried. Finally he climbed out of the shower, and dried off, wishing he could stand in front of his father's pyre again and let it...decontaminate him, after Saboac's touch.

He went still, no longer toweling his hair. "Chris?"

"What!" His brother sounded irritable.

His brother usually sounded irritable. No reason to let

that stop a conversation, or they'd never talk at all. "Did that thing say anything? The burning angel?"

"No, why?" Chris appeared in the short hall that led toward the bedrooms as Nick stepped out of the bathroom.

"Have you ever heard the word 'Saboac', then?"

"No. What's the deal?"

"It's…it's…in my head. The word. Like it put it there. I think it's its name."

"I never heard of an angel Saboac."

"Me neither. Look it up while I get dressed." Nick went into the bedroom he'd shared with Chris until he left, then froze, taken back in time and thrust into the future all at once. There were still posters on the walls from when they'd been teenagers, less of buxom babes than science fiction badasses. Nick guessed Chris still had a thing for Ripley. His own poster of Einstein's imagination quote was still up, hanging above a bookshelf that had a couple of his dusty high school sports trophies on it.

But everything else that said he'd once lived there was gone. To be fair, he'd taken most of it, and didn't know why Chris would keep the rest hanging around. There was a double bed now, instead of the two singles they'd had smashed up against the opposite walls with the piece of tape down the middle of the room to delineate *my side* and *your side*. The shelves below his trophies held knives, guns, and what Nick thought was a garrote, which seemed particularly gruesome. The closet door, partially opened, showed a limited number of coats and heavy shirts, rather than the jam-packed-full mess of clothes, shoes, random boxes, and general junk that had once been shoved in it.

Folded on the foot of the bed were sweatpants, a t-shirt he'd owned when he was fifteen, and socks and underwear so new they hadn't been taken out of the packages yet. Numb with the clash of past and present, Nick got dressed and padded out to the living room, where Chris was scowling over his phone. "You said Saboac? S A B O A C?"

"I don't know how it's spelled, but yeah, that sounds right."

Chris turned the phone toward him, displaying a Wiki page. "Well, that sucks, because Saboac's a fucking fallen angel."

# CHAPTER 5

"A f—" Nick took the phone out of Chris's hand, sitting as he skimmed through the article. "Not a fallen angel. A reprobate angel. No. Reporbated. What the hell is that." He trailed off, reading it more carefully while Chris sat back down and pulled his feet up on the couch like a kid.

"It's fallen, man. Nobody except some old guy at the Vatican cares what 'reporbated' is."

Nick, softly, said, "Shit," then shook his head. "No, I think it makes a difference. Fallen's a big deal, like, that's defying-God territory, right? But this says God *desanctified* Saboac."

"Fallen, desanctified, what's the difference?"

"Did you read this or not?"

"I'd just found it when you came out!"

Nick pulled a hand over his face and offered the phone back so Chris could read it, but Chris just stared at him expectantly. "Lucifer fell, Chris. He defied God and was cast out or fell or whatever you want to call it, and a bunch of others went with him. But they're still angels. This one isn't. God took away its sanctity, its angelicness. I think it's, like… pure evil."

Chris squinted dubiously. "I thought that was Lucifer's whole gig."

"I mean, I don't know, man, it's not like I've interviewed the devil, but can an angel even *be* pure evil? But this thing—" Nick shuddered, suddenly remembering the oily feeling of its touch. "I think this thing can be. Is."

"Well, if it used to be an angel and God took away its angelness, how can it even be anything? Wouldn't it just like shrivel up into cosmic nothing?"

"I don't know! It doesn't say!"

"What the hell good does that do us, then? What did pure evil want with Dad? Or us?" Chris inhaled sharply. "With *you*?"

Ice dotted down Nick's arms and spine, like the shower he'd just taken had been a cold one. "Me?"

"It grabbed your head, not mine."

"I was the one holding it!"

"You friggin' straight-armed it after it grabbed you!"

"What's that got to do with anything?"

"I don't know, Nick, are you in the habit of lifting people ten inches off the floor with one hand?"

Nick reeled back. "...no..."

"So I'm guessing it's got something to do with you! And you knew its name. And I didn't." Chris's voice cooled suddenly, down-shifting from aggravation and confusion into something Nick recognized as much more dangerous. "It wanted something to do with you, Nicky. And I didn't stop it."

"You blew up the house it was in."

"Think that's enough to stop a fallen—a *desanctified* —angel?"

"No." Nick closed his eyes. "No, I don't."

"So we gotta figure out—Jesus, I don't know. Who knows about angels, for God's sake?"

Nick opened his eyes again to give Chris a flat look. "I dunno, maybe God?"

Chris gave him a filthy look in return. "Right, 'cause you've got him on speed dial? No? That's okay, 'cause I've got the Pope in my contacts, I'll just call him up like 'yo, dude, reporbate angels, tell me the story there.'"

"All right! All right, Jesus, you don't have to lean in to the smartassery. What about...I don't know, what about Grandma?"

Chris's eyebrows shot up. "Why would Grandma know about fallen angels?"

"I don't know, except she always seemed like she knew everything, and...I don't know. It was a dumb idea." Nick pushed his hands through his hair and sat there, caved in over himself. "Does she even know about Dad?"

"I called her, yeah."

Hurt and anger crushed the air from Nick's belly. He tried to inhale around the emptiness, and pushed grated words out. "You called—"

"Look, okay, I know, okay? I get it. I called Grandma but I texted you, I get it, I'm an asshole." Chris slammed out of the couch and stomped toward the kitchen like accusations were stalking him.

"You really are." Nick stayed where he was, still trying to breathe around what felt like a gut wound. "She couldn't come?"

Chris banged things around in the kitchen, maybe emptying the dishwasher. "She's got a cow that's had a hard pregnancy and it's supposed to give birth any day. She was afraid if she left it she'd come back to two dead animals."

"And she didn't like Dad much anyway."

"She said she was sorry and we should come out to the farm," Chris said, on top of that. "Just like she's been saying since Mom died."

"She was probably right."

The banging went quiet, and after a minute, so did Chris's voice. "Yeah. Probably. Do you wanna go?"

"I can't. I gotta go back to..." A different kind of twist hurt Nick's belly again. "Back to school. At some point."

"With a desanctified angel on our asses? On *your* ass? How're you gonna explain that to pretty little Stephanie?"

"Chris, I swear to fucking God, if you can't stop being a dick…"

His brother crossed into Nick's line of sight to offer him a cheeky, asshole smile. "You know it's part of my charm."

"It really isn't."

Chris's smile fell away and he went back to unloading the dishwasher. "I'm not wrong, though. I mean, maybe we killed that thing and it was just an extra-special freak and you can go back to your nice life with your nice girlfriend and your nice…whatever. But maybe we didn't, and it comes after us again. Or you. What are you gonna do then? Tell her there are things that go bump in the night? Or about the freaks, since they're actually scarier, 'cause they're still people?"

"No! No. No, Stephanie's…she's my normal, Chris. She's everything I'm aiming for. I don't want her pulled into bounty hunting, much less vampires and whatever Saboac is."

"Your normal, huh." Chris sounded like he was looking toward Nick. "How long've you been together?"

"About eight months."

"Wow. And she's everything you're aiming for? So, what, you really are gonna marry her?"

"I mean…maybe? I don't know, man. But even if I don't, or especially if I don't, she doesn't need to know about all the crap we've seen. Our lives here, they're fucking weird, Chris. Even without the grendels, bounty hunting can get kind of monstery. I don't want her to be involved in monstery."

Chris came to the kitchen entrance, drying his hands. "'Grendels?'"

"The freaks. I don't like the word freaks and there's the Bhuntr Beowulf board and I thought…grendels."

"Hnh. Yeah, okay. That's kind of cool." He went back into the kitchen and Nick heard the scrape of one of the chairs against the linoleum floor. "This is more than 'kind of' monstery, though, Nick. I know you want to go back to Cali, but I think we really have to figure out this Saboac thing first. Maybe we *should* call Grandma. She's old and weird. She knows stuff."

"No." Nick got up to change the laundry as the washing machine started beeping. Chris was working on his jacket on the kitchen table, scrubbing ichor out with strong-smelling leather cleaner. "No, you were right, why would she know about reporbate angels. Besides, she's part of normal, too, Chris. I don't want to screw that up. I'd like to go out to her farm. Maybe this summer. I'm supposed to intern, but...I don't know. Maybe some family time is more important. I already—" Nick leaned heavily on the washing machine, head dropped as his throat went tight. "I already screwed that up big time," he managed after a minute. "I can't fix it with Dad. I shouldn't blow it with Grandma, too."

"So you're not gonna ask Grandma anything and you're not gonna tell Stephanie anything and you think *I'm* the one who thinks he has to do everything on his own?"

"Historically, yeah." Nick finished putting the clothes into the dryer and joined Chris at the kitchen table, watching without seeing as Chris scoured gunk out of his jacket. "I mean, when was the last time you asked anybody for help?"

"You, this morning."

"Before that!"

"S'not the point, is it. Point is, you're gonna have to tell Stephanie and your boyfriend someth—"

"He's my roommate, not my boyfriend. Tyler."

"Whatever, man. You're going to have to tell them something. If you're staying."

Nick, sharply, said, "I'm not *staying*," then both heard and felt himself lose the edge as his shoulders slumped. "I'm just... not leaving yet. Because you're right. Saboac being there doesn't seem like a coincidence, so I want to know if it was after Dad, or after us. Need to know," he amended more quietly. "'Cause if it was after us, I can't go home until it's dealt with, or I'll endanger everybody around me."

"Yeah, well, lucky me, I don't have that problem 'cause I don't have anybody around me." Chris wiped a clean cloth over the coat's leather, then rose to hang it in the laundry room, where he cracked a window open to help dissipate the smell. He pulled the door closed behind him, mostly keeping the cold out of the rest of the house, although Nick could feel the breeze from below the door skating across his toes.

"Why don't you?"

"You left."

"Man, I'm your brother, not your prom date. Why don't you have somebody else?"

"I had Dad."

"Are you being deliberately obtuse?"

"I don't even know what that means." Chris stumped past him into the living room, leaving Nick to put his head in his hands again and wonder when, exactly, his brother had gotten so stubborn. Except Chris had always been that way, and if Nick was honest, he might acknowledge it was something of a family trait. Even their grandmother had a mile-wide streak of stubborn that had driven her into the edge-of-nowhere farmhouse after her husband had died. Their mom had grown up out there, 'cause Grandma said cities weren't safe enough these days, never mind that the old lady had run off more than one rustler with her shotgun and had stories that raised the hairs on Nick's nape when he was little.

She would hear him out, if he called. She'd tell him he was crazy, after that, but she'd hear him out, and Nick almost wanted to get her reassurance that he *was* a little off the deep end.

Except she didn't know about the vamps and the freaks, which meant he already had more information than she did, so he knew he wasn't crazy, and her reassurances wouldn't do as much good as he wished they would.

And arguing with Chris would do him even less good than that. Nick sighed and went to look for his phone, which turned out to be in the laundry room, getting cold even though the dryer was running. There were a couple of text messages from Stephanie that he answered with a promise to be back in town soon, and an appalling gif from Tyler that he deleted without responding to. Then, laundry room door closed and the dryer running at his back, he sat on the floor and called Jake. "You with Stephanie and Ty?"

Jake's surprise came across the line. "Nick? No. Is Chris okay?"

"That's probably a question for a therapist."

A bark of laughter answered him. "I meant, are you calling because something went wrong, but valid point. What's up?"

"I don't know. I'm worried about him. Everything sucks. I miss Dad." The answers came in a rush, none of it what Nick had intended to say.

Jake sighed. "Yeah. Yeah, I know, buddy. I'm sorry. Are you guys done, then? Did you take care of the problem?" The slightest hesitation before the final word filled in all the details that couldn't be said aloud on the phone.

"Part of it," Nick said quietly. "It turned out to be more complicated than we expected."

He listened to the silence while Jake assimilated that. "Come in to town," the other hunter said after a moment. "We'll talk about it in person."

"As soon as the laundry's done. I'm wearing clothes from high school. Thanks for cleaning the house, by the way."

"Me? I didn't. See you in a while." Jake hung up and Nick sat, not hiding, in the half-frozen laundry room, until Chris pounded on its door.

"Nicky? You okay?"

"Sure. Just waiting for the clothes to finish."

"Well, come wait out here. I found some stuff on the

Beowulf board." The dryer beeped as Chris spoke and Nick rose, taking the clothes out and carrying them into the living room to dump on the couch and root through them for his own stuff.

"Lemme get dressed and you can tell me on the way into town. I have to talk to Stephanie."

"You are not going to leave those on the couch."

Somehow Chris managed to get all their dad's disapproval into his tone, even if Nick had never heard their father say anything remotely like that in his life. He paused with the armful of his own clothing to stare at Chris. "The rest of them are yours?"

"So? You took them out, you can fold them."

Nick's jaw worked a couple times before he muttered, "Fine. Let me get dressed first," and stomped into the bathroom.

———

Earthquakes would rattle the trailer less than Chris's baby brother clumping down the hall. When they'd been kids, everything Nicky did was a galumph, all energy and elbows that Chris guessed he should've realized would turn into about six and a half feet of brother-shaped muscle that could shake the ceiling. Nick had been about Chris's height when he went to college. He'd seemed smaller to Chris, though. For one thing, he'd been slimmer, but mostly it was that Chris had thought of Nick as his soft, sensitive little brother.

Nick was probably still sensitive, but he'd never really been soft, not the way Chris imagined he was. Not with their dad, and their lifestyle. And he sure as hell wasn't little anymore. He looked young, to Chris. Older than he remembered, but still young. But he'd been barely seventeen when he left for college, so most of four years later, he wasn't quite legal to drink yet.

Thinking about it, Chris probably shouldn't have handed him a beer when he'd shown up at the funeral.

Or fifty other times when they were teenagers, but their old man probably shouldn't have been giving Chris beers then, either.

Chris muttered, "Lousy fucking role model," and went ahead and folded his own clothes. Nick came back down the hall as he finished, and stopped dead.

"I was gonna do that."

"I know, but you wanted to get going to see Samantha."

"Stephanie, you dick."

"Whatever. Go get in the truck."

Nick headed for the door, obediently, then stopped and glared at Chris. "I don't have to do what you tell me to anymore."

"Then walk to town!" Chris marched past him and out the door, not quite making the effort to slam it in Nicky's face when he sullenly followed. He didn't make the effort not to, either, though, and Nick swore as it bounced back at him. He was still glaring when they got in the truck, but his sulk turned to reluctant interest when Chris muttered, "The Beowulf board's been seeing a bunch of extra-weird stuff in this part of the country. Vampire hives like the one we ran into. Freaks —" He shot a look at Nick, and as a peace offering, said, "*Grendels*. Grendels gathering, but not for any violence or crime. More like for protection, the boards say. They're not causing trouble, just hunkering down and looking scared."

"Anybody else seen this Saboac?" Nick still sounded sulky, but he usually did, at least to Chris.

"Not as far as I can tell. Nobody's mentioned a single big bad, just that the things we usually think of as the big bads are teaming up for moral support. There's a lot of chatter about why, and obviously people are imagining that there's something pretty bad coming, but nobody knows what."

"You mention Saboac?"

"Not yet."

Nick nodded stiffly, like he approved, or was relieved. "I guess we'll know if we killed it by whether the vamps and grendels disperse."

"Disperse." Chris shook his head and cast a glance out the side window so he wouldn't roll his eyes at Nicky. "You and your fucking vocabulary, man."

"Disperse is a totally normal word!"

"Normal people would say 'go home' or something."

"That could have a completely different meaning. They could all go home together, with that phrasing. We want them to go back to how they were. We want them to *disperse*."

"Like I said, you and your fucking vocabulary. Where's your girl, the Super8?"

"Holiday Inn." Nick frowned as Chris gave him a sharp look. "What?"

"Pretty fucking fancy, that's all."

"It's just a Holiday Inn, Chris."

"Yeah, whatever." Chris took the right that brought them over to the Holiday Inn and watched his little brother tumble out of the truck, all knees and elbows like a puppy dog again, as his girlfriend ran out of the hotel to meet him.

Nick didn't look right in Sterling anymore. When he'd layered up with the flannel and canvas, that had been okay. That had been the Nick he knew, the one who belonged here. But his *clothes*, the stuff he actually wore...somebody who knew how to shop for the good stuff had bought them for full price, not at an outlet store with last year's styles at a discount. They were flattering, Chris guessed. Fashionable. Like the hotel, Nick was real fucking fancy now. Soft. A college kid, not a bounty hunter.

The fact that that had been the whole point didn't make it any easier to look at.

Chris got out of the truck, hanging back until Stephanie

stopped fussing over his brother, or at least until Nick, sheep-ishly, made her stop. "You remember Chris."

"Hard to forget." Stephanie offered her hand the way she hadn't the night before, and Chris took it.

"Hey. Sorry about being a dick last night."

Surprise flitted through her eyes and she glanced at Nick, the same way she had the night before, before she nodded at Chris. "Apology accepted. We probably shouldn't have butted in."

"No, you were with Nicky. You were welcome."

A smile pulled at her mouth. "I've never heard anybody call him Nicky before."

"Well, you never met anybody who changed his diapers, either."

"Chris! You did not!"

"No, I didn't." Chris pulled up a grin for Stephanie. "The real stories are much worse."

Her smile broadened. "I look forward to hearing them."

Nick's voice went high-pitched. "But not right now. Can we go in, Steph? I gotta talk to you about some stuff. Is Ty here?"

"He's in the restaurant with your friend Jake. He's nice." Stephanie tucked her arm into Nick's and they went across the parking lot ahead of Chris. "He took it on himself to keep an eye on us, when I'm sure he's got a lot of other things to be doing instead. You've known each other a long time?" She glanced back at Chris, including him in the conversation.

"Since we were kids. We used to cut school together."

"I bet you got into all kinds of trouble."

"You have no idea. Not Nicky, though. *He* studied."

Stephanie dimpled. "Still does. We met in the library."

"Guys, you could try not talking about me like I'm not here."

"Not sure we can," Chris said, but Stephanie smiled up at

Nick again and they went into a clean white and blue lobby like that, arm in arm and cute as freaking buttons.

The restaurant at the far end of the lobby wasn't really a restaurant, just a place for hotel guests to eat their breakfast buffet. Jake and Nick's roommate had pushed two of the tables together and spread about forty cartons of Chinese takeout on them. Jake waved them down with a pair of chopsticks, like there was anybody else in the restaurant, or the lobby, for that matter. "I didn't know if California had made Nicky go all vegetarian so I got everything. Come eat."

"It didn't." Nick sat beside Stephanie and lifted his chin at his roommate. "How's your head?"

"Jake here wouldn't let me drink any more of that moonshine last night so I'm okay. You?"

"Slept off the worst of it. Chris, you remember Tyler?"

"Sure." Chris nodded as Tyler waved chopsticks like Jake had done. "Sorry if I was a dick last night."

Tyler finished his bite before giving Chris a blinding grin. "No worries. I mighta kinda been one myself. The cashew chicken is good."

"Thanks." Chris sat with the rest of them and for a few minutes everybody was more or less quiet, eating. Nick managed to put away about five cartons' worth of spring rolls, rice, and Mongolian beef even though it hadn't been more than a couple of hours, maybe three, since they'd stopped at the diner on their way home.

Maybe that was why he finished eating and pushed his plate away first. "Steph, I think you and Ty maybe better head home without me. Chris can drive me back in a few days, but we've...there's still stuff we've got to do."

Stephanie was shaking her head before Nick finished talking. "It's the weekend, and spring break starts soon anyway. We can stay. Or I can, at least."

Nick shook his head, too. "Spring break doesn't start until Thursday and we've got midterms. I can let them know my da—" His voice broke, and Chris started to reach for his shoulder, but Stephanie put her hands over Nick's first. Chris knotted his hand in a fist and retreated, feeling heat burn his jawline. Jake's gaze flickered past his, but if he'd noticed, he wouldn't mention it. Nick, almost in control of his voice again, said, "That my dad died. They're not going to let you skip them because you were driving somebody else home."

"They might," Ty said around a mouthful of rice. "'Specially if I get Dad to drop a donation in their coffers, huh? Anyway, I can hang out until tomorrow afternoon, anyway."

"My first exam is Tuesday," Stephanie said encouragingly. "I can fly back Monday night if I have to, or even really early Tuesday. Where's the nearest airport?"

"There are a couple regional ones a little closer than Denver, but you'd probably have to go through Denver to get back to San Francisco anyway, so you might as well start there. Hundred miles or so." Jake was making a real effort to keep his attention on the food, like he didn't want to get in the middle of Nick's friends being helpful versus Nick needing to go monster-hunting. Chris couldn't blame him.

"There," Stephanie said to Nick with obvious satisfaction. "I can fly back Monday night, if I have to."

Nick smiled carefully at Stephanie. "It's just that I might not be around a lot, you know? It's okay if you want to head home so you can study."

Tyler reached across the table to punch Nick's shoulder. "Nah, man. We've here for you. We'll study here and you can hang out when you need a break from everything." His gaze bounced toward Chris and away again.

Nick met Chris's eyes with a helpless expression, then smiled weakly at his friends again. "Thanks. I…thanks."

"Of course, babe. Do you have anything else you need to do tonight? Can you—I mean, do you want to stay at the hotel with me?"

"Or me?" Tyler fluttered his eyelashes and Nick snorted.

"Lemme talk to Chris about it. We haven't figured out—" Nick broke off as Chris's phone rang, drawing everybody's attention. Chris muttered, "Sorry," and took it out of an inside pocket, ready to hang up.

Except the caller was familiar, and he knew what it meant. He said, "Sorry," again, and got up to move a few feet away before he answered. "Chris Cassidy."

"Hey, Chris. It's Lauren at On Call Bail Bonds."

"Yeah." Chris could hear the rumbling smile in his own voice. "I got you in my phone, Laur. What's up?"

"Got a job for you and your dad, if you want it."

A fist closed in his chest, squeezing the smile away, although the roughness sure as hell stayed in his voice. "Dad died a couple days ago, Laur."

"Oh. Oh, fuck. Shit. I'm sorry, Chris. I didn't know. I'm sorry, I'll call somebody el—"

"No! No, look, I could use the money. What's the deal?"

Lauren sounded distressed. "Destruction of property, assault, good stuff like that. Your cut would be five grand, but—"

"Five—" The word cracked. "Yeah, I can't turn that down. Go ahead and send me the info."

"Are you sure? I'm so sorry, Chris."

"I'm sure. Thanks. Just send it to my phone." Chris hung up and came back to lean heavily on the restaurant tables, not quite looking at Nick. "I got a job that I have to take."

Nick inhaled to speak and his buddy Tyler beat him to it. "The fuck, man. I thought you guys had so much shi—" His wince suggested Stephanie had kicked him under the table. "So much *stuff* to take care of that Nick had to hang around. How can you go on a job?"

Chris couldn't even pretend that the expression he turned on Tyler was a smile. "*My* dad couldn't donate enough money to a college to make them look the other way if I skipped out on midterms, that's how. I've got a mortgage to pay."

Stephanie, more cautiously, said, "But..." and glanced at Nick.

"Chris is right." Nick spoke in a low voice. "We have a lot to sort out, but it's not gonna go away, and it's not gonna be made any easier by falling behind on the mortgage. You two should go home, and I'll come with you," he said to Chris.

"It's not like you can help."

"I got licensed in Cali, Chris."

Stephanie and Tyler both said, "You *what*?" as Chris straightened, surprised, and looked down at his little brother. Jake sat back, his eyebrows rising but his mouth still shut.

"I got my bounty hunter license in California after I moved there, as soon as I turned eighteen, and I've kept it up." Nick shrugged one shoulder uncomfortably. "I didn't know if school was going to work out. I figured being licensed would be a backup plan. So I can do the job. Legally, even."

Chris, softly, said, "Well, shit. Arright, Nicky. Let's do it, then. Maybe we can work out some of the other stuff too."

"Well, we can come with you," Stephanie said brightly.

"On a *bounty* hunt? No offense, but what the hell good are you going to do on a bounty hunt?"

Stephanie's shoulders tensed as she met Chris's eyes. "Supporting my boyfriend in a lousy time is enough good."

"Besides, it sounds badass," Tyler said. "Bounty hunting, man. That'll be cool. One for the bucket list."

Chris, through his teeth, said, "It's a lot less cool than you think, and you need a license to do it, so you can't just tag along. Why don't you go back to California and your scholarships and your rich daddy and y—"

"Chris." Nick sounded tired. Chris's phone buzzed as Lauren's email came in and he scowled at it.

"Bounty's almost five hours away. If you're coming with, pack up. I'm leaving in half an hour."

Nick said, "Chris," again, but he was already halfway out the door.

# CHAPTER 6

Stephanie dropped her head, watching Chris leave through her lowered gaze, then, lips pressed together, looked at Nick. "I know he's under a lot of stress, Nick, but…"

"But nothing." Jake's voice was gentle, as usual, but carried a warning. "No offense, Stephanie, but you and Tyler don't belong on a bounty. I know why you want to go, and I'm not gonna stop you, but you're going to make things harder for Chris."

"And what about Nick?"

"That's for him to decide." Jake, the traitor, got up and followed Chris out, leaving Nick to face his college friends alone. Stephanie turned an expectant look on him.

"It's not that I don't want you to come, Steph."

"But you don't want us to come," Tyler said.

Guilt surged through Nick. "It complicates things. And things are pretty complicated with me and Chris anyway."

Steph echoed, "'Complicated,'" in a flat tone. "Not the word I'd used. Toxic, maybe. Look, Nick, I'll stay out of the way. *We'll* stay out of the way, if you have to go. I think it'd be better if you came home with us, but if you're going to stay, I think you need a buffer between you and your brother right now. You're both running high, emotionally, and it's obvious one wrong word sets him off."

A smile flicked across Nick's mouth. "Unlike me, who is rational and reasonable at all times."

"You look a lot more reasonable to me. I don't want to leave you with him, Nick."

"I spent most of my life with him, Steph. He's got my back."

"Does he?"

"Yeah." Anger sharpened Nick's tone. "Yeah, Stephanie, he does. Maybe not in a way you exactly recognize, but yeah. He'd die for me."

"I'm more afraid he's going to end up killing you," Stephanie replied quietly. "Dragging you out bounty hunting when you're both grieving? Isn't bounty hunting dangerous?"

"Mostly it's studying digital footprints and personal habits. Figuring out where people go when they're not in trouble, and looking in all of those places, or following leads you pick up there, until you find them. Sometimes, depending on who you're looking for, it can get dangerous, but Chris and I can take care of ourselves."

"You tell me that," Steph said with a rueful smile. "But I see my big lunk of a squishy boyfriend and don't exactly believe it."

"Go to the gym with him," Tyler said dryly. "He doesn't look so squishy when he's benching two twenty."

Stephanie gave a slow leer. "Pretty sure I've seen more of him than you have."

"Not sure you have. Roommates, man. They get an eyeful whether they like it or not."

Steph laughed. "Okay, maybe not. But I don't mean squishy like that, anyway. Emotionally squishy."

Nick made a face. "I'm flattered."

She put her hand out, curling her fingers around his when he took it. "Just let us come along, okay? We'll keep out of the way, but you can stay in my hotel room and just...get a break from him, if you need it."

"Yeah." Nick lifted their hands to kiss her knuckles. "Okay."

Tyler stuck his lip out. "Who'm I gonna sleep with, then?"

Nick and Stephanie both squinted at him. "Are you implying you've been sleeping with my girlfriend, Ty?"

"Or my boyfriend?" Stephanie grinned.

"With all due respect, ew."

Nick put on a hurt expression. "Which of us gets the ew?"

"I'd say both of ew!"

Nick groaned and Stephanie clutched at her heart. "Wounded! How could you!"

"Honestly? It wasn't hard." Tyler made finger guns and shot at both of them. "Not my type one, not my type two, should we be packing up to go bounty hunting with you three?"

"Yeah, I guess." Nick looked out the doors toward the dark parking lot. "I'll probably ride with Chris for a while, though, unless Jake's gonna."

"Is he coming too?" Tyler asked.

"I dunno, but he's actually a bounty hunter, at least. Why, you decide he's more your type than us?"

"You all need more melanin, man. That lady last night, though, yeah, if she'd have me."

"Cheyenne? I'm not sure she's ever met anybody she considers worthy."

"That's 'cause she's never met me."

"Except she did, last night." Stephanie got up to give Nick a kiss. "I'm gonna go get my stuff and check out. Think they'll let me get away with not paying for tonight?"

"Probably, if you go ask Chris to charm them for you."

Stephanie laughed incredulously and left with Tyler trailing along behind. Nick cleared all the empty Chinese food containers off the tables, packed what was left back into the takeout bags, and put the tables back where they belonged before going out to the parking lot.

Chris and Jake were both leaning against the driver's side door of the truck, their heads ducked together in quiet conversation and their breath steaming in the cold air. Chris backed off a step when he saw Nick, and Jake clocked himself on the side-view mirror when he moved back. "Ow."

Chris, perfunctorily, said, "You okay?" to him, and, "So what's the deal? You shake them or what?" to Nick.

"They're still coming." Nick shook his head. "Sorry, I guess."

"Aw, your little college friends are determined to stick with you no matter what. It's kinda cute." The thinnest thread of admiration laced Chris's sarcasm.

Nick understood that, actually. Whether Chris believed it or not, he understood. Steph and Ty's insistence on tagging along was as generous as it was frustrating. "Look, I know it's a pain, but they're worried about me. They're my friends."

"Yeah, yeah, I get it. Probably a shit ton of people would drop everything and get their daddies to pay off the school so they don't get in trouble for me, too."

His brother, on the other hand, mostly just frustrated him. "*Jesus*, Chris, can you ever give it a rest?"

"Pretty much no."

"I would," Jake said a beat too late, then sucked his teeth, annoyed. "Drop everything, I mean."

"You'd give it a rest, too," Nick said dryly.

Jake quirked a faint smile as Chris punched his shoulder. "Yeah, you would. You got my back."

The way Chris could hit below the belt every time, without even trying, amazed Nick. He braced against the sting, but it had already scraped through him, leaving raw spots behind. He looked down, and Jake, who had always been more observant than Chris, said, "Nick does too, man."

"I know that." Chris sounded baffled, like Jake had seen fit to inform him that the sun would come up tomorrow. A little of the sting faded, and Nick could lift his head again.

"Chris was telling me about the vamps and Saboac," Jake said. "I assume that's what you wanted to talk about when you called."

"Wait, you're calling Jake now? How long has that been going on?"

"For god's sake, Chris. I haven't been sneaking around calling your best friend behind your back for the last four years or anything. I called him while the laundry was finishing."

"Oh." Now his brother sounded about twelve and vaguely embarrassed. "Okay."

Jake apparently thought so too, because he grinned broadly at both of them. "You're both idiots, you know that?"

Chris muttered, "Takes one to know one," cementing Nick's conviction that he had the emotional maturity of an average twelve year old.

"Anyway, if you're right and this Saboac thing is after one or both of you, probably getting out of town for a few days isn't a bad idea. I'll stick around and see if anything weird turns up here, if you want."

"Weird wasn't happening here, though. It was up over the state border in Bridgeport, where Dad died." Nick pulled his coat around himself, wishing he'd gotten a heavier one from the trailer. A California winter coat didn't cut it in Colorado, especially as the sun went down.

"The boards say it's happening all over the midwest."

"Is Colorado really the midwest, though?"

Chris stared at him, and Nick rolled his jaw. "Okay, maybe not important right now."

"You think?"

"The point is, I'll hang around and see if anything turns up here, since if Saboac is after you, this could be considered the epicenter." Jake spoke in a patient tone that indicated long-honed practice at stopping the Cassidy brothers from arguing with each other. "If it stays quiet while you're gone, maybe it was just a freak encounter."

"I don't think that thing was a freak," Chris said dubiously. "They look human. This didn't."

"No, an unusual one, not a *freak* encounter."

"Not a grendel encounter," Nick said with a note of triumph that made him think maybe he was about twelve, too. "See, that's one of the reasons I don't like using 'freak' for…freaks."

"A grend…oh, because of the Beowulf board? That's pretty good. Look." Jake's eyebrows drew down, digging serious lines into his forehead. "Are you two going to be okay? You've got a lot on your shoulders right now."

"We'll be fine." Chris shifted those shoulders, but Jake, still concerned, looked at Nick, and only relaxed marginally at Nick's nod.

"Call me if you need anything." Jake reached over and grabbed Chris by the back of the neck, almost rattling him. "Anything, okay, man?"

"Yeah." Chris stepped in for an awkward bro hug, pounding a knotted fist against Jake's back a couple of times. "You keep us posted too, huh?"

"I will." Jake nodded at Nick and went off to his own car, leaving Nick shivering in the cold beside Chris's truck.

"I'm glad you're still in touch with him," Nick said when Jake was out of earshot. "I didn't know if you'd stay friends after he moved south."

"He talks to me more than you do."

"Low bar."

Chris gave a quick, hard laugh. "Yeah, I guess so. Look, are they driving with us, because that's gonna get uncomfortable real fast."

"No, they'll follow in Ty's truck, and please don't try to

lose them, Chris." Nick sighed as guilty-as-charged humor twisted Chris's face. "Where are we headed, anyway?"

"Steamboat Springs."

"Isn't Shy living there? Maybe she'll know something about our bounty."

"There's twelve thousand people in The 'Boat and if she's hanging out with one of them who's up for assault and battery we gotta have a talk with her."

"To be fair, that does sound like something Cheyenne would do."

Chris chuckled. "It sounds like something Shy would want you to think she does. What she'd actually do is beat the ever-loving shit out of the guy we're looking for, if she got hold of him. Well, depending on who he assaulted, I guess. And then I guess she'd patch him up because of whatever code paramedics have about not hurting people."

"Yeah, okay, legit, except if Shy beat the shit out of somebody I don't think there'd be anything left to patch up." Nick went around to the passenger side door and put the Chinese leftovers behind the front seats. "I'll call her anyway, when we're on the road, and see if she knows anything."

"Yeah." Chris swung up into the truck, starting the engine as Nick went to meet Stephanie and Tyler as they left the hotel.

Stephanie looked dubiously at their old Dodge. "Is that thing really okay for a long drive, Nick? Maybe you should come with us."

Nick glanced back at the truck, which had been around a couple decades longer than he had, and had both the paint job and the rust spots to show it. "It's actually in great shape. I know it looks a little rough, but Chris is good with cars."

Tyler's lip curled. "If he's so good with them, why does it look like that?"

"Ever painted a car, Ty?"

"No?"

"Try doing a good job yourself someday, and then decide whether it's worth the bother. I'm riding with Chris." He gave Stephanie a brusquer kiss than she deserved—she wasn't the insensitive one—and went back to the Dodge, with Tyler's bewildered voice turning to Stephanie behind him.

"Why would you paint it yourself? Just bring it to a shop."

Steph grated, "Jesus, Ty, when are you going to get," and Nick didn't hear the rest as he climbed into the Dodge and closed the door.

Who was he kidding. Slammed the door. Slammed it on the beat of an AC/DC song on the radio, which somehow increased his frustration. Chris's momentary silence said a lot, and the caution in his voice said even more. "You okay?"

"Yeah. No. No. I don't know."

"Ty's kind of a dick, huh?"

"Ty thinks you're a dick."

Chris smiled faintly. "He's not wrong."

Nick made a short, startled breath that bordered on laughter, and turned the radio up. "Let's go."

———

Nick fell asleep about ten miles out of town, despite having turned the radio up to bone-shaking. On the plus side, that meant Chris could sing as loudly and as off-key as he wanted to for most of the three hundred mile drive across the state. The north route, avoiding Denver, kept him on the open road and made it harder—probably—for Nick's friends to lose him in traffic. Everybody stopped for a pee break around Walden, and Nick got back into the truck looking groggy. "You want me to drive a while?"

"I'm good."

"C'mon, Chris. You didn't get any more sleep than I did last night."

It was hard to believe the funeral had been only yesterday.

Chris put that aside, pretty sure that if he started to think about it too much he'd stop being able to function, and he needed to get through the hunt and back home again before he could fall apart.

Not that he would ever, ever fall apart when Nicky was around. "I'm good," he said again. "Been singing."

"No wonder I was having nightmares." Nick scrubbed his hands over his face, finishing waking himself up, and nodded. "Okay. Lemme see your phone so I can start looking for this guy. What's his name?"

"Derek Emerson. White, thirty-eight, concealed carry license, got fired from a trucking job a while ago."

"Stealing or accidents?"

"Road rage. Got in other drivers' faces a lot and it finally blew up. He got off without any jail time, but it was pretty bad." Chris unlocked his phone and handed it to Nick. "He's bounced from job to job since, mostly security. He got in another fight as a bouncer and actually burned down the whole bar. He got out on bail, but he skipped out and here we are."

"Jesus." Nick read the file as they drove through the dark night, then got his own phone and started searching on the guy. "He's got a bunch of social media profiles and his location turned on," he said disapprovingly after a minute. "Finding him shouldn't be too hard. Got a map?"

"Bought one at the service station back there. It's in the glove compartment."

"Shoulda known."

"Yeah you should have." Chris turned the radio back up and Nick spent the last hour of the drive using his phone as a flashlight and mapping out the coordinates that Emerson posted from most often.

"He hasn't posted for about five days," he said as they pulled into town. "Maybe he's smarter than I thought. You wanna check out the bars he hung out at, or call it a night?"

Chris glanced at the truck's clock, which was about as vintage as a bluetooth connection. "It's already eleven and we haven't slept much. Last thing we want is to get stupid with somebody who might be packing. Shy's not back yet, but she said we could crash at her place."

Nick said, "Uh," in a weird tone. "All of us?"

"Shit." Chris looked over his shoulder like he'd see the big SUV Tyler was driving. And did, actually, because it was riding his ass, but since the two in that vehicle obviously thought he'd ditch them at the first opportunity, he guessed he wasn't surprised by that. "No, not all of us. Shy's place isn't that big. I guess we can look for a motel."

Nick's silence was as momentarily weird as his tone had been, and for once, Chris wished he couldn't read anything into it.

He could, though. Stephanie and Tyler-whose-dad-could-buy-off-the-university weren't going to stay somewhere Chris could afford. Even with a big bounty coming in, blowing it on an upscale hotel—and most places in Steamboat Springs *were* upscale, because it was a skiing town—was a dumb-ass way to spend his money.

"Pull over at the gas station up there. I'll go with them tonight. You stay at Shy's. We'll meet up tomorrow." Nick sounded exhausted. Way more so than he'd sounded a minute ago, like it wasn't from actual tiredness at all. Chris pulled into the station and killed the engine, trying to figure out what he wanted to say, or how he wanted to say it. Or whether he should at all, because even he could see how it was a fight in the making.

Still, he finally said, "Is it like this a lot?"

Nick looked out the window as Tyler's big-ass Toyota Highlander pulled up. It wasn't brand-new-straight-off-the-lot, but it was only a couple years old, and Chris bet it had been new when he'd gotten it. "Not always," Nick said quietly. "But a lot."

Chris, carefully, said, "I'm sorry."

Nick gave him a brief, tight smile that went farther than words, and grabbed his bag out of the back of the cab. "I'll call you in the morning."

"Arright, man. G'night."

He drove to Shy's apartment alone, and slept on the couch.

———

Nick called at about nine-thirty, voice apologetic on the line. "They got up late. Not used to driving all over hell and breakfast, I guess. Where you at?"

"He's not home and I already hit the McDonalds and I'm at the diner he likes to have breakfast at. It's awesome. I had a thing called a 'Mountain Man Deluxe' that was like the best chicken-fried steak I'd ever had. Waitress gave me a chocolate milkshake, too."

"What, for being cute?"

"Why else?"

Nick snorted. "What about Emerson?"

"No joy. You did a good job with the tracking, though. Waitress here knew him, and so did the staff at McDonald's. He likes Egg McMuffins and his eggs over-easy. Never trust a guy who likes his eggs over-easy, Nick."

"I like my eggs over-easy!"

"Gross. Anyway, I'm heading to his gym to see if any of the rats there know where he'd go to ground. You coming?"

"Let me know how it goes and I'll meet you after? We can either follow the trail or hit the next place. There's a coffee shop he likes to go to on Saturdays."

"Meet you there unless I get something good at the gym." Chris hung up and left enough on the table to cover his bill, the milkshake, and the tip, just in case somebody gave the waitress hell for being nice. Emerson's gym membership was for a place a couple miles away, not a bad distance to walk for a warmup or after a big breakfast, but the only path was the road's shoulder. Chris wouldn't have walked it himself, especially in winter. It only took a few minutes to drive, though, and the staff at the desk really wanted to sell him a membership. He took a guided walk through, then asked if he could try the equipment. The kid trying to land his business gave him a day pass, and he grabbed workout gear from the truck before spending about forty minutes doing some serious lifting between short conversations.

A couple friendly guys got a lot less friendly after he mentioned he was thinking about joining the gym because his buddy Derek Emerson worked out there, and one guy just walked away. A woman in her thirties stopped her treadmill and put her hands on the arms, shoulders high as she studied Chris curiously. "You don't look like somebody who'd be friends with Derek."

"No? What do the rest of his friends look like?"

"Trouble. The bad kind," she amended after a brief examination of him. "You look like the fun kind."

"I'll break your heart," Chris promised. "But you'll have a great time, first."

She grinned. "I've had much worse offers. Seriously, though, you must not have known Derek long? Yeah," she said when Chris nodded agreement. "Take my advice and stop knowing him now. He's the type who brings people down around him."

Chris folded his arms over the top of her treadmill display, chin on them so he could look up at her through his eyelashes. "Truth is, we're less friends and more 'he owes me money.' I've been hitting his haunts, the ones I know about, at least. Got any ideas where I should look?"

She set her jaw forward, looking him up and down again. Differently, this time. First time, it'd just been appreciation. Chris was cool with that. This time, though, it was more appraisal. Tension increased in her shoulders, still high from how she'd braced herself on the treadmill's arms, and she sounded wary as she said, "Is he likely to be around less if you get your money out of him?"

"If things go right, yeah."

She pressed her lips together, then nodded. "He's got a thing for a girlfriend of mine who works evenings at the 8th Street Steakhouse. Like…a bothersome thing."

"A won't take no for an answer kind of thing?"

"Yeah."

Chris was just liking this guy better and better. "Your friend working tonight?"

"Yeah."

"I'll see what I can do to convince him she's not interested."

A smile rushed out on the woman's breath. "That'd be great." Her shoulders dropped and she looked him over again, the smile warming. "I don't suppose you're free until then?"

"I wish to hell I was. What's your name?"

"Rhonda."

"Maybe another time, Rhonda." Chris winked and went to shower before heading out. The woman waved at him as he left, and he called Nick, muttering, "You guys probably don't just want to just hang out in The 'Boat for the afternoon, do you," when his brother answered.

"What? No. Why, you got a booty call?"

Chris looked back toward the gym as he got in the truck. "I could."

"What?! How? What? Jesus, Chris, you didn't even bring the slutmobile. I mean I guess that's probably *why* you've got a booty call, nobody would actually hook up with you if they saw that thing, but—"

"Just shut up, Nick. I've got a good lead on Emerson. You didn't mark the 8th Street Steakhouse on his haunts."

"What? No. If he goes there, it's without his phone. Dammit, I like it better when they're totally stupid. What's the deal?"

"He's got a thing for a woman who works there and might be there tonight."

Nick fell silent a few seconds. "Well, shit. I mean, I guess you could go hook up with your new friend, then, unless you wanna spend the afternoon looking for him just in case?"

"I would *so* much rather get to know Rhonda better."

"Fine. I'll call the restaurant for reservations at what, seven?"

"Reservations?"

"We gotta eat, don't we?"

"Yeah, all right, man. Shit, there she is, I gotta go." He hung up and opened the cab door, standing in it and waving. Rhonda, her dark hair tied up in a sweaty knot he bet she didn't think was sexy, hesitated, then, smiling, came across the parking lot toward him.

"I thought you were busy."

"You know what, I had a good think about it and I realized some people are worth making the time for. Can I drive you home?"

Rhonda's eyebrows shot up. "You think I should let a man I just met know where I live, and leave my best way to escape behind?"

"Right. No. Bad idea. You tell me how this should work, then."

Her eyebrows went higher. "I'll be damned. You're not an asshole."

"Oh, I am, but not about this."

"Hah! Okay. That's my car over there." She indicated a Honda Civic with a nod. "Follow me?"

Chris gave her a lazy smile and sank back down into the truck's cab. "Anywhere you want to go, ma'am. Anywhere you want to go."

# CHAPTER 7

IF SOMEONE HAD ASKED NICK TO DESCRIBE THE MOST Colorado restaurant he could imagine, he would have come up with something close to the 8th Street Steakhouse. Stephanie, staring at the rough-wood-paneled walls and the moose heads and the antler chandeliers, exhaled, "They use antlers in all of their decorating," in a soft sing-song, then laughed. "Smells good, though. Looks like a good thing we made reservations, too." She gestured at the bustling space.

"I think I came here once when I was a kid," Tyler said thoughtfully. "Dad brought us skiing up here in Colorado somewhere. I didn't remember where, but I think it must have been Steamboat Springs, unless a lot of steakhouses around here have paintings like that one." He nodded at an Old-West-style bare-shouldered woman and grizzled cowboy on a sign with the restaurant's name on it. "I remember looking at her a *lot*. I was only like eight," he added defensively.

Nick grinned. "Sure, but what's your excuse now?"

"Oh, shut up."

A breathless hostess came up with a smile. "Do you have reservations?"

"Cassidy, for four," Nick said.

"Oh, yes, the rest of your party arrived a few minutes ago.

This way." She led them through the restaurant to a high-backed booth covered in what Nick suspected might be real cowhide. Chris was already there, facing the doors, a half-finished measure of whiskey in a tumbler. Nick hesitated, looking toward the doors, then took the opposite side of the booth, gesturing Stephanie in first. Chris got up and nodded Tyler toward the inner seat on his side.

Tyler stared at him. "Why?"

"So I can keep an eye out for our guy."

"You think I can't pick some white dude out of a crowd?"

"I'm sure you can, but it's not your job, and I might need to move fast." Cords in Chris's neck stood out as he waited for Tyler, who shot a skeptical look at Nick that grew more incredulous as Nick nodded.

"Are you serious?"

"Please, Ty."

Tyler muttered, "Whatever," and slid into the booth. "What's wrong, your hookup go south?"

Chris sat back down, keeping enough distance for the holy ghost between them, and spoke tightly. "She was great. That leggy redhead over there is her friend, the one Emerson has been harassing. I asked for her table and Rhonda told her to let me know if he came in." He drank the rest of his whiskey in one swallow and tapped the glass against the table like he was asking for more. After a minute the redhead—her name tag said T.J.—came over with a tray of water glasses and menus for everybody, and a second whiskey for Chris. Nick caught his brother's eye for a moment as he took another swallow, but Chris shook his head once and looked away. "What'd you guys do this afternoon?"

"Those two nerds studied," Tyler said. "I went looking for a ski bunny but I guess you got the only one hopping."

Chris said, "For Christ's sake," finished his drink, and got up for another.

Tyler, watching him go, said, "What's his problem?" and

Stephanie sighed loudly.

"His dad did just die, Tyler."

"Shit." Tyler shot a guilty look at Nick. "Sorry. It's not that I forgot, it's just he was such a dick about how he told you, and...I dunno. You don't stand up for yourself around him like I'm used to you doing."

"I'm fine, Ty. I don't need your protection. I don't need Chris's, either, but he's spent his whole life keeping an eye on me and I don't think he knows how to stop. Don't worry about me. Not on that count, anyway." Nick managed a fragile smile. Stephanie's hand stole toward his and wrapped around his fingers. They'd broken the books out *to* study that afternoon; that much Tyler had right. But the pages had started swimming under Nick's vision, and by the time he realized he was falling apart, it was too late to get himself under control. His eyes still burned from crying, and all he really wanted to do was go home and crawl under the covers.

Except he didn't know which home he meant, and that only made it worse.

Chris's laugh, familiar and startlingly warm, washed over the general noise of the restaurant. Nick looked over to see him grinning at the bartender like nothing was wrong. A minute later he came back with another drink, though his smile had disappeared. "Bartender says Emerson usually shows up around eight-thirty or nine and that he'll tell the chef to cook dinner our slow so we have an excuse to stay that long. He says if we order appetizers it'll take forever anyway."

"He told you that in two minutes?" Tyler sounded incredulous again.

"Some people think I'm charming."

"Some people haven't spent enough time around you."

"Maybe not. Hard to say which people, though." Chris gave Tyler a cold smile and nursed his drink through the appetizers, then got up and went back to the bartender, who poured the most generous finger of whiskey Nick had ever seen. Chris flirted his eyelashes at the guy and came back to the table swirling the over-filled drink.

Stephanie's eyebrows rose over a terrible job of hiding a grin. "I think the bartender's trying to get you drunk."

"Oh, I know he is. I might even let him." Chris took a significant swallow of the booze and barely even winced as it went down.

"I get the urge, Chris, but if Emerson shows up you'll need to be sober." Nick sighed as Chris, glowering, drank most of the rest of the whiskey in a second swallow.

Stephanie, very quietly, said, "At least dinner's coming," and Nick gave her a weak smile.

Their steaks arrived a minute later, and Derek Emerson didn't, so they had twenty or thirty minutes to eat, if not sober up. The bartender sent another whiskey over to Chris just before the waitress took their plates away, and wouldn't let Nick catch his eye to stop the drinks from coming.

Chris gave a short, sharp laugh as lifting the glass revealed the bartender's number written on the napkin below. He folded the napkin, hiding the number, and put it aside.

Tyler smirked. "What's the matter, he not pretty enough for you? I thought you were into random hookups."

Chris glanced at the bartender like he was considering him. "He's plenty pretty. Just not my type. Too pushy."

"Yeah, I bet you'd totally hook up with him if he wasn't pushy."

Chris finished the new shot of whiskey and gave Tyler a dangerously tight smile. "See, I figure you're gonna say something homophobic if I say 'sure, I'd do him,' and you're gonna say something homophobic if I say 'no way,' so how about instead of either of those things you shut the fuck up?" He stood up just a little unsteadily, announced, "I gotta take a piss," and headed for the bathroom with the overly-cautious walk of someone who had drunk too much too fast.

Tyler muttered, "Your brother's a whole bag of dicks," to

Nick, who stood almost as carefully as Chris had done, like it would help him control his temper.

"I don't think it's Chris who's being the dick here, Ty. Excuse me a minute." He followed Chris to the restrooms, earning a spit of laughter when he entered.

"Coming to tell me to be nice to your boyfriend?"

"No. He's being a real asshole, and I'm sorry. He's not usually this bad," he said more quietly. "He's out of his element and he thinks I take too much crap from you so he's trying to draw your fire."

"He's gonna draw more than fire if he doesn't shut his trap. I don't know why you hang around with that guy, Nicky." Chris went to wash his hands, not meeting Nick's gaze in the mirror.

"Reminds me of home, I guess." Nick grimaced as soon as he spoke, regretting it even before hurt curdled Chris's features. For once, though, his brother didn't have a quick comeback. Nick frowned, worried. "Are you okay?"

"I'm a fucking delight. Bartender says so."

"What happened this afternoon?"

"Nothing happened. I mean, plenty happened, but nothing bad." Chris dried his hands and headed for the door.

Nick stopped him with a clothes-line, or what would have been, if either of them had been moving faster. Caught him across the front of the shoulders, anyway, and flexed enough to slow him down. Confusion slid across Chris's face, like a friendly puppy had unexpectedly nipped him. "What happened, Chris?"

Chris shook him off, stepping back. "Why's anything have to have happened? Is there a new law that I can't have a few drinks when my dad's just kicked the bucket?"

"No," Nick said steadily, "but you drink between jobs, not on them. So what happened today?"

"Man, you haven't been around to see what I do on jobs for years, okay? You don't know shit."

"Jake would've told me if you were drinking on the job."

Chris's lip curled like he'd been caught. "Right, you and Jake got all buddy-buddy sometime when I wasn't looking, I remember now."

Nick, watching the tightness in Chris's throat and color rising along his jaw like he was fighting to suppress emotion, let that pass. "What happened, Chris?"

"Nothing!" Chris tried shouldering past him again, and this time Nick caught him with both hands, holding him back. His expression darkened as he tried and failed to shrug Nick off with a casual twist. His second attempt had more strength behind it, and his face grew more disbelieving as Nick held him in place. "What the hell, man, let me go."

"Tell me what's going on and I will."

"Nick, lemme go." Chris broke free with enough violence to send himself stumbling, and Nick caught him again, this time just to keep him upright. Chris snarled and jerked away again, hard enough this time to knock himself against a bathroom sink. He let go an inarticulate howl of pain, and Nick blurted, "Chris, what *happened?*"

"I fucking cried on her, okay?" The confession burst like a dam, releasing a wash of tears laced with grief and frustration and humiliation. Nick stared at him for a disbelieving, confused instant, then stepped forward and pulled his brother into a hard hug, half-hearing Chris's torrent of words against his shoulder. "I don't know what happened, we were having a great time and then I just fucking *cried* like some kind of goddamn baby—"

"You're allowed to cry, Chris." Nick's voice cracked even though he wasn't sure he spoke loudly enough to be heard. Words muffled against his brother's hair, he mumbled, "Dad died. You're allowed to be sad. It's okay. It's okay."

Somebody walked into the bathroom and reared back like he'd walked onto a porno set. "Jesus, in the restrooms? I'm calling the fucking cops, what the hell—"

Nick snarled, "Fuck off. Our dad just died," and the guy went white, face drawn with horror as he backed off.

"Shit, I'm sorry. I'm sorry, man. I didn't know." He fled the bathroom and Nick, teeth bared, hugged Chris harder when he tried to get away.

"It's okay, Chris."

"It's not okay. That woman didn't deserve me turning into a total girl on her."

Nick choked on a mixture of laughter and sobbing. "Women bleed for like seven years of their lives, man. If you think turning into a girl means you're not metal as fuck, you gotta think again."

Chris's own laugh sounded as fucked up as Nick's had. "Yeah, okay, fair. Still." He shoved away, wiping his hand across his eyes and under his nose. "She didn't do anything to deserve me falling apart on her. Except a hell of a bl—"

"You can stop right there!" Nick said hastily, his hands lifted in protest. Then he dropped them again, sighing. "She didn't do anything, but you…you have feelings too, Chris, you know? And sex is pretty vulnerable anyway, even if you're not mourning. What'd you tell her?"

As soon as he asked, an awful suspicion hit him, but Chris swept it away by muttering, "The truth, man. What else could I do? Making up some shit or running away without explaining would've fucked her right up and she didn't deserve that either."

A breath of relief escaped Nick. "That's good. I was afraid you just bolted."

"I'm not that much of an ass," Chris mumbled sullenly. "Despite what your pal out there thinks."

"Screw what he thinks." Nick pulled Chris into another hug that his brother elbowed his way out of.

"Let go, Nicky. You're not supposed to have to take care of me." He wiped a hand under his nose again, looking more like a kid than he would want to imagine.

"Everybody needs taking care of sometimes, Chris. Even you."

"I'm fine."

"You are a *terrible* liar."

"I'm an awesome liar." Chris rubbed a hand over his hair. "Just not right now, maybe. I swear, Nick, I'm not trying to pick fights with your buddy, but if he doesn't lay off…"

"I expect Stephanie's read him the riot act by now, but if she hasn't, I will. He's mad at you for how you told me about Dad dying," Nick added quietly.

"Well, fuck him. I owed you an apology and I gave you one. I don't owe him shit."

Nick could debate whether 'look, I get it, I texted you, I'm an asshole' qualified as an apology, but he doubted he'd get a better one, so he left it alone. "I'll tell Tyler you did. Maybe it'll help."

"If it doesn't he's gonna end up with a mouth full of broken teeth."

"You know, there might be a reason he thinks you're an asshole."

Chris gave him a brief, startlingly bitter look. "And I guess there's a reason he reminds you of home. Are we done having feelings? Can we go back to dinner?"

Nick sighed. "People don't just get over having feelings, Chris."

"Maybe not, but I'm gonna try. Come on, let's—"

The bathroom door slammed open and two guys beating the shit out of each other landed on the floor at their feet.

———

Chris bounced back with a yell, ready to stomp the idiots on the floor if they did anything stupid. Stupider than beating each other up, anyway. Stupid like going for him or Nicky. They were pretty focused on each other, though. He snapped,

"Stay here," to Nick, like he was five or something, and stepped over the fight into a full-on bar brawl.

The smart people were screaming their way out the doors and hiding under tables while enough jackasses with a chip on their shoulder threw elbows and knees and fists like they were auditioning for the next Robert Rodriguez movie. The Mexico trilogy style movies, not Spy Kids. Although the spy kids were pretty cool, to be fair.

Stephanie was in the corner of their booth, pale and quiet, which meant she had a pretty good head on her shoulders. Tyler wasn't, but Chris didn't think great choices were part of Tyler's lifestyle. Somebody veered near the booth and Stephanie grabbed one of their dinner plates, clearly ready to bash it over somebody's head if necessary.

Chris said, "I'm starting to get what you see in her," over his shoulder, then waded onto the restaurant floor. The roiling fight was already breaking up by the time he was a few steps in, without him having to personally knock any heads together. By the time he got to the middle of the room, almost nobody was fighting anymore. They were mostly groaning or staring at broken hands and bleeding knuckles, although a couple of people were laid out and didn't look like they were getting up soon. Not unconscious, just dazed or damaged.

That was the thing about fights outside of a movie set. They didn't last very long, even if there were a lot of people involved. Hitting things, and getting hit by things, hurt.

Nick's idiot friend Tyler wasn't one of the people on the floor, either in the 'hiding under a table' or the 'laid out' sense. Chris glanced at Stephanie, who didn't even notice him, and at the bartender, who pointed at the back door. "They went that way!"

Chris breathed, "Who the fuck went," and headed out the back door at a run, aware that Nick was a few steps behind him. "Man, go make sure your girl's okay!"

"She said she was." Nick passed him in like five strides,

those long gangly legs moving him like a race horse. He bolted up to the street, Chris on his heels, and they stopped for a heartbeat, looking both ways along streets lit by amber-colored lamps before Nick pointed. "There."

"I said go back, Nick!" Chris got off the starting block faster, but Nick passed him again. Chris was gonna throw a bolas around his damn ankles to slow him down. Later. Nick skidded to a stop where Tyler was leaning against a building, gasping, about three-quarters of the way down the block.

"Sorry," Tyler wheezed. "He got away."

"Who got away?"

"Your dude! Emerson! He came into the restaurant while you guys were in the bathroom, so I thought I'd do a citizen's arrest thing—"

Even Nick said, "God damn it, Ty," and Chris, furious, ran up the street to see if he could catch a glimpse of Emerson anywhere. A turn-of-the-century Jeep matching Emerson's personal report drove by on the main road, and Chris let out a shout of frustration.

His footsteps slapped against the pavement as he ran back to his brother and his brother's goddamn roommate. "What the hell were you thinking, Tyler?"

"That it'd be cool to catch him! That I'd be helping!"

"Well, great goddamn job, you spooked him instead."

Tyler straightened up, still wheezing. "I'd have caught him if I'd remembered my asthma meds."

"Maybe, but you didn't, did you. God damn it. He's on the move. Nick, you coming with me or what? We gotta haul ass if we're gonna catch him."

Nick started to speak, but Tyler waved it off. "Forget it, man. No big deal. I screwed it up and I'm sorry, okay? I'll just pay you the bounty so you're not out any cash, and we can forget about it."

"What?" Disbelief tasted like blood in the word, tight and raw. Chris couldn't even swallow, his throat was so tight.

"So what if the guy got away, is what. I get you need the money, so I'll pay it, but he's gone now, and we gotta go back to Cali, so forget it, okay? No big deal."

"This is my *job*." Chris's voice cracked and Nick took a couple steps away from Tyler. Distancing himself from him, or maybe getting close enough to Chris to keep his brother from cleaning Ty's clock. Fifty-fifty odds. "I can't just let him go. For one thing, he's dangerous, and for another, I let him go, that's my reputation down the toilet. You can't just throw money at me and make your fuckup go away." The whole world had turned into a couple bright points surrounded by so much anger Chris couldn't keep his speech steady. "It must be nice living a life where you can buy off anything that goes wrong, but that's not how it works out here in the real world."

He turned and walked away before the hands that had turned into fists decided to do any damage. Reminded himself that Derek fricking Emerson was getting away, and that walking gave him more of a head start. That running might burn off some rage. That running would definitely cover the sounds of whether Nicky was following him or not, because finding out the answer was 'not' was more than Chris thought he could handle right then.

Didn't matter. He'd done the job on his own plenty. Nick had a life to go back to.

A life filled with pricks like Tyler, but then, Tyler reminded Nick of home.

It wasn't that far to the Dodge, but Chris wasn't entirely sure how he got there. The distance between the back road and the parking lot just disappeared into a wall of anger, and if all he could see was pinprick points in the midst of blind fury, at least that was enough to get the keys in the ignition.

"Scoot over," Nick said. "You've been drinking too much to drive."

Relief hit in a wall of white, so hard that Chris didn't even argue. He just moved over and Nick climbed into the driver's seat. "Which way?"

"South," Chris said hoarsely. "Anywhere on his haunts he might be heading?"

Nick slid his phone out of his pocket and handed it to Chris, rattling off the passcode.

Chris almost fumbled the phone. "Really?"

"Yeah. It needed six digits." Nick's tone warned him to not make anything of it, so Chris didn't as he punched his own birthdate into Nick's phone to unlock it. The numbers swam, though, and Chris told himself it was the whiskey.

"There's a place about ten miles out of town where his phone checks in from a lot," he said after a minute. "Map says there's nothing there, but it could be a cabin? I should've tried finding him this afternoon," he said in low voice. "Could've at least lowjacked his truck or something."

"Might be lowjacked already. Did you talk to his car insurance? They might be able to kill his engine for us."

"No, his truck's too old. Not this old, but old enough." Chris patted the Dodge's dashboard, then held on to it like it might somehow stabilise him.

Nick breathed, "Crap," then glanced at him. "You okay?"

"Oh, I'm peachy."

"You shouldn't have, you know. Looked for him this afternoon," Nick clarified when Chris side-eyed him. "Pretty sure you needed what you did a lot more than you needed to go chasing after this dude."

"Ah, c'mon, Nick, the last thing I want right now is my little brother commenting on my sex life."

"Just saying." Nick hesitated. "Thanks for letting me drive."

"I wouldn't have if you weren't fucking right."

"But you would've driven if I hadn't followed you."

"Yeah." Chris looked out the window. "Yeah, probably. But I'm not the smart one."

"Chris..." Nick sounded tired, but didn't take it any farther. A minute later, Chris said, "Turn here," and they drove up in to the hills on a road that got less-traveled by the mile. "Should we park and walk the rest of the way in so he doesn't hear us coming?"

"There's ten inches of new snow out there and I'm wearing tennies, Chris."

"Man, you've gotten soft."

A quick smile darted across Nick's face. "Steph says I'm squishy."

"Squishy is not a word I would want my girlfriend to use about me. Hard. Virile. Manly. Vigor—"

"Dude, shut *up*!"

Chris cackled, then twisted, looking behind them. "Back up. There was a trail back there, just about wide enough for a truck, and the road up ahead doesn't have any tracks. I bet that's where he's gone." A minute later Nick drove them cautiously down a road barely two feet wider than the Dodge, following a single set of tire marks cut into the snow. Nick killed the headlights and hunched over the steering wheel, following tracks barely lit by the running lights. The moon had come out, sending fingers of brightness to slide between bare branches and evergreen needles, but not much of the blue light reached the snow.

Not until it found a clearing ahead of them, anyway, one just barely bigger than the cabin that stood in it. The night shadows were just different enough that Nick killed the engine instinctively a hundred feet or so from the cabin. The silence was so loud Chris knew Emerson couldn't have missed their approach, but they got out and pressed the truck doors closed gently anyway, and walked through the fresh snow so their shoes wouldn't squeak on the stuff packed down by the tires.

Moonlight made a block of Emerson's Jeep, and if there were lights on inside the cabin, there were also well-blacked-out windows that didn't let a hint of that light leak through.

Nick, his voice no louder than the hiss of wind over snow, said, "He could've gone out the back on skis."

"We can track him, if he has." They went up the two cabin stairs and put themselves on either side of the door, listening. Thumps inside suggested there was somebody in there, after all. Chris caught Nick's eye and gestured.

Nick stared at him, pointed first at his own sneakers, then at Chris's sturdy boots, then stared at him again. Chris bugged his eyes, mouthing, *It's my bounty!*

Nick pointed at his own feet repeatedly. *My feet are freezing!*

Chris rolled his eyes and held up two fingers. *Fine. Two minutes.*

Nick, satisfied, stuck his jaw out, and Chris slunk down the steps and around the back of the cabin through thigh-deep snow, silently muttering, *God damn it Nick, at least you're so frickin' tall your balls wouldn't be freezing off doing this shit, and what's more important, your frickin' feet or my goddamn nuts*, although by the end of that he wasn't even mouthing it any more, just thinking furiously as he waded through the snow.

At least the cabin had a back door. It would've really pissed him off if he'd gotten literal blue balls for no goddamn reason. He counted down the last thirty seconds of their two minutes in his head, trying not to shiver.

Just before he reached zero, Derek Emerson bolted through the back door and slammed into him. Chris yelled, more surprised than hurt, and heard Nick's voice shoot up in panic. "*Chris?*"

For a second, Chris saw everything with unnatural clarity. Emerson, silhouetted against the light from the cabin. Nicky, bursting into the cabin through the front door, looking too big for the small interior space. He looked scared, like little-kid scared, and then angry, the kind of angry that came from being scared and helpless. He bellowed, "*Chris!*" again, and before Chris could catch his breath to tell him everything was okay, the cabin exploded.

# CHAPTER 8

TIME WENT FUNNY AFTER THAT. CHRIS KNEW WHAT THEY *DID*: they did the job. They collected Emerson, who was too stunned to be combative. They put him in the truck. They drove him all the way down to Denver to deliver him the bail agents. They got their check. They drove away again, back up toward Steamboat Springs at two in the morning. They did the things they were supposed to do.

Through it all, Chris could see almost nothing except the image of Nick hanging there in the air, the epicenter of an explosion of light and chaos. Arm-length splinters of wood radiating out from him as the cabin erupted around him. Furniture shattering into pieces. Glass and metal and ceramic, deadly shards that shone with light and raced out against the darkness, making cuts against the night.

Every direction except where Chris was.

That was what stood out in the memory. The mess went *everywhere*. Down, up, sideways, into trees, into the earth, into the Jeep, into the sky to come raining back down again. But none of it went toward Chris.

If any of it had hit him, or even aimed at him, he could have almost pretended it had been a regular explosion, that Emerson had rigged the place to blow. But he couldn't shake the picture of Nicky at the center of it all, making sure, some-how, that Chris didn't get hurt in the outburst of power.

Nick hadn't said a word since then.

When they were far enough out of Denver that it seemed safe, Chris pulled over at a rest stop and killed the engine. "Nicky."

His brother was balled up as small as he could go and still be buckled in. He'd hit the ground that way after the—after-ward. He'd gotten up because Chris made him, and he'd gotten in the truck for the same reason. Emerson hadn't fought about it either. He'd just stumbled to the Dodge and crawled in, staring vacant-eyed at the burned hole in the ground that used to be his cabin.

Except it wasn't burned. Not like fire, anyway. Nothing else had caught. The forest wasn't in danger. It was like—like a sound bomb, Chris guessed. Scarred earth, broken trees, everything in shards and pieces, but no scorching. Just raw and mangled.

Emerson hadn't asked. Hadn't complained.

Hadn't dared look at Nick, not even once, on the whole drive to Denver. Nick sat sideways on the truck's bench seat, arms folded around his knees and head down for the four-plus hours it took to drive out, and Emerson had kept his eyes averted the whole time. Chris knew for damn sure, because he was watching Nick more than the road, and Emerson, behind him in the truck's narrow extended cab, almost as much.

Time was still going funny, like he was only realizing now what he'd been doing then. Like it was all still happening, and he was disjointed, out of place in his own life. He said, "Nick," again, and his voice cracked. "Nicky."

"Are you okay?"

A knot of fear untwisted itself from Chris's gut. "Yeah. Yeah, Nicky, I'm okay. Are you?"

His brother's head shook, hardly more than a shift in his stupid long hair as it fell over his arms. Chris breathed a curse and unbuckled so he could scoot across the bench and try to put an awkward arm around his gigantic little brother. "You're okay," he said quietly. "Nobody's hurt. Are you hurt?"

Nick shook his head again, this time more something Chris felt than saw. "Arright. You're not hurt, I'm not hurt, we got paid. Everything's okay."

"I blew up a house. I'm a *freak*."

Chris dared a tiny smile, even if Nick couldn't see it. "Thought we were calling 'em grendels now."

Nick lifted his head, gaze bleak as he met Chris's. He looked like the five-year-old Chris had treated him as earlier, when he'd told him to stay behind. Five and scared, like he'd been after riding his bike off a jump that led into a hollow where a bunch of their dad's rusted out cars had been dumped. Chris had caught hell for that, like it was his fault their old man kept his own personal junkyard, or that older kids had built a jump over it. Chris had been the one who found Nicky, screaming in a hole on top of one of the cars. Nick's bike had fallen below him, and he'd landed on it. He'd broken his arm, but the bike had stopped him from being run through by a jagged piece of metal a few inches lower down.

Chris had been the one who had called Jake's mom to drive them to the doctor, too, and Nicky's eyes had been like they were now the whole time while his arm got set and they gave him a tetanus shot. When their dad got back the next day he'd made it clear that none of it would have happened if Chris had kept a better eye on his little brother.

None of *this* would have happened if he'd sent Nicky back to California where he belonged, or kept him safer on the hunt.

"It's going to be okay." Chris reached for his best big brother voice, the one that usually calmed Nick down when they were kids. To his surprise, Nick's eyes closed like he really was calming down a little. "Nicky, can you tell me what happened?"

Nick shook his head, most a shift of his hair against his sleeves. "I heard you yell," he said, muffled. "I thought you were in trouble. I thought I couldn't get to you in time and I freaked. I *freaked*."

The second time he said it, he obviously didn't mean panicked, the way people usually did when they said they freaked. He meant he used power in a way that normal humans couldn't. And there was no point in denying that, so Chris just said, "Yeah," quietly. "But that's new, right, Nicky? It's never happened before?"

"No." Nick shook his head again, too, but spoke like he needed to convince himself of the fact.

Chills drained through Chris so fast he almost felt hot. "Then Saboac did something to you. Because freaks—*grendels*—don't just randomly start displaying powers when they're just about legal to drink. They—"

"Can manifest when they're under stress, Chris, you know that." Nick's voice cracked, but Chris laughed. It was a hard, broken kind of laugh, not a good one, but at least he laughed.

"Nicky, if you were gonna *manifest* because of stress you'd have popped off when you were studying for your finals." Or in one of a million fights with their dad, but even Chris knew saying that wouldn't be helpful right then.

Nick lifted his gaze just enough to stare at Chris. "You don't have to say 'manifest' like that. Normal people say manifest."

"Uh-huh. Sure they do. Point is, Nicky, you've been under a lot of stress lots of times. This only happened after Saboac." Chris took a deep breath. "So what we're gonna do is find that son of a bitch and take him out."

"What if it doesn't help?"

"Then we'll figure out what does." Chris reached over and grabbed the back of Nicky's neck, like he'd drag him closer. "It's gonna be okay, Nick. Okay? You hear me?"

"I blew a cabin up," Nick whispered. "I don't think that ends with 'okay.'"

"You didn't hurt anybody," Chris said. "You made sure not to. It'll be okay."

"Did I? Or was I just trying not to hurt you, and Emerson got lucky?"

"I'm gonna give you the benefit of the doubt. Either way, you were trying not to hurt somebody, and that matters." Chris leaned over until he could put his forehead against Nick's momentarily, then let go and backed off. "Think you can rest?"

"No."

Chris breathed a smile. "Try anyway. It's another three hours back to the 'Boat and you look like hell."

"You should let me drive if I'm not sleeping anyway. You had all that whiskey."

"That was a long time ago now." Chris sighed, looking toward the dark highway. "I can probably find a motel to pull off at if you want. I'll text your girl and let her know what's going on."

"At two thirty in the morning?" Nick's phone buzzed, like it had been doing every twenty minutes for the past five hours, and Chris spread a hand like 'see?' Nick took it out of his pocket this time, glanced at the messages, then called Stephanie with the phone to his ear and his eyes closed. He didn't say much for the first few minutes, then offered, "We got Emerson," after Stephanie either wound down or drew breath for another rant. "We just dropped him in Denver. We're gonna—"

He went quiet, his expression crumpled as Stephanie spoke to him. Chris scowled out the window, trying not to watch or listen, but his gaze kept going to the mirror, where he could see a glimpse of his brother's miserable expression as he said, "Yeah, I know yo—" and "We didn't really thi—" and "Look, Steph, I'm sorry, but—" to whatever she had to say.

After another long few minutes, he said, "I'll text you when we've got a place," and hung up looking exhausted. "She and Ty will drive down to meet us, since they're going to have to fly out of Denver to get back for mid-terms anyway."

"Please tell me they're smart enough to at least stay where they are for the night."

Nick shrugged. Chris sighed and pulled back out onto the highway, taking the first exit that promised motels. They were in a room less than half an hour later, and Nick was too tired to complain that it still had the faint smell of a decades-old former smoking room. He sent a text, then dropped onto one of the beds without taking his shoes off or pulling the covers up. He was by all appearances asleep before Chris got done using the bathroom.

Chris got an extra blanket from the closet, draped it over him, and went to bed himself. A few minutes later he heard the thump of Nicky's shoes hitting the floor, and then he could sleep.

———

Slashes of light lanced Nick's dreams, sharp and piercing and cutting hazy nightmare narratives into shards. He woke up bleary to see Chris, fully dressed, including his boots, still lay sprawled across the other bed, although Nick would lay money on him waking up as Nick got up and made a cup of genuinely awful coffee from the motel's instant fare. He poured it out after two sips.

Chris said, "That bad?" into his pillow. Nick nodded, not caring that his brother couldn't see it. Chris obviously didn't care either. "When they gonna be here?"

"I don't know. Soon."

"Go back to sleep."

"Can't."

"Arright." Chris sat up, rubbing his face. He looked five

years older, hollows under his eyes and his skin visibly dehydrated. Nick shuffled to the bathroom, got a cup of water, and walked it back to Chris, who drank it without any more comment than a look that said he didn't need taking care of. "Bad dreams?"

"Did I keep you awake?"

"Nah." Chris pinched the insides of his eyes, then rose and stretched himself like a cat, working out the kinks of having slept fully clothed. "But you always could sleep, no matter what else was going on, unless you had bad dreams." He went and got more water as Nick sat on his own bed, shoulders slumped.

"I kept dreaming about…what happened."

"'k. Tell me 'bout it."

"I dunno. I don't really remember much. Just there was a lot of light, and maybe…maybe Saboac."

"What do you remember about last night?" This time Chris handed *him* a glass of water. Not the same glass; he still had the one Nick had gotten for him in one hand, and drained it for the third time in as many minutes. Nick drank his, then handed the glass back to his brother with a pathetically hopeful look. Chris refilled it and brought it back before Nick even tried to answer anything about the night before. "I know I asked you already," Chris said, almost gently. "I know you told me a little already. But tell me anyway. Anything you remember, so we can figure out what to do."

"I was counting down two minutes. About ten seconds before the mark, I heard the back door break open and you shouted. And then…" Nick closed his eyes, the light marking the backs of his eyelids again. "I kicked the door open. I must have kicked the door open. It was broken and I was inside and it looked like Emerson was on top of you and I…"

"Exploded," Chris said, helpfully.

Nick lowered his head, frowning uncertainly at the half-empty water glass. "I guess? I wanted to get to you. I wanted to get him off you. And I felt..." He put a closed fist over his sternum, like he could capture the sensation that had been there. "I felt like I couldn't move fast enough, even if I didn't really know how I even got where I was. I felt like I could tear Emerson apart, like I could tear...everything apart. Like if I got hold of him I *would*. And I didn't want to do that, I just wanted you to be safe, but it was like there was all of this... energy? I guess?"

He looked up at Chris, who leaned against the motel room's desk, just a few feet way, with his eyebrows drawn in concentration. Not judging, just listening. Listening hard, and trying to understand. "It felt like I had to do something," Nick said helplessly. "Like...like a natural disaster or something, right? When something's happened and you can't fix it but you feel like you need to run or hit something or scream so you don't erupt?"

"Like you felt at the funeral." Chris hesitated. "Like we felt."

"Yeah." The small word came out in a desperate rush. "Like that. Like I didn't know what to do with it and if I didn't let it out somehow something...something bad was going to happen. And I knew I could've gotten to Emerson. He was just a couple steps away and he looked so insignificant and weak. He would never have even known I was coming, and then he'd have been..."

"Dead," Chris supplied. "But that's not you."

A bleak knife went through Nick's chest, cutting away at the certainty he might have taken from Chris's confidence. "I wanted to, though. I wanted to and I didn't, and then...I don't know, Chris. It's like I didn't move fast enough for the power to be satisfied but I couldn't hold it in. It just... exploded. Like you said. And then I was so tired. I'm still so tired."

Chris took a deep, careful breath. "Do you still feel it?"

Nick, lips compressed, nodded. "It's not as bad. It doesn't

want to get out as much right now. But it's there and I'm afraid if I get scared again..."

"You're going to have to learn to control it." Chris sounded so much older than he was, implacable and almost angry, like their dad, although he walked back what he'd said almost before he'd finished saying it. "You *were* controlling it, Nicky. You didn't let all that shrapnel hit either me or Emerson. You know that, right?"

"I know that's what you think. I think Emerson got lucky because he was next to you."

"Doesn't matter," Chris said with absolute conviction. "Even if you're right and you were only trying to keep me safe, you *did*. Which means you controlled it. Which means you'll be able to, Nick. We'll build on that."

"How can you be so calm?" The sensation of something building in his chest woke again, stronger than just the dull, tired presence he'd felt a moment earlier.

It dissipated, though, as Chris let out a quick bark of laughter. "I'm not. I'm pretending so we don't both flip out, Nicky. Last thing you need is me going haywire on you now."

"You're allowed to have feelings too, Chris." It seemed to Nick like he'd said that to him already, recently, but Chris only chuckled quietly.

"Right now you need me to be your cool, calm, collected big brother." He paused, then admitted, "And maybe I need that too. I mean, this is pretty weird, man. You look bad," he said after a minute. "You should try to sleep again. I'll keep watch."

"No." Nick sounded hoarse and wrung out, even to himself. "No, I gotta...I gotta figure this thing out now, Chris. I can't be around Stephanie if I don't know if I'm going to explode."

Chris stared at him a few seconds, then let go a slow exhalation. "Yeah, okay. Look, there's a...there's an old quarry up the road a ways. I'll check us out of the motel and we can drive up there and…I don't know, but there won't be anything to hurt out there, anyway. You can text your girl and tell her to meet us there."

"Arright." Nick closed his eyes. "Chris?"

"Yeah."

"Thanks."

Chris pushed away from the desk and put his hand on Nicky's shoulder briefly, then left the room. Nick packed up what little they'd brought in and met his brother at the truck a couple of minutes later. The drive to the quarry took longer than he expected, or felt like it did, at least, but that happened when you didn't know where you were going. He bet the drive out would seem shorter. He closed his eyes, resting his head against the window, and Chris, in the same voice he'd used when Nick was a kid, said, "Almost there, buddy."

"We're in a state park," Nick said, mostly to the window. "You sure we're supposed to be driving up here?"

"Pretty sure we're not." Chris flashed him one of those damn grins that got him in and out of trouble with equal ease. "On the other hand, it's winter, the road's big enough to drive on, nobody's looking, and some days it's easier to get forgiveness than permission."

"The Chris Cassidy Life Story," Nick muttered, and Chris's smile flashed again. A couple minutes later, the trail they were following stopped in a rough mass of carved-out marble that, despite its soft pale tones, looked dark compared to the snow heaped all over the place. "Tyler's gonna pitch a fit about driving his Highlander up here."

"How sad for him."

A betraying wheeze of laughter escaped Nick's throat, and Chris grinned. "I won't tell him you giggled."

"I didn't *giggle*." Nick paced forward, snow squeaking under his sneakers. They'd crushed cross-country ski tracks coming in, and there were more spreading across the quarry, giving him something more solid than powder to stand on. A wind cut through the pine trees, hissing between needles so dark they were almost black, beneath the cloudy winter sky. It smelled fresh and cold, with a promise of new snow. Nick stopped, and with the cessation of movement, his shoes stopped squeaking, which left him in a space of more complete silence than he'd heard in years. He could hear his own breathing, and Chris coughed once on the bite of cold in the air, but otherwise there was nothing but the wind scraping over the snow, and a sudden caw from an unseen raven.

The pressure, or the presence, of power inside of him seemed to wobble, in all that silence. Like it was equalizing, or something. Like it had room to expand, in the quiet. Or like it was looking for something to affect.

The last thought made Nick shudder, and he spoke too loudly, his voice cracking through the silence. "Great, here we are in the middle of nowhere with a bunch of snow and rock and trees. Now what?"

"You still feeling that energy, or whatever?"

Nick pressed the heel of his hand against his sternum. "Yeah. It's—" The answer turned to a yowl as a snowball slammed into the back of his head and melted directly into his collar. Scraping snow away, Nick spun on his brother, offended and borderline hurt. "What the hell, man!"

Chris, packing another snowball, actually looked a little guilty. "Sorry. I kinda didn't think it would hit you. Like you'd have a spider-sense or something."

"Well I didn't!"

"I said sorry! Try to stop this one." He lobbed another snowball, and Nick stopped it all right, but in the traditional way, by crossing his arms and ducking and yelling and generally protesting the entire process. He scraped up a handful of snow himself and flung it at Chris, who ducked behind the Dodge and yelled, "Neener neener!" because apparently they were five.

For a couple of minutes they just threw snowballs,

laughing and howling and swearing at each other, until Chris slipped on a slick patch, went down hard, and didn't get up again. After a couple of seconds Nick heard the rough catch of his breath, and went around the truck to find Chris sitting with his jaw clenched and his hands in fists, glazed gaze locked on the quarry walls a little distance away. Nick slid down to sit beside him, neither of them speaking or—quite, Nick thought—crying. But he would break if either of them spoke, and he thought Chris might, too. So they just sat until it passed, or at least until Nick's butt was so cold he couldn't feel it anymore. Just before he had to give up and get to his feet, Chris grunted, "I got an idea," and stood abruptly.

Nick rose, rubbing his frozen butt, and, baffled, watched as Chris found a semi-scalable chunk of quarry and began to climb. He slipped a couple of times, making Nick hiss with concern, but he caught himself both times, with a casual ease that made it look like he wasn't worried. But muttered curses bounced around the stone, so at least he had some modicum of sense remaining. Nick's own hands hurt with the idea of how cold the rock must be. After a few minutes, Chris had climbed maybe ten or fifteen feet, and found a ledge just about wide enough to stand on. He looked around a minute, said, "Nice view," then, "Ready?"

"Ready? For what?"

Chris jumped off the ledge.

# CHAPTER 9

PANIC AND POWER EXPLODED FROM THAT AWFUL SPACE INSIDE Nick's chest. He didn't think there were words around it, or inside it, just a raw need that erupted into action. Into form. Into something that leaped from him, as if the physical action he took—throwing his hands out like could catch his stupid-ass brother—shaped an impossible strength that would do what he otherwise couldn't.

Snow and air and Nick didn't know what else swept up together and caught Chris in a cushion just a few feet above the ground. Nick felt the impact, like he'd caught Chris physically, and the air rushed out of him. So did the unnatural power, like it couldn't withstand the shock. Chris fell the last couple of feet and landed hard in a pile of snow deeper than it had been before.

Landed hard, but not *nearly* as hard as he would have if Nick hadn't broken his fall. Nick's voice shot up, cracking the air and his throat. "What the *fuck*, Chris! What the fucking fuck!?"

After a moment's silence, a cackling groan emerged from the snowdrift, followed by a raspy, "Ow, man, that hurt."

By that time Nick was there, hauling him out of the snow-bank with both fists so he could yell in his brother's face.

"*That* hurt? What if I hadn't been able to catch you, *Jesus*, Chris, you could have been killed, you—"

"Get off." Chris tried to knock Nick's hands loose from his coat without much success. "Get off. I knew you'd catch me."

"How in ever-loving *fuck* could you know that?" Nick did let go then, explosively. Chris staggered backward a step or two and collided with the rock wall he'd just climbed. Snow from a tree above them collapsed and dumped heavily on him, and he yelled, "Hey!" like *that* was the unreasonable thing that had just happened. Then he shoved past Nick, knocking snow off as he went. "I knew it because you were trying to keep me safe with Emerson. What'd it feel like?"

"It felt like panic, you fucking idiot, what the fuck were you thinking—"

"Aren't you the one who was giving me shit about using 'fuck' too many times in one sentence like two days ago? Or yesterday? Jesus, when was that?" Chris pulled his jacket off to shake the rest of the snow off.

Nick stared at him blankly a few seconds, the mundanity of the question knocking him out of his anger. "It was…it's Monday morning. That was Saturday. Two days. Chris…" Nick sat down hard in the snow again, shaking all over as he buried his face against his knees. "Don't do that again. Jesus, man, don't do that again."

He heard Chris's boots squeak on the snow, and a moment later the heat of his brother's hand warmed his shoulder. "I gotta admit, there was a split second there where I thought I'd made a terrible mistake. You caught me, though, so I'd do it again."

"*Chris.*"

"Maybe not unless it was an emergency," Chris conceded. He crouched, his hand still on Nick's shoulder. "What'd it feel like?"

Nick snarled, "Terrifying," against his knees, then looked up. His brother's gaze showed a trace of sympathetic apology, but mostly held a familiar sharpness, an intensity that said he was on the hunt, searching for answers, and that he wouldn't let it go until he had them.

Sometimes, Nick thought, Chris reminded him too much of their father. He put his head back down against his knees, but this time he was searching for the right words, not just rattled beyond being able to speak. After a minute he lifted his head again. "Do you remember when we were kids and we spent like half a summer just lying around staring at things, convinced we could move them with our minds if we tried hard enough?"

A brief smile slid across Chris's mouth. "Yeah. You'd read some book where the kid could do that. I told you like half the X-Men could."

Nick, distracted, said, "I think like *two* of the X-Men could, at least on the main teams. Anyway, yeah. Aside from the *panic, dude*, it felt like that. Like that's what I was trying, except it worked this time. I…" He stretched out both hands, like he'd done when he'd tried to stop Chris's fall. "I reached, but my…my mind reached farther."

"And stronger," Chris said thoughtfully. "You wouldn't have been able to catch me with your arms. Anything else?"

"I don't know, man, I was really kind of focused on freaking out." Nick bared his teeth. "On panicking. Not, like…freaking."

"Not grendeling," Chris said, and shrugged when Nick gave him a hard look. "Yeah, it doesn't exactly flow, but we'll get used to it. How you feel now?"

"Exhausted."

"Too exhausted to try again?"

Nick's spine stiffened, angry dismay washing through him. "You just said—"

"No, not like that, yeah, no, I'm not jumping off another cliff today. But you have more of an idea of what you did, now. Basically telekinesis, right? So, I dunno…" Chris looked around, then packed a snowball together and stood up. "C'mon, stand up and see if you can stop it from hitting you."

"Why would standing up matter?" Nick rose anyway, and Chris backed off to give him some reaction distance before throwing the snowball.

It hit Nick square in the middle of the chest. They both looked at the blob of white breaking in pieces and sliding down his coat, and then Nick lifted an accusatory stare toward his brother.

Chris offered a wide cheesy smile. "Try again?" After a few more successful hits, Nick muttered, "You're enjoying this, aren't you," and Chris's smile went crooked before he said, "Lemme try something."

"Oh, sure, go ahead, this is obviously great, I'm having lots of fun, you do you, man, whatever."

Chris cackled and made a whole stack of snowballs, then scooped as many as he could hold up into one arm, and began throwing them at Nick with the other. The first couple hit while Nick stood there feeling mildly abused, and then a barrage flew at him. He raised his arms, trying to protect himself, then growled, "Hey...*hey*!" as they came faster. Then angry pain erupted in him as a snowball caught him in the ear, and his next protest came as an incoherent shout. He threw his arms down, apart, like he might if he was holding swords in both hands and making a last stand, and roared, as if the sound alone could end the bombardment.

An almost-visible wave of power, like frustration embodied, bubbled in front of him. The snowballs smacked against it harmlessly, disintegrating in soft poofs. The bubble didn't quite hit Chris, but it displaced air and snow, spitting a spray of white over him. He stepped, almost staggered, back, as if he'd been pushed, but the surprise that flashed over his face was replaced almost instantly by delight. "Yeah! There you go! Arright, what else? You straight-armed Saboac, go see if you can pick up the truck!"

"The truck weighs a literal ton, Chris, the angel thing didn't weigh that much." Nick tried anyway, with exactly as much success as he expected, but Chris waved it off.

"You can't do it if you don't believe in yourself, man. Try a rock instead. Or me, your buddy Tyler says you can bench press more than I weigh anyway."

"You want me to straight-arm you?" Nick asked incredulously.

"Sure!"

"Dude, you know you aren't meant to be experimented on?"

"Better me than Stephanie," Chris said cheerfully, and it turned out Nick *could*, in a flash of anger, straight-arm him, although at least he didn't grab him by the throat. Chris, dangling in his grip, said, "What's it feel like?" and Nick put him down to stare at him.

"It feels like straight-arming my brother, and it's not cool." He stepped back, slipping in the snow, and rubbed a cold hand over his face. "I know that's not what you mean. It feels like I'm using my muscles, but not as much as I should have to. It's easy, and I don't...I don't like it."

"And how do you feel? Still tired?"

"Not as tired as before. I don't like that either." Nick folded his arms around himself, staring at the snow, now broken with their footprints and snowball-collecting marks. "I don't want to be a freak, Chris."

"I don't know, man, it's pretty cool to be able to lift somebody like that." Chris's voice softened, though. "I know. But I think freak powers—grendel powers—are better if you know how to use them than not. You gotta be able to control that shit. So now we know you get explosive if you get mad or scared, but you can pick me up like I'm a rag doll without being pissy."

"You were being pissy," Nick announced. Chris rolled his

eyes, and Nick looked away. "No, I was mad, though. Mad at the idea I might hurt Stephanie."

"Oh. Okay, so it's still emotion-driven. But that's a lot more than we knew. That's good information. You wanna try anything else? Like a thunderclap or something?"

Nick, feeling like he'd regret it, said, "A what?" and Chris's smile brightened.

"You know, a thunderclap. Like Hulk does. Whoom!" He brought his hands together in front of him, hollow palms making a surprising amount of noise in the quiet quarry. "Focusing the power to see if you can knock trees over, or something."

"Trees."

Chris, defensively, said, "Sometimes he knocks trees over," and Nick chuckled despite himself.

"Yeah, all right, yeah. Get out of the way." He waved Chris to the side, then walked a few steps ahead of him to make sure he wouldn't be caught in the by-blow. Assuming there was any. He brought his hands together lightly a couple of times, feeling like an idiot doing a practice run for a stage fight, but trying to concentrate on what it would feel like to have that rush of power focused through the concussion of his palms. It felt almost alive inside him, like it would oblige because it was eager for him to try it out. "I don't like this, Chris."

"I know," Chris said, surprisingly quiet for a guy who'd just been geeking out over a Hulk-style thunderclap. "But you know I'm right, too. Honestly, Nicky, I don't care if you decide never to use it, once you've got a handle on how *not* to. But you gotta know how."

"Yeah." Nick exhaled, focused on a darker cut in the quarry up ahead of him, and forcefully brought his hands together.

A *thoom!* of power thundered out, cutting a thin focused line through the snow and kicking up a glittering spray of ice and pine needles. It hit the craggy wall of stone with enough force to send shards exploding from the rock, hard enough to shake the walls of the quarry. Snow collapsed from ledges and trees, hitting the ground in clouds of white that rolled back toward Nick and Chris, who both stood frozen in an aftermath that still rattled the air.

An unexpected thrill of glee shot through Nick, so bright and sharp and unlooked-for that it felt like someone else's emotion, something alien and intrusive in his own mind. He inhaled too sharply, trying to banish it, and the sensation grew even more alert, then fled abruptly, lost beneath Chris's awed, "Holy shit, man. You've got defensive and offensive moves."

"Yeah." Nick watched the snow settle as the reverberations faded away, and shook his head. "I don't think I want to do any more right now, Chris. This is…something happened in my head just now and I didn't like it."

Chris sharpened. "Something like what?"

"I don't know. It felt like…" Nick closed his eyes, trying to chase the feeling that had popped up. He could almost see a streak in his mind, a path where it had gone, and a presence at its other end. "I think maybe it was Saboac. I think maybe…maybe it knows where I am. I think maybe…I can find it, too."

"That—what? Where is he?"

"I don't know. North? Still north," Nick said with more confidence. "Maybe homing in on Sterling. We can find him, Chris. I can find him so we can kill him and get this over with."

"Nick, I don't think—"

The sound of a distant vehicle cut through Chris's opinion. They both fell silent, turning toward it, although Chris cut a look toward Nick that said the conversation wasn't over yet. A minute or two later, Tyler's SUV pulled up behind the Dodge, and Stephanie spilled out of it before the engine was dead. She flew at Nick for a worried hug, and he caught her, burying his face in her hair.

"We're fine. Things just moved fast last night and we didn't have time to call. Sorry." He met Chris's eyes briefly, but his older brother shrugged it off, obviously not caring how Nick spun the story.

"It's a four hour drive to Denver from Steamboat Springs!" Stephanie protested. "How could you not have time to at least text?"

"It's not a good idea to make personal connections in front of bounties," Chris said unexpectedly. "Nick called as soon as he could."

Stephanie's eyebrows drew down. "Oh. Okay, I guess that kind of makes sense. Still, I was worried! And what the hell are you guys doing out here? This is the middle of nowhere."

"I know. I needed some air to get my head clear after the bounty."

"This is Colorado," Tyler said as he got out of his truck. "There's nothing *but* air out here."

"Okay, so I needed some space."

"There's nothing *but*—"

Stephanie ducked, without really leaving Nick's arms, and pitched a handful of snow at Tyler. His "Hey!" sounded injured, but Stephanie shrugged unrepentantly. "I wouldn't have had to if you'd been going to keep your damn mouth shut."

Chris gave Nick a quick, cocky half-grin. "I like her."

"Me too."

Steph shivered. "Is there some reason we have to be standing out here freezing to death? Can we go now?"

"What happened here?" Tyler had gone past them and was walking heel-to-toe along the sharp line that marked the path Nick's thunderclap had taken. "That doesn't look natural."

A band of heat warmed Nick's chest from within, like a

warning. "Who knows? Yeah, let's go. I'll drive out with Chris and we can head for Denver International."

Stephanie's gaze went careful. "I'd like you to come with us, if we're going to leave. I don't want to spend our last couple hours together, uh, apart."

Nick glanced toward Chris, who shrugged. "Whatever."

Still carefully, Stephanie said, "Maybe Ty could ride out with Chris."

"What?" Tyler's voice shot up high enough to startle birds, and Chris's expression went black with irritation, but Steph sparkled her eyes and her voice went sweet and cajoling.

"C'mon, you're not going to kill each other if I'm alone with Nick for a while, are you?"

"Nah." A sharp-edged grin slid across Chris's face. "Not worth my effort."

Tyler bared his teeth, making an obvious effort to not come back with a pointed rejoinder. "Look, I'm sorry about last night, okay? I didn't mean to be an ass."

"I know," Chris said, shortly. "That's part of why you were. Go on," he said to Stephanie. "Fine with me, whatever."

That was hardly a ringing endorsement, but Nick gave his brother a tight smile of thanks. Tyler curled his lip but sighed. "Fine, whatever, okay. But I'm taking the doughnuts with me."

"Oh, see, breakfast of champions," Chris said. "Maybe you're okay after all, Ty. Did you bring milk? Coffee? No? Never mind. You're a lousy date." He went and got in his truck with a martyred expression, while Tyler got doughnuts from the back of his truck, then handed Stephanie the keys.

"Don't wreck it."

"Oh, well, I was totally going to, but now that you've said not to…"

"Yeah, yeah." Tyler sneered and headed for the Dodge.

Stephanie watched him get into the truck, then turned to

Nick with a rueful smile. "They're going to kill each other, aren't they."

"I seriously doubt it. Ty wouldn't stand a chance." Nick crawled in the Highlander's passenger seat and checked the back seat, where an entire box of bakery-style doughnuts still sat. "I thought he was taking these."

"We bought a lot. Give me a jam one, will you? Or maybe wait until we're off these skinny trails. I don't think we're supposed to be driving up here, Nick."

"No." Nick smiled faintly. "Probably not. Is it okay if I eat one now?"

"Eat as many as you like." She got the SUV turned around and drove out, silent while they followed their own tracks back, and finally, once out on the main roads again, said, "What happened, Nick? You look awful, and I didn't want to leave you alone with your brother for that long. Are you okay?"

"I'm fine. It's not Chris. But what we gotta do isn't going away, Steph. This is going to take more than a couple of days. You and Tyler need to go home."

"Well, I'm okay with driving in to Denver so we're not going back and forth all over the place before flying out, but we can squeeze out today before we start being in danger of missing mid-terms, Nick. And even if it's not okay or fair, you know Tyler's right. His dad or my parents can probably make it good with the school if we miss the tests."

"Don't do that. First off, you shouldn't because it *isn't* right or fair, and second, if you do and keep hanging out it's gonna be rubbing Chris's nose in it the whole time you're here. But also…" Nick looked at the sugar-coated surface of his doughnut, trying not to feel the flutter of energy inside his chest. It didn't feel drained from their experiments, and he wasn't confident that it wouldn't erupt into explosiveness again just because he'd directed it a couple of times. It felt like imminent danger, coiled within him.

"I don't care about Chris except as an auxiliary to you," Stephanie said with quiet intensity. "I'd rather not make him uncomfortable, but it's more important to me to be here for you."

"Right now I need Chris." Nick glanced sideways to see hurt and confusion flicker across Stephanie's face. "I know you don't understand why, since I haven't said much nice about him, but I need him, not you. You should go home." The energy in him didn't take up as much space as the too-hard beating of his heart, or the anguish that squeezed his lungs. "This thing here could take quite a while, and I don't want you dragged into it. You need to go home, and we should—" He drew a ragged breath. "We should stop seeing each other. You shouldn't be stuck waiting for me, when I don't know how long this is going to take. Go back to California and have fun."

Steph's confusion remained, but the hurt slowly morphed into outrage, and she actually pulled over to the side of the road so she could turn toward him. Nobody would care. They weren't on the main road yet, just a smaller one with trees on both sides and very little traffic. "Do you think you're breaking up with me? *Now?*"

"I am breaking up with you," Nick whispered hoarsely. "Steph, what's going on, I don't want you to be a part of it. It's dangerous and it's—"

"You always do this," Stephanie said, rough with emotion. "You've talked about it. You talked about it being part of why you went to college as early as you did, and why you never came home again until now. I've seen you do it with friends when you felt like they were getting too close. I've even seen you drop a psych class because it wanted too much of *you*. You run instead of dealing with it, whatever 'it' is. I don't want that to happen with us, Nick. I get that you and your brother have some major shit to work out. I don't get why you won't let me in on all of it—"

"Because it's a lot worse than you think it is, Stephanie!"

She paled and he saw her pulse leap in her throat, but her eyes were worried, not afraid. She reached for his hand with cold fingers. "What is?" she asked, very softly. "It's obviously got to do with your dad, Nick, and...look, the way Chris is protective of you? The way you got out of the house as soon as you could? The way you two clearly have a shit-ton of trauma to unpack now that he's dead, and the way you shy away from anybody *really* getting to know you? Nick, were you...what did he do to you?"

The feeling in his chest convulsed, like bands of plasma shooting off the surface of the sun. It clawed into the places inside him that held the answers Stephanie was looking for. He thought it would launch from them. That maybe that's where it had started the night before, when he'd thought Chris was in trouble, or just a while ago, when Chris had jumped off a damn cliff. The out-of-control sensation was much worse—much stronger—than it had been when he'd tried the thunderclap. Stronger, even, than when he'd blocked the barrage of snowballs. The feeling of being watched returned, and Nick took a shaking breath, then another one, trying to hollow the power out before it erupted again, and finally said, "Nothing anybody can change."

"You can change it," Stephanie said gently. "Maybe you can't change what happened, but you can change it by talking to me about it, Nick." There was an ache in her voice to match the one in his chest. "Or to *somebody*, if not me."

"I can't—!" The words burst out of him and he dragged them back, breathing hard. "Chris is the only one who can understand, Steph."

"Chris is even more messed up than you are! At least you got out of whatever happened with your dad. He stayed. He needs at *least* as much help as you do, and I don't see how you're going to get it from each other." Stephanie's hands tightened over his. "Please don't push me away, Nick. Let me help you get through this. If you've got to stay with Chris, okay. But let me stay, too, okay? And when you can...*if* you can...you tell me what you can. Okay?"

Nick closed his eyes, pushing the bands of fire within him down. Hoping they wouldn't surge and destroy everything around him again. Wondering how the hell he could say that to his very stubborn girlfriend, and being fairly certain he couldn't. "It isn't safe, Steph."

"I'm old enough to decide that for myself, babe."

"Not in this case," he whispered, opening his eyes again. "I...I know more about what's going on than you do, and..."

"Nick, he's dead. Your dad is dead."

The grendel power twisted inside him again, searching for something to hold on to. "It's not just my dad, Stephanie."

Stephanie, sharply, said, "Is it Chris?"

"What? No!" Nick recoiled, staring at her in genuine distress, then slowly folded in on himself, shoulders sagging. "No. No, it's *not* Chris, okay? Chris is...Chris is good," he said more softly. "Better than he thinks he is. Better than I give him credit for. And he understands."

"And I don't. And I won't, unless you decide to explain things to me." Stephanie looked back as Chris's truck pulled up behind them. Tyler got out, but Chris, visible as a shadow in the driver's seat, just leaned over the wheel and waited. Nick could all but feel his brother's gaze, in the same way he could feel that other presence watching him.

Tyler pulled the back door open and stuck his head in. "Everything okay? What's going on?"

"Nick thinks he's staying in Colorado without me."

"Oh, yeah. Good luck with that." Tyler closed the door and went back to the Dodge.

Stephanie snorted. "At least somebody's on my side here."

"Steph, if I knew how to explain it to you without you thinking I'm nuts, I would. But I don't, so can we just...can we just move on, please?"

"Move on with breaking up, you mean?"

Regret lanced through Nick and he felt his expression collapse, although he managed to say, "Yeah," loudly enough to be heard just before Chris opened the door behind Nick.

"What the hell is going on here? Are we just hanging out on the roadside all day now or something?"

"I told you," Tyler said, opening the Highlander's back door again. "Steph doesn't want to go home."

"Of course I don't! I want to help Nick—"

"I get that, and I appreciate it, but Nick and me, we gotta…we're going to try to find the guy who killed our dad, and that's…"

Stephanie breathed, "Oh, shit," and shifted her gaze to Nick. "That's what this 'stuff' you've got to take care of is? Nick, that could—that could take forever."

"I *know*. That's why I told you to go home without me!"

"Well, why didn't you tell me what you were going to *do*?"

Nick rolled his jaw, looking for an answer that would make sense. The *reason* was he hadn't been thinking of it like that, exactly. Not as something he could explain away as easily as a manhunt. He'd been thinking of it as a monster hunt, and that took too much explaining.

Chris came to his rescue. "Because we're bounty hunters, Stephanie, not cops. We're supposed to collect people who've skipped out on bail, not go out and find killers ourselves. Tell me you're not about to argue with him on this."

A flush of confusion ran over Stephanie's cheeks. "I…well, I mean…"

"So if we could just talk you into going home, it would be easier," Chris said. "We could do what we have to do, and—"

"And fuck up Nick's whole life?" Tyler asked. Chris's shoulders tensed and he pulled away from leaning in the truck door and turned toward Tyler with a kind of control Nick recognized. Tyler either didn't recognize it, or didn't care. Smart money was on getting out of the way, when somebody looked at you with that kind of control, but Tyler swung out of the back door and squared up with Chris.

"You know I'm not wrong, man. I get that finding whoever killed your dad is important, but realistically it could take months or years or even never happen. You're really gonna talk Nick into staying with you to do that when he could go to med school and make a difference in hundreds of lives? *Thousands* of lives?"

"It's not like that, Ty——"

Tyler, eyebrows rising, turned on Nick, who edged Chris aside to climb out of the Highlander. "Isn't it? Are you telling me you won't stick it out until you find the guy, no matter how long it takes? I know you're telling yourself you'll just take a couple weeks and then if it hasn't worked out you'll come back to school, but do you even believe that?"

Guilt surged through Nick, heating his face the same way Stephanie had just flushed. "Maybe? I mean, I did…"

Stephanie climbed out, too, and came around the front of the SUV. "Look, Chris, I know you don't think you're trying to hold Nick back, but——"

Alarm flared through Nick, trying to get its claws into the grendel power inside of him. "Steph, he's *not*——"

"Then he should be letting you come back to Cali to finish your degree, Nick," Tyler snapped. "He's got to let you be who you are, not who he wants you to be."

Chris, almost beneath his breath, said, "Jesus, what do you think I've been trying to do his whole goddamn life," then half-shouted, "Fine, all right, *fine*, go with them, Nick, I'll figure it out on my own. I always do."

"No! No, Chris, look, I think I've got a line on this——on what happened." Nick stumbled over the explanation and cast a frustrated look toward Tyler and Stephanie. "I think I can track him, with——with——you know, with what I learned."

"Oh, yeah, that's clearly a great idea. We'll just use——" Chris, too, broke off, struggling for a way to refer to Nick's grendel power without giving everything away to the other two. "No. It's a shit idea. I don't want you doing that."

"See?" Tyler snapped at Nick. "He doesn't think you can make your own decisions."

"That is *not* what I said—"

"Whose side are you on!" Stephanie yelled at Tyler.

"Nick's! I'm on Nick's side!"

"Then why are you trying to get him to do whatever his terrible idea is that Chris doesn't think he should?"

"Because it should be his decision!"

"It should be his decision, but that doesn't mean you should be encouraging him to make stupid decisions!"

Chris flung his hands up. "I don't even know who I'm agreeing with, but all three of you should just go back to goddamn California—"

"Chris, what if I'm the only one who *can* find—him?" Nick's voice rose and broke, frustration building like a warning in his chest. He tried to take a deep breath and nearly choked on it as Chris bellowed, "I'm pretty sure *he* isn't gonna be that hard to find, Nick, given the—"

He broke off for the second time, although his hands finished the sentence, indicating wings and fire. Not that Stephanie or Tyler would understand that, but Nick did, and the ball of frustration inside him grew larger. Beyond frustration into resentment, bordering on anger. "So, what?" Nick yelled back. "You want to go deal with that alone? You think that's going to work out for you?"

"I want you to stay safe!"

"That's all any of us want!" Angry tears were shining in Stephanie's eyes. "Nick, just come—"

"Let the man make his own decisions!" Tyler yelled, and above him, above all of them, Nick roared, "*Enough!*"

Grendel power smashed out of him with the word, rolling over them, and blew the windows out of the Dodge.

# CHAPTER 10

GLASS SHATTERED, BREAKING IN CHUNKS AND SHARDS THAT flew outward in a glittering hail. Screams, louder than the fracturing glass, echoed off the cold road as Stephanie and Tyler ducked away, disbelief and panic in their cries. Chris ducked, feeling glass bounce off his leather jacket, and straightened to stare from the Dodge's blown-out windows to his whey-faced brother.

Nick stood rigid with shock, hands spread wide, cords visible in his throat. Of all of them, only he hadn't turned away from the explosion. Bits of faintly green tempered glass gleamed in the folds of his clothing and hair. Stephanie was still screaming, and Chris's own throat was raw from a yell, but Nick hadn't moved or made a sound. Chris opened his mouth to say something—to ask if Nick was okay—but what came out was, "What the hell did you do to my truck?!"

Nick's gaze snapped from the Dodge to Chris, whose fingers clawed like he could pull the question back in. Hurt, then anger, slammed through Nick's expression, before it settled on cold fury.

Stephanie's fury wasn't cold at all. She whirled on Chris, hair flying loose from its ponytail. "What do you mean, what'd he do? He didn't do anything! How could he have done that? That was a freak fucking accident, you stupid son of a bitch!"

Chris closed his eyes, trying to unknot his hands from the fists they'd become. Trying to relax the angry tension from his face, from how he held his jaw, from his shoulders. He needed to apologize, to make his first, asshole response right again, but his heart was beating so fast and his face was so hot with blood that even breathing steadily seemed hard. He had to get through it, had to man up for Nick, and despite all the bullshit their dad had fed them, *manning up* didn't mean blaming him for an accident, or refusing to ever say sorry. He just had to do it, so he could help his brother.

By the time he got enough breath in his lungs to speak, though, Nick was saying, "It *was* a freak accident," in a low, thick voice, full of despair. "Because I'm a fucking freak."

"You're not, Nicky." Chris sounded as thick and slow as his brother did.

Nick turned a look of scathing disgust on him. "Don't be stupid, Chris. I just fucked up your truck."

Chris inhaled. Deep breath, through his nose, bringing it way down into his lungs, like it could wipe out hurt. He wasn't stupid. Not that stupid, anyway. "It's a truck. It doesn't matter. Are you okay?"

Nick's voice broke as he gestured at the Dodge. "Of course I'm not okay!"

Tyler breathed, "What the hell is going on?" and Stephanie gave him a filthy look.

"Chris has lost his goddamn mind, that's what. I don't know what just happened—"

"I happened." Nick's flat tone cut through Stephanie's protestations. "That was me, Stephanie. That's why I wanted you to leave. I told you I was dangerous."

"You said it wasn't safe, not that you were dan—"

"Stephanie." Nick sounded desperate. "Please."

She stopped hard, like it took a lot out of her, which Chris could understand. She tried twice to start again, failing both times, and finally said, "I don't understand," in a thin voice. "How could you have done that?"

Chris watched his brother gather himself, and took a step forward, like he could stop Nick from doing something idiotic. But it wouldn't help. Stephanie wasn't going to understand unless she saw, and Nick's normal was already blown to hell.

"There are monsters in the world, Steph," Nick said very, very quietly. "Monsters like from stories, but some of them are just people with dangerous power. Freaks. Like me."

Chris bit back a protest at the term, and Stephanie, eyes bright with fear and anger, began one. "You're not a freak, Nick, you're—"

Nick didn't say anything else, just turned toward the black-branched trees that stretched away from the side of the road. He glanced at Chris just briefly, like he was looking for —Chris didn't know what. Permission, maybe, but more like absolution. Either way, Chris dropped his chin in a nod, knowing what to expect.

There was no way at all Stephanie could expect Nick to slam his hands together in a thunderclap, though, and for the line of trees straight in front of him to simply…cease to exist.

Branches, splinters, clumps of earth, sprays of snow, all erupted in a thin narrow line, stretching dozens of feet out from where Nick stood with his hands clasped together. The boom reverberated, shaking the earth, making Chris's knees buckle. Tyler grabbed the front of his SUV to stay on his feet, and Stephanie screamed, a clear bright high sound, a perfect counterpoint to the ground-rumbling burst of power that Nick had displayed.

He turned back to Stephanie, who'd fallen to her knees and was staring up at him, snow and dirt clutched in white-knuckled fingers. He drew breath to speak, but she shook her head, short sharp frantic motion, then scrambled to her feet.

She ran past Tyler, snatching at his arm, although he stood frozen, staring in something like awe at Nick.

"Tyler, come on, come *on*!"

"But that was—that was—" A wide-eyed smile of delight formed on Tyler's face, but Stephanie cried, "Come *on*," again, and he muttered, "Fine, *fine*," and got into the Highlander. A moment later they disappeared down the road, and only then did Nick crumple, very slowly, to the ground.

Chris didn't get there quite in time to catch him. Didn't matter. He got there fast enough to hold him, fast enough to bend his head over Nick's and feel his brother shaking with rage and fear and frustration. Got there and held on until Nick threw him off, yelling, "Aren't you afraid? You should be afraid! Look what I did to your truck!"

"It's just a truck, Nicky." Chris fell back onto his butt by the roadside, not caring about the ice or cold or snow or the rounded edges of tempered glass that lay scattered like pale green gems across the frozen earth.

"It's not just a truck, it's your—it's your fuck you to Dad! It's—" Nicky doubled over, hands knotted against the snowy ground, forehead pressed against bits of glass.

Chris chuckled. "It's one of them, yeah, I guess." He gazed toward the truck, more or less sightlessly. "I don't know if he ever even knew that, or cared. I didn't know you knew." After a moment's silence, he said, "I don't know if I knew."

"How can you be so calm?" Nick's words bounced off the asphalt and came toward Chris as flat despairing things. "I blew up your truck. I scared Stephanie away. I fucked up, Chris." His voice broke, and he repeated, "I fucked up," through choking tears.

"Yeah, well, it's gonna be a cold drive home," Chris admitted. "C'mon. C'mon, buddy. Get up. Let's get out of here before…"

He didn't even know how to finish that. Before the cops came? Before somebody happened onto the edge of Route 57 at eleven in the morning in the middle of winter? Before Stephanie and Tyler got back to civilization, and told everybody that Nick Cassidy had grendel powers?

Didn't matter. They just needed to get out of there before any of that happened. Before it got any colder, or the wind picked up any, because it really was gonna be a crappy drive home, with no windows in the truck. "Let's see if I've got any plastic sheeting in there. Cover the side and back windows, anyway."

"You do," Nick said dully, to the earth. "You know you do."

"Yeah. I know." Chris offered Nick a hand, and pulled him up whether he wanted to rise or not. It took a solid half hour to get the sheeting out from under the seat and tape sections to most of the windows. They were both sweating by the time they finished, and Chris stared at the open windshield glumly. "Think we'd get arrested for driving with a Visqueen windshield?"

Nick pressed one hand against the sheeting they'd put in the side window, judging its clarity. "It's not technically illegal to drive without a windshield, just stupid. So it's probably slightly less stupid to have Visqueen in front of your face so bugs or rocks or whatever don't fly in and hit you in the eye."

"Arright, well, you're the smart one, so that's what I'm telling the cops if they pull us over."

"What the fuck are we *gonna* tell the cops if they pull us over?"

Chris, pulling a new sheet of Visqueen across the Dodge's broken windshield, glanced at his brother. "The truth. We were out on Route 57 and something blew a line of trees and our windows out."

"'Something?'" Nick's voice cracked, and Chris shrugged.

"They're not gonna believe the details, so why bother with them? We'll tell 'em we're going home to get it fixed 'cause we can't afford to stay overnight in Denver, which they're gonna believe because I'm driving a forty year old truck in the first place."

Nick said, "Chris," and then obviously ran out of steam, because they finished stretching the plastic sheeting over the windshield in silence. It didn't make the best window ever, but it was better than driving a hundred and fifty miles in seventeen degree weather with no windows at all.

"Two hundred miles," Chris muttered to himself a minute later, as they got in. Nick glanced at him, then sighed.

"I guess so, yeah. We're definitely gonna get stopped if we drive through Denver, but if we take the back roads...."

"Yeah." Nick wet his lips and turned his face toward the blurred-out window. "I'm sorry."

"Shit happens, man. Wasn't your fault."

"It's not like it was somebody else's fault, Chris."

"It's not like you can be expected to be in perfect control of a weird-ass new power set like thirty-six hours after you got them, Nick. Believe me, if anybody could it would be you, and you're not, so it's not possible." Chris pulled back onto the road cautiously. He could see, kind of. Well enough to not get in a wreck, if he drove slowly and no bison or deer jumped out in front of them. They might make it home before dark.

No, they *had* to make it home before dark. No way was he driving in the dark with Visqueen windows, and sleeping in the truck was bad enough with one person and windows. Two of them without them...

They would make it home before dark. Simple as that. They just had to. Chris concentrated on the road, driving slowly, and forgot about most everything else.

"Why would it be me?" Nicky's voice cracked like he hadn't spoken in a long time. Maybe he hadn't. Chris's shoulders ached from hunching over the steering wheel, like being six inches closer to the plastic window would make it easier to see through. The odometer said they'd only driven about thirty miles, deeper into the mountains, but he had no sense of how long it had taken.

"Because you're—" Chris coughed on the answer and made himself sit up straighter, trying to loosen his spine. "Got any water?"

"Yeah, there's a…" Nick reached for a water bottle, opened it, and handed it over.

Chris took a couple of long gulps, swallowed hard, and handed it back. "Thanks. Jesus. How long have we been driving?"

"About an hour, but you're going slower now than when we started."

"More snow." Chris puffed his cheeks and sighed the air out. "Because you're good at everything you do, Nick. You study hard, you fight hard, you work hard on…relationships." Even he thought he said that last word like it had a bad taste. "So if anybody could figure out how to use grendel powers in a day and a half, it'd be you. Me, I'd be fucking it up all over the place for years, but you…."

"You wouldn't. You learned how to rebuild an engine in a weekend when you were about twelve. You could do this." Nicky wasn't really arguing, though. He thumped his head against the headrest and fell silent again for another long time as the truck crept up mountain roads, hugging the white line all the way in case they needed to ditch. There wasn't much traffic, and what there was didn't seem to care that they were going like nine miles an hour, as long as they stayed out of the way. "I can still feel…it. Him. Saboac."

"That's not creepy at all." Chris forced himself to straighten up again. If he only did that when Nick spoke, he'd be permanently hunched by the time they reached Sterling again. "Seriously, man, is he like…watching you?"

"I don't know. Maybe. I think I can watch him, too, though. If I keep my eyes closed it's almost like I can see through his eyes."

"Yeah, *don't do that*."

"We gotta find him somehow, Chris."

"Yeah, okay, sure, but how about you don't give him a direct line to blowing up your brain or whatever when we're on a twelve-inch wide mountain road where a bunch of truckers wanna drive ninety miles an hour?"

Nick rotated his head like his neck was an iron bar, and stared at Chris for a couple seconds. "I haven't seen any truckers out here."

"I swear to god, Nick, the Iranian yogurt is not the issue here."

"*What?*"

"The Ir—" Chris risked a glance at his brother. "Never mind. You have the internet. Look it up. The point is not the truckers, that's what I'm trying to say. Do not invite the reprobate angel into your head."

"Reporbate."

"Man, is there actually a difference? You've got the internet," Chris muttered again. "Look it up."

This time Nicky did, and a minute later he shrugged. "Means rejected by God, either way. That's the second definition. Rejected by God and beyond hope of salvation. Wow. That's…wow."

"So that's the difference between a fallen angel and a reporbated one? I mean, you said that God desanctified the reprobate angels, but, I don't know, *rejecting* them seems even bigger than desanctifying them. Maybe it's the same, if you're God. I'm not," he added, in case that wasn't obvious. "Does that mean like, Lucifer or whatever has the hope of salvation, and our new buddy Saboac doesn't? That's…" Chris grimaced, unable to do better than Nicky had. "Wow."

"Yeah." Nick went quiet again for a long time, and they crept through a stretch of road labeled as the Peak to Peak Highway. Chris had driven it at least a dozen times, and never felt like it was trying to kill him until now. It took almost two hours to get to the other end, but at least they were heading out of the mountains. His hands felt like ice clubs, wrapped thickly around the steering wheel, forever stuck. Nick finally muttered, "You should let me drive," and Chris, to his own surprise, muttered, "Yeah, okay," back without an argument.

They pulled over at a gas station, refilled, got some snacks that were mostly jerky, sugar, or coffee, and switched places when they got back in the truck. Nick sat in the driver's seat, gazing blankly through the plastic sheeting. "I think that's what it means, yeah. I mean, we read that they were pure evil, nothing redeemable left in them, but…rejected by God without hope of salvation, that seems worse somehow, you're right. So, yeah. The Devil himself has a chance at redemption but Saboac doesn't. And he's in my head."

"We're gonna get him out," Chris said flatly. "Just don't give him any more air time than you have to. Don't try to find him, Nicky. I'm pretty sure he's gonna come find us anyway."

"Me," Nick whispered. "He's going to come find me."

"Yeah. And I'm gonna be standing in the way. Now shut up and drive, okay? At the rate we're going it's gonna be another five or six hours before we get home already."

"Should be a little faster once we get out of the mountains," Nicky said, but that was all. He got them most of the way back to Sterling in silence, but Chris kicked him back out of the driver's seat about an hour out of town, knowing his hands would be blocks of ice like Chris's had been. Nick didn't object any more than Chris had, and hunched in the passenger seat with his hands stuffed in his armpits as Chris drove them home.

"Can you let me out here," he said in a low voice, as they hit the edge of the property. "I need to walk for a while. Get out of my head."

Chris crooked a grin at his brother. "Just keep that angel out of your head, man."

"Yeah." Nick slid from the truck and tucked the plastic

window back into place. "I'll be home in a while."

"Arright. Call if you want me to come pick you up."

"Only if you find a car with windows," Nick closed the door carefully and trudged ahead of the truck. Chris passed him a couple seconds later, and rumbled up to the trailer twenty minutes after that. He was half frozen. Nicky would be better off having walked. At least it'd get his blood going.

A thousand degree shower and twelve hours of sleep would get Chris's going. He staggered into the house, feeling thick and clumsy, and a blade of fire pinned him to the wall.

———

There had been nothing *wrong* around the trailer. Between bouts of pain, in moments of coherency, Chris kept coming back to that. He couldn't have known. There were no footprints outside, no windows broken, no lock jimmied. The door had been closed, the lights off, no new tracks anywhere to clue him in. Just his own stupid thick self walking into home territory like it was safe.

His dad would have been disgusted with him, but no matter how many ways Chris went over it, he couldn't think what he might have done different. Not unless he treated his own home like it was enemy turf.

Obviously, he should have.

Saboac kept letting him off the wall. Letting him get to a weapon, even, and then slamming a wing or a knife or a taloned hand toward Chris, and throwing him up against a wall again. There were burn scars on the walls now, and holes, and some of those on Chris, too. He wasn't sure about his left shoulder, anymore. Some of the muscles there were cut. Cauterized, so he wasn't bleeding out, but he couldn't lift the arm very well, and the pain ran through him in waves that had made him puke twice already.

He gotten in one good counterblow when the fucking

angel shook him by an ankle and laughed. He palmed a vial of holy water from inside his coat and rolled, when Saboac dropped him. *Stop, drop, and roll.* Maybe if he could get Saboac to do that, the fire would go out and he'd have a fighting chance. Anyway, he rolled to his feet and smashed the vial into the reporbate's chest.

The fire *did* go out, just briefly, and just where the holy water splashed. Black ice formed in its wake, spilling in dots across the thing's burning wings, and Saboac screamed.

That was a win, Chris thought. He hadn't screamed yet himself, he didn't think. But he'd made the angel scream. He'd take it.

There was a broken window after that, and Chris was lying in the glass and the snow and the blood, all of which, he was pretty sure, was his own. The sky above him was grey with cloud cover, and an ashy pink, like his blood on the snow, at the horizon.

If he could get enough holy water, he could probably fry the reporbate angel. 'Course, now that Saboac knew Chris knew that would work, getting that much holy water was going to be hard.

Like getting that much holy water was gonna be easy anyway. Right now getting *up* was gonna be hard. Chris forced himself up to sitting, feeling glass crunch beneath him. His left arm was working even worse than before, and he couldn't think about the concussive landing on his spine. It was lucky he hadn't cracked his head open on a stone.

He had to get out of there. Into town, where he could fill a gas tank or a giant squirt gun with holy water. Although it wasn't like Saboac would be sitting around waiting for him to come back and kill him.

He had to get out of there, and get Nicky off the property. That was more important, way more important, than anything else. Chris shoved to his feet, stood there a heartbeat waiting to see if he was gonna fall down again, and managed to turn toward the truck before what felt like a cannonball hit him between the shoulders.

At least this time his arm cushioned his head as he smashed to the ground.

Shards of pain shot through him, burning points that felt more vindictive than before. Like, having unexpectedly hurt the reporbate angel, Saboac now wanted to make sure Chris suffered for his…audacity. That's the word Nicky would use. Chris would just say for his balls.

For some reason that made him laugh. A harsh, croaking laugh, like he'd swallowed some of Saboac's fire along the way, but a laugh none-the-less, and he thought if he could laugh, then maybe he could get up. Tried the left arm. Didn't work. Tried the right one. Didn't want to work, but after a couple seconds, it did. Chris pushed up, first into a ball, then, with effort, backward onto his heels, even if his chin dropped to his chest, and his chest heaved with the effort.

His shirt was wet. Shirt and coat both, now that he noticed, what with staring down at himself and all. Pin pricks of pain amidst the wet, like ice had poked through his layers to scrape at him.

Except no. The thought came slowly, thickly, but hey, it came, and Chris felt that was pretty good.

It wasn't melted snow soaking his coat, or ice pricking his chest. It was broken vials of holy water, the ones from his coat lining. Those things were tough, but not meant to take a hundred and ninety pounds of handsome man landing full-force on them. So Chris was dripping with holy water now.

And holy water hurt the reporbate angel.

He laughed again, somehow. Climbed to his feet, aware that fiery wings were pummeling him, that claws and blows were landing, and—on some level—that the angel was getting mad. Not just 'puny human hurt me' mad, but 'why won't this motherfucker stay down' mad.

"Because fuck you, that's why." Chris spun—wobbled, but

god damn it, he got to tell this story, so he spun around like a fucking superhero—and lurched toward Saboac. Not trying to hit the angel. Not trying to dodge its blows. Just ran at the fucking thing, and hugged it.

It didn't even try to block him. Which made sense: Chris wouldn't know what to do with an enemy that ran at him with its arms open and no visible weaponry, either. So he collided solidly with the skinny bastard, and wrapped his arms around it with all the strength he had left. That wasn't much, to be fair, and his left arm didn't do much wrapping, but the important part was that he pressed his holy-water-soaked chest against the monster, and for a second, the monster was so surprised it let him.

Then Saboac began to scream. Bone deep banshee screams, so loud Chris's ears rang and popped and pain pierced through his skull. If he hadn't been holding on to the reporbate angel, he would have fallen, but since he was, he just held on harder, and it screamed louder. It felt like the earth broke apart beneath that scream, like the trailer would blow up, like vibrations would melt Chris's eyes and teeth and brain and guts, not necessarily in that order. He couldn't even tell if he actually heard it anymore, or if he just felt it, but it felt awful enough that if he didn't hear it that was okay, really, he was going to die of a melted brain in a minute anyway so it didn't matter very much.

What did matter was that pock holes of horribleness were opening up in Saboac's chest, that black ice chewed its way through the fallen angel, that maybe, *maybe*, if Chris could just keep not dying for long enough, he might at least take the feathered fiery monstrosity out with him, so Nicky would be safe. That, by Chris's standards, would be as good as it got.

Just before he realized that unconsciousness was only a breath or two away, he discovered he could still hear, after all, because he heard Nicky yell, "Get the fuck off my brother!" and then the space between Saboac and Chris exploded.

# CHAPTER 11

THE EXPLOSION THREW CHRIS...AWAY. BACKWARD, PROBABLY. He couldn't tell anymore. He hit something hard with his spine, anyway, and his head cracked against the hard thing and he slid to the frozen ground and sat there stupidly as Nicky stormed up the driveway toward Saboac.

Nicky looked weirdly big. Bigger than usual. Too big, like something dark and dangerous rode him. His eyes seemed bright, even in the darkness, and his hands were clawed. For a blurry, uncertain moment Chris thought that might not be metaphorical. Saboac staggered in a half-circle, turning away from Chris toward Nicky, and Chris swore he saw a daggered smile cross the fallen angel's gaunt face.

Something much worse than Chris had happened to Saboac. He could see the damage he'd done, sort of. Everything was dark, which, well, the sun had gone down, and reddish, which was neither good nor normal. He didn't want to feel his face to find out *why* his vision was red. Either way, Saboac's chest was marked with the black ice where Chris had squeezed holy water onto it, but Nick had done something...*else* to the monster.

The pressure that had separated Chris from Saboac had left wounds in the fallen angel's chest, like Nick had grabbed it with those too-clawed-looking hands and sank the talons in, leaving long rendered tears through its torso. Fire leaked through the holes, although where the fire touched the holy water, it froze, which seemed to be hurting the creature. Chris, on a cough, said, "Go me," and wondered why the cough tasted like blood.

Saboac hunched inward, like it could protect its tenderized guts as it lurched toward Nicky. It had lost all its smoothness, all the speed that had made it so hard to fight, and even the battering strength of its wings. Chris wanted to get up, to attack the thing from behind to give Nick a better chance at killing it from the front, but nothing would respond anymore, not his right arm, not his legs, nothing. It all hurt, so he probably hadn't broken his neck, but nothing would move, either.

Nick's voice cut across the darkness. "Chris? You okay?"

He tried to say *yeah, of course*, and only coughed again, more weakly this time, instead. Nick's face went blank and Saboac gave a thundering hiss that had none of the power of its earlier scream. It leaped at him, suddenly fluid again, and Nicky simply…stopped it.

Stopped it like before, with a straight arm to catch its throat, except he never touched the thing at all. Saboac's pounce ended ten feet away, the fallen angel dangling in midair, with Nicky's clawed hand lifted skyward as if he held something in it.

Punctures appeared in Saboac's throat, cutting off the rest of the noises it made, and Nicky, his voice low and angry and dangerous, said, "You should have left my brother alone."

He turned his hand in the air, but Saboac didn't turn with it. Just the rips in its throat changed position, worsening, as Nicky lifted his other hand to hold it back-to-back with the first. Then, with a single violent motion, he ripped them apart.

Saboac tore to shreds with the motion, pieces of black-ice-fire scattering across the yard, flames guttering and flickering in the wind as they landed and searched for something to catch hold of. Nicky, teeth bared, turned to each of those shattered pieces and ground them to dust with nothing but his anger, extinguishing the fallen angel's remains. Grendel power washed off him in waves, hammering at Chris, who thought he would disintegrate if Nick turned that anger on him.

Of course he would. A fucking *angel* had disintegrated. Chris would probably just disappear like he'd never existed.

He felt like maybe he was gonna do that anyway, except Nicky was not in a good place and Chris couldn't just go and die on him when he was like this. Especially when it was his own damn fault Nicky was *in* such a bad place. If he hadn't fucked up, if he'd paid attention so Saboac couldn't blindside him, if Nicky wasn't so stupidly heroic that he came to help Chris *anyway*....

He would've been fine. Nicky would've been fine, if Chris had just died. If he'd gotten there too late to use his grendel power to fight a fallen angel, it would have been *fine*. He'd have been sad, but he would have gotten over it, and now, now everything was fucked up. Chris croaked, "Nick," and wasn't really sure if he'd made a sound, but after a few heartbeats—he counted every one—his brother turned his head toward him.

Nicky's eyes were *definitely* bright with power, glowing with it, like it burned him up from within. Chris wheezed his brother's name again, and Nick took a few dangerous steps toward him. The grendel magic he carried bore down on Chris, like he would be ground to bits like Saboac had. He shook his head, or tried, and Nick pulled up abruptly, the fire fading from his eyes.

The magic stopped, too, and Chris was able to take one easier breath. One: then he knew how badly hurt he was, and the next breath was a hell of a lot harder. He thought he made a sound, probably a whimper, and Nick shook himself like he'd just woken up. "Oh, shit, Chris. Chris!"

Nick ran to his side, and Chris had maybe three seconds to be real glad his baby brother had grown up so strong, but then the agony of being picked up swept over him and he faded into red-edged unconsciousness.

———

The house was filled with blood and fire.

Nothing really burned: it smoldered, thickening the air with smoke, but Saboac's flames apparently weren't as good at setting a house on fire as a little gas left in the pipes was. Lucky for Chris. Lucky for Nick, who would have been way too late if Saboac had just blown shit up.

There was a darkness in his mind, a stain that he flinched away from whenever he thought of Saboac's name. He couldn't stop thinking it, though, like the reporbate angel's presence was an empty tooth socket that he had to keep worrying at.

Maybe, just maybe, it was easier and safer to think about the mark Saboac had left on him, instead of the ones he'd left on Chris.

It seemed like not much more than stubbornness was keeping Chris alive. He was full of holes, mostly shallow, like Saboac had been toying with him, but a few terrifyingly deep ones, and more burn marks than Nicky could count. The layers of leather and wool flannel had gone a long way toward protecting him from the burns, but nowhere near far enough.

And there was all this power bubbling in Nick's chest, in his mind, in his hands, in his whole body, and none of it wanted to do anything about his brother bleeding out in his arms. He got clean bandages—Dad always kept a lot of those around the house, with good reason—and rubbing alcohol to wash the wounds with, and put as much pressure on them as he could, but all the goddamn power running through him wasn't doing him any fucking good at all, not now, not with Chris...like this. He couldn't put words to what *like this* meant, not without shutting down. He piled blankets on his brother and fumbled for his phone, actually putting a call through to Cheyenne, instead of just a text.

She picked up with, "This better be an epic fuckup, Nicky, like what the hell are you doing calling, you're scaring the shit out of me."

Nick said, "Chris is dying," and then it was all too real.

———

It took three hours for Cheyenne to get there. Not her fault: she was at home, over in Steamboat Springs, and that was a four and a half hour drive on dry roads. *Keep him alive,* that's all she'd said. *Keep him warm, keep pressure on the wounds, keep him alive. Talk to him. Keep him alive.* She didn't tell him to call the local paramedics, didn't tell him to bring Chris to a hospital, didn't tell him to do anything that would end up having to explain why the house was half on fire and how Chris had ended up full of puncture wounds. *Just keep him alive.* That's all she'd told him to do.

So he did. Three hours and some change, huddled beside Chris on a bed to keep him warm, mumbling stories about college and not even caring, right then, that most of them involved Stephanie, whom he'd scared off with grendel power. Just anything to keep Chris listening and alive.

Chris roused a couple of times, half conscious, then out again, and Nick's heart went colder and faster with fear every time he fell silent again. Chris's pulse was getting worse. Nick didn't know how to fix it. Being pre-med seemed pretty fucking useless right now. Chemistry and biological principles didn't help him put his brother's guts back together. He wasn't supposed to spend an internship following a doctor around to be sure this was what he wanted to do until this summer, although right now the *only* thing Nick wanted to do was be able to help people heal—

He was pretty sure he was saying all of this aloud. Less sure it was helpful, but Cheyenne had said to talk to Chris, so Nick was talking and talking and couldn't shut up.

Then the bedroom door banged open and Cheyenne was there, her face set behind a medical mask and her gaze already focused on Chris. The light seemed to change with her presence, growing warmer, safer. She had her paramedic bag with her, and handed Nick a saline drip like she expected him to know what to do with it. Get it up high, that's all that mattered. Higher than Chris's arm. He got a hanger and hooked it over a dresser knob. Heard Shy snapping latex gloves on, and turned back to see her bent over Chris's wounds, examining them. Her skin looked exceptionally dark compared to Chris's pallor. She was carved of midnight, and he was made of shallow blue-lit water.

"He's got so many burns." Shy breathed the words, probably not meaning for Nick to hear. "Get the burn ointment, you did a good job packing these wounds, he'll probably need blood, do you know his blood type—"

"We're both O positive. I can—" Nick didn't finish, just sat down and put an arm out.

Shy swore. "I'm going to need your hands right now. I'll stick you when Jake gets here."

Guilt lanced through Nick. "I didn't call him. I should have."

"Jake's not a paramedic," Cheyenne said flatly. "You called me, the person who could save Chris's life. And I called Jake. He was out east on some job, so he couldn't have gotten here before me anyway. He's on the way now. Should be here soon. Wash your hands and put a pair of gloves on, then get back out here and help me."

By the time he came back with the gloves and a medical mask in place, she had the saline drip in Chris's arm, and the light in the room was definitely warmer, like her just being there helped. "You did a good job," she said again, more quietly this time. "Most of these are shallow and at most need a stitch or two. There are two that are a problem, though, and you're going to have to help me. Can you do that without melting down?"

"Yeah. Just tell me what you need."

The next minutes passed in a blur as Shy sewed wounds with surgical precision. The light kept changing, wavering, turning gold and brightening, then fading back to normal. Nick shook his head, trying to steady it, and Cheyenne gave him a filthy look that told him to hold still. Even her eyes seemed bright with the gold light, like it was leaking around her irises. Nick lifted his head, looking blearily for light's source, then bent over Chris again, doing what he was told. Cheyenne turned her intense focus back on Chris, and the brightness glimmered again, like it was showing them where work needed to be done. "Okay," Shy finally breathed, and sat back. "Okay. If we can get blood into him, I think he'll be all right. Go wash up and then I'll stick you."

"Thank you." Nick sounded rough, close to tears. Cheyenne gave him a hard smile from behind her mask.

"Don't thank me yet. Later I'm going to want to know what the fuck happened here. Jake!" The last word came on a burst of relief as Jake came in, worry making him almost as pale as Chris. "Jake, what's your blood type?"

"A positive. Chris is O positive."

"Right. You wash," Shy said to Nick again, and he went to the bathroom, hearing Shy's low quiet voice updating Jake on what she knew.

Jake was lifting a couple of Chris's bandages, examining the lesser wounds, when Nick came out again. There was new pink skin there under one of them, the cut more a memory than an actual hurt. Nick stared at that without fully under-standing it, sat where Shy told him to, and put an arm out so she could give his blood to his brother. Somewhere in there, Jake got him orange juice and he drank it slowly, waiting for it to warm in his mouth before he swallowed it. Chris looked better, but not good. Nick's head hurt. He couldn't remember when that had started. Had an awful feeling it had been during the fight with Saboac. It wasn't safe to think about Saboac. Just safer than thinking about Chris, dying.

"He's going to be okay," Cheyenne finally said. She'd never really stopped working on him, treating burns, checking his breathing and his heart rate, unhooking Nick from the transfusion with a muttered promise that it was enough. The bedroom's light still seemed warmer than it had been before she arrived, but it was dimmer now. "He's warm, he's topped up with new blood, the worst of his injuries are stitched or bandaged. Let's take five outside."

"I'd like to stay," Jake said, and Shy shrugged.

"You do you, buddy. Nick, out."

He got up obediently and left the bedroom. The rest of the house was noticeably colder, although nothing was on fire anymore. Maybe Jake had taken care of that. Maybe Saboac's death had. Nick didn't know. Shy threw herself heavily into an armchair and pointed at another. "Sit."

Nick sat, and all at once the glimmer of warmth, the gold hint to the light, went out, as did any gentleness in Cheyenne's voice. Not that 'gentle' usually played in the same arena Shy did. "Talk."

"I've got powers," Nick said flatly. "Freak powers. And—"

Shy held up one finger, stardust paint on the nail. "Powers since when."

"I don't know, Friday? Saturday morning? I don't even know what day it is."

"It's Monday. Monday evening. Okay, so this is a new thing, which means you two assholes aren't keeping secrets. Fine. Go on."

"We went looking for the thing that killed Dad and we

met a…" Nick shrugged. It sounded stupid, but the truth didn't care what it sounded like. "A fallen angel. A desanctified angel. And it came after us again today and I wasn't here to protect Chris."

"You two fuckers and your protection thing. So it's what happened to the house? To Chris? What happened to it?"

"I killed it," Nick said flatly. "I used my power and killed it and then I called you to help Chris."

Shy stared at him for what felt like a long time, then nodded. "Okay."

"Okay? That's it? Just 'okay?' I'm a fucking freak and it's okay? Chris almost died and it's okay?" Anger built behind Nick's eyes, filling his head and throat and spilling toward his chest.

"Don't be a fucking moron, Nick. You know what I mean. What else am I supposed to say? Are you okay?"

"No. I don't know. I'm not hurt."

"Close enough. You did good in there," she added, voice softening. "You're going to make a hell of a doctor, Nicky."

"Freaks don't heal people. They hurt them."

"Guess you're going to have to change that, then." They stood, glaring around the house. "Come on, let's get this place sealed up so you two idiots don't freeze to death tonight."

Nick stood, glancing hesitantly at Chris's bedroom. "Can I check on him first?"

"This mess isn't going anywhere."

Jake looked up as Nick came into the room, then stood. "He's woken up and gone back to sleep a couple times already. Wait for a minute and he'll probably come around."

"Thanks, man." Nick grunted as Jake gave him a quick, hard hug, then left the room so Nick could sit at Chris's bedside.

Chris looked so much better and utterly terrible all at once. Nick could see the blue veins in his eyelids, and even the green of his eyes looked drained when he opened them. "Ayyyyyy, Nicky. You okay?"

"Me?" Nick's voice cracked. "I'm fucking peachy, thanks. What the hell were you doing, fighting that thing alone?"

Chris's eyes drifted shut again on a whispered chuckle. "Wasn't my idea, bro. Got blindsided. Dad'd've hit me alongside the head for that."

"Yeah, well, Dad was an asshole."

A twitch of Chris's eyebrows agreed before his breathing steadied out into sleep again. Nick drifted off for a minute, too, or maybe longer: when he opened his eyes again, Chris was pulling at bandages, trying to remove them. Nick leaned forward to catch his wrist. "Cut it out, you need those, you're all fucked up, man."

Chris rolled a shoulder, showing Nick the sticky spot where he'd taken a bandage off already. Tender-looking skin shone pinkly, new scars forming, but Nick knew for a fact that had been a two-inch-long cut a few hours earlier. "Where's the bandage for that?"

"I dunno, I threw it…" Chris made a vague motion and Nick stood to find the piece of gauze, which was streaked with old-looking blood, but not a lot of it. Way less than there'd been when Shy had removed the bandage Nick had put on, cleaned the wound, and rebandaged it.

By the time he looked back, Chris was out again. Nick took the bandage into the living room and said, "What the fuck?" to Shy, then, belatedly, "Thanks," as he realized most of the holes and fire damage had been roughly patched over.

"What the fuck, what?" She caught the bandage when he threw it at her, then shrugged. "What's this?"

"Chris just took it off his shoulder where that two-inch cut was."

"Looks more like an old period pad, with the blood that color." Shy went back into the bedroom and emerged again a couple minutes later, confusion written across her features. "What'd you do?"

"What'd *I* do? I didn't do anything. You're the one who came in all glowy and shit."

"All gl—what?"

"You were glowing," Nick repeated. "Or the light changed when you came in, I don't know. That's why I kept shaking my head, trying to clear it."

"I don't know what you're talking about, Nick." Cheyenne dropped into an armchair again, visibly tired. "You just said you had freak powers. You did something."

"I didn't." Cold certainty ran through the words. "I tried. I couldn't. I can tear shit apart, Shy, I can't make it better. You're the paramedic."

"I'm a paramedic," she echoed, stretching the syllables out to emphasize them. "I can't make cuts and burns vanish in a couple hours. Wouldn't that be fucking great! You said you got freak powers on Saturday. Maybe Chris did too."

Nick's heart clenched and he sat like his knees had been taken out. Missed the edge of the sofa, smashed all the way to the floor, cracking his tailbone when he hit. The next heart-beat felt too big, like it had to expand too far in order to make up for the tight squeeze it had contracted to. His head hit his knees and he mumbled, "Didn't think of that," around a sick feeling of relief. Maybe Chris hadn't been in so much danger after all. Still too much, but not as much. Maybe Nick hadn't almost let him get killed just 'cause he wanted to walk off his own drama.

"We can test that," Jake said from where he sat patching up another hole in the wall, then brushed off the scathing look Shy gave him. "Not now. When he's better. I don't propose we go stab him again right now."

"I don't propose stabbing him at all!"

"Stabbing who?" Chris's voice, raspier than usual, came from the hallway entrance. "Where's Nicky?"

"Here." Nick stood, moving into Chris's line of view. Chris limped over, grabbed the back of his neck, and examined him from up close, close enough that Nick could see how badly injured his brother still was. He was months past any summer tan anyway, but the new shining scars stood out vividly pink against too-pale skin, and his eyes were sunken with exhaustion. "You shouldn't be out of bed, Chris."

"Me? I'm fine. Who's getting stabbed?"

"*Nobody.*" Shy's voice bounced across the room. "Go lie down. You shouldn't—"

"Be out of bed, yeah, I got that."

"Be able to stand, you idiot. I don't know what it is with you Cassidy brothers, always trying to be the toughest son of a bitch in the room." A beat passed, and Shy muttered, "All right, that's a lie, I knew your dad, obviously I know what it is with you two, but you still need to get over it. Go lie down, Chris."

Despite the fact that Nick was supporting at least half of Chris's weight through that grip he held on his neck, Chris managed to a cocky, self-sure grin at Cheyenne. "Look, I know you finally had me in bed where you wanted me, Shy, but it didn't have to take this much effort. I'm easy for beauty."

"You're a shallow, self-centered prick who couldn't turn my head with a wrench," Shy said mildly, "and you're about to pass out."

Chris went, "Pffhhh!" dismissively and turned his attention back to Nick, the grin fading away. "Nicky—"

"Chris, I think Shy's right, you look really bad—"

Chris got about halfway through another *pffhh* before he went limp. Nick, half expecting it, mostly managed to catch him, although what started as a grab under the arms became a frantic hug around his brother's chest, because it turned out that if you just grabbed an unconscious person under the arms, their arms rose up like noodles and they kept right on falling. "Fuck!"

Cheyenne started giggling like an eleven year old, tears of laughter running down her cheeks. Jake came to the rescue, grunting as he helped take Chris's weight and staggered toward the bedroom. "I thought you were strong these days, Nicky."

"Dead weights aren't as easy to lift as barbells!" They pretty well threw Chris on the bed, there being no less awkward way to get him there. He bounced once and made a pained sound, but didn't come to in any meaningful way. "Shy, is he concussed?"

She came to the doorway, wiping tears away and sounding serious enough, despite the grin. "Probably should be, but no, not as far as I can tell. Guess you two can thank your dad for your thick skulls. Look, I'll stay in town overnight if you need, but I got a late shift tomorrow night and have to head home."

"Maybe stay," Nick said uncertainly. "He's better than he was, but he's still passing out every other minute."

"Yeah, well, I'm not staying on that ugly-ass couch of yours. The living room's freezing."

"Take...take Dad's room." Easier for Shy to sleep there than either Chris or Nick, and maybe if she stayed the night it would make it feel a little less like Dad's room, and more like a place one of them could someday sleep.

"You can stay at mine," Jake offered. "Walls are whole, there, and it's close enough for an emergency."

Cheyenne shot Nick a glance that almost looked apologetic. "Yeah, that's better. Sorry, Nick, I just, uh…"

"Yeah, no, I get it, we can't sleep there either."

"You want me to clear it out?" Jake asked quietly. "I won't throw anything away, but I can take it to mine for a while. Might neutralize the space."

Nick closed his eyes. "Honestly, that would be great. I know I should be able to, but I…can't. Not right now."

Jake knocked his shoulder against Nick's on his way past. "That's why we have friends, man. Come on, Shy, gimme a hand with it."

"What, *now*? What the hell." Cheyenne followed Jake, protesting all the way, and the last argument Nick heard from the other man was, "You don't want Nick sleeping in the cold either, do you?"

He wouldn't put money on Shy caring that much, but appreciated the thought. He sank down on the chair, half listening as their friends thumped and banged around, cleaning out their dad's room. Half listening, half sleeping. Half hearing Saboac's hissing laughter, the crackle of its power and its wings, and trying to shove those things out of his memory.

Somewhere in there, Jake and Cheyenne got quieter, or left, or maybe Nick just fell asleep, because the next thing he knew, weak early morning light seeped through his eyelids as Chris growled, "You should have just let me die."

# CHAPTER 12

"What?" Nick had heard Chris well enough. He just didn't believe what he'd heard. Except he did believe it, because of *course* his asshole older brother would decide —"Why the actual fuck should I have let you die?"

"You had to use that grendel power to save me," Chris said hoarsely. "That can't be good. And maybe all that thing wanted was me. Maybe you could've gone back to Cali after that."

"Yeah, back to college and the girlfriend who's terrified of me now, that'd be great." Nick was on his feet somehow, bubbling over with anger. "You can't really think I'd be happier with you dead."

"It'd get you out of this life. All I'm supposed to do is keep you safe, Nicky—"

"Bullshit! Jesus, that's such bullshit! You—" Nick's hands turned to claws, throttling the air, and he had to back off, trying to find a way through anger to speech. By the time he trusted himself to speak again, Chris was sitting up. Pale and shaking, but sitting up and prodding at the wounds Shy had tended to the night before. "You're alive," Nick said, trying to sound calm. "And that's good, Chris. You've got to learn that you're more than just my guardian angel."

"You gotta learn I never needed to be anything more than that."

Frustration flooded through Nick again, turning his thoughts sharp and dangerous, like they'd cut *him* apart, never mind Chris. "Maybe you didn't, but I'm trying to build a life, Chris. You have to build one too."

"I've *got* a life, Nick!" Chris stood like he was seeing if he could. He could. Just. He knocked away Nick's offer of help, because of course he did, and Nick stood back, eyes closed and mouth pinched while he worked through not feeling childishly rejected. Chris limped to the bedroom door—Nick could hear it in his uneven footsteps—and stopped there like he wanted to be dramatic. Nick bet he just needed to lean against something and rest for a minute.

"I know my life looks like shit to you, but I'm fine with it. And I'd be fine dead, too, Nick. It doesn't matter that much. It doesn't matter if you don't like it. I get to decide what's worth dying for."

Losing his temper wasn't going to help. A fight wasn't going to help. Nick set his teeth together, trying to hold anger back. It fought to get free, feeling like the grendel power, pressing within him, bubbling up, ready to be used. He opened his eyes again, in case that helped. It did, maybe a little, or maybe being able to see Chris made it worse, like his brother was a focal point to explode his frustration toward. "Don't I get to decide what's worth fighting for?"

"Not if it's me!"

"Who the fuck else am I supposed to fight for?" Nick's voice rose and cracked, his control slipping. "Dad's dead, Stephanie's gone, Tyler's a dick, you're all I've got left! Family is all I have left!"

"You left your family!" Chris had to be running on willpower alone, the way he turned on Nick, fury flushing his skin and exhaustion weakening his actions. "You fucking left,

Nick, you don't get to decide you stay and fight for family now!"

"You *told* me to leave!"

"I did more than goddamn tell you, I signed every piece of paperwork you needed signing—" Something happened behind Chris's eyes, a panicked retreat, like he hadn't meant to say that, and Nick caught his breath, trying to parse that before Chris doubled down. "But the point is you *left*, Nick, you left me here with Dad and you went off to have a life and you were supposed to, you should have stayed there, if you had stayed you wouldn't have this grendel problem—"

"What'd you think I was going to do, not come to Dad's funeral? You're the one who told me about it!"

"That's exactly what I thought!"

"Well why the hell did you even tell me about it then?"

"I don't know!" Chris slammed his hand against the door-frame, like the pain could drown out emotion. "But you should have stayed away!"

"Well it's too fucking late for that now isn't it! Christ, Chris, you just—I can't win, can I? I betrayed you by leaving, I betrayed you by coming back, what the actual fuck do you want from me?" Nick slammed past his brother, just enough in control to keep from smashing his shoulder into Chris's.

The sound Chris made indicated he wished Nick *had* bashed into him, and Nick pretty much wished he had too. Maybe it would knock Chris on his stupid ass hard enough to keep him down for a minute, until he started thinking again. "Not that thinking is your strong suit," he snarled, probably not enough under his breath.

Definitely not enough under his breath. "Yeah, we *know* you're the smart one, Nick—"

Nick bellowed, "I'm not goddamn smarter than you, Chris, I'm more studious, there's a fucking difference—"

"Oh yeah, more fucking *studious*, let's split those hairs, you roll out that dictionary vocabulary you've got and make me look like an assh——"

"Believe me, you're doing that all on your own!" Nick stomped through the living room like he could find something to wreck, barely fighting a boiling darkness inside him that wanted to do nothing else. Except that would be infantile and he was a goddamn adult and besides Chris was shouting and stomping out behind him and he sure as hell wasn't going to give his jackass older brother the satisfaction of watching him melt down. He raised his voice, deliberately drowning Chris's lecture out. "I'm sorry, I don't even know what you said, I can't hear it over the sanctimonious prickitude!"

"Oh, just fuck off, Jesus, if you came back to be a dick I'll be glad when you're gone——"

Guilt and anger spiraled in Nick's chest, flaring toward destruction. Self-destruction, maybe. Anything was better than screaming, though he couldn't stop himself from that, either. "You've always been glad when I'm gone! I know how much fun it was for you, watching out for your nerdy little brother when we were kids——"

Chris yelled again and Nick still couldn't hear it past the tide of anger in his mind, the blind rising rage that felt like Saboac cackling somewhere at the bottom of his soul. "Shut up shut up just *shut up*!"

"Like I started this bullshi——"

"Shut up!" Nick swung wildly, like he'd shove his brother away. Power arced, the same as it had in the remote cabin, except no, it was worse, that had only erupted, this was directed, this——

——this caught Chris in the chest, threw him backward, slammed him into the wall. The whole trailer shuddered with the impact and he fell, not even making a sound. Other things made sound: the tv, wobbling and then crashing to the floor; a couple pictures thumping against the walls without quite dislodging; the floor itself, creaking.

The heat in Nicky's chest turned to ice, lining his insides, quenching the anger and the power all at once. If he had heard Saboac before, and maybe he hadn't really, the fallen angel's voice was gone now. Empty fear filled him, and he didn't dare look toward Chris and couldn't not, all at the same time.

Through a fog of frigid terror, he could see Chris's chest rising and falling. That was something. Not enough. He moved mechanically, coldly, going to Chris's side. Kneeling beside him. Trying to see if anything was broken, if anything was more hurt than Chris had been before. As if he hadn't been hurt enough. Nick didn't know his own voice as he whispered, "I'm sorry."

Maybe really didn't know it, not at all. Maybe he'd become someone else. Maybe Saboac was inside him, talking through his lips.

It might be worse, if he'd done this himself. Was worse. If it was Saboac, if the grendel power had a mind of its own, then Nick could blame it. But he couldn't, not really. He'd done it. He'd blown up the cabin and he'd scared Stephanie off and he'd killed Saboac and now he'd maybe killed his own big brother, although Chris groaned and shifted enough to suggest he was alive and probably going to stay that way.

"Come on," Nick whispered. "Can you get up? If I help you? Come on. Let me help you. I'm sorry. I'm sorry, Chris. I didn't mean to. I'm sorry." Cautiously, carefully, he got Chris to sitting, and nothing seemed too broken or out of place. Getting to their feet was harder, but Nick pushed them up using the wall and after a minute could limp his brother to the bedroom, still whispering, "I'm sorry."

"S'okay." The rough reassurance sounded like Chris still hadn't drawn a full breath. "'S'an accident. S'okay."

"It's not okay, I *hurt* you, you thought I couldn't—"

"Nicky." Somehow Chris pulled himself together, pulled himself upright enough to clasp the back of Nick's neck and draw his forehead to Chris's own. "It's okay. It was an accident. You would never hurt me on purpose. You don't have a handle on this power yet. It's okay. I'm fine."

He lost strength at the end of that, buckling, then visibly braced himself, obviously not willing to fall, regardless of the effort it took. Nick's heart wrenched, leaving him barely able to breathe; his whisper came in cracks and falls. "Let's get you back to bed."

The fact that Chris didn't argue, that he went willingly, said how much he hurt, even if he'd never admit it out loud. He winced when Nick lowered him onto the bed, and brushed it off with an almost-convincing grin, if you didn't know him well enough to see its glittering hard edges. "Go get some sleep, Nicky. I'll be fine."

That really meant *let me lick my wounds in peace*, and Nick, guilty, slunk away to let him do that.

———

It hadn't been Nicky.

Chris kept telling himself that, like he might believe it if he said to the backs of his eyelids often enough. It hadn't been Nicky that had thrown him across the room. It had been the grendel power, power Nick couldn't control yet. It had been anger. Anger as triggering as the fear Nick had felt when they'd gone after Emerson. They shouldn't have been fighting. Chris should have known better, should have known to keep a lid on it while his little brother figured this new power out.

He hurt everywhere. He'd hurt everywhere *before* Nick had thrown him into a wall. He half remembered Shy being there. Mostly the warmth of her hands and her steady low swearing, which Chris found more reassuring than actual reassurances. Swearing meant she wasn't lying, that she knew just as much as Chris himself did that he was all fucked up. He'd been unconscious a lot of the time, and just as glad about that. It would've been better if Nicky'd left him for dead, though.

Yeah, that hadn't been a useful road to go down, even if he'd been right. Chris whispered a reassuring, "Fuck," to himself, and after that, slept.

It was dark when he woke up, which maybe wasn't saying much in northern Colorado in March, but it had been daylight when he fell asleep, so he'd probably fucked up his entire schedule. On the other hand, sitting up hurt literally every single part of his body, even his hair, so honestly if he could piss and go back to sleep, maybe after half a bottle of Jack, that would probably be fine and maybe tomorrow he'd be back on schedule. But there was noise in the living room, so after he went to the bathroom, Chris lurched down the hall.

Nicky's shoulders were caved with guilt as he put the tv back up on the wall. Chris grunted, "Lemme help with that," and staggered over. He wasn't much help, but Nick nodded and accepted the offer, which was all that really mattered. After more effort than it was worth, they got it up again. Nick sat on the floor beneath it and Chris, trying to move like he didn't hurt, went into the kitchen to see if he could find that bottle of Jack.

There wasn't any, but there was a bottle of bourbon. He muttered, "Close enough," and poured at least two shots into a cup before saying, "You okay?" aloud.

"No." Nicky sounded like a kid. Chris bared his teeth, swallowed the bourbon, poured a second glass, and waited until Nick said, "Are you?" in a small voice before gathering himself to back to the living room.

"I'll live." He handed Nick the glass and remembered afterward, again, that his brother wasn't even actually legal to drink yet. "Jesus, they should give you a pass for body weight or height or something."

See, if Nick didn't follow, it would be easier, or something, but his little brother's broad shoulders shook with a single short laugh. "I don't get carded a lot, yeah."

"You still got a baby face, though." Chris drank straight from the bottle and Nick drained the glass without even wincing.

"So does Leonardo DiCaprio and he's ancient."

"Yeah, but he'd date you."

Nick coughed like he'd just drunk the whiskey, then really laughed. Enough to look up at Chris with a grin still on his face. "Dude, I'm young enough but I don't think I'm his type."

"No accounting for taste." Chris offered a hand up and Nick took it, leaning in a little as he stood, almost like a hug. Enough that everything was okay again, anyway, even if Chris still couldn't identify a single part of himself that didn't hurt. "Where'd everybody go?"

"Back to Jake's place. Shy had to drive home this morning for her shift tonight. They cleared out Dad's room so I could sleep in it."

"That was decent of them." Chris took another swallow of the bourbon, weighed the likelihood that he'd pass out if he sat down, and did it anyway. The couch sucked him toward unconsciousness immediately and he sat forward, trying to stay awake. "What time is it?"

"About eight."

"At night?" Chris's voice cracked and Nick twisted to look back at him.

"Yeah, at night, Chris. You got the hell beat out of you." Guilt seared Nicky's face.

Chris ground his teeth together. "It wasn't your fault, Nicky."

"Some of it was."

He wasn't doing this again. He couldn't. *They* couldn't. Chris clenched his eyes together, too, trying to figure out a way past it, then did his best to just bypass it entirely. "I could go back to sleep, too."

He could just about hear Nick's brain skipping around, trying to find the track if they were gonna just move right past the fight. After a couple seconds, awkwardly, he said, "You probably should. I ordered pizza, though. It's in the fridge."

Previously unnoticed hunger roared through Chris's belly and he stood up. Too fast, as it turned out. Probably too fast even if he hadn't taken about five shots in as many minutes, but definitely too fast with that and every part of him including his toenails hurting. The couch swam up and caught him again as the room went blurry.

He was pretty sure that more than a few seconds had passed when he opened his eyes again, but he couldn't tell it by his own sense of time. But the pizza box was on the couch next to him and Nick was sitting on the floor beside him like a very large worried dog. Chris mumbled, "Aw, good boy," and ruffled his brother's hair.

Nick knocked his hand away with enough force to suggest he was relieved, not mad. "Eat and go back to bed, man. You're a mess."

"Yeah." Chris couldn't even manage an argument about who was supposed to take care of who, this time. He just ate the pizza, and meant to go to bed, but he woke up on the couch with a blanket over him when the sun crawled far enough past the horizon to get in his eyes. Winter cold leaked in around the patched holes in the wall until his breath hung on the air. After a minute he pulled the blanket over his head like the world would go away if he hid from it.

After another minute he got up, or at least sat up, because that wasn't gonna work anyway. Sitting up reminded him that everything hurt, although not half as bad as when he'd passed out the night before. A shiver ran down his spine, cold air creeping from the walls like it could coil around him. He got up, pulling the blanket over his shoulders against the chill, and padded down the hall to find Nick.

Both the bedroom doors were open, and their dad's room

had been mostly cleared out, like Nick had said. Even the blanket was different, like Jake and Shy had gone to the trouble of changing the sheets. Chris went for his pocket like he'd find his phone in it, so he could send a text and say thanks, but god knew where the phone actually was, he sure didn't.

Nick wasn't in their dad's room, though. He was in Chris's room, looking too big for the bed, and coiled up like it would help him fit better. The blankets were a wreck, worse than Chris ever woke up to, and one hand was a fist in the pillow by his face. Nick had always slept like that, thrashing around and finally curling into a ball. Chris used to be able to tell how bad a day it'd been by how small Nick made himself.

Maybe not that much had changed, after all. He went in, threw his own blanket over Nick, and checked back again when he got to the door on the way out.

The hand knotted in the pillow had already relaxed some, and a line between Nick's eyebrows was gone. Chris closed the door quietly and dragged his own sorry ass off to the shower. At least the hot water didn't rely on the house being warm to work, and it beat some of the ache out of his body.

Nick was up by the time Chris got breakfast on the table, and out of the shower before Chris looked at what he'd cooked, thought about how much he'd watched his brother eat, and gone back to cook more. Nick came to the table as he got the last of it on, ate about three-quarters of what Chris had laid out, and finally said, "Thanks," in a low voice.

That was a better greeting than Chris got most days. "Had enough?"

A brief smile ran across Nick's face. "Thought I'd better leave you some."

"Here and I thought I was gonna hafta fight for the scraps."

Nick's smile strengthened and Chris grinned. "I'm fine. I don't eat as much as you do."

"'Cause you're little."

Chris barked a startled laugh, and Nicky looked pleased with himself before shivering. "It's colder than a witch's tit in here."

"Hey. I know at least two witches personally and their tits are nice and warm." Chris grinned as Nick threw a napkin at him, although the expression faded into a scowl as he glanced around the room. "You're not wrong, though. They did a decent job patching it up for the middle of the night, but it's gonna take some actual work."

"Got anything else planned for the day?"

Chris's eyebrows rose. "Guess not." He threw the napkin back at Nick and got up to clear the table.

"I got it. You cooked." Nick waved him off, collecting dishes and sliding them into the sink. Chris stared at him a minute, then mumbled, "Okay, I guess I'll go see what's in the shed."

"Get the toolbox from the Dodge, too."

"Yeah." He went out and dug around, hoping for some decent building materials lying around. Nothing that was gonna work well in the long term, for sure, but plywood and some filler would keep the heat in better than plastic sheeting or the one place Shy had stuffed a pillow into a hole, anyway. It took a wheelbarrow and a couple trips back and forth to get enough into the house to make a difference, and by that time Nick had finished the dishes and gone to turn some music on.

He came back into the kitchen with a stack of records and a curious expression. "When'd we start doing vinyl again?"

Chris shrugged, piling timber inside the front door. "Found some of Dad's old stuff a while ago. Thought I'd go retro."

"Nerd." Nick left again, grinning, and Muddy Waters rolled through the trailer a minute later.

"Now who's a nerd?" Chris yelled, and Nick's voice drifted back toward him.

"The hoochie-coochie man! Ma-nah-nah-nah-nah!" The latter was obviously supposed to sound like a harmonica doing a blues riff, and Chris guessed if he could tell what it was supposed to be, it was probably close enough.

He muttered, "Dork," anyway, before yelling a couple lyrics back.

"You know the lyrics, dude, so if I'm a dork you're an uber-dork or something. Gimme a hammer, I'll get this mess under the window fixed."

"Why do you think I'm carrying more than one hammer?"

"Because you're wearing a tool belt and I can see one, you tool."

Chris grinned and handed the spare hammer over. "Don't smash your thumb."

"Dude, I'm not seven." Nick threatened Chris's foot with the hammer instead, then got to work, singing off-key more often than not, and going inside to flip or change records when one of them noticed the music had stopped. Most of the day got eaten by repairs, although Chris went in to make something hot for lunch as an excuse to thaw his hands. Nick came in with red cheeks and a redder nose and flipped his soup spoon across the table because his fingers were thick from working outside.

"What was that about not being seven?" Chris threw a dish towel at him. Nick cleaned up and did the dishes again, which Chris thought he could get used to. By dinnertime the trailer was patched up enough to do until everything thawed and they—*he*, Chris reminded himself grimly—could do a better job.

Nick's phone rang during dinner and a shard of hope so sharp it hurt to see cut across his face before he said, "Oh. It's Shy," and put it on speaker. "Hey, Shy."

"Try not to sound so happy to hear me," she replied sharply. "How's our patient?"

"Your patient is fine," Chris said. "Been finishing patching up the house. Thanks for saving my fine, fine ass."

"You were supposed to keep him in bed!" Cheyenne's accusation was clearly meant for Nick, who made a face at the phone.

"You wanted him kept in bed, you should have stayed and kept him there. I'm just his brother."

"You outweigh me by…" Shy fell silent, obviously trying to decide how much Nick weighed, and eventually said, "Probably forty pounds, anyway."

"Dude," Chris said. "He outweighs *me* by forty pounds."

"How much do you think I weigh, Chris?"

Nick's eyes bugged and he shook his head rapidly. Chris bugged his eyes back and shook his head too. "I'm not touching that with a ten foot pole, Shy."

"Well, his brains weren't knocked entirely loose," Cheyenne conceded, a grin audible in her voice. "Maybe fifty pounds, then. You sure you're okay, Chris?"

"Yeah. Thanks. And thanks for checking in."

"Yeah, no problem. Look, I gotta go, I'm starting my shift, but Jake's supposed to check in on you before he heads south again. Don't be all macho and stupid, okay?"

"Never," Chris said insincerely.

Shy swore as she hung up, and Nick said, "How much do you think *I* weigh? I don't outweigh you by forty pounds!"

"I dunno, like two twenty?" Chris curled his lip. "Oh. Okay. That's only like thirty pounds more than me. Should I call her back and say maybe you do outweigh her by only forty pounds?"

"That depends on how attached you are to being alive, man."

"She wouldn't kill me after all the effort she just put into patching me up."

"Are you sure?"

Chris rolled his eyes up like he was consulting the inside

of his head, then shrugged. "Yeah, maybe not." They finished dinner in more or less companionable silence, until Nick got up to clear the dishes away. He brushed off Chris's offer to help, but caught his breath like he had something to say. Chris waited a second, then said, "Okay, spit it out."

Nick, leaning over the sink, shook his head, but after a minute, barely audible over the sound of running water, said, "What do we do now?"

Chris shot a look at Nick's phone. "Maybe now you call your girlfriend."

"That'll go over like a lead balloon."

"You were hoping that was her, when Shy called."

"Yeah, but it wasn't. I—" He fell silent abruptly, turning his head, and Chris stood, hearing the same thing his brother did: an engine in the distance, coming closer. Nick dried his hands and they both went for handguns, with Nick muttering, "Although it's not like Saboac drove up," which was close enough to Chris's own line of thought to send a pang through him. It would be *so* much easier if the time Nicky had spent in California had changed him enough that they weren't…

Chris didn't even know. 'Weren't brothers anymore' was stupid. Weren't in sync, he guessed, although that sounded practically the same as not brothers, to him. Either way, they took up positions on opposite sides of the door, Nick flicking the window shade on his other side to glance out. "Old Jeep Cherok—oh, it's Dayton."

"It's Dayton's car, maybe," Chris muttered, and after another glance at him, Nick nodded and kept his guard up, following Chris's lead. A few seconds later, though, the Jeep door banged shut and Nick exhaled.

"Yeah, it's Day. What're you doing here, Dayton?" He pulled the door open for Dayton as Chris, sliding the gun into an inner waistband holster, stepped away.

Her eyebrows rose as Nick did the same. "Are those guns in your pockets, or are you boys just happy to see me?"

"Little bit of both?" Chris tried for a leer that made Dayton roll her eyes so hard it looked painful. She still stepped in to hug Nick, then wormed her way through Chris's defenses to hug him too. "What're you doing here, Day?"

"I thought I'd come check up on you and if you weren't home yet I'd make sure the pipes hadn't frozen. What the hell happened here?" Day turned like she was just actually looking at the place, a frown marring her expression until she looked like an angry Tinker Bell.

Chris started, "There was a little acc—" and Nick said, "I'm a freak, Day."

"Yeah, I always knew it. Geek in the streets, freak in the sheets. You've got that vibe, Ni—"

Color rose in Nick's face and Chris had about enough time to say, "Nick, we just fix—" before his baby brother raised a hand and blew out the goddamn window.

———

"Niiick!" Chris's yowl almost drowned out the shattering of glass. Freezing wind burst into the trailer, and Nick, far too late, thought about what he was doing.

It had been easy. So easy. Natural, comfortable, hardly even anger-driven. On one hand, he needed to be able to control the power without getting highly emotional. On the other, he needed to think about what he was doing, too. Either way, he just stood there with the biting wind whipping hair into his face and watching Dayton, whose own hair was suddenly wild and unkempt.

He had to hand it to her, though. She said, "Oh. *That* kind of freak," like he hadn't really done anything unusual at all. "Now fix it, it's fucking freezing in here already."

Embarrassment rushed Nick, heating his face again. "I don't know how."

"You just exploded the window for dramatic effect and

you don't know how to unexplode it? Man, next time, like, I don't know, break an egg, not your house. Is that what happened to everything else in here?" Dayton stomped around the dividing wall to the living room, disappeared for a minute, and came back wearing one of Chris's hooded sweat-shirts over her winter coat. It came to her thighs and dangled past her fingertips, making her look like a kid.

Chris made a not-great attempt to choke back a laugh. "You're adorkable, Day."

"Oh, fuck you. Where's everybody else? Will you please fix that window!"

"Don't look at me," Chris said to Nick. "That one's on you. Go get some plywood and I'll catch her up while you fix it. We'll be in the bedroom where it might be almost warm."

"Oh yay," Dayton muttered. "Just what I've always wanted, huddling in a bedroom with the Cassidy brothers." She turned on her heel and stomped back through the house, with Chris in her wake, claiming there were people who would pay good money for the opportunity she was dissing.

"It'd go faster if you'd stay and help hold the plywood!" Nick bellowed after them, and despite being unable to see them anymore, had the clear impression that Dayton flipped him off.

Ten minutes into trying to keep the goddamn board from slipping down the wall, he yelled, "Stay!" at it, and a thrum of grendel power lashed out to pin the wood in place. Nick's heart stuttered in his chest and the piece slipped again, but the second time he tried, with less anger and more intensity, it held. A stupid grin crawled over his face and he pointed a fingertip at a nail. "Bang!"

It shot through the wood. All the way through the wood, and out the other side. Nick grimaced and tried again, with less enthusiasm. The new nail tapped into place with a couple of finely honed strikes of power. He breathed a sound, almost a laugh, and tried again before trying to pick up several nails at once with the grendel power.

It almost worked, the nails falling like rain when his concentration wavered. He held his breath, trying again, and got several up and nailed in place that time. Half aloud, like Chris would hear him, he said, "I think maybe I can control it," before putting in the last few nails the more conventional way. He pushed the toolbox under the window instead of putting it away, and headed deeper into the house, calling, "Hey, Chris, I think you're right, maybe I can learn to control it without getting pissed off!"

Chris, through his bedroom door, said, "Yeah, I know you can, man."

Nick went in, closing the door behind him and snickering at Dayton, who had pulled Chris's sweatshirt over her knees and turned herself into a little ball of warmth in the middle of the bed. "Did you get cuter while I was gone, Day?"

Dayton curled her lip. "I was always this cute. You're just an idiot. I was just telling Chris you shoulda told Stephanie in the first place."

"About what, being a grendel? It only happened a couple days ago." Nick stopped in the process of sitting on the bed, backing off with his arms folded across his chest.

"No, you idiot. About what you and Chris were really out there hunting all those years."

"No." Nick shook his head, backing off another step. "The whole idea was it was supposed to be normal with her, without any of that crap following me around."

"And how'd that work out for you?" Dayton gave him a hard stare from inside the puckered circle of the sweatshirt's hood. She looked like a cartoon character, or maybe a Pokemon: all face and scowling eyes in an otherwise amorphous dark mass.

Nick's defensiveness fizzled out under the cute factor, and

he had to search to find it again, finally muttering, "Not great."

"So you should've told her. If you want a long-term relationship, that's not the kind of secret you should keep, Nick."

"Yeah, and when was the last time *you* had a long-term relationship, to know so much about it?"

Dayton released her legs from the sweatshirt and pulled the hood back to glare at him, her hair turning to blonde static wisps all around her head. "Whaddaya mean, I thought I was in a long-term relationship with you two jackasses."

Chris snorted. "Not sure found-family-siblings counts, Day."

"Found family," she echoed. "You been reading fic again, Chris?"

"What are you talking about, found family, we all just basically grew up together, we're just family," Nick said, bewildered.

"First, I'm not your family, you Cassidys are definitely a league of your own, and second..." Dayton turned her gaze toward Chris, brushing her wild hairs down with her palms. "Why doesn't he know the found family trope?"

"Because he only reads books, not stuff with Ao3 tags."

"What," Nick said to the ceiling, "is Ao3, or do I even want to know? Never mind." He finally did sit down on the edge of the bed and dropped his head into his hands. "Maybe you're right, I should have told Steph in the first place. It's too late now."

"So what're you gonna do now?"

"I donno." He lifted his head enough to glance at Chris, who shrugged.

"I donno either. Saboac's dead. Maybe that's the end of it. Maybe you do get to go h—back to Cali."

"Chris." Nick heard the weariness in his own voice. "If Saboac wanted me, or us, for a reason, I can't go back until we figure out what it is. You know that."

"Maybe your dad just pissed off the wrong people or something," Dayton said. "Sins of the father and all that crap."

"Who do you piss off enough that they call a desanctified *angel* down on your ass?" Chris demanded. "Like, that's not normal-level trolling. I didn't even know it was possible."

"Yeah, okay." Dayton tucked her legs back under the sweatshirt, which was never going to regain its shape at this point. "I dunno either. You said at the funeral that the pyre was a family tradition. That's not normal either, so maybe there's something in your whole family that makes you desanctified-angel-worthy. Doesn't your grandma still live in Nebraska or something?"

"Montana, yeah."

"Come on." Nick shook his head. "You're the one who said Grandma's normal."

"She is!" Chris's shoulders fell. "Unless Dayton's right and there's some kind of family bullshit tied into all of this."

"Why would it have to be her side of the family? It could be Dad's."

"Yeah, well, Dad was the only one left on his side of the family so I guess it better be Mom's side because we don't have anybody else to ask. And it was Grandma's husband that got the funeral pyre, not Dad's parents."

"Oh." That hit Nick like a swift punch to the diaphragm, popping the word out of him. "Shit. Yeah. I guess so. I don't know, so, what, should we call her?"

"This seems like a face to face conversation."

"The Dodge is wrecked, Chris."

A line of tension thinned his brother's mouth. "We can take my van."

"The shagmobile?" Dayton's soprano shot above Nick's tenor, but their voices both broke on the second word. "Oh my God," Dayton went on. "I'm totally coming with you. I've always wanted to see the inside of that thing."

"You *really* don't," Nick promised. "That thing is a rolling crime scene."

"There's not room for three anyway," Chris muttered.

"Oh, but I bet you've fit three." Dayton's voice dropped suggestively below her normal register and she waggled her eyebrows. Nick snickered, she grinned, he grinned bigger, and a couple seconds later they were both giggling like tweens while Chris's expression grew increasingly grim. Nick laughed harder and Dayton leaned over to punch his shoulder, then turned her face against it and giggled until she shook the whole bed.

"Okay, fuck you both." Chris got off the bed with a chorus of Nick's *ewwww* and Dayton's sing-songy "I've never been able to make that work in my head without it getting incesty," following him.

Nick pushed her over sideways as Chris stomped out. "Ugh, that suggests you've even thought about it."

"Oh yeah." Dayton pulled her hood up again, still cackling. "Hours of my life, Nick. Days. Whole weeks, even."

"So gross."

"Uh huh. Yeah. Super gross. Like dudes and their twins fantasies."

"I don't have twins fantasies!"

Dayton eyed him from inside her hood. "What about the Thompson twins in seventh grade?"

Nick felt heat crawl up his collar. "Okay, but I was like *twelve* and they were really cute and I was stupid!"

"Uh huh." Dayton leaned over, knocking her shoulder against his before her voice softened. "You doing okay, Nicky? Both of you, you doing okay with your dad and everything?"

Pain twisted Nick's chest hard enough to take his breath away and he had to stare at the wall a minute before he trusted himself to speak. "No. No, but I guess we're managing, because we have to."

"Yeah." Dayton sighed. "Yeah, that's the really shitty thing about death. The whole world should stop and wait for you a while and it doesn't. You guys…" She shrugged like she didn't know what to say. "You want me to hang around for a while or anything?"

Nick snaked his arm around her shoulders, and she squirmed to hug him hard, like she thought it might give him an excuse to hold on hard, too. She wasn't even wrong, and Nick guessed it took a while before he was able to mumble, "I don't think so, but thanks," in a too-rough voice. "I think we're probably gonna head out in Chris's nasty-ass van pretty early. Grandma lives way up north."

"Okay." Dayton wriggled away, tugged Chris's sweatshirt off, pulled the coat she'd never taken off back down around her hips, and leaned over to kiss Nick on the cheek. "Text or call or something if you need anything, okay? Even if it's just to scream about your dumb brother."

"I will. Thanks, Day." Nick walked her back into the living room, where she said exactly the same thing to Chris. Nick, laughing, said, "Hey!" and Dayton smiled unrepentantly on her way out the door.

"She knows about all this and still likes you," Chris said in her wake. "Maybe you oughta date her instead."

"What're you talking about? She's had a crush on you her whole life. *You* date her."

"Dude, what are *you* talking about, she's had a crush on *y*—" Chris broke off, obviously hearing himself repeat exactly what Nick had said. Then his face curled in a dismay that Nick felt his own expression reflecting, and they both looked after Dayton. "Oh. Oh shit. Did we, uh, did we miss that?"

Just as aware he was echoing Chris, and equally unable to stop himself, Nick said, "Oh, shit," in agreement. "Shit. Dude. I thought she liked you."

"I know she liked you!"

"Shit! Did you ever like her? Poor Dayton. Shit!"

"I dunno! She was like my little sister! Who was into my

little brother! Shit!" Chris pointed at him. "We can never speak of this to anyone."

"Yeah, no, they'll all think we're idiots."

"They already do!"

"Apparently they're right!" Nick spread his hands like he'd settled the point.

Chris made a motion suggesting he couldn't argue, then, with a shrug, said, "Nothing we can do about it now. Go get some sleep. We gotta leave pretty early if we want to get up to Maddock tomorrow."

Nick made a face. "There's really not another working car? We have to take the slutmobile?"

"Give it a goddamn rest, Nicky."

"Jeez. Okay. Fine. See you in the morning, I guess." Nick stomped down the hall, hesitated between the bedrooms, and in a fit of pique took Chris's, leaving his brother to deal with being the first one to sleep in their dad's old bed.

# CHAPTER 13

"C'MON, NICKY." CHRIS'S VOICE CAME OUT OF THE DARK NOT nearly long enough later. So, though, did the smell of bacon, and Nick rolled out of bed toward the promise of food before his brain could register a meaningful protest. "You got time to shower, if you're quick," Chris called, so Nick stumbled directly into the bathroom and was more or less awake, whether he liked it or not, when he sat down for breakfast several minutes later.

There was a *lot* of bacon. Enough that he could eat as much as he wanted without feeling guilty, which didn't usually happen except in a cafeteria, and not always then. A tall stack of buttered toast and mostly-full carton of orange juice sat beside the plate of bacon. Chris said, "Might as well drink it, it'll go off if we're gone more than a couple days anyway. Two eggs or three?"

Nick gratefully poured half the carton into a large glass as he wrapped a piece of toast around some bacon and folded the whole thing into his mouth. "Freeh peefh."

"'k." A minute later Chris slid three over-easy fried eggs onto Nick's plate and went back to cook himself a couple.

Nick dipped another piece of toast into a yolk, then

paused, staring at his plate. "I thought you said eggs over-easy were gross."

"Shut up and eat." Chris came back to the table with fewer eggs, longer cooked, and sat down to eat like he was facing a firing squad at sunrise. "Got your stuff together?"

"All I even brought with me was a backpack, so yeah, I guess so. And it'll fit under the front seat so I don't have to crawl around in your shag carpeting. The bacon's really good."

Chris's eyebrows twitched downward and he glanced at the rapidly-diminishing pile of bacon. "Thanks. I couldn't remember how crunchy you liked it. Dad was 'cook it till it shatters.'"

"No, this is good. Hurts my teeth when it's shattery."

"Yeah, me too." A few minutes of concentrated silence later, Chris pushed his plate away and stood. "I'm gonna grab a shower so we can be on the road by six."

"Can I finish the bacon?"

To his surprise, Chris chuckled and smacked, almost patted, his shoulder on the way past. "Yeah, Nicky, you can finish the bacon. If there's any left over when the bottomless pit is satisfied I'll throw together some BLTs for the road."

"We have fresh lettuce and tomato?" Nick asked incredulously, and, forewarned, left enough bacon for BLTs. He got the dishes done, dried, and put away while Chris showered, and went out to see if the shagmobile needed to be dug out or anything.

The Dodge, with its big wheels and high chassis, could've gotten over the snow berm that had piled up in front of the garage door, but a van wouldn't. Nick broke the snow and ice up, shoveling it out of the way, and pulled the garage door open as Chris crunched through the snow behind him. "Oh, thank God, you painted it. And changed the license plates."

"Did you really think I was gonna drive around in something that said SLTMBILE on it?"

"I mean, yeah? This is better, though."

"No shit."

It had always been a large van, with a pop-up roof for more light and headroom, and Nick couldn't remember if it had had windows in the body or not. Probably, since there were windows now, with inside shades drawn down, but mostly all he could remember was there had been some kind of horrific mostly naked woman and an eagle and maybe a wizard hat, he wasn't sure anymore, painted down one side of the van. The other side had been comparatively tame, if a howling wolf and an American flag could be called tame.

Since then, though, it had been professionally repainted in two tones, kind of olive green and cream that looked pretty normal for a vehicle twice as old as Nick was. The paint job didn't cover the dings and signs of age, but it looked a hell of a lot better than it had. "Is it still all shag inside?"

Chris sighed and pulled the back door open. A ceiling light splashed on, brightening the interior, and Chris stomped around the door toward the front to throw a cooler onto the seats. Nick cringed in anticipation, then flinched upright and stared.

If the exterior had been bad before, the interior had somehow been worse. Three-inch orange shag everywhere, including on the step up to a shag-covered bed that had belonged on a 1970s porn set. Despite the orangeness, it had also managed to be a dark, dank space that Nick hadn't even wanted to breathe near, never mind think about what nastiness was *in* that carpet.

All the stuffy, muffling shag had been stripped away and the van's interior had been lined with light-colored wood. A halo of soft gold Christmas lights stuttered on around the pop-up roof as Chris started the van's engine, casting a warm glow on sanded wooden countertops over rough-wood sectional cabinets. A narrow sink and a two-burner stove took up part of the counter, and a bed filled everything from the side doors to the back of the driver's seat. The bed had storage beneath it, more wooden cupboard doors that caught the light from above. A blue and gold rug was tacked to the floor, and the window shades, which were reflective on the outside, were lined with dark fabric on the interior to keep light from shining through.

"Holy shit, Chris. Did you do all this yourself?" Nick reached out to brush his fingers over the nearest wall, then leaned over to examine the construction. There was enough depth between the wood and the van wall to suggest the whole space was insulated. He stepped up inside, ducking so he would fit, but lifting a hand to the pop-up roof, which was lined with silk-soft wood, too. "This is beautiful. Why the hell didn't you say something when I was giving you shit?"

"What was I gonna say, it doesn't suck anymore? Like you'd believe that?"

"Yeah, well, you're right, I wouldn't have, but I should've. *Did* you do all this yourself?"

Chris's shrug said 'yeah, like it matters,' and Nick shook his head. "It does matter. You did a great job."

His brother half scowled back at him, like it bothered him that Nick understood the shrug. "You coming up here or what?"

"No, man, I got a lot of looking around to do here! This is amazing! Yeah, yeah, okay, fine. Pull out and I'll move the Dodge in and close the garage door." Nick climbed out the back of the van, closed the doors, and went to start the half-frozen Dodge so it could be parked inside until it could be repaired. A minute later he climbed into the passenger side of the shagmobile, muttering, "I'm gonna hafta give it another name. When did you do all this?"

Chris shrugged again, stiffly. "Since I bought it. I still got a little left to do."

Nick turned around, peering down the van's now-dark interior. "What's left? It looks great."

"Working on a table that slides out from under the bed, for one, or changing the whole top to put a high roof on so the bed can go up there."

"You'd have a shit ton more room on the floor if you did that. But you'd have to rearrange everything."

"It's all modular anyway. Anyway, If I don't do that, I gotta figure out a solution for at least one permanent chair. The bed's fine as it is if it's just me, but sometimes it's not."

"I bet not. This is, like, a non-terrifying shagmobile." Nick elbowed Chris, or at least made the motion, since he was about two feet away from him in the driver's seat.

"Oh, shut up. Put some music on and shut up."

"Yeah, okay. Got bluetooth in this thing?"

"Dude, it's from 1973." Chris waited a beat. "Of course it's got bluetooth. Should be under—"

"Shagmobile?" Nick asked hopefully.

"Mystery Machine, you jackass."

Nick cackled, turned the stereo on, and a few seconds later, *Let's Get It On* rolled through the speaker system. Chris bellowed incoherently and Nick, laughing, found a classic rock mix instead.

"Thank you! Jesus! I do not need that playing when the only other person in my van is my brother!"

"Shaaaaagmobiiiile!" Nick cackled again as Chris made a threatening gesture at him, then settled down in the seat to watch the miles creep past under their wheels. He fell asleep somewhere past the Wyoming border and didn't wake up again until they stopped for gas in Casper. "Shit." He sat up groggily, fumbling for a water bottle that Chris handed to him. "Sorry. You shoulda woken me up."

"If I'd known you were gonna pass out like a four year old I'd have told you to take the bed. S'fine. You want coffee?"

"No, I'm good. Lemme fill the tank, I gotta move." Nick got out to fill the tank and Chris, moving stiffly, went in to pay. "Lemme drive a while," Nick said when his brother got back.

"You got less sleep than I did." Which was true, if not exactly the truth about why he thought he should drive.

"You think I'm gonna let you drive—my van after all the time you spent insulting it?"

Nick felt a slow grin creep across his face. "What's her name?"

"What makes you think it's got a name?"

"'Cause you almost said it. C'mon, what's her name?"

Chris sighed. "Lucille."

"Please don't you leave me, Lucille?" Nick half sang the words, and his brother looked pained.

"First, those aren't the lyrics, and second, no, not that Lucille. She's not gonna leave me, are you, Lucy." He patted the van as he walked back toward the driver's seat.

Nick marched out in front of the van and spread his arms, palms up. "Lucy, I'm sorry for all the jokes I made at your expense. I didn't know my dumb big brother was gonna treat you like a lady, and I shouldn't have been slut-shaming anyway, that was a dick move. If you don't mind, though, Chris needs sleep as bad as I did, so if you could see your way clear to forgiving me and letting me drive for a while, that'd probably be good for all of us."

Chris hadn't yet opened the driver side door by the time Nick finished. He just stood there, giving him a hard look, before finally saying, "I can't tell if you're fucking with me."

"I am not fucking with you," Nick said with genuine sincerity. "Seriously, man, I knew you worked on this thing—on Lucille—some in high school, but I had no idea she was, like, a passion project. She's amazing."

Chris's shoulders hunched. "It's not that big a deal."

Chris was obviously full of shit, but Nick doubted that argument would win him much ground. "Just go get some sleep, dude, okay? I promise not to drive past..." He rolled his eyes up, trying to figure how far they'd come and how much farther they had to go. "Billings, okay? That's about as far as

Casper is from Sterling. I'll give your baby back in Billings. That sounds like a country song."

"Number one hit in 1977," Chris agreed, but tossed Nick the keys and went around Lucille's back end to open the far side door. By the time Nick got in the driver's seat, his brother was sacked out across the van's bed with a muttered, "Drive carefully," before silence fell.

Nick waited to queue up *Let's Get It On* until he was pretty sure Chris had fallen asleep.

———

They'd both been awake for hours by the time they hit the outskirts of Maddock, not that there was much to Maddock, Montana except outskirts, anymore. It had been a gold rush town, big enough that they ran the train to it back in the late 19th century, but it had dried up with the rush and there wasn't much left except some tumbleweeds and a couple ghosts. Nick, watching the greyed out buildings go by, said, "I wonder what it was like here, back in the day."

"You've wondered that every time we've come through here since you were five, Nick. You have the internet, look it up."

"I dunno, I think maybe it's better to wonder. Y'know, like, that was the saloon, that was the whorehouse, that was the general store…."

"That's still the general store, man." Which was true, although Nick didn't think it sold anything but tinned milk and a couple of souvenirs about the little town's long-ago glory days. Less than three minutes later they'd passed through the little town, leaving dust to hang on the faded boards and greyed-out signs. Their grandma lived another twenty miles out of town, on a ranch Nick remembered as having visibility for a good solid ten of those miles.

Of course, he'd been a lot younger and smaller, the last

time he was on Grandma's land. It probably wasn't really possible to see more than a couple miles in any direction, but when he'd been a kid, it seemed like the old lady had been able to see him get into mischief anywhere.

Or trailing along behind Chris, watching *him* get into mischief, and then the both of them getting in trouble for it. Nick chuckled at the memory and Chris glanced at him. "Lemme guess, you're remembering when you fell in the creek."

"I'm remembering when you *pushed* me in the creek."

"Potato, potahto. I should've pushed you, since I got my hide tanned for it, anyway."

"You really didn't?"

"No, it was one of the other kids who grew up out there that Grandma let play on the land. I don't think she really meant to. The kid who pushed you, not Gramma, she knew what she was doing. You just didn't know how to walk on a wet log and she bumped into you. I almost caught your shirt trying to grab you when you went in, and you decided I'd pushed you."

"In my defense, it sounds plausible."

Chris cast him a brief look Nick couldn't read, then lifted his chin at the road in front of them and the distant house at the end of it. "Grandma's waiting for us."

"Did you call, or will she have a shotgun?"

"Why not both?"

"Hah!" Nick grimaced at the laugh's sharpness, but Chris smiled briefly.

"No, I called from Billings. She said we could come up and stay as long as we wanted."

"Not too long," Nick said without thinking. "I mean…"

"Yeah, no, we don't know if another frickin' angel is gonna come after you. Us. We'll stay overnight, maybe, and head out tomorrow. She'll be mad, but I'd rather she was mad than caught up in all this crap."

"Maybe we shouldn't have…"

"No, man, we can't explain what's going on over the phone. I mean, what're we gonna do, text 'hey gramma, know anything about killer fallen angels?' If she doesn't know about it, it's too weird, and if she does, *I* don't wanna get, like, a text message about that."

"Like y—" Nick bit his tongue on that and Chris shot him a glare.

"Give it a rest. I said sorry."

"You said you were an asshole."

"All right so I'm *sorry, fuck*."

Nick's shoulders hunched and he muttered, "Thanks," at the window.

Chris said something under his breath, and a chill of cold anger slid up Nick's spine. He pressed his eyes shut, felt his jaw tightened, and looked for a way to shake it off. A couple of bumpy minutes later the van slowed as they reached the house, but the emotion wouldn't let go, and he didn't want to go see his grandma while he was still spitting fire. Especially with the grendel magic poking at him, looking for a chance to explode. Chris killed the engine and Nick heard him thump the heel of his hand against the steering wheel a couple of times before he said, "I'm sorry, Nicky," more quietly than before. "I should have called."

A knot untied itself under Nick's heart and he exhaled some of the anger away. Most of it, maybe. "Thanks."

"Grandma's on the porch looking at us like we're a couple of idiots."

A little grin fought its way up and Nick opened his eyes to see the old lady doing just that, standing cross-armed in her doorway with a shotgun leaning on her hip and a dog staring intently past it. "She might be on to something, you know."

"I get that impression sometimes, yeah. You ready for this?"

"I haven't been ready for a single goddamn thing that's happened in the last week, Chris."

"Has it been a week?" Chris still had his hands on the steering wheel, his gaze locked forward like he was looking at their grandmother, but his eyes looked unfocused. "I guess so. Dad died a week ago yesterday, the funeral was a week ago tomorrow. I'm having a hard time with days right now."

"Well, letting Grandma's house get cold 'cause she's standing there with the door open waiting for us isn't gonna help that."

"Yeah. I guess not." Chris moved his hands like he'd turn the van off, discovered he'd already done it, and stared blankly at the keys for a couple seconds before removing them from the ignition. "All right. Let's go."

Nick finally opened his own door, like he'd been waiting for permission. The dog shouldered past their grandma, hackles rising and a low warning growl echoing over the snowy landscape. Grandma said, "Calm down, Bill," and the dog eyed her, then lay down with its chin on its paws, tail brushing her feet warily. She stepped over him, leaving the shotgun in the doorway, and came down a short set of steps to crunch across the snow toward them. "Hello, boys."

"Grandma." Nick felt a stupid smile crease his face, and stepped up to hug her. She'd gotten *tiny* since he'd seen her last, not just short like everybody else, *tiny*. Some of that was age peeling away everything extra, although she'd never had much extra to begin with, being one of those old ladies who got increasingly whip-like instead of softening into Mrs. Claus.

She hadn't lost any strength, though, as she returned his hug and chuckled as he lifted her up. "You got tall, boy."

"I guess you didn't sneak me enough coffee when I was little."

"I still make it with all that milk and sugar you liked." She smiled as he put her down again, and turned to Chris, who folded her into an even longer hug. She murmured something into his hair after a long moment, and when he released her, it was to brusquely wipe his hand over his eyes.

"'s good to see you too, Gramma. How's that cow?"

"Learning that motherhood is no bed of roses. Come on inside, boys. You probably want something to eat."

"It's been a while since the BLTs," Nick admitted.

Chris looked at him crossly as they followed their grandmother into the house. "We ate in Billings and then again in Great Falls, Nick. Both of those were after the sandwiches."

"So? It's still been a while since the BLTs."

Chris muttered, "I swear to God," but crouched to let the dog sniff his hand while Nick passed the animal and went into the house, following the scent of meat loaf and baked potatoes.

He guessed the decor was last-century, because nothing had changed since he'd been there last: a living room with over-stuffed couches and striped covers, low square coffee tables, table lamps that cast warm incandescent light over the room. The kitchen was brown wood and white counters and linoleum, although he guessed the table could have been a hundred years old, for all he knew. There were three bedrooms down the hall, and just the one bathroom, unless she'd had a new one put in, but she'd been living alone out there for a long time, so it didn't seem likely. "It looks just like I remember, Grandma. So do you."

"Not shorter?"

He ducked his head and smiled at his feet. "Everything seems smaller, yeah."

"I'll let you in on a secret. I've been painting it all with shrinking dust for twenty years now. It's not you, it's everything else."

Nick laughed. "Yeah? How come Chris got short, then?"

"I did not." Chris, having apparently made friends with

the dog, came inside with the dog on his heels, and pulled the door shut behind them.

"Oh, I sneak down to Sterling once a year or so and give him a good dusting, too. Used to do it to you, but San Francisco's too far a drive for an old lady like me, so you escaped my wicked ways. And now look at you, too tall to hug unless you pick me up." Grandma clicked her tongue and pointed to the kitchen chairs. Nick slunk to one, almost feeling guilty for having gotten tall. Chris sat in another, and for a moment their grandmother stood and studied them.

"What a couple of handsome boys you turns out to be," she finally said. "How are you, under the circumstances?" She turned away to open the oven, a wave of heat and stomach-rumbling scent rolling out as Nick exchanged glances with his brother.

"We're okay," Chris said after that silent consultation. "Mostly. Um, Grandma, I hate to jump into the deep end—"

"Then don't," she said briskly, putting the meat loaf on the table. "Eat dinner. Eat cookies."

Nick, unable to help himself, brightened. "There are cookies?"

"There will be after dinner. And then get a good night's sleep, Christopher. You can dive in the deep end tomorrow."

"Grandma, I think we need to leave in the morning. There's—"

"You're going to drive thirteen hours, stay for twelve, and leave an old woman alone in winter?" Grandma delivered half a dozen large baked potatoes to the table and Nick, belatedly, got up to help. "Sit back down," she told him. "Nothing's more tiring than sitting for a whole day. You can fuss over me tomorrow."

"Grandma, some stuff has happened. It might be dangerous for us to stay," Chris protested as Nick, feeling like he was about nine, obediently sat again.

A scowl passed over their grandma's face as she returned

to the stove for a pot of vegetables. "What bullshit did your father leave you to deal with?"

Chris, cautiously, said, "I'm not sure it's his bullshit," and for the first time since they'd arrived, Grandma stopped moving. Arrested, so fully that it looked like something external had grabbed hold of her, but so briefly that Nick almost wasn't sure he'd seen it.

Then she was back in action, draining the vegetables and bringing them to the set table, telling Nick he could get up after all, and get some drinks for everybody and put the butter on the table. He did, but not without glancing at Chris to see if he, too, had caught Grandma's momentary hesitation.

Chris dropped his chin, barely a nod. Nick half wished he hadn't, that he'd imagined the whole thing, but they'd seen the same thing, and that meant maybe Grandma knew something after all. But she sat down, saying, "Tell me about college, Nicholas," and for a while, at least, they all pretended everything was normal. The dog put his head on the table and looked absolutely tragic when Grandma snapped at him. Nick was pretty sure she noticed, but ignored, Chris feeding the animal scraps off his plate. By the time dinner was over, the dog was Chris's best friend in the world, and followed him around the kitchen as he cleaned up.

Grandma watched that with clear amusement. "You were always good with the animals, Christopher. You should come out here and help me on the ranch. Those cows don't have babies by themselves."

"Pretty sure they do, Gramma."

"Well, all right, most of the time, they do. Still, it's a better life up here than chasing bounties around, my boy. Your father never should have brought you up like that."

"You're probably right." Chris went silent a minute, dishes clinking together as he washed them. "Nicky, you wanna dry these? How come you and Dad never got along, Gramma? I mean, was it…Mom?"

Nick got up to help while their grandmother frowned at both of them. Then, like she couldn't talk without moving, she got up too, taking a bowl out to start cookies. "Not because she died, no. We never liked each other much before that, either. He was very handsome, your daddy, and girls came easy to him. I was raised not to trust a man like that."

Chris grinned at the dishes. "You were raised not to trust a man like that because your mom was gay, Gramma. She didn't have time for any men."

Grandma sniffed. "Having been married to a man for the better part of thirty years, I see her point."

"Hey!" Both the brothers protested, and their grand-mother laughed.

"You boys don't seem too bad. Doing dishes and every-thing without even being told. Somebody raised you right, in the end."

Nick said, "Chris did," without really meaning to, and his brother gave him a sharp, startled look.

"Then I suppose if he has kids of his own, he'll do all right by them," Grandma said. "Turn the oven back on, will you, Nicky? Three fifty."

"Yes, Gramma. Are those gonna be chocolate chip cookies?"

"Are they still your favorite?"

"Yeah…" Nick smiled sheepishly at his toes, then bright-ened as Grandma said, "Then I suppose that's what they'll be. Chris, what about you?"

"What about me? Chocolate chip is fine. Nick eats more cookies than I do."

"Nick eats more everything than you do," Nick said.

"Nick eats more than an average moose."

Nick made moose antlers with his wet hands and soapy water dripped down his temple and forearm. "Ew. Look what you did."

"How is that my fault?" Chris asked, outraged.

"I don't know. It just is. Thanks for the cookies, Grandma."

"Don't thank me yet. They might turn out to be terrible."

"Unlikely."

"More unlikely things have happened."

Chris shot Nick another look at that comment. Nick bugged his eyes in return, shrugging. People said that kind of thing. It didn't necessarily *mean* anything. Chris cocked a skeptical eyebrow, as if arguing it didn't *necessarily* mean anything, but given how Grandma had gone still earlier about the 'maybe not dad's bullshit' line, it could add up to a pattern.

Nick, out loud, said, "Two points don't make a line," and Chris made a what-the-hell face.

"Dude, I'm the one who skipped half of high school, but I'm pretty sure two points *exactly* make a line, that's, like, the point."

"Or two points."

Chris threw a handful of soapy water at him and their grandmother barked a warning that made the dog stand up, bristling. Chris mumbled, "Sorry, Gramma," and cleaned up the mess he'd made while the dog licked his ear.

"Go put your things in the bedrooms," Grandma said sternly. "I'll call you two young men when the cookies are ready, assuming you can behave."

They both mumbled apologies and left the kitchen, although Chris's expression grew increasingly affronted. "What does she think we are, little kids?"

"We were kind of acting like it. Look, Chris, can't we just…she wants us to stay a couple of days. Can't we just stay tonight and tomorrow and talk about it all then?"

Chris eyed him, then sighed as they went out to the van to get their stuff. "I don't know, Nicky. How are you doing? Like, with, you know."

"It's still there. I can kind of ignore it if I'm trying to be really, I dunno, normal."

"Normal like hanging out with Grandma for a couple days?"

Nick nodded, and Chris sighed again. "Arright. Arright, Nicky, you win. We'll stay until Saturday, okay? We'll pretend everything's cool tonight, and eat cookies and get some sleep, and tomorrow we'll see what she knows. Just let me know if anything gets, like, you know. Weird."

"Thanks." Nick gave his brother a weak smile. "I will. Thanks, Chris."

"Yeah, well, I'm gonna eat more cookies than you, so that'll show you."

"What, exactly, will it show me?"

"I don't know, man, like how I get indigestion or something. C'mon." They brought their bags into the house. Grandma called them for cookies as Nick unpacked his stuff, and Chris, true to his word, ate enough of them to impress even Nick.

Also true to his word, he begged off half an hour later, looking queasy, and staggered to bed, which left Nick and Grandma grinning after him. "He's a good boy, your brother," Grandma said once he'd gone. "Looks after you."

"I know. Drives me nuts, but I know."

"Well, family's like that." Grandma considered Nick for a long couple of moments, her gaze thoughtful. "I know you boys want to get answers and get out of here, Nicky. Thank you for giving an old lady time with her grandsons. I do miss you kids, you know."

"I know. I'm sorry, Grandma. We're—"

"You're living your own lives," she said firmly. "Which is what kids should do. I might not have gotten on well with your father, but I can't put all the blame on him for us not having a closer relationship. I could've taken myself out of the back of beyond to come see you, too."

"Was it hard?" Nick asked quietly. "With Mom gone, and everything?"

"It was, and that's probably all the more reason I should have made an effort for you kids's sake. Sometimes it's too easy to let the years slip by up here. You're grown men now, for heaven's sake." She examined him critically again. "Grown men who need more sleep. Go to bed, Nick. There'll be more cookies in the morning."

Nick, surprised, laughed, then stood to kiss her cheek. "Okay, Grandma. Thank you for dinner and dessert. I love you, you know that?"

"I do, sweetheart. Now go on to bed. Sleep well."

"I'll try." He left her sitting in the living room with her book, and fell asleep faster than he expected to after doing more or less nothing all day.

Something woke him in the small hours of the morning, a coyote or maybe just the silence, and Nick went from asleep to hot fast tears before he knew he was awake. He rolled over, burying his face in the pillow, but couldn't muffle the ache of loss or regret, or the sobs that sounded loud as thunder to his ears. He got up, scuffing his shoes on at the door, and went out into the night without a flashlight or coat. Just about enough moon reflected off the snow to help him navigate, and he followed the only sound that wasn't wind: water, running above and below ice in the creek half a mile from the house.

It was too cold to keep crying, which was something, at least. The air cut his lungs if he breathed in too deeply or sharply, and tears smeared and froze, so he kept wiping his face until they were gone, and by that time, he'd reached the creek.

The log they'd crossed all those years ago was still there, or maybe another one had replaced it, but it made a dark, slick line across the iced-over creek. Nick could almost step over the water now, but it had seemed like a mile across when he'd been little. The water broke through the ice in places, spilling out onto the ice in narrow fingers before crawling back. The creek bed dipped on just that side of the log, dropping several inches in depth. It had felt like an endless fall, when he'd been six, even though he hadn't really gotten wet past his chest. Chris had pulled him out while the other kids screamed.

His chest ached like he needed to move, and after a minute he did. He crouched by the creek, pushing his fingertips against the ice. Water rushed past, bumping against the ice enough that Nick thought he could feel it from this side. He pushed a little harder, trying to make the ice crack. It wouldn't be hard to break through it, although with the way ice shattered, he'd probably overbalance and fall in. It had been deep enough to drown a kid in. Nick didn't know if it would be as dangerous to an adult. Part of him wanted to find out. He pushed harder, feeling it bend under the pressure. The ache in his chest swelled to fill his whole body, and the ice melting under his fingertips felt hot. It was stupid and risky and weirdly tempting to keep pushing. Nick shoved his hand down, not entirely sure if he was using his own strength or the aching magic inside him, but the ice cracked sharply, and freezing water engulfed his hand, the current trying to grab his fingers.

Familiar footsteps sounded, Chris's voice carrying over the squeak and crunch of snow. "What're you doing out here, Nicky?"

Nick yanked his hand out of the water, guilty, angry, relieved, and looked over his shoulder to see his brother draped in the Dodge's scratchy wool blanket. Chris's eyes were tired and worried. "It's two in the morning, bro."

"What are *you* doing out here?"

"Heard you get up. Followed you." Chris shuffled over and dropped the blanket around Nick's shoulders. He, unlike Nick, had a coat on beneath it.

"I didn't know you'd grabbed this from the truck."

"Hate traveling without it. It's the worst, it itches, it's stiff and doesn't bundle up good, but damn it's warm. Come on back to the house, Nick."

"In a minute." Nick stood and stuck his cold wet hand in his armpit, watching the water spilling by. Rivulets spun across its surface from where he'd broken the ice, clearing frost and snow so that the dark, almost invisible shadow rush of water was visible beneath it. His chest hurt less, but his heart crashed against his ribcage. Chris had pulled him back from something that he couldn't even recognize, much less name. Chris was always doing that for him. "I was six when I fell in, wasn't I? It was the summer after I crashed my bike and broke my arm."

"Yeah, I guess so."

Nick nodded. "Yeah, I thought so." He took a breath. "I'm sorry. I'm sorry I thought you pushed me."

Chris went still for a moment, then nodded. "S'okay. Thanks. C'mon, Nicky. You shouldn't be out here alone at this hour."

"I'm not. My big brother's watching out for me."

"Fuck, man." Chris rolled his head, looking the other way, but Nick caught a glimpse of a smile. "C'mon. There's nothing out here. You're not gonna learn anything standing on the riverbank."

"I dunno, I kinda already did."

"Ugh." Chris rolled his head again and turned away from the water, creaking back across the snow. "Fine, stay out here all night, whatever, I'm going back where it's not balls-freezing cold."

"Hey, wait up. Wait up, Chris. Wait for me." Nick turned and hurried in his brother's wake, obscurely relieved to catch up and fall into step with him. Chris knocked his shoulder against Nick's, and they walked back across the snow to Grandma's house in the dark.

# CHAPTER 14

CHRIS WOKE TO A PAIR OF BROWN EYES GAZING SOULFULLY across the bed at him. After a couple of seconds, a regular thump started, then sped up as the dog became more certain he was awake. Chris chuckled and reached over to scratch the animal's ears, mumbling, "Bet Gramma would kill you for being on the bed, Bill. Shh, though. I won't tell if you don't."

Somehow Grandma, elbow deep in flour and shortening, still gave him a sour look when he went into the kitchen, Bill on his heels. "You let that dog sleep on the bed, didn't you, Christopher."

He raised his hands in a show of innocence. "In my defense, I didn't *let* him. He didn't ask. Nicky still sleeping?"

"Mm. You boys were out late last night." Grandma nodded toward a chair, and Chris sat to watch her putter around making biscuits.

"He was having trouble sleeping. I just went to make sure he was okay. Sorry if we woke you up. You need help, Gramma? I can cook."

"Somebody in your house must have been able to," his grandmother said with a sniff, then clicked her tongue as she dumped the biscuit dough onto the counter and kneaded it a few times. "No, I can spoil my grandsons for a morning or

197

two. I'll let you cook next time, see if your bite is as good as your bark."

"Most ladies say it is," Chris said modestly.

To his relief, Grandma laughed. "You remind me of my mother, Christopher. She was a firecracker."

"I don't really remember her," he admitted. "I know there are a couple pictures of us, but I was really little."

"She was only a couple of years older than I am now when she died." She cut biscuits with an easy, habitual twist, dropping the dough onto a cookie sheet. "It seemed old at the time. To me, at least. Not so sure she felt the same way, now that I'm coming up on that age myself. How's your brother doing?"

Chris frowned at the table. "Okay, I guess. I was kind of a dick, telling him about Dad, so that sucked. I sucked."

"Most of us aren't at our best in that kind of situation," Grandma said, more gently than Chris thought he deserved. "What matters is you were both there for each other. Right?"

"Right. I guess."

"So why don't you tell me what's been going on?" The biscuits went into the oven and Grandma sat down across from him, dusting her hands.

Chris shot a look toward the bedrooms. "I dunno, maybe I should wait for Nicky."

"S'okay," his brother said groggily from down the hall. "Go ahead. I'll be there in a minute." The bathroom door closed, swallowing the last of his words.

Grandma looked expectantly at Chris. He sank into his chair, fingers knotting and tangling and drumming at the edge of the table until he realized he was doing it and made himself stop. "Grandma, I...look, if you don't already know about what I'm gonna talk about I'm gonna sound crazy."

"One of the wonderful things about being old is everything the younger generation says sounds crazy, or at least detached from the reality you knew as a child. Go ahead."

"Well, like—I mean, why *do* we have funeral pyres, Grandma? That's not normal. I mean, do you *know* why we do?"

Obvious weariness passed over the old lady, making her smaller and older before she took a deep breath, clearly preparing herself. "Are you asking me because you think I don't know, or because *you* don't?"

"I *don't* know! Or I—I know why Nick and I did it. I don't know if it's the same reason you had a pyre for Grandpa, or if…did Grandma Jean get a pyre too?"

"She did."

Chris stared at Grandma for a minute, then exhaled so long he thought he might cave in on himself. "Then either you guys think you're a bunch of Vikings or it's the same reason. We burned Dad's body because he was killed by vampires, Grandma."

His grandmother said, "Well, *fuck*," and got up to take the biscuits out of the oven. Chris sat in silence, watching her with his jaw dropped. No matter how many times he tried to crank it back up, it went back down. Nick came out of the bathroom, looked between them, and sat down to find out what he'd missed.

It took a couple minutes for Grandma to gather herself again, and it involved getting the biscuits into a basket, taking a pot of homemade cinnamon applesauce off the stove, putting it all on the table, and going back for everybody's drinks. Then she sat, stared at the breakfast food, and said, "Your god damn father was supposed to keep you boys out of all that. That was the entire point of…dammit. Damn that man! Eat," she snapped. "Eat. I can't think with you two staring at me like that."

Nick reached for biscuits at the same time Chris did and they spent a few seconds fighting over the one that had a little crescent in one side, where Grandma had overlapped two circles with the cutter. She'd always done that, not on purpose because there was only ever one or maybe two at most. On some level Chris believed those were the *best* ones, because they meant Grandma had made them by hand just for her grandsons.

He got the crescent-cut biscuit, then, with a surge of suspicion at the childhood memory that told him Nick *always* got those ones, he handed it to his little brother.

Nicky brightened like a kid, then, sheepishly, said, "Those ones are best."

"Yeah. I know." Chris took another one and they concentrated on buttering and applesaucing them until Grandma said, "It's been in the family as long as I've ever known. I don't even know what 'it' is, but my mother guarded me against it my entire life. Her wife, her friends, all of them, they went half crazy keeping me safe as a kid. Mom thought I might inherit it, but I guess it passed me by. It got your mother, though. It got my Ruth."

Chris's appetite vanished, although the food smelled amazing. "What do you mean, it got Mom?"

"Oh, honey." Grandma braced her head in her hands. "She believed in all sorts of nonsense that *my* mother wouldn't deny. Angels. Demons. Possessions. She used to see them, she said, and Mom—my mother—believed her. She taught her how to…she couldn't defend herself. Ruthie couldn't defend herself. Mom didn't understand that, she said she should be able to. It drove Ruth crazy, in the end."

"Grandma?" Nicky's voice cracked. "What happened to Mom?"

"She died," their grandmother said wearily. "Your father brought her to a—he called it a religious order. A cult. They said they could exorcise her. They couldn't. She died."

"What the—what the fuck, Grandma?" Chris pushed his chair back from the table, sick energy boiling through him. The horrible idea that *this* was what Nicky's grendel power felt like hit him, and he turned to his brother, who had gone sheet white and unmoving. "Why the fuck didn't anybody *tell* us that? Nicky, are you—are you okay?"

Nick didn't even really answer, just kind of shuddered, but he obviously wasn't *okay*. Chris didn't know if *okay* even existed anymore. He thought he was going to have to hit something, or throw up, or both, and he didn't know how to do any of it without falling apart.

But he couldn't fall apart, because then Nicky would. He dragged in a breath that felt like it should hurt, and it was awful that it didn't, like he shouldn't be able to even breathe anymore, and his hands were cold and his stomach kept twisting and his heart thumped like it needed to escape.

"Because the one thing your father promised after that was to keep you away from that whole world," Grandma said bitterly. "Even me, because I guess I was part of it, even if it skipped my generation."

"*It didn't skip ours!*" The words burst from Nicky like an eruption of power themselves. Chris pulled his brother out of his chair and got between him and Grandma, saying, "Nick. Nick. Nicky," until Nick's glazed gaze snapped to him.

"C'mon, Nicky, hold it together. I'm here, okay? I got you. It's gonna be okay. This explains a lot, man. It's shit, it's shit we didn't know, but this crap, it didn't come out of nowhere, we got a whole family thing around it, okay? So you're okay, Nicky. You're who you always were, all right? You're you, buddy. Okay? Nicky?"

The tremble of a nod was enough. Chris's knees damn near buckled, but he couldn't hold Nicky up if he fell, so he didn't. "Arright. Arright, Nicky. It's gonna be okay." Over his shoulder, to their grandma, he said, "We went to kill the vamps that got Dad, and got our asses hand to us by an angel. A fallen angel."

"Reporbate," Nicky said hoarsely, and Chris nodded encouragement.

"Yeah, that's right, reporbate. Not just fallen, but, uh, cast out, castigated! By God."

Nick managed a brief, weak smile. "Castigate means scolding. Desanctified's kinda worse, Chris."

"You and your fucking vocabulary, Nick. I thought I was doing pretty good there." He got a little nod for that, another almost-smile. "Yeah, so shut the fuck up, man. You okay? You okay?"

Nick trembled again, definitely not a nod or a yes in any way, so Chris kept his grip on his shoulders. "You are, though. You're okay. The thing woke some kind of power up in Nicky, Grandma. Like big power."

"Freak power," Grandma said, and Chris bared his teeth.

"We're calling it grendel power these days, but yeah. You know about that? *What* do you know about it?"

"My mother said it was demon blood in humanity. Or demon essence. Coming out in us. That there was more and more as she got older. She thought maybe it was because there was more of it that Ruth couldn't defend herself. It hadn't been that way when she was young, she said. She said back then there weren't many demons, but there were even fewer people who could fight them."

"So I'm *demon-powered*?" Nicky's voice cracked and Chris swore the whole house rattled with it.

Grandma snapped, "Sit down, boy, and eat. Get yourself grounded. It'll help."

"I'm gonna puke if I eat."

"That'll ground you too," she said unsympathetically. "Sit."

Nick met Chris's eyes, then nodded, still not much more than a tremor. Chris let him go and Nick all but dropped into his chair, falling so fast Chris wished he hadn't let him go. "'s'okay," Nick grated. "'s'okay. 'm okay." He didn't bother with a fork, just picked up an applesauced-biscuit and shoved the whole thing into his mouth.

Half a second later he looked like he wished he hadn't, but it was too late by then. He chewed his way through it as Chris cautiously sat, ready to jump to Nicky's aid again if necessary.

"You eat too," Grandma said.

"I'm gonna p—" He cut himself off, pretty sure she'd tell him the same thing she'd just told Nick, and instead ate a bite of applesauce and biscuit.

His appetite came back and for a couple minutes he and Nick ate without speaking. Grandma watched them, apparently until she was sure they wouldn't stop until they'd had their fill, before saying, "You boys already knew your mother was ill. There didn't seem any point in explaining the terrible details, not when you were meant to be kept out of it all. I thought your damn father was *bounty* hunting, and that was bad enough, but…."

"He said somebody had to take the freak bounties," Nick said roughly. "Somebody who knew what was really out there. So he did it, because he knew."

"And he still wouldn't bring you boys to me." Grandma's voice was filled with contained rage. "I'm sorry. I should have come and taken you."

A twist of regret hurt Chris's chest. He shoved it down, trying to breathe past it, and muttered, "Spilt milk, Grandma. You didn't know. Neither did we."

"Why didn't he tell us?" Nick sounded young and lost. "I mean, why didn't he at least train us better, if there were angels and demons and shit to hunt?"

"I dunno if it even matters, Nicky. Tracking skills are tracking skills, right?"

"Tracking an angel is tracking a falcon on a cloudy day level shit, Chris."

"Yeah, all right, you're not wrong." Chris put his fork down and rubbed a hand over his forehead. "Grandma, is…is there anything else you can tell us about Mom? Did she have the same kind of power Nick does?"

"I blow shit up," Nick supplied grimly, when Grandma looked like she'd ask.

"Then no. She seemed possessed, Nick. I'm sorry, but it's true. Like something dark would find its way into her, and eventually leave again. Not leave. Be burned out. She did have that power."

"Only dark things?" Nick asked hollowly, beneath that.

Grandma shook her head slowly, like she didn't know, not like the answer was no. "Mom believed the dark things came to Ruth because she was a beacon they couldn't resist. She would burn them up eventually, but Mom didn't understand that. She thought Ruth should just be able to fight them immediately, be able to…"

"Exorcise them?" Chris asked, and Grandma shrugged.

"She called it something else, but yes. But Ruthie never could, and finally something she couldn't burn away got into her."

Nick, grimly, said, "Was she pregnant with me then?"

Grandma sat back, surprise washing over her face. "I don't know, Nick. I don't think so, but she was strong. Maybe she hid it for a long time. Or maybe she didn't know. My mother said they were insidious, those things that took over human bodies and fed on their souls."

Chris said, "Jesus," to his biscuits, and Nick gave a short, dark laugh of agreement, then raised his head to look at Grandma again.

"Is that why you moved way out here after Grandpa died? To get away from those kinds of things? From that legacy?"

"I tried." The old lady sighed. "I should have come for you boys. I'm sorry."

"It's not your fault, Grandma." Chris looked at Nick. "But what the hell do we do now?"

"I can't hurt anybody out here. Maybe I should stay."

"Well, then, I'm staying with you. But you can't stay out here forever, Nicky, you're gonna go be a doctor."

"Just what people are gonna want, Chris, a doctor who accidentally blows shit up with demon magic."

"Grendel power," Chris said sharply. A little to his surprise, Nicky dropped his gaze, then nodded.

"You're welcome to stay," Grandma said. "I still think Chris ought to come out and see to that cow."

Chris laughed roughly. "Just like that? All back to normal?"

"That's the thing about life, my boy. It keeps coming, so you might as well adapt to whatever is happening as normal."

"Yeah, I'm not sure I've got that much philosophy to spare." Chris bared his teeth and stood. "Look, I'm gonna go call Lauren and see if there's any work coming up. I could use something that wasn't full-on crazy pants." He left the table to Nick asking Grandma something about the burning it up thing. The dog followed him into the bedroom and sat to watch as Chris put in his call.

Lauren picked up with her usual, "On Call Bail Bonds, what can I do for you?"

"Hey, Lauren, it's Chris Cassidy."

"Chris, hey, honey. How are you holding up?"

"I could really use some work to take my mind off everything."

"Mmm." She went quiet a minute, although he could hear paperwork and then the clicking of her keyboard. "You sure? I do have a job, if you want it. Dumb-ass kid who skipped bail on her third felony drug charge and disappeared."

"Third offense. So that's some real money." He sat on the bed, waving to the dog, who came over and puts his head under Chris's hand.

"You know I always try to give you the good ones, Chris."

"'cause I'm your fave."

"Because you're my fave," she agreed with an audible smile. Then her voice gentled. "You sure about this?"

"Yeah. There's a lot of shit going on and I just need some work to get my head out of it."

"If you say so." She hesitated before hanging up. "You and your brother doing okay, Chris?"

A spasm of grief hit him so hard he was abruptly glad he'd called, instead of video-phoning. "As good as we can be," he said in a voice gone suddenly tight. "Thanks for asking."

"Gimme a call if you ever just need to talk," Lauren offered quietly. "Or come on down to Denver and I'll buy you a drink."

"Might take you up on that," Chris said, still hoarsely. "Thanks."

"All right. I'll send those files on now."

"Thanks." Chris dropped the phone on the bed and the dog leaned against his knees, rolling its eyes up at him sympathetically. "Hey. That's a good boy. Who's a good boy, huh?" Chris lowered his head against the animal's furry shoulders, concentrating on its smell and warmth as he tried to get ahold of himself.

"Chris?" Nick stood in the doorway, sounding worried.

"'m fine. Lauren's got work for me."

Nick sighed. "Okay. I'll tell Grandma we're leaving this afternoon."

"What? Nick, no—"

"Well, I'm not staying up here twiddling my thumbs, Chris, and I don't think she knows any more secrets that are going to help me figure this out."

Chris dropped his head again, trying to decide if he had a headache or just felt like he should. "What'd you think about all that," he said in a low voice. "About grendel stuff being demon-powered. Or maybe angel, I guess, 'cause there was sure as shit an angel after us."

"A desanctified one," Nicky said harshly. "Whatever it did

206

to me, or found in me, it wasn't good news, Chris. I mean, I believe it. What else can I do? Grandma said Mom used to be able to burn them out, kind of. That she'd kind of fill up with light and the possession would burn away. That's what happened to you when you got hurt. Or when Shy was working on, you, anyway."

"I filled up with light?" Chris lifted his head incredulously.

"Maybe you got the angel powers and I'm a fucking demon."

"Man, if either of us is gonna be an angel, it sure as shit isn't me."

"The thing is, does it even really matter? I still have to control it, right? And I can't go back to school until I'm in control, so I might as well go with you."

"Yeah, but Nick, up here there's nothing for you to—"

"Hurt?" The word came out like a knife, cutting at Chris for having the nerve to even start down that path. "No, just Grandma and some cows and the dog, right? I'm not gonna be any use in the world if I can't go anywhere except a ranch on the edge of nowhere, Chris. So I might as well go with you and get a handle on this thing and, I dunno, move on with life."

"Did killing Saboac level you up?"

Nick leaned back, like the question had been an attack. "What?"

"Are you stronger now than you were before?"

"I..." A frown line appeared between Nick's eyebrows and he pushed his hand through his hair. "I don't know. I did some of the repairs with the grendel power, but that was, like, practice. I was seeing if I could do something without losing my temper."

"Are you still hearing it?"

Nick's gaze skittered away, then came back defiantly. "No."

"Dude, don't fucking lie to me."

"Well, I'm not! Not...like before." He closed his eyes, rocking against the door frame. "The creek water, all deep and cold and fast and dark and able to sweep me away? That's what the power felt like." His eyes opened again and guilt creased his face. "I'm glad you came out to find me. Something...I think something was going wrong out there. But you stopped it. You stopped me." He rubbed his chest like he didn't know he was doing it, and took a deep breath. "I can still feel something in me. It's not as uncontrolled, though. I was just freaked out at Emerson's cabin, right? And at the trailer when Saboac hurt you. It was all panic and adrenaline and a storm inside me. But it's colder now. Calmer. Maybe stronger, yeah, I don't know. Like I could..."

Worry spiked in his gaze, making him look a lot older all of a sudden. "Like I could do some really terrible shit and not even care very much. Or at all, maybe."

"Well, that's not gonna happen. First because you wouldn't, and second because I won't let you."

"Yeah." Nicky refocused on him. "So I gotta go with you."

Chris squinted, then waved a hand. "Okay, you won that one somehow, but don't let it go to your head."

Nick produced a lopsided smile. "No way, man, I'm putting that down in the calendar. 'Today Chris said I won a round.' I'll be buying drinks to toast myself every anniversary of this date for the rest of my life."

"And I'll be buying 'em to drown my sorrows for letting it slip." Chris's phone buzzed and he picked it up, scrolling through the incoming email. "Daddy's little rich girl, it looks like. Rich enough to buy off bail but dumb enough to keep getting caught running drugs."

"Rich means hard to find," Nick protested.

"Rich *could* mean hard to find, but dumb usually means pretty easy to find. I can do it myself and come ba—"

"No."

Chris looked up at the set of his brother's jaw, then back at the phone. "So I'll tell her we're taking it?"

"I don't know, Chris, lemme see the files first. I'll get my computer. Easier to type in search stuff that way."

"Some of us have joined the modern world and use voice recognition."

"Some of us think we're real fucking funny."

Chris grinned at his phone. "Some of us do. That is true. Some of us are right, too."

Nick threw an imaginary object at him and Chris batted it away, grinning. About forty minutes of research and cross-referencing later, he texted Lauren to say they'd take the job, and went out to the kitchen to find out Grandma had packed up enough food to last them two days on the road. "It doesn't take a genius to realize you were leaving," she said to Chris's surprised protest. "I want you boys to come back soon, though, do you hear me?"

"We will." Chris folded the old lady into a hug and held on until she smacked his shoulder and made him let go.

"You'd better get going, if you're going to. I expect you've got a long way to travel. I wish you'd find a job that would let you settle down, Christopher."

"I'm good at this, Gramma."

"You're good at it because it's the only thing you've ever tried."

"Jeez, have you been talking to Nicky or something?"

"Not about this." She handed him a bag of food and he went out to the van as Nick came in to say goodbye. The dog followed him mournfully, as if they'd been best friends forever, and watched sadly from the porch when they drove off.

"There's an off-the-books property in Idaho that her Dad's second ex-wife has the title to." Nick had his computer in his lap and the wifi hooked up to his phone, after bitching that Chris didn't have a hotspot set up in the van. "She's got social media pictures from there, hashtag secret hideaway."

"Subtle," Chris said. "Anything recent?"

"Does a livestream count?" Nick turned the computer screen toward him and Chris glanced over to see a woman about his own age in a hot tub, waving champagne at her phone.

"Doesn't that just look like the life," he said under his breath. "Think Daddy's girl will marry me if I promise not to turn her in? I don't need much, just alimony and a beach house."

The camera turned to a young man also in the hot tub, and Chris shrugged, bringing his eyes back to the road. "Oh well, a guy could hope."

"Looks like that's her brother," Nick said after a minute. "For what it's worth."

"As long as it gets me the alimony, sure, I'll marry him instead. I'll even wear white to the wedding."

Nick cackled and turned the screen back toward himself. "Every bride deserves to wear white, eh?"

"Damn straight. All right, where we going? Idaho, right?"

"Practically on the border, yeah. Who the hell goes to hide out in northern Idaho?"

"Rich people, I guess. It's way up on Upper Priest Lake, dude, I'm not even sure you can drive there."

Chris shot him a look. "Then how the hell do you get there?"

"I dunno, a boat? Float plane?"

"Well, fuck, Nick, can you fly a float plane?"

"No I cannot," Nick said, almost cheerfully. "Guess we'll have to cross that lake when we come to it. Except I guess we'll have to go around it, really. This drive is gonna be like Lombard Street."

"Like *what*?"

"That really crooked street at the top of the hill in San Francisco."

"Oh. Oh, yay, great. Boy, she better come easily after what it'll take to get to her."

Nick said something under his breath and Chris, pretty sure he didn't really want to know, said, "What?"

"Nothin', I just thought getting girls to come easily was part of your charm."

Chris leaned over to turn the radio way, way up, drowning out Nick's laughter with the music, and refused to turn it down until they'd been on the road a good couple hours. Nicky finally yelled, "I'm gonna get some of the lunch Grandma packed us," and Chris had to turn the music down so he could say, "I'll find somewhere to pull over," without bellowing.

Nick still looked pleased with himself as they parked the van, which was annoying and a relief all at the same time. It was *normal*, that's what it was, and even if everything was fucked up, Nick acting normal helped, even if it was at Chris's own expense. He bounced out of the passenger seat and into the back of the van before Chris had even killed the engine, saying, "I still can't believe you did this whole thing, Chris, it's so cool," from behind him. "Is there beer in the fridge?"

"You're not twenty-one for like three months, Nick."

"That doesn't answer the question, and you've been giving me beers since I was twelve." Nick opened the fridge as Chris crawled through the seats onto the bed. "Dude, there's no beer in here."

"I don't usually take her out in the winter. She's not stocked the way she would be in June or something."

"Yeah, no, that makes sense, no real clearance. Is she gonna be okay driving up to the lakes?"

"As long as the roads are maintained, yeah, probably. I mean, I'm not taking her 4-bying."

"Speaking of which." Nick settled down with a plate of food and waved one foot in the air. "I'm gonna need boots if we're trekking up to collect this girl. I can't hike through snow in sneakers."

"Wish you'd thought of that back at the trailer."

"I did. All my old boots are too small for me. So's the rest of my winter gear. We can hit a Goodwill or something and see if we can find anything to fit me."

"So you're telling me we're not going to get up to Priest Lake tonight 'cause we gotta drive into every podunk town between here and there to see if they've got a decent thrift shop?"

"I can look online so we don't have to drive around *everywhere*." Nicky sounded a little offended.

"You could call anywhere that looked promising and ask, too."

Nick recoiled. "Call? With a *phone*? And my *voice*?"

Chris grinned. "Yeah, yeah, I know. It's the worst."

"It's a good idea, though." He finished eating and scrolled through his phone, obviously searching for thrift shops, and even called a few. "Good news. There's a Goodwill in Ponderay that's gotten a bunch of men's winter gear in recently. They'll put the boots aside for me. And it's on the way, but we gotta get there before five or we'll have to stay there overnight."

Chris glanced at the time and muttered. "We'll probably just about make it. I'd rather camp out closer to the lake and get an early start, if we're gonna hafta hoof it up there."

"Yeah. Sorry."

"Yeah, well, the cushy college boy life in Cali doesn't really need winter boots, does it." Chris crawled back into the driver's seat and headed west again. And south. And north. And west. And way the hell south, until he said, out loud and uselessly, "Why'd they have to put all these fucking mountains in the way, anyway."

"Builds character."

"Builds continents, anyway."

Nick laughed. "We're almost there, anyway, and we can get the stuff and head…"

"Farther south," Chris said, glancing at the map.

Nick wrinkled his face. "But then we get to go north?"

"Very exciting. I know we were going this way anyway, but it better be worth it."

Maybe an hour later, looking at the sleek 'neon sunset' printed snowsuit that the thrift shop had proudly brought out for Nick, Chris, straight-faced, said, "It's worth it."

"Oh, shut up."

"It's very you."

"I said shut up!"

"I can't imagine why anyone would want to get rid of that."

"Chris, I said shut up!"

"Too bad about the boots, though." They were solid brown workman-style winter boots, not unlike the ones Chris owned. But Chris's snow gear was brown and black, not neon blue shot with florescent purple and orange skyscapes.

"Chris, I swear to God…"

"At least I won't lose you in the woods," Chris said cheerfully. "Or in the dark. Or in a cave. Or—"

"Caves *are* dark! And it's not my fault this is all they had that would fit me!"

"Oh, no, it's not your fault. It's not anybody's fault. It's a *gift*."

"Ugh! I hate you, man!"

"Yeah," Chris said happily. "I know. Now get in the van, we've got another hundred miles to drive." He headed around to the driver's side, singing *True Colors*, and the snowball he caught to the back of the head was absolutely worth it.

# CHAPTER 15

TECHNICALLY, NICK GUESSED, *TECHNICALLY* YOU COULD DRIVE most of the way to Upper Priest Lake. In summer, anyway. In winter you had to park at a comparatively nearby park'n'ski, which hadn't even been something he'd known existed, and then hike a couple miles up to the campground you could drive to in the summer.

*Then* you got to hike another couple miles, or take a boat, up the still-water thoroughfare to the actual lake, but there were no boats in the winter and Chris gave him a filthy look when he suggested ice skates. Nick kept grinning about that, even if it made Chris pissier. The thoroughfare wasn't kept clear, so there'd be too much snow for skating, but Chris's expression was funny anyway. He had *not* been happy about driving Lucille up increasingly blue roads to get to the park'n'ski in the first place, and having to get up and hike four miles before he even got to the lake that he also had to hike halfway around to get to his quarry was not improving his mood.

Nick had to say *his* morning, on the other hand, was going pretty great. Even the potshots about his ski suit—Chris kept calling him 'Sunset Boulevard' weren't landing. He did eventually say, "Shut up, Chris. Look around and enjoy being outdoors," which surprised his brother into silence for a few minutes.

Just a few, though. After a bit, Chris started muttering again about soft California lifestyles and how he got plenty of time outdoors and a bunch of other shit that started to get on Nick's nerves. Something—not anger, exactly, but something dark started crawling up his spine, like oil seeping into his thoughts and blackening them. It followed his nerves and blood vessels and spilled gradually through his whole body, filling him with—not Saboac's voice. Not again. Flashes of fire, of wings, like if he extended his hands he might see the flames in his palms, or fiery feathers if he hunched his shoulders. "Chris, stop."

Chris, obviously satisfied he was finally getting under Nick's skin, *didn't* stop, of course, because bitching about being inconvenienced by the hike and half-blinded by the snowsuit was—well, it was a way to take his mind off a hard, sweaty slog through a couple feet of snow, really. Nick knew that, but it didn't help, any more than trying to focus on a step at a time was helping. Inverse color kept switching in, outlining the shapes of their steps in the snow, or turning trees into white shapes against a black sky.

After a while, Chris fell silent, more, Nick thought, because breaking trail was difficult work than out of any concern for Nick's feelings. It helped less than he'd hoped, the sensation of filling with darkness and the flashes of inverted colors still plaguing him. "Chris, I don't feel right."

To his brother's credit, he stopped immediately, bitchiness fading into concern. "Talk to me, Nicky. What's up? Is it Saboac?"

"Maybe? I feel wrong," Nick said miserably. "Color keeps going inside out and I feel like I need to—hit something? But not with my hands, with..." He made a short motion with one hand and watched a blur of power, like sticky black tar, smear after it. "Did you see that?"

To his surprise, Chris said, "Yeah," in a low voice. "Yeah, it looked kinda like cutting a hole in the sky. There were stars inside. Nick, maybe you better go back to the van."

"I don't want to be alone." Nick could have swallowed his own tongue, but an awful look of grown-up weariness shadowed his brother's face.

"Yeah, no, that seems legit. All right, look, why don't we sit down for a while? Wait it out. And I'll stop being such a dick," Chris conceded grimly.

"You already did. It didn't help." Nick did sit down, though, just straight into the snow, which was heavy enough to make a stab at supporting him before it gradually gave way to his weight. Chris sat, too, but didn't sag so much, so he was surrounded by it like the back and arms of a throne.

Except a throne should be metal or wood or something, Nick guessed. Something ostentatious, proclaiming the importance of the person sitting in it. It should have a dais, and light, and stairs rising toward it, so anyone approaching would appreciate their lowliness, how they were inherently unworthy to be in the presence of—

Power flooded out of him, a thick ugly rush of darkness that made him dizzy, and Chris blurted, "What the fuck, Nicky?!" as the snow he sat in reshaped itself. Compacted, almost to ice, with cloudy blue shades in its depths. It crumbled almost as fast as it came together, a throne made of little more than snow and imagination, but it changed enough that Chris scrambled to his feet, brushing its remains away and staring at Nick.

A patch of wet frozen earth, all alone in an otherwise snowy landscape, lay where Chris had been sitting. Not a big patch, maybe about the circumference of Nick's arms, if he made a circle with them. About as big as Chris had been, sitting there in the snow.

"Sure," he said aloud, much more to the damp earth than his brother. "Only the snow you were touching transmuted. To make a real throne it would have taken a lot more."

"What the hell are you talking about, Nick? What throne? What the hell?" Chris waved his hand in front of Nick's face, breaking his locked gaze from the ground. He snapped his attention up to Chris, then crushed his eyes closed, trying not to shudder.

"I thought you looked like you were sitting a throne. And then I think I tried to make one. The...I don't feel as sick anymore."

"Oh, well, that's..." Chris's silence suggested he was thinking better of saying 'good' or 'better,' and after a moment he finished with, "...fucked up," which at least made Nick cough laughter.

"Yeah it is. I think...do you have water?"

"Yeah, man." Chris got a bottle from his pack and handed it over without reminding Nick that he was carrying a couple himself. Nick drank most of it before he remembered, but when he started an apology, Chris cut him off. "You good to go?"

"I think so. Just..."

"Don't be a dick. Yeah, yeah, I got it. Arright, c'mon, Nicky. Let's get you up." Chris offered a hand and pulled Nick to his feet, winced at getting an eyeful of Nick's snowsuit, and visibly checked himself from commenting. Instead, with equally visible effort, he said, "You good?" again.

"Yeah. Yeah, I'm good."

"Right, well, I guess if you start building up grendel power again maybe you could blast a path through the snow so we can walk easier instead of building a snow palace or whatever."

"My frozen soul in flying fractals all around, huh?"

"Man, you do not know the right lyrics to *anything.*" Chris shook his head and struck out again, moving faster after the brief respite. Maybe moving faster so they could get the job over and done with, Nick figured. So Chris could go back to figuring out what the hell to do with his fucked-up baby brother. Bleak tendrils attached themselves to that thought, and Nick shook them off almost literally, with a sharp jerk of his head. Do *for* his fucked-up baby brother, maybe, but not 'with.' Their dad had been the one who didn't know what to do *with* him.

"Nicky?"

"I'm good."

"Lemme know if you're not." Chris fell back after a while, letting Nick break snow. He squelched the impulse to see if he *could* draw on the grendel power, more afraid he'd be able to than not, and just did it the hard way, one step at a time, although once he fell and broke through six feet of snow with a thump, leaving Chris laughing in the background. "Dude, if I could just flip you end over end this would go a lot faster."

"Like a cartoon," Nick agreed, grinning as he brushed snow off his suit and kept going. It took longer than either of them wanted to reach the lake, with Chris casting a quick, grim look at the sky, and then the time. "It'll be faster going back," Nick offered. "We won't have to break the trail."

"Maybe they'll have snowmobiles we can…borrow."

"Pretty sure 'borrowing' a bounty's property goes beyond any of the legal grey areas bail bondsmen get to exploit, dude."

"I won't tell if you don't." Chris had taken the lead again, and groaned suddenly with relief. "There's a trail up there, along the lake. That'll speed us up. How far was it?"

"Couple more miles. The whole upper lake's only a couple-three miles long anyway."

"Well, which is it, a couple or three, because if it's a couple miles farther and a two mile lake then we're gonna be off the lake before we find the place."

"Pedant," Nick muttered. "Lake's about three miles on this side, the other side's longer, so it's a couple miles."

"I'm not a pedant!"

"A pedant, dude, not a pedo. A pedant nitpicks irrelevant or boring details."

Chris said, "Oh," sullenly, and Nick grinned, betting Chris couldn't decide which was worse, that he'd gotten the word wrong or Nick had known what he actually meant. He didn't ask, though, and another forty minutes of less-hard slogging along the already-broken trail brought them to an A-frame house just about literally a stone's throw from the water's edge.

They slowed on the approach, sticking to the cover of trees, although the land had only been cleared enough for the house, and had no significant yard space either in front or behind it. A broad deck—the site of the hot tub—covered what might have otherwise been the front yard, with stairs down to the ground and a mostly-cleared pathway to the frozen water, where a skinny iceboat was lashed to a dock. Chris said, "Oh, I am *definitely* taking that," and Nick couldn't even blame him.

"Yeah, I'd take the house, too." Warm yellow light blazed through every window, and the front of the house was all window, casting gold shadows on blue-white snow. Open stairs swept up from a huge living-dining area, with a professional-grade kitchen gleaming under the interior lighting. The front half of the house didn't have an obvious second floor, just an open, partially floored area the stairs swung through on their way up to what had to be the master bedroom overlooking the lake.

"I mean, it's not too late," Chris said. "We could just go propose to Dumb and Dumber in there and live the rest of our lives as kept men."

"I'm having a hard time seeing the downside of that, yeah. What if they say no, though?"

Chris shrugged. "Then I guess we arrest them. That's a totally reasonable response to rejection, right?"

Nick laughed. "Yeah, maybe it's no surprise you don't have a girlfriend. All right, what's the plan?"

"I was gonna go knock on the front door and get down on one knee and ask the first person who answers to marry me."

"Uh-huh. And what am I gonna do?"

"You're gonna go around to the back door so when they run, it's straight into your arms. You can propose if you want, that's cool. We'll be brother-husbands or something, it won't be weird at all."

Nick ducked his head, trying to keep his laughter quiet. "You don't quit, do you, man."

"And that's the actual reason I don't have a girlfriend. They just can't keep up with me. We ready?"

"You know they're gonna flip out," Nick said. "They think they're all alone up here."

"Which is why you're taking the back door," Chris said patiently. "I give it seventy-thirty odds they don't even open the front door."

"Pretty sure their only getaway vehicle is that skimmer."

"Dude, this girl has been arrested like eight times as a drug mule. I don't think unbelievable genius is one of her selling points."

"Must be nice to be rich," Nick said under his breath as they stepped out of the tree cover and split up. Chris gave him a moment to get halfway behind the house, then jogged out of sight, although his footsteps creaked audibly on the snow-covered deck stairs for a moment.

———

Somebody—Chris was willing to put a small bet on it not being the two rich kids in the house—had been shoveling the walk and deck regularly. Not all of it: a couple feet of snow lined the way to the hot tub, the door, and the path. But enough that either there was a third or even fourth person at the house—cook, groundskeeper, maybe somebody who did both—or someone came in regularly to do the dirty work. Better if it was the second one, and he probably should have talked it out with Nick, done some more recon to see if there was evidence of a third party around the place before they split up.

That kind of reckless shit had gotten their dad dead.

Chris hit the door probably harder than he needed to, trying to shove that thought off. The triple-paned glass, good for keeping the place warm when the front was all windows like that, rattled under the force of his blows. Somebody inside shrieked and he tried the door, finding out *after* he'd announced himself that it was unlocked and he could have just gone right in. Dammit, he sucked. This could've all been over with his bond in handcuffs before she even knew he was there, but instead he was making a hash of things, just like always. Guilt rose in a tidal wave and he buried it, as always, with the anger, crushing the doubt and fear as best he could.

By that time he was inside, yelling the usual bullshit about being a bail bondsman and how it'd be better if she didn't make things worse and just came with him. Instead her stupid brother came charging out from the back of the house and actually tried to tackle him. Chris waited until he was almost on top of him, stepped aside, and stuck his foot out.

The brother tripped and smeared himself face-first across the hardwood floor. Chris clicked his tongue. "Now, see, you're not gonna be able to do a video for your followers for days, dude, you messed up your pretty face. Although, I dunno, I guess you could film yourself from the neck down or something, they'd probably be into that? You look pretty stacked, not that I'm checking you out or anything." He shook himself, trying to break the flow of verbal diarrhea. He was usually mouthy, but this felt like he couldn't stop himself from verbalizing every feeling that ran through him. Nick would probably say he needed therapy. "Anyway, where's your sister?"

"What the hell is wrong with you?" A woman's voice, breaking over his shouting, although he hadn't meant to be shouting. He turned away from the guy sprawled on the floor to find the bounty on the stairs above him, her hair wild and fury radiating off her in almost visible waves.

"Kayleigh Dawn Parker? I'm here to bring you to justice." Damn, all he needed was a ten-gallon hat and bow legs and he could walk right into a Western. A twist of something that bordered on laughter spiraled through him, pulling his veneer of anger with it in corkscrew turns. He clawed back at it, preferring the anger to everything underneath, and snarled, "Come on, bitch, this is gonna end with you in cuffs anyway so why don't you just come down here." The words tasted bad, bitter and wrong in his mouth.

She smirked. "Your mama know you call women names like that?"

"I *don't*." He didn't. Cheyenne would clock him. All the Geography Girls would, and he'd deserve it. But he didn't, even if they *wouldn't* belt him one.

He didn't, because his dad would have.

"Sure you do," Kayleigh said. "I just heard you. What are you, some kind of scared little dick who can't control his temper and has to hunt women down to feel big? Fucking pathetic. Get out of my house." Her eyes blazed with right-eous fury, and Chris buckled under the overwhelming sense that she'd nailed him, she knew him inside and out, that there wasn't anything under his shield of anger but more anger. She knew he carried that shield so he could hide behind it, so nobody could see there wasn't anything else to him. Chris Cassidy, anger machine.

"No…" Well, he sure as shit didn't believe that protest. Miss Kayleigh with her frothy hair and big eyes wasn't gonna, either, much less her brother, who was groaning now and trying to get to his hands and knees. Chris put his foot in the small of the brother's back and flattened him again. "Stay down."

"Kayleeeiiiigh." The brother's whine could set a monk's teeth on edge. Chris drew his foot back, ready to kick him, then forced himself a couple of steps backward instead, lifting his hands to his temples.

His mind was *boiling*. His head actually felt too hot, like a shitstorm of conflicting emotion would explode through in a mess of blood and brains and shards of glass, every one of them carrying some fucked-up bit of feelings, so regret could pierce its way into fear that would slice into uncertainty that would cut so deep that the anger would start to bleed until he couldn't risk anything more being exposed because he might just die of it. He should have just fucking called Nicky, but he'd been, he'd been scared, so scared he wouldn't come to the funeral that trying to drive him away was safer, yeah, even if that cut at *him* as bad as it did Nick, he should have *been* there for their dad, shouldn't have let him get killed in the first place, should never have helped Nicky go to goddamn California, shouldn't have said no back when Jake asked him t—

Somehow he'd dropped to his knees, still holding his head. His scalp was so hot his hands felt cool against it, but somewhere in the cacophony of guilt and anger he heard himself say, "No," out loud, in a voice that sounded almost normal.

No, he definitely *should* have helped Nick get to Cali, to get out of this stupid fucking awful life. He hated it. God, he hated it, he missed Nick like he'd miss his own heartbeat, but if there was one right thing he'd ever done in his own disaster of a life, it was getting his little brother out of it. Yeah, he still wanted him back more than just about anything, he *hated* not talking to him, but that was on himself, too, he could have sent a fucking text instead of trying to suck it up and be a *man* about it all, being a *man* about this kind of thing was their father's bullshit, not—

"Oh, it's you," Kayleigh said from up close, and there were fingers in his mind, trawling for those easy spikes of emotion. Dragging them up, tangling them together, until the world went white with pain and confusion.

It wasn't him. That was a thin line to hold on to, nothing against the weight of freak power scrambling his skull, but it was something. Kaleigh was a freak, a grendel, not one of the all-out monsters like the vampires or whatever, but like Nick, human but…gifted. Cursed. Powered, anyway, whether for good or bad.

Definitely bad, Chris thought, and it felt like something of a triumph, having a thought of his own. In this case, the grendel power was definitely bad. Or at least, how it was being used was bad.

Too bad that didn't help one good god damn little bit at all. Guilt surged through him, drowning out every other memory, tainting anything it touched, and where guilt couldn't reach, anger or fear did, until it felt like there wasn't anything left. Black dog on his shoulder, turning decent memories murky and bringing worse ones to the front. He wanted to scream the way he had at the funeral pyre, and couldn't even tell if he did or not.

It was cold. Colder than it had been, making his head and face feel hotter still. It felt good in his lungs, though, cutting and sharp, clearing them until he didn't feel like he was drowning in emotion inside his own body. If the rest of him could get cold, he might be okay. He knelt, not really sure if it was his own idea, but there was ice under his hands, and that helped too. The impulse to smash his hands against the ice rose, faltered, and strengthened again, although the first crash of his fists told him it was way, way too thick there. He'd never break through. If he could get his head under it, though, into the cold water, the sensation of boiling his own brain might stop, and that would help. He got up again, following an ideation that felt both intrusive and like a huge fucking relief, toward the distance.

Not just following it. Running after it, like something was after him. That black dog, maybe, its weight starting to crack the ice as he ran. Part of him was screaming now, probably not the out-loud part, but part of him didn't like what he was doing, and the rest of him said *nah, it's fine, keep going,* in a way that didn't use words, just overwhelming, convincing emotion.

The ice snapped, radial crack beneath his foot, whiter cloudy lines shooting through the its wider translucent body, and black water seeped over the fresh lines. Even the black dog couldn't keep him moving forward then, a survival instinct shrieking inside him, freezing him in place. Another horrible crack sounded, and panic clawed at his mind, trying to get him to back up. He couldn't even do that, not even when the water crept toward the sole of his boot.

Right about then the mental fog cleared, the black dog backing off, as somewhere behind him Nick said, "Get your *fucking mind* off my brother," and made all the darkness stop.

———

The good news was nobody had tried to use the back door as an escape route. The bad news was, it was locked and Nick spent a couple precious minutes looking for a key before wondering if he could just…break it. He'd put nails through wood, using the grendel power. Breaking a door lock couldn't be that much harder. Or at all harder. And the power was there, waiting, without any siryn songs of warning or darkness tangling up in it. Nick took a breath, put his hand on the knob, and turned it with all his strength, trying to back it up with the power.

It screeched under his hand and the whole lock dislodged inside the door, twisting and breaking into pieces. Nick stared at it a couple of seconds, then shook the bits free of his hand

and pushed the door open, stepping inside as quietly as he could.

Because silence was important after making metal scream with his bare hands. He mumbled something not even he could understand at himself and crept forward, listening toward the front of the house. Chris was out there, talking— arguing—yelling at—somebody, probably the bounty. The door between the front and back halves of the house was closed, presumably trapping warmth in the front, because the air in the back felt somehow both thick and cold as shit. There were skis for both snow and water in the dimness, boxes, various warm-weather gear, like this room was meant primarily for storage. Nick glanced around, looking for some-thing weapon-like, because if there was one thing snowsuits weren't good at, it was making weaponry easily accessible.

Fishing poles. A badminton set that looked like it had never been opened, which made sense because there was nowhere to play badminton here. Same with the croquet set, like somebody had an idea of what a hideaway house should have in it, without any concession to where the house was situated. There was a telescope with enough dust on it to suggest it hadn't been used since it was purchased, too. Nick thought he'd spend every night with that thing set up, if he lived on a lake thirty miles from the nearest meaningful light pollution, but maybe being rich meant not appreciating the stars, he didn't know.

In the meantime, at least he could hit something with the croquet hammers, if he had to. He opened the package, took one out, and went forward as Chris's voice faded.

The damn interior door was locked, too. Nick stared at the handle a moment, irritated. Locking even one exterior door seemed ridiculous for the only house on the lake. Locking an interior door spoke to a kind of paranoia that made no sense at all. It wasn't as if anybody was going to break in out here.

Anybody except him and Chris, obviously. The irony, Nick thought, was palpable. He glanced around for a key, didn't find one—it was probably on the *other* side of the door —and broke the handle again, stepping through with what felt like a dramatic flourish.

There was no one in the front room.

For a couple of seconds Nick couldn't process that, even staring at the emptiness where only his own faintly neon reflection looked back at him from the windows. The windowed door stood open, but the air in here felt thick, too, like it had in the back room. Thick and hard to breathe, like mugginess hung in the cold air, carrying a bad taste into the back of his throat. The bounty's brother—Nick couldn't remember his name from social media—stood on the deck, looking over the lake. The bounty herself was on the dock, which stretched several feet out over the frozen water.

And Chris was out in the middle of the fucking lake.

Panic and anger spilled through Nick in equal parts, clawing for dominance, and the bounty turned toward him as if she knew he was there. Her eyes looked bright under the cloudy sky, like the snow was reflected in them. Panic won out, clutching Nick's chest with a spiked grip, crushing his lungs like the thick air couldn't be breathed, and the croquet mallet fell from fingers gone suddenly numb. The bounty turned away, now smiling with a satisfaction visible even at the distance. Chris took a few more steps out there on the ice, then braced, arms going wide as the ice began to change color as water spilled over it.

Mindless terror shot through Nick, liquifying his guts and turning the protest he started into a tiny, frightened sound. The air weighed him down, disintegrating his ability to think, leaving overwhelming emotion in thought's place. He'd been scared before; he'd been miserable with fear, even paralyzed with uncertainty. But this felt external, like he was being pushed into a too-small space that he didn't belong in. He felt squeezed, almost the opposite of the grendel power erupting out of him.

That idea snaked through his mind, catching fire, waking that power and burning away the weight of fear, the weight of the *air*. The air wasn't heavy: the bounty's *magic* was. She was using grendel magic somehow, fucking with his mind. Fucking with Chris's mind, sending him out to where the ice grew dangerously thin.

He saw her realize it when he threw her enchantment off and burned it away. He could almost see the shape of her magic: it was the tendrils that had sunk into Chris's mind, the thin whip-like strands that had tried to seize his own mind, but lost their grip when they met *his* magic. Nick chased those strands back, following the shape and the form, studying them as he stalked onto the deck with rage and retribution on his mind. The bounty's brother yelled, either warning his sister or trying to scare Nick off, but brushing his attack away was effortless, thoughtless, a swing of unseen force that knocked him into the snow piled across the deck's surface. A few more long strides took Nick to the dock, and by then the bounty had turned away from Chris, her hands curling as she faced Nick.

She knew how to use the magic she commanded. She lashed it at him in vicious coils, searching for an entry point to his mind. He followed them back, finding vulnerable points in her own mind. She was scared of going to jail, of losing her cushy life, of the people she ran drugs for. But she also didn't believe she would ever be caught, not permanently, because manipulating emotion was so very easy. Just as manipulating Chris's guilt was easy.

*That* was an easy thread for Nick to follow, that contemptuous pride she had in turning Chris's mind against himself. There was so much darkness buried under Chris's surface, it hardly took anything to set it free. Nick couldn't quite hear her thoughts. He could just feel—sense—her emotion, her strength of conviction in what she was doing. A flick of her hand sent another coil of weighted emotion toward Chris, and Nick heard himself snarl, "Get your *fucking mind* off my brother."

It wasn't so hard, really. Mostly just copying what she did, but he had more raw strength, the angel fire burning under his skin, dark streaks of magic eager to be used. Her talent folded under his, crumpling back into her mind, and the rest of her, he seized, making it impossible for her to move beyond breathing, beyond blinking. She was a marionette, a puppet, easy to manipulate. He could almost use the power like that, as strings, tugging at her foot, moving it forward. She made a terrible noise deep in her throat, rage and fear tangled up into one. The temptation to let her drown in her fear, the way she had nearly drowned Chris, the way she'd tried to drown *him*, rose in Nick's chest. All it took was chasing down the emotion, giving it more to feed on, and he could make someone do nearly anything. As could she. No wonder she kept getting away with her crimes, even if she kept getting caught.

Nick shuddered. All he needed to do was get her back to Denver for processing, not turn her own mind against her. She wasn't about to walk out of here under her own volition, though, and the iceboat was right there. Nick came down the deck steps toward her, hardly recognizing his own voice. "You can get in the boat or I can make you get in it."

For a heartbeat, he almost admired the defiance in her snarled, "*Make me.*"

In the next, another sound like a shot cracked across the ice as it weakened further, and the smug, superior sensation he'd been reveling in shattered. Alarm replaced it, followed by a bitter sort of appreciation for the woman's skill. She'd nearly had him again, more subtlety this time. She had *wanted* him to concentrate on her, because after a few seconds longer of focusing solely on her, the ice holding Chris would break.

Disappointed fury flashed across her face. Nick growled,

wrapping power around her in a way similar to how he'd held Saboac in the air: telekinesis, he guessed. She bellowed with outrage, trying to free herself from his psychic grip as he stalked out to the end of the dock to yell, "Chris?"

A low growl of Chris's own came back, carried only by the echoing ice and the thin winter air, like he was afraid an out-loud answer would send him into the water.

"I'm gonna grab you, Chris, like I did at the quarry." More like he was doing with the bounty, really, but it didn't seem like the time to explain all the details. Chris growled again and Nick stretched the grendel strength toward him, not actually certain it would reach that far. Maybe it didn't have to, or at least, maybe not enough to grab his brother. Maybe he could make a sheet that would slide under him, shore up the ice until Chris could get himself back to safer ground.

The ice cracked again, sending Chris lurching downward this time, and Nick forgot about the best way to do something, or testing his skills, in favor of dropping the grip he had on the bounty and grabbing for Chris with all the power at his disposal. Black water surged up as he yanked his brother forward, pulling him across the ice with grendel magic, until the bounty picked up the croquet mallet he'd dropped and hit him in the back with it.

Nick, bellowing with pain, dropped Chris and spun on the girl, who let go of the mallet and backed off. Power roared through him again and he grabbed her, much less carefully than he'd grabbed Chris, and marched her, shrieking and furious, into the iceboat. She thrashed on its floor, screeching, and he kept her pinned down with threads of power that looked back at him with burning eyes. Chris, sliding on the ice with wet feet, skidded to the dock a couple of seconds later, panting with effort and residual panic. "Dude, you okay?"

"Bitch hit me," Nick said through his teeth. "Right in the fuckin' ribs." He could already feel a bruise starting.

"Yeah. Good thing she didn't aim three inches lower and get your kidney."

Nick, wheezing, stared at his brother, who shrugged. "I'm just saying. If any of the Geography Girls had picked up that mallet you'd be a bloody pulp on the ground by now."

Despite the pain radiating near his spine, Nick gave a cracked laugh. "You're not wrong. Even Dayton would've hit harder, and not stopped. Go. Go. C'mon. Go get in the boat."

"What about the brother?"

Nick looked that way, at the kid—'kid,' like the guy wasn't probably older than he was—sitting up in the snowbank on the deck. "He can stay here. Somebody will come get him before it thaws."

A smirk twisted Chris's mouth and he nodded. A couple seconds later they were both in the iceboat, Nick unfurling the sail as Chris said, "How the hell do you know how to do that?" and almost literally sat on the still-shrieking bounty. "You shut up," he told her. "I've had enough mind-fuckery today."

"Stephanie's dad has a sailboat." Nick heard his own voice go tight and tried to loosen it, but at least Chris didn't push it. It took a minute or two, but he got the sail correctly situated and shoved the boat away from the dock. Metal scraped across ice, a low hiss that somehow sounded too much like Saboac. The bounty shrieked again, overpowering the sound. By the time she lost her voice, they were speeding down a channel of ice that the wind had blown more or less clear of snow.

Chris yelled, "We shoulda taken one of these up here!" gleefully as they sped past the trail they'd painstakingly broken.

"Well, if you'd thought of it…!" Nick's teeth got cold in the space of a grin, but it was worth the dirty look Chris shot him. Getting back to the campground where they'd started their snow-breaking hike from took almost no time, compared to the journey in; the ice, while too snowy for people on ice skates, was plenty clear for the iceboat's larger blades and greater speed.

And at least there was a more or less clear trail back to the park'n'ski. Their bounty—Kayleigh—kept shrieking about not being dressed for this, until Chris snapped, "You would have been if you'd just come with and not tried mind-fucking me."

"Oh, I didn't try, bitch," she said with a sniff. "You were full-on mind-fucked."

"I don't like her very much," Chris muttered to Nick, and stomped ahead, leaving Nick as a buffer between them.

A couple of times he felt tendrils of her power trying to catch hold of his emotions, and put up a wall that felt like cold flame between her attempts and himself. When her focus moved to Chris, Nick, in a low voice, said, "Don't even think about it."

Her gaze skittered off his uncomfortably, and she stopped.

It was still light when they got back to Lucille, and Chris dragged Nick aside, staring grimly at their bounty. "If we just hand her to local LEOs she'll manipulate her way out of custody before they can get her to court."

"Which means you won't get paid."

"We," Chris corrected. "But yeah. You don't have anything that'll knock her out for eighteen hours or so, do you?"

"Just the power of my mind."

Chris stared at him. "Can you do that?"

"I...don't know."

"Man, I do not think you should try."

"It'd make the trip back a lot easier." Nick lifted his eyebrows hopefully.

"Dude, that is one hundred percent the path to the Dark Side."

"Nah, that's fear."

"You telling me you're not afraid?"

Nick's breath caught in a hitch and he scowled, looking away. "I don't know."

"You frickin' well should be, if you're not."

"You're the one who told me I had to learn how to use it so I could *not* use it."

"I didn't mean by taking over people's brains!"

"She did!"

"Dude!" Chris threw his hands up. "If she jumped off a bridge, dude?"

"Oh, come on, that's not the same thing at all."

"It totally is. You," Chris snapped at Kayleigh. "Get in the van and, like, sit in the cast iron frying pan."

Both the bounty and Nick gaped at him. "What?"

"Iron's supposed to disrupt magic, right? It does in fairy tales, anyway, right?"

Nick, thoughtfully, said, "Well, fuck. That's a pretty good idea." He herded Kayleigh into the van and actually made her sit in, or at least on, Chris's frying pan while Chris, from the front seat, said, "Well?"

He could feel her grendel power stuttering and scraping, not entirely obstructed, but unquestionably disturbed. "Know what, I think it'll work? We should get some iron handcuffs if we're gonna run into more grendels."

The bounty's eyes flashed with suspicious interest. "Grendels?"

"Freaks like you and me."

She scowled, looking away, and muttered, "Grendels is cooler. I hate being a freak."

"Yeah. I get that." Nick lifted his voice. "C'mon, Chris. Let's get this done."

# CHAPTER 16

THE DRIVE BACK TOOK FOR-FRICKING-EVER, MOST OF A DAY even without stopping for food, bathroom breaks, or the sleep Chris so desperately needed. Lauren at the bond agency gave him a weird damn look when he told her Kayleigh Parker needed to be kept in iron cuffs, if at all possible. "This some kind of weird sex thing, Chris?"

"Oh, darlin', you'd be the first to know." Lauren was just about old enough to be his mother, but she laughed anyway as Chris shook his head, unsure of how much he should tell her. "She's just…she's unusual, all right? The iron makes her less dangerous."

Lauren's gaze went past him to the slender young woman sitting in the corner of the bond office, then came back to him. "What is she, like, a White Walker? Susceptible to dragon glass or something?"

"Um, something like that, yeah."

Lauren's eyebrows rose and she shrugged. "I'll let them know. Dunno if it'll do any good, but I'll try."

"You be careful with her around. You start getting any dark thoughts or going on an emotional roller coaster, either hit her in the head or get out of here."

A faint smile pulled at the corner of Lauren's mouth. "You're serious."

"As a heart attack, okay?"

She studied him a moment, then nodded. "All right, kiddo. Let me get you your check, in the meantime. Then you and that brother of yours look like you could use some sleep."

"Yeah." Chris cast a glance toward the van, where Nick had been way too quiet for a long time. Hopefully he was sleeping already, but Chris kinda doubted it. He'd had that look he got when he was studying, except the only thing Chris could figure for him to study was Kayleigh's grendel power, and that just seemed like a bad idea. "Thanks, Laur."

"Not a problem. You boys are my favorites, you know." She handed the check over a couple minutes later with a promise to call when she had another bounty, and Chris went back out to Lucille, where, yeah, Nicky was in the passenger seat, thumping a rhythm on the dashboard and not sleeping.

"Talk to me, Nicky." Chris pulled Lucille's door shut behind him and slumped in the seat. "What'd you learn from that girl?"

"I can do what she does." Nick sounded light, almost hollow. Almost thin. "It's not that hard, really. Emotions just roll out, you can push them around w—"

"Yeah," Chris said, "so the thing is, every freak I've ever —*grendel*, god damn it—every *grendel* I've ever heard about, they could do, like, one thing. Like Kayleigh in there fucks with emotion, okay, I'd never met that one before, but…" He shuddered, trying not to remember the freezing wash of water into his boots as the lake started to rise through cracks in the ice, and how he'd been willing to just let the ice break and the cold water take him. He would have said he'd never do something that fucking dumb, but she'd found some part of him that was ready to.

The worst part was, if he let himself linger on that realization, it wasn't really much of a surprise. It took effort to shove that away, and he felt Nick's gaze slide toward him, like his little brother was wondering if he could fuck with Chris's mind, too.

"So they're strong," he said harshly. "Or they can mind-fuck you, or they can turn invisible or whatever, but they can't mind-fuck you *and* use telekinesis *and* thunderclap *and* get a bead on somebody else's power *and* figure out how to use it themselves."

"I'm special," Nick said in a falsely bright voice. "Must be the family legacy of demon blood. Lucky me."

"Are you okay, man?"

"Sure." Nick sank into his seat. He'd abandoned the neon snowsuit as soon as he could and looked thin and tired now, in ordinary colors after a long day. "It'd just be so easy. I see why she did it. And I'm a lot smarter than her. You could get away with murder, easy."

"Not exactly what you want on your doctor resume, Nicky. 'Gets away with murder easily?' Yeah, no, I don't think so."

"Make catching bounties easier. Frogmarch them into custody with my mind, that was pretty cool, wasn't it?"

"Dude, I'm glad we got her, but no, it wasn't cool. It's freaky, and not like grendel-freaky, like freaky-freaky. And what she did to me was worse, but that doesn't fucking excuse it, okay?" Chris sat up, glaring at Nick uncomfortably. "Like, she just about killed me, you get that, right? You can't really think using a power to fuck with somebody's emotions is okay."

"I bet I could get Stephanie back," Nick said almost distantly. "Bet I could. Be really easy. Wouldn't make her forget, you know? Just kinda smooth it over. Remind her of the good times. Make sure she focuses on those."

"*Jesus*, Nicky, are you hearing yourself? Rapey incel much? What the *hell*, man? You can't *coerce* your girlfriend into coming back to you, what the actual fuck!"

"No, I'm not—" Nick flinched upright, offended, although the offense slid to horror after a few seconds, and then to sick-edged paleness. "I don't know what that was."

"That was the fucking power! That shit is not okay! It's screwing with *your* mind, never mind mine or Stephanie's or whatever. Dude, man, I thought you were like, incorruptible, but what the actual fuck!"

"They say everybody's got a price," Nick said thinly.

"And yours is getting your girlfriend back? Seriously, I thought better of you. What the hell, Nick!"

Nick, in the same thin voice, said, "I think something's wrong with me," and somehow all of Chris's anger and disgust vanished into worry.

"Yeah. Yeah, fuck, um. Okay, look. It's gonna be okay, Nicky. We'll figure it out. Look…"

"I better stop using the power. You told me that in the first place. Just get a handle it, that's what you said, but I'm out here experimenting and shit. I broke their door with it. And then she went after you and it was like I could see it, so I copied it, and…I shouldn't have done that." Nick leaned forward, making himself into a ball that didn't really fit in the passenger footwell. "I can see the eyes and the fire in the power. The wings. It feels like Saboac, Chris. I think I'm in trouble."

"It's gonna be fine," Chris said again. He could hear his own big brother voice, calming Nicky, even if it didn't work on himself. "Okay, look, I think we should get out of Denver, okay? And then maybe find—a church, I think, yeah? Priests should know about demon stuff, right?" He tried for a little grin, felt it fail, and pushed it harder. "It'll be okay. What churches ordain women? We'll get you a hot priestess exorcism or something."

To his relief, Nicky's shoulder's twitched with amusement, if not exactly laughter. "I think the only people who call them priestesses are witches or druids or something."

"Okay, so, we'll find a coven or something. I'd hate to spoil your chances of finding the light with the holy thirteen, right?"

"Dude, you are…" Nick lifted his head, a mortified smile on his face. "I don't even know. Incorrigible."

"If that's anything like encouragable, I'm good. Seriously." Chris lifted his chin, indicating Nick's phone. "See what you can find about churches around here, on the outskirts, maybe, that deal with exorcisms or demons or whatever, okay? Churches or covens or circles or whatever the hell they call how druids worship. Somebody's got to have some answers," he said more softly, "and in the meantime, probably being on consecrated ground's worth something, right?"

"Man, how can you just take this in stride?" Nick took his phone out like he was told, but his voice broke. "I'm all fucked up, Chris, and you're just chill."

Chris put the van in reverse, getting out of the parking lot, and headed north, figuring home lay that way, at least, and if push came to shove, there were churches in Sterling. "Fucked up is the one thing I'm good at, Nicky. Fucked up is my whole life. That's all."

"It's not, you know." Nick didn't say anything else, though, at least not about that, and Chris didn't want to argue with him. After a while, he did say, "There's a little old Orthodox church I think maybe nobody's using anymore up north toward the mountains. There's hardly any town there anymore."

"Orthodox? Yeah?" Chris glanced at him. "You feeling that vibe, or something?"

"I always liked the onion tops," Nick mumbled. "And if nobody's there I can't…"

"If nobody's there we can't ask questions," Chris said, but it wasn't much of an argument. "But if it's quiet, maybe we can sit this out for a while, figure you out. Good thing is you've obviously got more control than you had, right? You

wouldn't be able to copy her if you were just flailing around in the dark."

"I'm not sure that's comforting."

"I'm doing my best here, man."

"Yeah." Nick chuckled roughly. "Yeah, I guess so. Sorry. Look, we're going a couple hours north here, can we get food first?"

"That's a really good idea. And…maybe if we need to hide out we should go that far up, but I kinda really think we need to talk to somebody who's got, I don't know, a direct line to God or something."

"Fine, just pull over at the next church then, I guess." Nick banged his head back against the seat, winced, and pressed his lips together. Chris, grimacing, kept an eye out for either a diner or a church, and found the second one first.

"Ten minutes," he promised. "We can just ask if they have anybody who knows about…"

"Demonic possession?" Nick asked sharply. "Like that's not gonna get some funny looks?"

"They're priests. I bet they get weirder questions than that every day." Chris pulled into the parking lot of a white-walled church that looked to him like it had been picked up out somewhere in South Carolina and replanted halfway out of Denver on the north road, columns around the door and a white steeple and all.

"I bet they're pastors, here, not priests," Nick mumbled as they got out of the van.

Chris shrugged. "It's all the same thing, isn't it?"

"Dude, how do you know *nothing* about church hierarchy?"

"You were the one telling Stephanie how I skipped out on Sunday school."

"I think I was telling *you* how you did that."

"Well, whatever, it's not like you went either, so how come you know the difference between a priest and a pastor?" Chris took the couple steps up to the door in one step and turned to wait on his brother, who had stopped abruptly at the leading edge of the first step. "Come on, let's go."

"I can't." Color blotched Nick's face, red and white patches underwritten by queasy yellow. "I can't step up."

"What, you hurt your knee with all that stomping through the woods? You're still practically a teenager, dude, shake it off."

"No." Nicky's voice rose and broke. "I *can't*. It's like there's a—wall."

Chris barked laughter. "You telling me you can't walk on holy ground?"

The laugh dissolved into sickness as Nick's wild-eyed gaze rose to meet Chris's own. "Holy shit, you can't walk on holy ground?" Nausea plunged through him, breaking a cold sweat on his skin as he took the couple steps back down to the ground. "Nick, I'm sorry, I'm not trying to be a dick, but —seriously?"

"I'm fine here in the parking lot," Nick said hoarsely. "But if I try to step up…" He did, pushing his foot forward like he'd take a normal step, but just couldn't. He lifted both hands, pressing them forward until they reached the edge of the step. Chris saw the strain in his arms and throat as he pushed forward, and a brightness of panic in his eyes as he leaned into the effort like a mime going all-in on his performance. "I can't. I *can't*!"

"Stop." The word came out harder than Chris meant it to, as he grabbed Nick's arm and pulled him back a couple of steps. "Come on, Nicky, stop it. You're gonna hurt yourself."

"*Why can't I go in a church, Chris?*"

"I don't know." The nausea in Chris's belly felt like it was trying to get out but couldn't decide which way to go. "I don't know, but we'll figure it out. Just not here, okay? Right now we're gonna go get some food and give you a chance to breathe—"

"I don't *want* to breathe! I want to know why I can't go in a fucking church!"

"Probably because God doesn't like you using that kind of lan—" Chris's head snapped back with the impact of a punch he didn't even see coming. A punch he wasn't sure Nick had used his fists to throw. He staggered, catching blood from his nose, and stared disbelievingly at his brother through a haze of pain and tears. "Man, if you just broke my fucking nose—!"

"Oh, you're too goddamn vain about your face anyway." Nicky lashed out again, and this time Chris saw the movement, but his fist didn't connect. Just power did, catching Chris right in the gut, shoving him backward another couple steps.

"At least." It took two tries to get enough air to get beyond that. "At least my face is worth being vain about. I'd'a broken up with you too, if I had to wake up to that every day."

Nick bellowed and Chris bolted back toward Lucille, skidding on patches of snow and hoping that Nick just chased him instead of remembering he could probably grab Chris by the ankle with his mind and smash him around the pavement.

As luck would have it, Nick just chased him. If getting tackled by an angry, linebacker-sized brother counted as luck, anyway. Chris hit the icy asphalt with a bounce that did another number on his nose and howled with pain. "Dude! My nose!"

"Screw your stupid nose, you—"

Chris flipped over and threw a handful of snow in Nick's face, hoping the cold would at least startle him into calming down for a second. Nick flinched away, clawing at the bits of gravel that stuck in the snow, then fell backward, confused dismay beneath the melting ice on his cheeks. "What the... what am I..."

"We're getting you a burger," Chris grated. "Or six. You

gotta get grounded." He got up, afraid to touch his face, and offered his brother a hand.

Nick stayed where he was, sprawled on his ass on the half-frozen pavement. "I hit you."

"Twice. Get up."

"Are you gonna hit me?"

"Not while you're expecting it." Chris tried a smile, hoping it would show that he was kidding, but it sent a stab of pain up his nose into his brain and he grimaced instead, trying to bite back a snarl. "Man, I think you broke my goddamn nose."

Nick, almost writhing with guilt, climbed to his feet without Chris's help. "It's swollen," he reported miserably. "Don't touch it. Get a doctor to look at it in a couple days."

"No? Don't do the…" Chris made a motion like they did in the movies, although he didn't actually grab his nose for fear he'd pass out.

"No! No, it doesn't really work that way and it's hard to tell if a nose is broken until the swelling goes down. I'm sorry, Chris."

"Just get me an ice pack from the van and…" Chris hesitated. "I was gonna say you drive, but…"

"But I'm going off the deep end," Nick said with a tight smile. "Can you see okay?"

"Sure, except for the tears." Chris tried to make a face and the world spun dizzily. "Ow."

"It looks like it's almost stopped bleeding," Nick offered. "That's a good sign."

"Oh good." Chris braced himself and tried one more time to move the rest of his face. It worked better when he was prepared for the pain, although tears sprang to his eyes again. "I swear to God, if you broke it…"

"Then you'll be ruggedly handsome instead of picture perfect." Nick went to the van and got the ice pack Chris had asked for, and he spent a few wincing minutes holding it to his face before he dared look in one of the van mirrors to assess the damage, which looked a lot better than it felt.

"But that's good," Nick said apologetically. "It's probably not broken. And it stopped bleeding and there's no clear stuff coming out—"

"Of my *nose*? What clear stuff would there be?"

"What clear stuff *usually* comes out your nose?"

"Snot, I guess." Chris touched his nose, trying not to cry again, and mumbled, "It doesn't feel like anything's moving, and I can see if I don't touch it, so let's go, I guess. I want you to be fed and sleepy. Like a hibernating bear. There's a diner about a block up from here."

"You want to walk or drive?"

Chris squinted painfully, then sighed. "Walk, I guess. Probably the longer I wait for this to calm down, the better." He put the ice pack back on as they headed down the street, muttering, "'course, this look isn't gonna help me charm an extra cup of coffee out of the waitress or anything."

"Coffee refills are usually free," Nick said. "Don't tell me you've been putting 'getting extra refills' on your scoreboard."

Chris sniffed and regretted it profoundly. By the time the pain faded enough to say, "A gentleman never tells," it wasn't as funny anymore, and they were at the diner. Nick at least had the decency to hold the door for him, and the first waiter inside it said, "Oh, you poor thing, what happened?" and led them to a table right away.

"Slipped on the ice and caught myself with my face."

"Ooooh." The pitch of the waiter's sympathy practically vibrated through Chris's nose. He wanted to cry, or worse, vomit, but the idea of that much extra pressure in his head made him want to cry even more. He tried to smile as they sat down. It hurt. He stopped.

Nick muttered, "I bet he'll give you free coffee," as they sat.

Chris snickered after all, regretted it even more than the

sniff, and tried not to have any expression at all. "I'll take it, I'm easy. I wonder if he's got any aspirin."

"You can ask when he comes back." Nick picked up the menu at the side of the table, but frowned over it at the diner. Chris followed his gaze, clocking mostly older people at the free-standing tables and the bar counter, and a handful of families in booths like the one they sat in, with old dark grey pleather seats and heavy ripples in the backing. The staff were busy but not yet overwhelmed, and Chris checked the time—pushing 5pm—to see if they'd probably be expecting a rush soon.

"Think we got here before it got busy?"

"Huh? Nnh." Nick shook his head and frowned at his menu instead. "No, I just feel creepy, but it's probably me, not the diner. I've been in much creepier diners."

"Remember that one in—"

"With the gold fixtures and the clown in the bathroom?" Nick shuddered and Chris laughed even though it made his nose hurt.

"The part I remember was the stains on the floor. I was only like twelve but I was frickin' *sure* that was blood—"

"Dude, it absolutely was. It absolutely was. The clown killed somebody, man. The clown killed everybody."

Chris laughed again, then whimpered and tried to keep himself from hiding his nose under his hands. "God, that really hurts. Stop making me laugh."

"You brought up the creepy clown diner!" Nick looked up, worry cutting lines into his forehead before he stood. "Something's wrong, Chris. Something's—get out!" He lifted his voice, drawing attention as he braced himself. "Everybody get out! *Now!*" The last word carried power, enough power that Chris found himself on his feet, ready to bolt for the door.

He fought it, but others didn't. Couldn't. A few actually ran, then shrieked as the diner doors slammed shut in front of them. "Not that way." Nick gestured toward the back of the restaurant with one hand, the other clenched like he was trying to keep the doors closed. "Chris, help."

"What do you need?" There was nothing out in the parking lot besides cars and a handful of people heading toward the front door. Before Nick could answer, he was at the door, wedging it shut, yelling for the cute waiter to bring the keys. The waiter yelled back, clearly thinking they'd lost their minds, and for a bad moment it struck Chris that he and Nick were both visibly armed young white men a handful of miles from Columbine. Yeah, he couldn't blame the waiter for flipping out. "Just get out! Get everybody out!" He got the door jammed shut and began pulling the shades down, clipping them in place where they could be. The diner became a lot less airy and friendly with the shades drawn. By the time he returned to Nick, his brother had both hands extended, power wobbling visibly through the air.

"There's something out there," Nick grated. "It wants in. It wants—"

The windows exploded inward, most of the glass caught by the drawn shades, although a few of them blew in so hard the shades shredded or ripped free, spraying and raining shards into the room. Chris caught his breath, about to ask a stupid question, when the first of the things flowed over the broken glass, and all the stupid questions were answered.

He'd never seen a demon, not as far as he knew, so his certainty that *that* was a demon was arguably unfounded. The first of them was a sleek thing with oily claws, with blackness where the eyes belonged, although it turned its head like it could see. Then it jumped, and if Chris had doubted what it was before that, it didn't do something normal like tear into the diner patron it landed on. It *sank* into her, disappearing like it had never been. She went rigid, then screamed, but not a strong sound, just a thin wail of pain and fear. The next demon took another customer the same way, and then there were too many to count, too many to see.

Chris grabbed holy water from inside his coat, trying to count the vials by feel and hoping it would work as well against demons as it did against vampires. They reminded him of vamps, a little. Something about how they moved, something about their sightless eyes. He vaulted a table to pour holy water down the first victim's screaming throat, and almost wished he hadn't. Her eyes bugged and she began to cough, clawing at her own skin so hard it raised welts, then bloody streaks. But between that, and between the screams, she rolled over and vomited the demon back out. It reared up, clearly nowhere near dead enough, and he poured another vial of holy water, and then a third, onto it.

It died then, mostly. Turned into a feeble bubbling ooze of goo, anyway, and that would have to do. He was never gonna stop them with the vials, though, and shot a frantic look toward Nicky. There were what looked like hundreds of the demons in the restaurant now, crawling across the floor, seizing the customers who weren't fast enough to get away. Several of them died as Chris watched, absorbed by the things attacking them. One of them fought so hard the demon took her over, but didn't seem to be able to drain her life the way the others were doing. She staggered to her feet, twisted and obviously in pain, but also visibly stronger than the unbodied things around her.

There were a few others like that, becoming hosts instead of just victims, and Chris didn't know which was worse. He drew a knife and cut one of the weaker ones away as it jumped at him, and the steel at least made it flinch. The first of the embodied demons reached Nick. Chris let out a hoarse yell, and his brother's hand snapped out, catching the woman by her throat. She screamed, a wretched painful sound, and Nick's gaze turned toward her slowly, like she was a bug pinned to a board. Or worse, maybe, like she was a *snack*. Chris yelled, "Nicky," hopelessly, and for a moment Nick's gaze came to him. "Let her go."

As soon as he said it, it sounded like a really stupid idea. Nick dragged her closer, anyway, staring down at her with his jaw clenched and his neck corded, the strain visible enough that for a heartbeat Chris really thought he would unhinge his jaw and bite her head off or something.

Instead he clawed his free hand against her chest and *pulled*.

Demon essence—Chris didn't have another word for it— stretched under his hand, then sank into his fingers, slowly at first, then with increasing speed, until suddenly the woman gasped and Nick dropped her, panting. She scrambled away, running for the back, and Nick stretched his hand out to grab another one of the half-demon humans. This time the extraction went faster, but his grin went nastier, his eyes darker. Chris said, "Nicky," again, but there wasn't a hell of a lot he could do. Nick could stop the things, and he couldn't.

Instead, around a cold sick feeling in his stomach, he started looking for a way to stop Nick. The unbodied demons started pooling toward Nicky, like he'd become a vortex, too strong to avoid, and the newly-taken humans launched themselves at him en masse, obviously trying to break him down. From the corner of his eye, Chris saw him grab two of the host humans at once, and watched the darkness from them flood into Nick before he released the shaken diners.

"Can't." Nicky's voice, harsh with effort, broke through his search. "Too many. Chris—" The last word had a note of warning, and Chris spun, barely avoiding one of the unbodied things as it threw itself toward him. Nicky's howl of rage rose, splitting the air, and a burst of power slammed through the room.

Demon essence ripped out of the hosts, leaving them to collapse in screams, but alive. For a heartbeat Chris thought the crap that had filled them would just be obliterated, but at the end of that heartbeat it snapped back, much farther back than it had started, sinking into Nicky. His skin lit up from the inside with black power, with edges of fire and eyes, way too much like Saboac, and he fell into a pool of goo, swirling unbodied demon *grossness* that hadn't had the decency to just die or disappear when his power had smashed the diner.

He croaked, "Chris," and Chris stopped caring about getting any of that crap on himself, it would come off or it wouldn't, it would take him or it wouldn't, but he couldn't leave Nicky to just fight the stuff off on his own. He hit the floor on his knees, grabbing Nick's shoulders, then his face. His brother's skin was cold, clammy, nasty, like it had forgotten how to human. "Nick, come on, c'mon, Nicky, stick with me, all right? Stay with me, I can get you outta here but you gotta stay with me, okay? Come on, Nicky. It's you, right? It's you in there. Come on, buddy. Gimme a sign, okay? It's me, man. It's Chris. I got you."

Nick went, "Hhh," a little sound Chris had heard plenty of times when they were kids. It gave him just enough time to throw himself sideways before Nick hurled, although it wasn't the spew of demon essence he hoped it would be, just regular old barf. A look of revulsion crossed his face, and Chris had to laugh. Maybe so he wouldn't scream or cry, but he'd take it, whatever the reason.

"Yeah, that's right, man. I was trying to get you grounded with food but I guess puking will do. Okay? Okay?"

Nick barely nodded, and Chris got himself under his brother's arm before Nick full-on passed out. "C'mon. C'mon, let's go, let's get back to Lucille, let's get out of here, buddy, okay? Okay. We're good. We're good."

They got more than halfway down the block before Nick collapsed into a dead weight who clearly wasn't going anywhere under his own power.

# CHAPTER 17

GETTING A DEAD WEIGHT INTO A FIREMAN'S CARRY FROM HALF standing was slightly—slightly—easier than from the ground, and it was only half a block. Chris told himself that about a thousand times in the half block. He didn't want to haul Nicky's heavy-ass self for half a block, but he could, because it was better than any alternative he had open to him. He was gonna cut Nick's legs off later, though, because two hundred and twenty pounds of little brother slung across his shoulders was way the hell more than any reasonable person should be expected to carry. Nick had been a nerd when he left for college, for God's sake. He should have stayed that way, a skinny lanky kid who didn't turn into a dead weight slab of muscle and bone.

Never mind that a dead weight slab of muscle and bone was better than Nick getting totally absorbed by—or absorbing—any more demons. He'd *stopped*. He'd heard Chris and he'd stopped and if that was the case, Chris couldn't give up on him, so he could carry him for a hundred blocks if he had to. His head—his *nose*—hurt so badly from the extra weight that it was almost funny, if crying was funny, and every single etched-out word of thought and stab of pain and wave of emotion carried him another step back toward the van parked in the church lot.

It wasn't until he got there that he wondered what the hell he was doing. Lucille was not gonna cut it. Vans were never gonna keep demons out. Chris shot a despairing glance at the church, which at least ought to provide some kind of protection, except Nick couldn't cross the threshold.

Still, maybe being at the threshold would be better than in a stupid VW van. "C'mon, Nicky." As if saying *c'mon* would make his brother any less of a dead weight, but it helped him get the last couple dozen yards across the parking lot. He staggered to the steps, turned, and dropped onto them like he weighed twice what he usually did.

More than, actually, since Nicky outweighed him. His brother slid off his back, thudding onto the porch, and Chris went, "Woo," straightening as his weight changed and he felt suddenly and unexpectedly light. He was sweating like a horse and needed a drink of water, but the van seemed impossibly far away and he didn't want to leave Nick exposed on the steps even for a minute.

It took a very long time to grasp that Nicky was *on the steps of the church*.

A jolt of panic and relief sent Chris to his feet, not really thinking. He stepped over Nick, tried the church door, and found it unlocked, mumbling, "Thank you," to…he didn't know who. God, maybe, not that he generally considered himself on speaking terms with any celestial beings.

Except Saboac, obviously, and now a bunch of frickin' demons, he guessed. He muttered a curse, propped the church door open with a chair he found inside, and dragged his brother in before closing the door again. He didn't know if 'demon-infected but unconscious' was a holy ground loophole, or if carrying Nick across the threshold had made the difference, but it didn't really matter. Being inside a holy place had to be better than not.

Turned out there wasn't anybody there to ask about possessions, anyway. Just leaving a church unlocked and unattended seemed somewhere between stupid and appropriate, like, he was pretty sure Jesus or somebody would approve, but also it seemed like a good way to get stuff stolen or wrecked.

Not that there was all that much in this place to steal or wreck. Pews, yeah, but the interior walls were plain white, kind of bright and refreshing. There was a large, but very simple dark wood cross at the far end above a pulpit and what Chris guessed was an altar. There wasn't much else to steal. Whatever kind of church this one was, they apparently mostly went for the 'no graven idols' thing, and thought that random people in search of shelter should be able to find it in their place of worship. Chris was grateful as hell.

He sat down hard on the floor and dropped his head. "What're we gonna do, Nicky?"

Unsurprisingly, Nick didn't answer, and for a few seconds the only real sound in the church was Chris's own tired breathing, louder than Nick's. The walls must have been thicker than they looked, blocking out the sounds of evening traffic. Either that or it was just that serenity churches sometimes had, like they actually were a shelter from the outside world. Shelter was good. Shelter was great. Too bad Chris needed a god damn miracle.

A sharp laugh jerked through him. Well, he guessed he was in the right place for miracles. "Hey, God, you wanna..." For some reason, the faint humor of it fled, and he mumbled, "You wanna help out some? I mean, I'm not really into the whole God thing, but I guess if there's demons and shit there ought to be a god, so..."

Even he recognized that wasn't much of a prayer. With a worried, half guilty look at his brother, he got up and went to the front of the church, looking beyond the crucifix, but at the joining of the ceiling and wall beyond it. Somebody had done a nice job of lining those joins with sculpted moulding, concealing the actual join. There was a word for that stuff, like baseboards except for on the ceiling. Nick and his big stupid brain would know the word.

"I don't really know who I'm supposed to talk to," Chris growled toward the ceiling. "I don't know if you go straight to the top when you need something from God or if you gotta go through, like, middle management first. I don't think I've got time to Karen my way to the top, though. I kinda need…"

His shoulders rounded and he looked back toward Nick, still unconscious back by the door. "I need help. My brother needs help. He's a good kid, God, or whoever the hell I'm—sorry, whoever the fuck—I'm talking to, but I can't…this is above my pay grade, guys. I can't stop a demon horde. I can't protect him from that. I don't know what…" He sighed and knelt, not so much because of the supplicant-to-God thing as he was just frickin' *tired*, like, bone-weary and beat down. Sat on his heels and bent forward, hands under his forehead to support himself on the little step that led up to the altar or whatever it was. His jeans cut into the backs of his knees, slowing circulation immediately, but even so, he thought he could probably just fall asleep there.

Which wouldn't do him or Nicky any good, so he shoved back onto his heels, gaze fixed on the step in front of him now. "I don't know what I'm supposed to ask for. I don't know who I'm supposed to ask. But if there's anybody listening, angels, saints, gods, whatever…please help me. Help me help my little brother."

He waited a minute, then gave another sharp little laugh, loud enough to bounce off the walls this time. "Yeah, okay, I don't know what I expected there. St. Peter to waltz in through the door or something, I guess. Fuck." He got up, shoved his hand through his hair, and went back to Nick, who was still asleep. Unconscious. Part of him wanted to try waking him up, but there was a whole potential host of things wrong with waking him up, too, and maybe Nick knew it. Maybe he was just trying to stay out of the world until Chris figured out something to *do*. His breathing was steady, anyway, and his color didn't look bad, so short of going to a hospital, which could be full of potential demon hosts, Chris didn't know what the hell else to do but leave him on the church floor and try to come up with a plan.

The fleeting thought to call Jake or the Geography Girls crossed his mind, but none of them were close enough to help right now, and explaining the scene in the diner—which would probably end up on the goddamn evening news, or social media, now that he thought about it—was more than Chris thought he could cope with.

"'cause it's a lot easier to deal with it all myself," he muttered to Nick. "Super good coping skills there, right? Or whatever you'd call it. Using my support network." After a minute, he did text Jake, and then the girls, and by the time he finished he realized he should have used a group chat.

Four or five messages later, Dakota asked if he was updating everybody individually, and then a new group chat came up with "*Chris is an idiot, guys, he's talking to all of us, let's just congeal.*"

*Consolidate,* Jake wrote.

*You knew what I ducking meant, didn't you?*

*\*FUCKING*

Cheyenne came up as a series of dots that became *I just got you put back together, Chris, why are you getting Nick beat up now*

*Never mind why. Where are you? I'm in the truck.* That was Jake, and Chris exhaled a little stress. It didn't really matter that he couldn't do anything. The fact that he would come helped.

*Little church on, lemme check maps...* Chris flipped to a map app as the church door opened. He shoved the phone in his pocket, scrambling to his feet with his hands extended. A tallish white guy, good-looking, sandy-haired, wearing a good suit with a complicated belt under a long, expensive coat, came in, his eyebrows rising as Chris stepped protectively in front of Nick. "Look, I'm sorry, my brother's hurt, I know this isn't a great place to have him lying, but I couldn't figure out where else to go—"

"I know. You called me."

"What?" Chris felt for his phone, wondering if he'd butt-dialed somebody, and the guy grinned. Bright grin, friendly and welcoming.

"No, not that way. That way." He pointed up, and Chris looked up like there would be a cell tower there or something.

Obviously there wasn't, and half a second later the penny dropped with a rush of disbelief. Chris twisted toward the altar at the front of the church, then double-took at the guy. "No fucking way."

"I think the response 'way!' is several decades out of date, but…'way.' You said your brother needed help. That demons are…above your pay grade? You can call me Ari." The big guy—he was almost Nick's size, but paler—crouched at Nick's side, studying him without touching him. "What happened?"

"Uh." Nerves, part disbelief and part hope, ran through Chris, making his skin tingle. "I. How."

Ari glanced up, the grin returning with a crook this time. He had perfectly symmetrical features, so symmetrical he didn't look quite real. Heavy eyebrows, but not too heavy, like he kept them under control. Deep-set blue eyes and a straight nose that reminded Chris for the first time in several minutes that he'd been punched in the face recently. The grin was disarming, easy to trust, and both the first and the last thing Chris wanted to do was trust it. "You prayed. I heard."

"How do I believe you're—"

"An emissary of God? Well, for one thing, you're supposed to take that on faith, Christopher R—"

"Shut the fuck up."

Ari had an amazing fucking laugh that rolled right across the church. If he started singing, Chris thought it might sound like actual choirs, and hoped he didn't. "Faith is not our strong suit, I see. Very well. Will the halo do? The wings…are hard on suits." He *brightened* as he spoke, not a ring above his head, but a glow of power that spilled all around him, glimmering at the edges like starlight. It surrounded him, not quite touching even his suit, and faded in a stretch across his back like it encircled something Chris couldn't see. Just before it got too bright to bear, it winked out again, leaving the frickin' *angel* crouched at Nick's side, his expression one of amused expectation.

"Will that do?" Ari asked again.

"Uh." Chris swallowed. "Uh, yeah, I guess—I guess it will. Wh." There was probably a word or even a whole sentence he meant to say after the syllable, but his ability to think stopped there and didn't start again.

Ari's grin flashed a third time. "Good. Your brother is Exalted. Th—"

A hard, loud laugh burst from Chris's chest, hurting his throat. "He's fucking what? *Exalted?* Gimme a fucking break. He still eats Froot Loops for breakfast."

The angel's smile faltered and he looked taken aback. "That seems…ill-advised. They're mostly sugar, and hell on the roof of your mouth."

Chris's eyebrows shot up. "Angels can say hell?"

"The devil can quote scripture for his own purposes, Christopher."

"Do *not* call me Christopher again."

Ari, with visible, real curiosity, said, "Or what?" and Chris had absolutely no answer for that. "Exalted," Ari repeated after a long enough pause to be certain everyone knew where the power balance lay. "It means he's—"

His expression darkened and he stood, turning toward the door before it opened again and a Black guy in a flowing robe and loose trousers stalked in, snarling, "*Castaway.*"

Ari said, "Dogsbody," in a disparaging tone, and the new

guy—who had to be at least six inches shorter than the angel but made it up in shoulder width—said, "Don't trust *anything* the castaway says," to Chris. He wore his hair shorter than Ari's, close-cut on the sides with a little more length on top, but he had the same kind of impossible perfection to his features as the angel, with deep brown eyes and a flawless mouth currently set in a warning scowl.

"I assure you I haven't told him a single lie. Or do you intend to dispute the fact that this boy," Ari said with a languid gesture at Nick, "is Exalted?"

"This one is fallen," the new guy said to Chris. "*Don't trust him.*"

"What? No, dude, he had—who are *you*?"

"My name is Elemiah, and I'm an—"

"Honestly, if you say 'an angel of the Lord' I shall positively hurl, Eli."

Elemiah—Eli—gave Ari a withering look. "I *am* an angel of the Lord, and you no *longer* are, Arioch."

"Please." Ari—Arioch, apparently—sniffed. "I'm no less angelic than you. I merely have free will now."

"You only serve a different master."

"At least I do it because I chose it!"

"Will you two shut up!" Chris's voice cracked, which weakened its authority, but the bickering angels, if that's what they were, at least fell silent and gazed at him in something approaching hurt astonishment. "That one," Chris snapped, stabbing a finger toward Ari, "is definitely an angel. He had a halo. Who the fu—"

Eli, with the air of someone who didn't have time for nonsense, shrugged his shoulders as if an itch lay between the blades, and with a soft rush of sound, the entrance of the church filled with wings. Feathery, glinting with gold, absolutely vast. Almost as soon as Chris understood what he was seeing, they snapped away again, and he discovered he was on his ass on the floor without any real idea how he'd gotten there. "Turn around!"

The smaller angel lifted his eyebrows, but did, briefly, and Chris turned an accusing glare on Arioch. "I thought you said it was hell on suits."

"There may be some disadvantages to being castaway," Ari replied tightly. "Are we quite finished?"

"What the hell is castaway?"

"Exactly what it sounds like," Eli said. "He was cast out of Heaven. Fallen."

"I was not cast," Ari said through his teeth. "I *chose*."

"Is a fallen angel, castaway, whatever, even still an *angel*? Why would a fallen angel answer a prayer?"

"Your brother needs help," Arioch said. "Does it really matter right now?"

"It might." Chris, inspired, dipped his hand inside his coat, came up with one of his last vials of holy water, and stood to fling it in the blonde angel's face.

The angel—fallen angel—flinched irritably, but didn't scream or smoke or sizzle into a puddle of ichor, although faintly exasperated disdain did cross his face as he brushed the water away. "Look what you did to my suit."

Chris's confidence wavered. "Why didn't it affect you? It burned Saboac."

Ari's lips peeled back like an offended cat's. "Saboac is *unclean*. *I* am merely—" He cast a furious glance at the other angel. "Fallen."

"Was." Chris curled a hand into a fist, looking down at Nick. "Saboac *was* unclean. Nicky killed him."

"He what?" Both angels, fallen or not, were momentarily united in shock. Then Elemiah crouched over Nicky, just as Arioch had done, and said, "It may be too late, then."

"On the contrary, I'd say my timing is flawless." Arioch lifted his gaze toward the distance, then transferred it to Chris. "I understand you don't trust me, although I've hardly given you reason not to. Still, let me offer you another reason *to*."

He reached for his belt, and Chris's voice shot up. "What the fuck, dude!"

Obvious amusement flickered across the angel's face. He loosened and removed the belt, which did not, to Chris's huge relief, send his pants to the floor as he handed the belt to Chris.

As he handed the *sword belt* to Chris. A three-foot blade, previously hidden by the cut of Ari's long coat, hung from one side of the leather contraption. Eli hissed, and Chris took the thing, baffled. "What's this for?"

"For the oncoming fight."

"Dude, this isn't the crusades, okay? I don't know how to use a frickin' sword."

"I suggest you adapt. I believe our enemy is upon us."

Chris got halfway through, "What do you mean?" before the church door slammed open and more demons poured in.

———

Demons shouldn't be able to be able to come in to *churches*. That thought popped into Chris's mind and held there for far too long, wasting time during which he should have been fighting, running, or saving Nick. Demons should go up in flames on holy ground. That had to be in the rulebook somewhere. *Nick* hadn't been able to get into the church while conscious, and he wasn't even a frigging demon.

No, but he'd sucked up a lot of desanctified angel power, and the blonde fallen angel clearly thought Saboac was a whole lot worse than he was. Chris ground his teeth and shoved the whole debate away, trying to drive himself into action as bat-winged, screaming monsters flew at him from an otherwise-ordinary-looking evening. He took a step forward, meaning to protect Nicky if nothing else.

Elemiah knocked him aside with the same step, either finally in motion or Chris hadn't been frozen as long as he thought, and bent to scoop Nicky up effortlessly. His wings snapped open again, and this time the glimmers of gold at the edges burned, fire outlining feathers until they stood out individually instead of being a blurry soft-looking mass. Then he leaped with as much ease as he'd picked Nicky up, clearing the pews and—

—and Chris didn't know what happened next because the flood of demons didn't stop. He threw the sword's sheath off, swung with the blade, and overbalanced. "God damn it, I know how to use *knives*!" The sword's steel shone with a fiery light, giving the individual demons more edges and shadows than they'd had in the diner. That was something, at least.

Ari, from somewhere in the mess of rushing demons, said, "Well, excuse *me*," but the blade in Chris's hands twisted as if it had a life of its own, or heard him. Then he had two knives in his hands, flawlessly balanced, both with the same fiery shine as the original sword. His fingers went so cold he almost lost his grip on the hilts, then shook himself, muttering, "Fight now, freak later."

He tightened his grip again as a sleek narrow dark thing came for him, and swept the left-hand blade up, catching the demon in the gut. It erupted in a shower of sparks, obliterated instantly. He had almost enough time to admire that before there was another one on him. He sliced with the other knife, splitting the thing wide open. Thick sludge dripping from the wound and it gave a short, hard scream before his second blow killed it. "Babies, where have you been all my life?"

Arioch, briskly, said, "Hell," and Chris checked the impulse to throw one of the knives at him. He wouldn't be able to, anyway: the air was dense with things that stretched and pulled apart, or bubbled into another and expanded. He struggled to think of what they reminded him of, then coughed an unhappy laugh as he killed another of the ones that seemed to at least be able to remember what it was shaped like.

Lava lamps. That's what the blobby, shape-changing ones reminded him of. Except lava lamp goo didn't roll forward, claiming ground and pushing him back against a pew. Arioch didn't seem to be doing much better, although shadows blurred and brightened as he fought. Chris fell back another step, then had to climb over the pew to get away. They were starting to realize there were other aisles they could use, their attack scattering as they tried to get past Arioch and himself to the front of the church, where Nick lay. They didn't even try to enter him the way the ones at the diner had done to the customers there. He had a lot of questions as to why, and no time to ask. Sweat rolled into his eyes, stinging, but he was afraid to brush it away, afraid that even a single missed strike would lose the battle.

They weren't going to win anyway. He pushed the thought away. Even if it was true, it didn't matter. Every minute he kept these things away from Nick was a minute in which—

He didn't finish that thought either. Didn't know how. Slice and strike and jab, the knives moving in his hands, sometimes along his outer forearm like he was a weapon himself, other times turning so he could stab beside or below himself, trying to hold a line that kept falling back, step by step by step. "Where the hell are they coming from?"

Arioch, less briskly than before, said, "If only it were Hell, I might be able to stop them. Stand back."

As if there was anywhere to freaking go. Chris dared one glance behind himself, looking for Nick. He lay on the floor, partially hidden behind the altar. The other angel crouched over him, evidently not giving a shit about the fight going on in the back half of the church. "Hey!"

Eli didn't look up, but sudden brightness threw him into harsh relief. Chris turned toward the fight, a hand lifted to protect his eyes against increasing brilliance that almost cut the demons all on its own. It had the same clarity as Arioch's body-encompassing halo, like a star coming to rest inside the church. There was no heat, though, only light, almost too bright to look at before it flared, and Chris abruptly understood why the halo had thinned across Arioch's back.

He had wings. Fallen or not, he had wings, huge and carved of light, insubstantial, the opposite of shadows. They ghosted to the church walls, beyond them, pinion feathers stretching through physical matter, and the demons weren't falling to *nothingness*, they were stricken by the touch of those wings, burning in the same way they did when Chris stabbed them with the knives he'd been given.

And it still wasn't enough.

They kept coming, flooding in, threatening to overwhelm even the castaway angel's brightness as his wings swept inward, catching demons, frying them, and opened again, throwing them away. Chris surged in again, ducking beneath the wings, stabbing and cutting and, he thought, yelling. Yelling a lot. Mostly obscenities, but it drew the demons' attention, which kept them from swarming past him toward Nick. They funneled straight toward him, too many to fend off, but that was Arioch, keeping them from going down the other aisles now, his insubstantial wings enough barrier for the roiling mass of demonic bodies.

Well, if he was going to die, at least this one would go down in the history books. Not that anyone would believe it, but still, fighting demon hordes was a pretty epic way to go.

Arioch, sounding very far away, said, "*Elemiah*," through gritted teeth, and the world thundered to an end.

————

Wings. The sound of the world ending was *wings*. Elemiah's wings, clapping open with enough force to knock Chris aside.

To knock demons aside. To knock *Arioch*, who looked other-wise immoveable, aside: the castaway angel fell against the door, temporarily blocking the next wave of demons.

The rest of the thunder was Elemiah's landing, a deaf-ening crash of body and weaponry. He had a sword. A big fucking sword. Chris didn't know where it had come from, but then, the angel had wings, too, and Chris didn't know where he kept those, either, so he wasn't gonna worry about it too much.

And then there was the fire.

Unlike Arioch's cool light, Eli's fire had heat. Blinding heat, roaring from the gold-lined edges of his wings, rising around him in unrelenting flames as his wings closed into a cupola. The blaze shot upward, sparks darting into the air, catching bits of demon flesh and incinerating them, and for some reason Chris thought of kneeling in front of his father's pyre and screaming.

The pillar of fire inched out from where Eli knelt, then expanded in a single smooth rush. Chris caught one breath, expecting it to burn his lungs, and the fire passed across him harmlessly, even as it turned the demons in its path to ash. The whitewashed floor under his feet wasn't even scarred by the roaring flame.

It passed through the walls, through Arioch, through the door, before fading somewhere in the parking lot.

Elemiah rose gracefully, the wings and the fire and the blade all—extinguished, or vanquished, or something. Nicky would know the word.

"Nicky." Chris forgot about the angel's grace, about the roasted demons, about the castaway brushing non-existent ash off himself, and bolted for the front of the church. The angel said something, behind him, but he didn't catch it as he swung around the altar to find his brother stiffly trying to sit up.

# CHAPTER 18

A WHOLE BRASS BAND HAD SET UP IN NICK'S HEAD, EVERY instrument out of tune. Even the drum. Nick didn't know if drums *could* be out of tune, but the one in his head was.

There were probably more important things to think about, but he had a dark, hissing spot in his mind that he didn't want to even look at it, much less think about it. He sat up an inch at a time, a little disappointed to find out he could. "Chris?" The word didn't really make it out of his throat.

Chris appeared anyway, stumbling around the side of something big, something pale, something Nick didn't remember from the diner, and crashed to his knees. "Nick. Nicky, you okay?" His arm went under Nick's shoulders, offering support as he sat. Nick didn't want to think about how much it helped.

It seemed like there was a lot he didn't want to think about. "I feel like hell. What..." His head dropped, and he sat there, just about swaying in Chris's grip, before taking a deep breath and lifting his head again effortfully. "Not to be an ingenue about it, but where am I? What happened?"

Chris fell back with a hoarse laugh and rubbed a hand over his face. "We're in that church up the street from the diner. You kinda passed out after that demon fight."

"I don't...remember." Some of it hissed there, in the dark place in his mind, but he didn't want to look. "What happened back there?"

"You were pulling demons out of people," Chris said grimly. "And it happened like Gramma said did with Mom. The demon stuff went in you."

"Your *mother* suffered this as well?"

Nick didn't know that voice—deep, gravelly, reassuring— or the man it belonged to, when he came around the other end of the—altar, apparently, if they were in a church. "I couldn't go in the church." His voice cracked like he'd been asleep, or parched, for hours.

"I dragged you in while you were unconscious," Chris said. "I dunno why it worked then."

"A sleeping form holds no immediate threat," the stranger said. He was Black, good-looking, not very tall, but well-dressed in what looked something like a west African agbada made of silk and embroidered with gold and red threads. From Nick's perspective on the floor, he looked a little impos- ing. "And consecrated ground has only the most rudimentary of protective magic about it to begin with. Easily overcome by demon hoards, for example."

"Uh-huh." Nick lowered his head to pinch the inner corners of his eyes, then looked up again. "Sorry, you are...?"

"This is Elemiah," Chris said blandly. "He's an angel."

"Chris..."

"No, I know, but seriously. I prayed, dude, and an angel showed up."

"Two, actually." Another voice, this one silken smooth, preceded the arrival of another extraordinarily good-looking man, this one white, blonde, tall enough to *definitely* be imposing from Nick's seat on the floor. He threw an expen- sive-looking long coat over the altar, and shrugged his suit jacket off to drape it over his arm. "Arioch. You may call me Ari. Or Harry, if you must."

"I don't think I must." A throb of pain ran through Nick's skull. He thought if he could see inside his head, the pain would be red, dancing along the paths of darkness that were sinking into the wrinkles of his brain. "Chris…"

"Seriously," Chris said again, more quietly. "I prayed. They showed up. That one's, uh, what'd they call it, castaway? Fallen, anyway. I guess he works for the devil or something." He gestured toward the blonde, whose expression tightened.

"I was not cast out. I *left*."

"Sauntered vaguely downward, did you?" Nick muttered. To his surprise, Chris barked quiet laughter and elbowed him. The castaway angel, however, veritably smoldered with anger.

"I left," he said again. "Purposefully and deliberately, turning my back on hypocrisy that preached and punished—" He broke off, then visibly redirected his words, snapping, "There was no *sauntering*, Exalted. I *left*."

Chris whispered, "I didn't know you'd seen *Good Omens*," and Nick said, "I read the book," back, although he'd seen it, too. The point, though, was to make Chris's expression fall and for him to hiss, "You *nerd*," so it worked, and Nick dropped his head to cackle quietly.

When he looked up again, both the purported angels were staring down at them as if they were…humans, Nick supposed, and for some reason that struck him as funny, too. A sound perilously near a giggle erupted from high in his throat. Chris, clearly without knowing why, gave an almost equally high-pitched laugh. Half a second later they were leaning on each other, howling and hitting each other's shoulders, and barely thirty seconds after that, the hysteria fled and Nick found himself wiping his eyes, not sure if the tears were laughter or something else. It had only been a week since their dad's funeral. Eight days, maybe.

Chris knotted his arms around Nick, hugging him hard. "S'okay, Nicky. You're all right, all right? You're okay."

"'m not though. There's something in my head, Chris. It's

dark and it's trying to fill me up. I don't think I'm stronger than it is."

"'course you are. 'course you are. You're my baby brother. A Cassidy. You're strong as fuck. And these two good-looking bastards are gonna help, anyway." Chris loosened his grip on Nick's shoulders a little as he looked up. "Right?"

Elemiah said, "You are in no condition to," and Arioch, much more loudly, said, "Oh, yes, definitely."

Nick, aware he was missing the point so broadly it could only be deliberate, said, "They're like *weirdly* good-looking," and Chris snorted an agreement. "They're really angels?"

"That one's got a halo and the other one did the whole pillar of fire thing," Chris said, gesturing without much direction to indicate which of them had done which.

"Sorry I missed it," Nick said in a low voice. He wanted to stand, but wasn't entirely sure he could on his own, so he put some weight on Chris, who started to lever him up. "What's 'exalted?' You called me that." He lifted his chin at Arioch, who spread his fingers across his chest in a 'who, me?' gesture.

"It's—"

"Nothing to concern yourself about," Elemiah said shortly.

Nick gave a dubious grunt as the blonde angel turned incredulously toward Elemiah. "Nothing to *concern* himself about? What do you propose, Eli, that the Exalted return to his daily life? Pretend this isn't happening? How long do you imagine that will last? Weeks? Days? With the power this boy has taken into himself, you'd be lucky if it was *hours*. The second Sphere is tiresome by nature, Elemiah, but I didn't imagine you were *stupid*."

"He's better off knowing as little as possible—"

"When has that ever been true in the history of their miserable, petty, small-minded and," Arioch ground his teeth, "occasionally magnificent species? Not from the first damned apple, Eli, and you know it."

Chris stopped trying to get Nick to his feet and lifted a finger instead. "Wait, are you telling me that whole thing is true? The garden and the snake and everything?"

"It's a metaphor," Arioch said disdainfully. "Look at him, Eli. The boy can hardly stand, with the power coursing through him. You cannot possibly imagine ignorance is bliss. Or do you just intend for him to die? And I thought the fallen were supposed to be the villains of the piece."

"Nobody is dying here," Chris growled. "You hear me? Nobody."

"He's not wrong, though." Nick, uncomfortably aware of how much weight he was putting on his brother, tried to straighten on his own. He felt like he'd eaten too much, except in his head. Like a hangover, if his brain itself was nauseous. "I feel like I might explode. Or throw up. Or both."

"Tell me exactly what happened with Saboac," Elemiah said, but Arioch laughed.

"Can't you *tell*, little Power? He *reeks* of the unclean seraph. He stinks of demon flesh. And it hasn't killed him. He's going to rule the world."

"What?" Nick made it to his feet at that, sickness rushing through him like the grendel power jacked up on drugs. "No I'm not! What's wrong with me?"

"Nothing," Arioch said at the same time Elemiah said, "Everything." This time, though, the blonde castaway made a shushing motion with one hand, and either Elemiah heeded it or the action had some power, because Arioch went on without interruption this time. "You are so rare as to be a unicorn, my boy. You don't exist. Humans cannot survive demonic possession and wield demonic power, and yet here you are, doing both."

Chris, almost certainly without knowing it, stepped in front of Nick. "Then what were those things at the diner? The people the demons went into?"

"Lunch," Arioch said frostily. "Demons feast on human

souls, on their creativity and anger and madness. Once possessed, the soul is lost, save for an interference by someone like your brother here, and someone like him has not come along in—"

"Four hundred years," Elemiah said.

"At least that," Arioch agreed. "One of your kind, Nicholas, can undo the status quo between the realms almost without trying. Demons will be drawn to you for the rest of your life, desperate for the power you bear, as if they might somehow strengthen themselves on it."

Nick took a step back, embarrassingly glad that his brother stood between him and the other two. He didn't entirely want to believe they were angels, but the hissing presence of Saboac—what was left of Saboac, which was far too much *him* now—*felt* the truth of their divinity, and whispered its truth in Nick's mind. Even the fallen one burned with something that the threads of dark power yearned for, something it had once not just known, and which was now so far gone that only the memory of its memory remained.

He could take that power, Nick thought. He could reach out and grab Arioch by the throat and take that blinding power. Refill himself with it like a drink of cold water, feel it burn through his veins and bring him back to life. Somewhere through that wound the knowledge that it wouldn't last, that nothing lasted, not even the light of a sun, but for a while, a little while, he would be whole, and nothing on this or any other world could stop him.

"No!" He didn't know his own voice, cracked and scared. "No, I'm not going to—feed demons?" He hung onto that, trying to shove away the thought of drowning in angelic power. "How could I?"

"You can't," Arioch said, almost soothingly. "At best you can absorb them. At worst, you'll destroy them. But every one will impregnate you with power."

"Dude. Did you have to say 'impregnate?'"

Nick burst out with another one of those high shaky laughs. Chris's stupid mouth might keep him from falling all the way into whatever the hell it was Arioch was promising, whatever the hell it was the burgeoning power inside him wanted. Arioch ignored Chris, though, and Nick's own shriek of laughter. "All you have to do is give in to the dark power, and anything you want will be yours."

"Are you saying my baby brother is the Antichrist?" Chris's hands balled into fists like he would take on the fallen angel all by himself.

Nick thought he probably would.

"No!" Arioch sounded almost offended, but then his beautiful voice turned amused. Delighted, even. "I'm saying he has the *potential* to be the Antichrist. It's really all very exciting."

"Then what are you even doing here?" Nick, half aware he was copying Chris's stance, clenched his own fists, leaning in a little, like he could brace himself against whatever the angel said. "If you're a fallen angel, don't you want me to go all Antichrist and destroy the world?"

"Not even the Morning Star wants the world in ruins," Arioch murmured. "He only wants to be held above man in God's love, as a more perfect being should be."

"You know that's a bunch of eugenicist bullshit," Nick snarled, and Chris looked back at him with familiar fond exasperation.

"You and your vocabulary, man."

For the space of that brief smile, Nick felt almost normal again, stabilizing when otherwise he was sure he would come apart. Chris fell back half a step, coming alongside Nick again, shoulder to shoulder.

"His mother should *not* have been able to do this," Elemiah said, as if he was having an entirely different conversation with Arioch to the rest of them.

The big angel flicked his fingers uncaringly. "All the rules have changed, Elemiah. It's been decades since the demons were trapped on this plane. Their little freaks—grendels, is that what you're calling them? How charming—have been breaking the laws for most of a century now. I'm not concerned with one woman's ability to draw essence and expel it. She clearly had the blood, and now it's manifested in young Nicholas here."

"What blood?" Chris growled.

Arioch brushed him off as easily as he'd done the other angel. "Demon blood, clearly. Your lineage is lousy with it. Even you shine, although the power has nothing to take hold of, in you."

"But he healed," Nick protested. "Back after the fight with Saboac. He was almost dead and he healed."

Arioch's eyebrows rose. "Not at his own hand, surely."

"Nah, Cheyenne was there," Chris said. "Forget it. How can we be lousy with demon blood?"

"That's what your 'grendels' are," Arioch said with clearly waning patience. "Once, demons took human hosts, lived in them until the soul was devoured, and moved on. Sometimes they had children. Those children cannot be retaken by another demon, but they often had power, and that power now manifests in your grendels. And some of you," he said with a nod toward Nick, "are *rich* with it."

"What, precisely, could your mother do?" Elemiah's gaze swam between Nick and Chris, fixing on Nick as he shrugged.

"I don't know. She died when we were little. Something like what I do, I guess, except after a while she burned it up inside her or something." Even saying it made the power inside him hiss and writhe. It didn't feel like it had when it had first started. It was worse now, more powerful, and it had been bad enough to begin with.

Elemiah shook his head. "That makes no sense. There is no power of that nature that I know of."

"And you would know, little Power," Arioch said in a light voice.

"I would watch my epithets, were I you, Arioch. I am not the lesser of us in this time and place."

"Nor am I convinced you're the greater."

Chris said, "Do you guys need to get a room?" just as Nick was casting a look toward him to wonder something similar. Another giggle drowned out some of the darkness spinning through his mind. Chris's smart mouth really *might* get him through this.

That, and some food. "I didn't eat, did I," Nick said uncertainly. "I think maybe I should eat. Something that isn't demons." That struck him as funny, too, but even he knew his laughter had a hysterical edge. "Chris, I'm really not okay."

"I know, man." Chris's voice went quiet, serious with worry, and he turned a scowl on the angels. "So can you guys help, or what? Because if you can't, we gotta find somebody who will."

"Fighting demons again would be ill-advised," Elemiah offered. "If you were to return to your normal life—"

"I'd love to!"

"He can't," Arioch said at the same time. "Surely you know that, Eli. They will continue to come for him, until he's overwhelmed with their rage and greed and hunger, and then he'll turn that power outward so it doesn't destroy him."

"Sounds pretty much like being destroyed," Nick grated, and Arioch gave a graceful shrug of agreement.

"Would it work for a little while?" Chris's voice broke on the question. "If he went home, if he went back to school and pretended this wasn't happening, would it help for a while? Long enough for some of that crap in him to…I don't know, maybe it'd burn up, the way I guess Mom could do?"

"Your brother is a reservoir," Arioch said, almost gently. "There will be no burning through it, only a continual powering up."

"But it might help," Elemiah said. Arioch rolled his eyes and turned away as if giving up on the entire conversation, while Eli focused on Nick. "You're not an evil child, not by nature."

"Or nurture," Chris muttered, and Nick, surprised, put his hand on his brother's shoulder for a second.

"Not mostly, anyway."

"Dad was a bastard, but he wasn't…" Chris lost conviction and looked away, so Nick held on a second longer, then let Chris's shoulder go.

"I believe there's hope," Elemiah went on. Arioch turned back, eyebrows elevated in clear surprise.

"Why?" Nick asked. "Why do you think there's hope? Because as far as I can tell I'm pretty fucked up."

"You are," Eli echoed in measured tones, "pretty fucked up. But by all rights you should have fallen long since. You shouldn't have been able to return to yourself in the wake of fighting Saboac, and yet you did."

"Chris helped me." The defense, or explanation, Nick wasn't sure which, came to his lips immediately. "I couldn't, wouldn't, have been okay without him."

Arioch made a sound of long-suffering disbelief. "Please. A mere human is no match for the power of a reporbate seraph."

Elemiah's eyebrows drew down, though. "Not unless they're s—"

"That hasn't happened for untold generations!"

"Forty," Elemiah said steadily.

"That's longer ago than the last Exalted!"

"And that may be why there *was* an Exalted." Elemiah's patience clearly snapped as Chris muttered, "You feel like maybe we're getting the highlights reel and not the main story here, Nicky?"

"Go home, Nicholas," Elemiah said. "Live quietly. Survive. Keep your brother nearby, if you can."

"What?" Chris's voice shot up. "I don't belong in college—"

"We could argue about that again," Nick muttered, but Chris glared at him, then at the angels.

"Forget it, we'll figure it out. In the meantime how do I, like, unpray an angel? Banish you, or whatever?"

"*Banish?*" Arioch's nostrils flared. "We're not lapdogs to be called when y—"

"I mean, you called him a lapdog," Chris said, gesturing to Elemiah."

"I called him a *dogsbody*, you ignorant mortal, and—"

"Do I just say, hey God, never mind, they can go home now? Because if that works—"

"Tsssht!" The sound was equal parts reprimand and silencing as Arioch turned his attention elsewhere. "Elemiah, what have you done?"

The smaller angel turned away, too, tension riding through his shoulders. "This was not me, Arioch. What use have I for archangels?"

Nick said, "For *wha*t?" and the church doors burst open.

———

Chris said, "Again?" not so far under his breath that it couldn't be heard, and stepped in front of Nick, dipping his hands to his waist. He came up with knives Nick hadn't noticed before, knives Nick had never *seen* before, with blades that glimmered like fire and gold. "Stay back, Nicky."

"Chris, if they're archangels, you shouldn't—" Nick didn't know how to finish that sentence. "You should let me..."

Elemiah and Chris both barked, "No!" while the fallen angel tilted a skeptical eyebrow at that call. Nick, feeling a momentary solidarity with him, spread his hands a few inches in frustration, and the angel grinned. Then, as if in agreement that the other two weren't wrong while also not necessarily being right, Arioch looked to the back of the church, his smile falling away, and Nick followed his gaze.

If Arioch and Elemiah were handsome, the leader of the entering group was literally otherworldly. He was of medium build, medium height: nothing that would be noticed in a crowd, were it not for the beauty of his features. Roughly curled dark hair with touches of grey, even darker eyes, and a short-cropped beard that made Nick wish he could grow a decent one himself. He stopped a few steps inside the church, a host of others falling out behind him. They looked human, next to him, although the hiss of power in Nick's mind said they weren't. It said they were all ripe for plucking, easy targets, although that certainty faded when he glanced back at the leader, whose beauty was marred, he thought, by a streak of arrogance.

Like Elemiah, the newcomers wore something similar to agbada, with loose-fitting shirts and trousers under the flowing robe. Unlike Elemiah, though, they were all visibly armed, swords and spears carried with long-familiar ease. Nick's mind skittered over the name of the weapon the leader carried, and a thin strand of bleak recognition lifted it into his awareness: a halbert. Raphael carried a halbert, Saboac's knowledge told him, and that was far more information than Nick wanted, if it came from the dark angel.

Raphael's host filled the back of the church, echelons to the archangel's left and right. It wasn't, Nick thought, a strong defensive line, although what the hell that meant, when there were a couple dozen of them and four on his side, he didn't know. Still, somewhere within him, he thought he could take them without much effort.

As if that thought somehow conveyed itself to Raphael, the archangel slipped a thin, sharp smile, and extended his halbert, the pike pointed directly at Nick's chest. "That one."

Chris stepped in front of Nick as if it was the easiest, the most natural, thing in the world to do, and for an instant, Raphael's smugly certain expression twisted to surprised confusion. "Move, mortal."

"Sure." Chris stalked forward, knives spinning in his hands, moving to a throwing position. "How close you want me? 'cause I got a good angle from here."

Arioch said, "Christopher," and Chris said, "I got this," without looking at the fallen angel at all.

"You place yourself between a heavenly host and an abomination?" Raphael's voice, as beautiful as the other angels', also carried a vast weight of confusion.

Chris, clearly on purpose, muttered, "Abomination, that's you, right, Harry?"

"*Excuse* me?" Arioch, magnificently offended, stepped forward like he meant to take issue with Chris. The back of his shirt was shredded, two long thin cuts near his spine with myriad other slices, much smaller, lining the longer ones. Elemiah matched him on Chris's other side, eyeing them both.

Nick thought he saw it half a heartbeat before the archangel did, the way his brother and their angels had *all* put themselves between Nick and the host. He croaked, "No," but Raphael's grin broke bright and cold.

"You side with the abomination, Elemiah?"

"Still not clear on who the abomination is," Chris said brightly. Arioch hissed at him, cat-like, with his jaw dropped and the sound coming from deep in his throat. Chris shrugged easily, then, with only the warning of casual grace, flung one of his gold-tilted knives toward the sneering archangel.

Raphael's defense left a smeared afterimage in Nick's memory, as if he'd more imagined than seen it. A flicker, really, hardly anything more, a sweep of *wing*, if the blur in his mind could be trusted. Color, not fire, maybe feather, but bright and quick and taking the impact of the knife effortlessly. Nick tried tracking the knife's trajectory and couldn't find it in his memory, much less with his gaze.

Then the hilt clattered to the floor, the blade—melted,

although that suggested heat or fire or at least ice turning to water, and the knife didn't seem to have gone through that kind of transformation. It had simply disappeared, as if absorbed into the wing buffet. Chris said, "Fuck!" in surprise as Raphael laughed and Arioch yowled, "That was priceless beyond measure, you idiot!"

"It worked on the demons!"

"It worked on the demons because it was made from *angel feathers*!"

"Well, how was I supposed to know?"

"I warned you!"

"You said my name!"

"I said your *full* name!"

Chris made an explosive sound of derision and sheathed the second knife in favor of one of his regular blades. "I took those from *Hell*," Arioch growled. "You have no idea how much trouble I'm going to be in."

"Dude, I think we're in enough trouble already!" Chris gestured at the host of angels, whose anger-neutral expressions were fading toward incredulity.

"This is the defense you muster?" Raphael asked Elemiah, clearly amused. "You don't even belong here, Eli, ne—"

"This is precisely where I belong," Elemiah said with such soft conviction that even Raphael faltered. "My duty as a Power is to restrain evil where I find it on the earthly plane, Raphael. *You* have no business here, but this is *exactly* where I belong. And the situation is under control. You are most welcome to return to Heaven."

Raphael's lip curled, and Nick became aware that the angel host were shifting, preparing for a fight. His stomach clenched, grendel power equally at the ready, and his hands turned to slow fists. If he acted now, took them by surprise—

"An Exalted is an abomination before the Lord," Raphael all but purred. "You do not *contain* that, Elemiah. You do not *restrain* it. You slay it, as if it was a dragon."

"Even dragons are afforded a chance," Elemiah said steadily. "If I require your assistance, Archangel, I assure you that I'll call upon it. In the meantime—"

"In the meantime, nothing," Raphael snarled. "The abomination will die, and die now."

"You know," Nick said under his breath, "maybe I'd be less of an abomination before the Lord if things would stop trying to *kill me*."

"Kill him," Raphael said flatly.

For an instant Nick hardly understood what the archangel had said. The host did, though: they moved together, so smoothly that their advance felt like a kind of conviction of its own. Arioch and Elemiah both stepped in front of Chris, whose sound of protest almost made Nick laugh. Nobody got in front of *Chris*. It was his job to get in front of Nick, to be the protector, not the protected. "It's good for you," Nick said in a thin voice. "See what it feels like."

Chris cast him a brief, grim look, but his attention snapped forward again as a sound like rainstorms on tin roofs rumbled through the church, and impossible light erupted through it. The angels—*their* angels—were winged now, massive, fire-lined feathers on Elemiah and strains of light slicing through Arioch's shirt. A fallen angel shouldn't have wings like that, made of translucence, like the substance had been ripped away and only divinity remained. Those wings looked so much more celestial, so much more etherial, than the grey and gold and fire of Elemiah's.

Raphael's host didn't bother with wings, at first. They just roared forward like wind and snow and ice battering anything in its way, and the first clash of power shattered every window in the church. Angels, it appeared, could bleed, although Nick didn't know where the blood came from, whether it was their angels or the others. Elemiah had a blade now, a sword of fire that looked too big for anything mortal to wield, and it scythed through one of the angel host effortlessly.

Not scythed. That would require a scythe, not a sword. Nick hung up on the thought, trying not to go beyond it. Trying not to see blood as essence, as power that could be drained to strengthen him. The grendel magic burned for that essence, despising the limitations of a frail human body. Even a frail human body that could contain demon power, that could manipulate and employ that power, still had nothing on angelic strength. The strains of Saboac left in him craved that shit, longing for its own lost divinity, and Nick, trying to separate himself from the demon-fueled magic, wondered if the angelic power could shore *him* up, quench some of the demon essence he'd taken on. The knife made of angel feathers had killed demons, Chris said. Maybe the two conflicting magics would give Nick some space to maneuver in.

He hadn't quite believed Chris. Saboac, within him, had recognized the angels' divinity, but Nick still hadn't *quite* believed it. He knew that now, as Arioch sliced with one of those intangible wings and somehow scored a palpable hit despite its insubstantiality. He hadn't *not* believed him, but the wings were…

"Convincing, aren't they," Chris muttered as he retreated to Nick's side. "I didn't really believe it either until I saw the wings. They're gonna get their asses kicked, Nicky. I have a vial of holy water and a knife that angel wings absorb, so I'm about as useful here as a sack of wet shit."

"Delightful image, Chris, thanks, that's what I wanted to die thinking of."

"You're not gonna die."

"Yeah? What am I gonna do, then?"

"You're gonna power up and fight."

"Chris…"

"Nicky, there's like twenty-seven angels in here and most of them want to kill you, so unless you got a better idea, this is it." Chris almost contained a flinch as their angels met with

Raphael's host in a clash of metal, and a broken piece of weaponry sailed past the barrier of Elemiah's wings. "This is definitely it."

"I can't." Nick's voice sounded small, even to him, even considering the shouts and unearthly rumble of angels at war. "I can feel it all inside me, Chris. Saboac wants the angel power as much as the demon power. It wants me to go all Sith on them. I can't stay...me. I can't stay good."

"You can." Chris grabbed the back of Nick's head, pulling his forehead against his own. "I gotcha, all right? You do whatever the fuck you have to do, and I'll get you back, okay? S'what I do. S'what I'm here for, arright?"

"Chris, you—you kept Dad off my back, you kept me alive on—" Nick crushed his eyes closed, barely able to choose the words, so many of them rose to be spoken. "On freak hunts, on days when there wasn't any food, on...you made sure I got to college. This isn't the same. You know it's not the same."

"It's exactly the same, okay? It's exactly the same. You get in trouble, I figure out how to fix it. That's how it works. So if you got an idea what to do, Nicky, you gotta go with it, because your guardian angels are getting their fine asses handed to themselves."

Nick, entirely against his own expectations, burst out laughing. "Those are Heaven's asses, huh?"

"They really fucking are." Chris let him go and lifted his chin toward the fight. "Go on. Show 'em what you're made of, bro."

Nick hesitated one more moment. "It's a bad idea."

"I know." Chris's voice gentled. "Now go on."

# CHAPTER 19

THE WORST PART, LIKE SLIPPING BACK INTO HUNTING AND
fighting with Chris when they'd gone after the vamps that
killed their dad, the worst part was how *easy* it was. The
grendel power was there, right there, not something he had to
reach for, not something he had to try to find in himself. He
just had to stop fighting the impulse to use it, and there it was,
filling him, making his hands ache as it loosened in him, as it
tried to escape. *Directing* it was hard, Nick didn't know if he
could, didn't know if he could tell it the difference between an
enemy and an ally and have it care.

The answer, obviously, was to get in front of his allies, so
he wouldn't risk them. Couldn't risk them.

There were so many *wings*, though. Arioch's slices of light,
cutting so brilliantly it hurt Nick's eyes as he edged forward;
Elemiah's thunderous, fire-edged feathers, overwhelming with
the clap and swing of battle. Raphael hadn't yet unfurled his,
but the others, the host, they were now airborne and earth-
bound twists and storms of white wings, and it was so fucking
*loud*. Chris went sideways from where Nick went, not fighting,
and some thin nasty thread of betrayal whispered that in the
crux of it, Chris didn't have his back after all. The power did,
though. All he had to do was *use* it, and he would be unstop-

pable. Untouchable. He could take a stand, and the world would crumble around him. All he had to do was let go.

Elemiah's wings burned, where they touched his skin. Not even his skin: Nick wore too many layers for the wings to actually touch him, but the fire bled through canvas and flannel to scorch him anyway. Because he was demon-powered, of course. Because the grendel magic was anathema to angelic power. He would need to destroy Elemiah, too, then. Probably the fallen angel, too, and take their strength as his own. Power curled in his hands, almost physical in form, like whips of magic that he pulled back to release.

But then Chris was there again, in his line of sight. He had a weapon now, a—laughter scraped Nick's throat as he recognized it. An angel's weapon, the pike's head that one of them had lost to Elemiah's sword. He swung, huge upward movement, and an angel's wing split under the blade. Ichor sprayed and the angel screamed. Chris got an awful grin Nick had only seen a few times before, and threw himself into the fight with reckless confidence. Elemiah cried out hoarsely, a warning, but by then Nick was past him, past Arioch, and the immediate enemy—the ones Chris fought—was in front of him.

Nick cast that whip-like feeling of power forward, watching darkness streak from his hands, as if he'd unleashed the demons he'd absorbed. An angel turned, slamming their poleaxe downward, and Nick screamed as the holy blade effortlessly cut apart his attack and pain backwashed into him. The world around him went black, pinpoint fury that focused on the angel that had hurt him. Thunderclap, that's what Chris called it: Nick brought his hands together at speed, seeing nothing but the angel, and then nothing at all as power ripped through him, through the angel, ruptured it into a blaze of light and unearthly essence. He lashed a hand forward, trying to capture that fading glory, but it was gone so *fast.* He couldn't take it, if he destroyed them from a distance.

Somebody—the angel Elemiah—said his name again, from very far away. Not that far. Couldn't be that far. They were in a small building, so Elemiah couldn't be more than a few feet away, but he *sounded* a world away, a universe away. Far enough that Nick could ignore him, because what could the angel say that would help, when angels were the enemy here.

They weren't angry, the angels. Not most of them. The ones he fought now, the ones that were easy to destroy, they met the fight with implacable conviction. They were so singularly focused on their duty and the righteousness of that duty that there was nothing to gain hold of, nothing to manipulate or shift or change. Nick spat like he was hacking away the uselessness of the skill he'd learned from the female bounty they'd picked up. Rejecting it, if it couldn't do him any good on the battlefield.

Although Raphael. Raphael, who stood apart from the fight, sneering, smug, seething with hatred. Raphael had something that skill could hook into, something that could drive the archangel mad, if Nick got deep enough inside his head. A white-winged angel threw itself at him and he caught it by the throat, the motion familiar, although it took a moment to remember he'd grabbed Saboac that way in their first encounter.

Saboac had put its hand on Nick's forehead, then. Woken his grendel power, or maybe poured some of its own essence into Nick, into the human vessel that could contain and survive and use inhuman magic. This angel beat at him with its wings, tried to stab him, and died, if that's what angels did, when Nick dragged its ethereal substance from it the way he'd done with the demons that swarmed him. Its light went out, sank into him, and flared through channels of understanding of how to use that power. He flexed his shoulders, sharply disappointed to find wings didn't spring forth, and discarded the angel's body in search of more prey.

There was Chris again, bloody now, that demented grin still in place. He had a different poleaxe, an unbroken one, and used it with a violent skill that suggested years of practice. Nick didn't think his brother had ever picked up a poleaxe before. There were angels around him, dead or dying, and Nick—pounced, he thought he pounced, cleared more air than he should be able to—to get his hands on one of the dying ones, ripping its essence from him. Saboac's wisdom howled within him, gleeful with the influx of power, and then there was Arioch, brilliant and beautiful and bloody, grinning down at Nick with an awfulness that not even Chris's bared teeth could match.

"Exciting," the fallen angel said. "Very exciting. Can't wait to see what happens next." He spun away in a blur of slicing wing, leaving Nick to heave a breath and try, for one desperate scrambling moment, to remember who *he* was, what *he* wanted. The rest of the church came into focus then, just briefly, and Nick recoiled, falling onto his butt as he began to see what he—what they—had wrought.

The dead lay everywhere, in drifts of feathers that had little to do with power, anymore. There were still several on their feet, some surrounding Elemiah, who fought with blade and wing but not the pillar of fire that Chris said he could, and a few trying, but losing badly, to Arioch, whose ruthless brutality seemed like it might have been enough to win the day all on its own. Chris, in the moment, stood alone, beaten but nowhere near broken. On the surface, at a glance, it looked like the power now bleeding from Nick's hands hadn't even been necessary.

Except beneath it all lay gory lines, dark streaks where Nick had scraped away the angels' strength, gathered it into himself, weakened them enough to turn the tide their way, and it still called to him, begging, demanding, that he take what was left, and more. His hands glowed, black light that wobbled in his vision, blurring his very bones as it crawled through his body. His eyes were hot, dark fire dripping from them, flickering through them, like if he caught a glimpse of himself in the mirror he would see a blazing monster, its eyes alight with death. Even his throat tasted like fire as he tried to cough a denial, tried to voice a refusal, tried to say this wasn't *him*.

The word burned to death on his tongue as Raphael, a slow, poisonous smile baring his teeth, stepped into the fray with unfurled emerald wings. Literally emerald, Nick thought: certainly that color, but not soft like feathered wings, and with a translucent depth that looked like light through stone, or stone through water. There were flaws in those wings, cracks of lighter and darker shades that made up the lines of where pinions might be, and running along the heavy bones, giving the impression of innumerable battles fought and uncountable scars survived. The archangel clapped those wings and a sound like avalanches shattered through the church.

Nick heard Chris mumble, "Oh, fuck," and had just enough humanity left in him to agree before all hell broke loose.

———

The angels Chris had been fighting died too easily.

That wasn't right. It couldn't be right. There was no way battling an actual angelic host could be too *easy*, even if he'd picked up one of their own weapons to use against them. The broken pike had been good, but the poleaxe he took off one of the feathery bastards he killed with the pike was much better, like, why did this weapon ever go out of fashion levels of better.

The answer, obviously, was range weapons and guns, but that took away from the satisfaction of slashing and stabbing through a blood tide of anger that Chris didn't even think was about the fight at hand, or the enemy they faced. It had to do with keeping Nick safe, with blind fury at *anything* that threatened his little brother. Demons, angels, schoolyard bullies, their dad, it didn't really matter. He'd been fighting for Nick his whole life and he wasn't gonna stop now. Simple as that.

The poleaxe seemed to help focus the anger, though. It fit well in his hands, didn't weigh too much, could be used defensively, and killed the bad guys at a comfortable distance, or not, as he preferred. But they died too easily, and he didn't really understand why. It wasn't him. It wasn't even Nicky, although the glimpses he caught of his brother were terrifying, like his humanity was slipping. Like it *had* slipped, and everything left was a battleground between good and bad.

Then the archangel spread his wings, and Chris understood why it had been so easy. Whatever he'd been fighting, they were the little guys. The foot soldiers. More than human, sure, with their wings and their holy weapons, but maybe not much more than vampires, except on the other side of the equation. A little too fast, maybe. A little stronger than you'd expect. But not a *power*, not the way the archangel was.

That power flexed with the archangel's wings, the landslide-like sound only the smallest expression of his strength. Even so, you couldn't hear that sound and imagine anything human could stand up to it. The noise itself was crushing, never mind the battering sweep of dark green that cleared most of the floor of the fallen.

*Hah*! The sound barked in Chris's mind, although he didn't think it was audible. Cleared the floor of the dead, maybe. The *Fallen* leaped that wing sweep effortlessly, his own insubstantial wings flared in brilliant, if ineffective, glory. Only a few steps away, Elemiah leapt upward as well, but unlike Arioch, he didn't come back down again. His wings swept open too, but not just the broad two-wing spread of before. Six wings, like Saboac, except the resemblance ended there. Saboac's wings had been so closely entwined seeing that there were three to a side had been hard. Each set of Eli's was as massive as the first, and their beating against the air, against the church walls, against the threatening thunder of Raphael's wings, could bring down mountain ranges.

Chris had figured Eli could fly, on some level. He had to be able to, because he'd leaped over Chris's head while carrying Nick, earlier. That leap had more in common with flight than jumping, but it wasn't the same, it wasn't half the same as watching Elemiah take flight, watching him hang there in the air, and slam a pillar of fire toward the earth and sky.

Raphael shrieked, more fury than pain, and leaped skyward too. Another avalanche scrape rattled the church as another two sets of emerald wings burst forth, carrying through the fire without issue, although it ran gold over the green of his wings. The clash of weaponry, Raphael's halberd and Elemiah's sword, screamed through the church like it would take the walls down. The archangel's wings *did* batter the ceiling, powerful emerald bones cracking rafters and sending a rain of drywall and paint down to incinerate in Eli's flames. Eli's wingtips bent, though, his wingspan too broad to fit across the church, or even down it as they spun through aerial combat, but he stayed in the air, with fire roaring over everything it touched.

Nothing burned, as if the holy ground recognized its own, but the air got too hot to breathe, hot enough to taste as it crawled down Chris's throat, and battered away again by all of the wings. The world was full of wings and maybe nothing else, their sound relentless, and somewhere in the midst of the unforgiving noise he remembered that Biblical descriptions of angels tended toward the terrifying. Now he understood why. He croaked a protest even he couldn't hear, but Arioch looked his way, then leaped again, ephemeral wings spread.

This time he landed on Raphael's back like a cat trying to claw its way up a person to escape a bath. The archangel's wings collapsed into nothingness and they both fell, landing with shattering weight on pews that went up in a scatter of splinters. His halberd disappeared in the chaos, and Elemiah dropped, his wings, but not his fire, folding away. The church suddenly seemed much, much larger.

Not quite big enough, though, to contain Nicky.

Chris's brother looked like a wild thing, raw power barely kept in check by a human shape. He looked scraped thin, skin too tight over his bones, like Saboac had been, except once upon a time Saboac had had access to unearthly beauty, and Nicky was only human to begin with, so now he was cadaverous, blood-dark veins throttling his neck and face and even his hands. His hands kept opening and closing as if he couldn't control them, and he prowled forward like a predator, not like a human, but a cat or a shark or a frickin' velociraptor, Chris didn't know, but it looked dangerous and inhuman and blood-thirsty.

One of the few remaining angels put herself between Nick and Raphael as the archangel threw off the effects of dropping twenty feet into oak pews. Nick caught her by the throat and threw her aside effortlessly, but not before a glimmer of power surged from her into him and he *brightened*, then dimmed again like dense smoke was swirling in front of a lamp, except inside him. He stalked through Eli's fire, teeth bared in a hiss, and through the wall of flame Chris saw astonishment cross the angel's face. He reached for Nicky, then clearly thought better of it, even before Arioch growled a low sound of warning.

The castaway was on his feet again, his shirt in tatters and his face scarred with smoke and ash, even though he hadn't gone through Eli's pillar, not that Chris had seen. Raphael came to his feet with a roar, casting his wings wide again. They hit Arioch so hard the blonde angel slammed backward into a wall and slid down it, cartoon-like. Elemiah leaped after him without seeming to consider it, just the one set of his wings spreading to carry him over the archangel.

Which left no one between Nick and Raphael, because Chris didn't think he could get there fast enough. He tried anyway, launching himself over more space than normal with the poleaxe's haft as help, but Nicky had his hands in Raphael's robe before Chris was halfway there.

The shockwave of their engagement knocked Chris on his ass anyway, throwing him halfway back across the floor again. Pews didn't break when *he* smashed into them. The shock of pain screaming through every part of his body suggested probably *he* had broken, but in the moment his nerves were too stunned to try anything beyond sending pain and panic through his whole system.

Didn't matter. Didn't matter. Couldn't help Nicky if he was out for the count himself, so he made himself stand and decided he could, if only just. Nothing was broken, maybe. The poleaxe helped, he could lean on that and take a couple of shuddering breaths before pushing himself forward. Whatever was going on, Nick needed backup, and the angels were fucking around somewhere else. Chris couldn't see them anymore. 'course, he couldn't see much that wasn't right at the end of his own nose, except the blur and brilliance of his little brother throwing down with an archangel.

Raphael's wings wouldn't fucking stop battering the air, although he didn't seem to be able to buffet Nick the way he wanted to. Every time those huge emerald things closed, they bounced back again like they'd hit something invisible. Semi-visible. Chris thought he could maybe see a wall of smoke-stained power washing around Nick, almost like Eli's column of flame, except sort of...evil.

He hoped he'd just hit his head so hard he couldn't see anything clearly.

Nick, snarling, got one hand off Raphael's robes and planted it over the archangel's face like he might dig his eyes out. Instead power flared, violent green, with such a back-wash that Chris stumbled again, then gasped as the pain fled.

All of it, down to the blurry vision, down to the thick bone-bruised feeling in his spine, down to the spots in his hamstrings that were so numb from pummeling he'd hardly been able to feel them. Even exhaustion washed out of him, leaving him feeling like he'd had a great night's sleep and could maybe use a breakfast platter the size of Wyoming. His grim shuffle forward turned into a dead run, and all at once Eli and Arioch were coming from the archangel's other side, too, like they'd planned a coordinated attack.

And in the middle of it, Nick looked—better, almost. Burning bright, instead of stained with the dark threads of demon essence. Chris bellowed a warning at his angels, hoping they'd see it too, but almost as quickly as the improvement came, it faded again. Nick's lips pulled back, baring his teeth, and for a second Chris actually thought his brother was gonna bite Raphael's neck, like he'd turned into some ether-sucking vampire. Assuming angels had ether for blood, anyway. Something like that.

Nick didn't have to close his teeth on Raphael's throat, though: he visibly drew power with his grip, the same kind of surge as from the angel Chris had just watched him drain, except so much more. *So* much more, waves instead of glimmers, and it fought with the grendel power, rising in conquest and then falling into disarray, until the archangel's wings dulled, their glassy depths thickening from translucent emerald to opaque jade. It happened fast, so fast that Chris had barely made it to within striking distance with the poleaxe before Raphael shrieked and broke Nick's grip, flinging himself away.

"Abomination, unclean, befouled, desecration, profane." Each word came in a rough snarl, like the weight of them might drive Nick to the ground. And maybe it did, because Chris's brother dropped to his knees, screaming with power that rolled off him in pulses. Chris staggered the last step or two to get in front of him, to put himself between the archangel and his brother, and for the space of a heartbeat, and then longer, both the power roiling off Nick and the archangel's litany failed.

Raphael hissed, "Away," and Chris managed a laugh from somewhere deep in his soul, although it came out as more of a shudder than a sound.

"Like hell."

"You will die for this abomination."

"Every day of the week and twice on Sundays," Chris agreed, and the flash of confusion in the archangel's eyes momentarily made the flood of abject terror that Chris was trying not to notice worthwhile. Raphael's gaze darted to the poleaxe Chris held, almost reminding Chris himself of it, and, inspired, he spun it. It cut through the air, leaving a streak of gold in its wake, and he didn't think he imagined the light of caution that sprang to Raphael's face. "Or you could die instead," Chris suggested.

He almost thought it wasn't going to work, but then Arioch and Elemiah were there beside him, the three of them a wall of wing and weapon between Raphael and Nicky. Raphael shuddered, his face contorting with hate, and the glance he gave Eli warned of oncoming vengeance. "Do not imagine this has ended. This will be engraved against you in the Books of Law."

"This is my very purpose," Elemiah said with enough serenity even Chris thought it came across as snide. "Yours lies elsewhere. Whether my name or yours is written, or stricken, from the Books remains to be seen."

"He takes the very grace from our bones, Elemiah."

"Then best you return to the second Sphere before yours bleeds away in its entirety."

Raphael's face slackened with surprise. "You wouldn't."

"I?" Elemiah lifted a broad shoulder and let it fall again. "I would do nothing, but even Powers cannot contain an Exalted forever."

Nick screamed again, as if he'd been waiting for the cue. To Chris's not-particularly-secret delight, the archangel flinched, then snarled. "I promise you this has not ended, Power."

"Probably not," Eli said, still with that irritating serenity. "But it has ended *for now*."

Fire thundered around him, around all of them, a blazing tower that flashed over Chris's skin, over Arioch, who had kept uncharacteristically quiet for the last minute or two, and over Nick, who howled again. When it banked, Raphael was gone, along with the few other angels who had survived the attack. Elemiah sagged, and Arioch, breezily, said, "An admirable effort, Power. You'll pay for that."

"In all likelihood." Eli turned toward Nick, his expression breaking, and Chris's stomach clenched as he spun to see what was wrong.

Nick was on his feet, cracks of light breaking through his skin with dark boiling power rushing in the depths of those cracks. His hands, the palms upturned, were the color of blood and fire, split along the lifelines, skin looking like it rose away from his flesh and bones. He turned one hand left and right, examining it as if it was a tool to be dissected, then lifted an awful smile toward Chris. "I can see the heart of the universe."

Arioch made such a dismissive sound that even Elemiah shot him a look, but Nick tilted his head, eyes wide and blank with blazing power. "You think not?"

"I think no mortal can contain the knowledge to do so. If you even so much as looked upon the its edge, you would immolate wi—" The rest of his condescension was lost as Nick turned his palm toward him and light, laced with dark-ness, exploded out.

Chris gave a hoarse yell, shielding his eyes and twisting to follow the bolt's path. It shot through the church wall, blazed a mark across the night, and hadn't yet faded when Chris whipped back toward his brother. "What the hell are you doing, Nicky, that asshole is on our side!"

"Please." Nick's lip curled. "A castaway angel? The Fallen Throne? Even if he was, I would have to destroy him, but *really*, Chris, why would the castaway be on our side? We all know you're not the brightest, brother. Maybe you should sit this one out. Let your betters deal with the corrupted divine."

Pain as pure and clear as a knife's blade sliced so deep in Chris's chest he had to put his hand there, look down, to see if he was actually bleeding. No. No knives, no blades, just the fucking awful power of words, cutting away his breath, his heart, his belief. That last was always shaky, especially in himself. An easy target. Easier than the blood and bone and muscle, really, and he knew it.

Nick knew it.

Nicky wouldn't say that, though. Nicky who kept telling him he was smarter than he thought, that he could do more than he expected of himself. Nicky was full of shit, yeah, but he'd never admit that. He'd never tell Chris how fucking useless he was. He wouldn't, and Chris knew it, and the cut fucking landed anyway, punched right through him and made him forget how to breathe, made him forget he'd ever known how to breathe.

He looked up again, but it took such a long time to look up again, to meet the soulless glory of Nick's blazing gaze, and somehow he found enough breath to say, "Better to reign in Hell, right? Isn't that what Arioch said? That's enough reason for him to take your side, and if he took your side, he took mine, Nicky." That was it, that was all, there wasn't any more breath in his body, and that was okay because at least that way it couldn't be knocked out of him again.

A flicker of irritation darted across his brother's face. "And do you have an excuse for the Power, too? Perhaps the dogsbody wants to serve a different king? Why else would he let an Exalted live?" A noise came on the end of that, a hiss so broad and deep it didn't sound like it had come from a human animal at all. Nick's hand flashed forward, seizing Elemiah, who neither bellowed nor burst with power the way Raphael had when Nick had grabbed him. He only wrapped a hand around Nick's wrist, blocking some of the terrible glare that bled off Nick's skin.

"The judgement on your survival has not yet been passed, Exalted. But Arioch was right. You shouldn't have lasted this long, much less been able to do what you do now, and while I see all too clearly how dangerous is the path I've chosen, I am not yet, I think, at its end. There's time yet, to pass judgement."

"Not if I drain you of power," Nick whispered.

Eli's eyebrows rose. "I invite you to try."

"*Dude!* That is a *terrible idea!*"

It was also obviously too late, as power crackled around Nick's fingers and rage turned his mouth to a thin line. He clawed the fingers of his other hand, clearly trying to drag Elemiah's strength from him.

Instead, he drew fire.

That pillar of incorruptible flame scored across Nick's hands, down his arms, over his chest, singeing, snapping, incandescent, and catching bits of visible grendel power to ignite them. Nick screamed, a low hoarse sound, and Chris took a hard, uncertain step forward. "Eli—"

"He should burn," Elemiah replied softly. "An Exalted so far gone as he is should simply burn, Christopher. I am a Power. The least destructive aspect of my duties is to bind irredeemable evil on the mortal plane, and more often, it is my duty to destroy it. Your brother should burn."

"Well fucking stop it if you think he's gonna fucking immolate!"

The Power smiled briefly, glancing up at him. "And, you see, I begin to suspect why he does not."

"I don't see! Let him *go!*" Chris took another step, wanting to pull the angel off his brother and fairly certain that even if Nicky wasn't burning, *he* would, if he laid hands in Elemiah.

Eli murmured, "In a moment." The fire swallowed Nick whole, then faded as he yowled again, and Elemiah moved back. "I can do nothing more for him."

"Looks to me like you did too fucking much already!" Chris stumbled forward, catching Nick's shoulders. "Nicky, buddy, you in there?"

His brother's eyes were blank again, empty of everything that meant anything to Chris. "I need their power."

"You need fuck all except a sandwich and a good night's sleep." Chris's voice cracked and he swallowed down heartache. "Come on, man."

Anger twisted Nick's face again. "Get out of my way, Chris."

"On a cold day in Hell, man." Chris cast a desperate look over his shoulder, relieved to see Arioch, brushing at his shirt as if it wasn't already bedraggled, stepping through the gaping hole in the church's wall. "Is that a thing? Cold days in Hell?"

"Any unpleasantry you might imagine is a thing in Hell," Arioch replied airily, without looking up. "How deeply childish of you, Nicholas. Did you really imagine a little bolt of the corrupted divine could obliterate one whose entire self is made up of the same? Oh." The last word came more softly as he caught sight of Nick, and he came forward more quietly, as if finding himself unexpectedly at a memorial. Nick reached past Chris with shaking, clawed hands.

Chris grabbed his wrist with a lot less effect than Eli had done, although Nick at least looked at him. "Fine, you want them, you gotta go through me first."

A snarl twisted Nick's face again. "Don't be stupid."

"Oh, you just made it real clear that stupid is my only stock in trade, Nicky, so I guess this is the road I'm on. You want the angels, you can go kill them, whatever, but you're going to have to kill me first, because I'm not gonna let you do this shit while I'm still alive." There was a hollow place in his chest, his heart slamming around in it like it was looking for something to hang on to.

"*Rrrangh!*" The sound clearly came from Nick's belly, scraping his throat on the way through, and he shoved Chris hard enough to knock him backward, careening toward shattered pews. He caught himself and came forward again, shaking his head.

"Gonna hafta do better than that, Nicky. I'm st—hff." *That* sound came from Chris's solar plexus emptying out, leaving him no room to pull air in again, as Nick's fist caught him in the gut. He was a big kid these days, Nicky was, but the blow felt like a sledgehammer, not something human.

Probably about the same way that stupid fucking text Chris had sent about their dad's death had caught Nick. He sucked air in around his teeth, but couldn't get it farther into his body than his throat. Didn't matter. He stumbled forward again, and by the time he got hold of Nick's shoulders he could almost drag in a fresh breath. "'m still here. C'mon, Nicky, do it right or give this shit up."

The next hit was pure magic, and that almost made it easier. Not the impact, the impact hurt like fuck, he didn't even know what he'd *hit*, except probably not the pews, 'cause it hurt all over, evenly, instead of in a lot of painfully individual locations. A wall. Probably a wall. That was good, he could use the wall to push up to his feet again. It would have helped if there was something, anything, to sort of brace himself on, a chair or one of the pews or even another poleaxe, but either the angel weaponry had disappeared with them or he just wasn't close enough to see any.

That was about enough putting off the inevitable. He got up again, shaking his head like a bull. Feeling bull-headed, in fact. A grin slashed his face and this time he rushed his brother, tackling him with a shoulder in the belly, and the next couple minutes, seconds, eons, he couldn't tell, were filled with fists and elbows and one epic headbutt that left him cross-eyed and dizzy. He hadn't exactly shaken that off when Nick pinned him, raining hits down with the rhythmic certainty of inevitability. Oh, he was screwed. Totally screwed, couldn't get a defense up if he tried, so in the end he just mumbled, "'sokay, Nicky. 'sokay. Did my best. So'd you. Sometimes shit just happens, right? 'sokay. You do what you gotta. I love you, though, man, okay? Don't forget that. Don't forget."

Nicky went still for a heartbeat, then two, then three, until they stretched into enough time for Chris to start really feeling the jelly his face and torso and shoulders had been pummeled into. Then Nick threw himself backward with a terrible noise, anguish tied with rage and despair. "Chris?"

"Hey, good job." A tiny, broken laugh cracked Chris's throat. "Good job, man, you stopped. Good job, Nicky. But I gotta…I gotta rest now, okay, Nick? Just gimme…a minute, okay…?" He couldn't count the places that hurt. Could maybe count the places that didn't, if he remembered any of their names. Toes. Maybe his toes didn't hurt. Maybe. The world was kind of fuzzy, anyway, dim and getting dimmer, like he really did need that rest, except Elemiah came into his line of vision when all he wanted to do was pass out.

"I lack Raphael's gift for healing," Elemiah murmured. "I can't take all the pain away, as he did. But I can improve the situation, at least, if you'll let me."

It took way too long to even open his eyes again, much less vaguely remember the burst of emerald power that had filled the church, and that he'd gotten up again, unhurt, afterward. "Is that what happened?" It didn't matter. He tried to flap a hand dismissively, but the hand wouldn't flap. Or do anything else, either. No wonder he hadn't been able to block Nicky's punches. His arms didn't work anymore. "Do your worst, man, it's gotta be better than this."

Chris's vision faded out again, or maybe Eli just squinted. "I'm not sure how my worst could be better."

"Just heal him, Elemiah," Arioch said impatiently from somewhere out of sight, and an oddly soothing wash of flame flared over Chris's eyes, and then the rest of him. It burned the pain away, or at least most of it, like fire could somehow reduce swelling and bruising to days-old memories instead of fresh injuries. He grunted, checking to see if he could breathe easily again, then sat up and forgot everything else as he caught sight of Nicky, sagging on the floor like a rag doll without support. Only rag dolls would have caught fire by now from the heat and glow spilling off his brother's face and arms and body.

"I can't hold it." Nick's voice was thin and high and scared. "I'm going to burn up, I'm burning up, I can't hold it, Chris. It's too much, the angel...I can hold the demon but not the angel power, Saboac wanted the angel power but it's too much, I can't—"

"Why the fuck?" Chris swung his gaze toward Arioch, toward Elemiah, looking for an answer, and unexpectedly found one in Arioch's regretful voice.

"Saboac was *desanctified*," the fallen angel said softly. "Made unholy by God herself. The grendel power is demon-born, and because demons are born in turn of humanity, an Exalted can carry that magic, use it, wield it. But angels are another thing entirely, Christopher. Remove our capacity to touch the divine, and all we are is monsters. That's what desanctified is, to the Spheres. Even whole, even not scattered through your brother's mind and power, Saboac cannot wield the divine, not anymore, no more than a—" His hesitation as he searched for a metaphor was obvious, and wasted precious time. "No more than a corrupted battery could hold a charge," he finished after a few seconds. "The power might reside in it momentarily, but then it fails. Your brother is failing, Christopher. I'm sorry."

"*No!*" The word ripped from Chris's lungs, filling his throat with the taste of blood as he turned back to Nicky. Any lingering pain, any memory of it, disappeared in a rush of adrenaline, and his whole self was awake, more awake than he could ever remember being. "No. *No.* No, listen to me, Nicky." He grabbed Nick's shoulders, then his jaw, making his little—baby, younger, definitely not *little*—brother look at him. "No fucking way, Nicky. Look. Look."

Nick's jaw was hot, or maybe Chris's hands were cold. He felt cold all over, like hope and life were draining out of him all at once. "Look, you remember just before college, Nicky? You remember when you got so fucking drunk and smashed up that window? You were gonna lose your scholarships and everything? What'd you do? What'd you do then, Nicky?"

"I…" Nick's voice broke and cracked. Tears leaked down his cheeks but didn't make it to his jaw, to Chris's fingers. They burned up instead, his skin too hot to let them flow. "I asked you to help. I didn't know what to do. It was gonna…I was scared I wasn't gonna be able to do…anything, with that on my record."

"And what'd I do?"

"You took the blame. You fucked up your own life, Chris. You screwed yourself so I'd be okay."

"Nah." Chris managed a little grin. His heart was cracking right out of his chest. "Wasn't that big a deal. First offense, misdemeanor, all that. Paid a fine, did a few days in jail, no big deal. But it got you to college, didn't it, Nicky. Got you out of our stupid lives, that was the point."

Nicky gave him a broken smile in return. "Wasn't your first offense. Wasn't your offense at all."

"First one anybody ever pinned on me. Last one, too. It's okay, Nicky. This is too much for you to handle, all right? So I'm gonna take the heat. I been watching you, Nicky. You're throwing that power around like it's a baseball. I just need you to lob it into me."

"You'll *die*." Elemiah's shock obviously overrode any diplomacy he had left, and even Arioch's voice rose with incredulity. "You're human, Christopher. You share none of your brother's Exalted status."

"'cept I'm lousy with demon blood too, you said," Chris said steadily, without looking at them. Nick was shaking his head, violent little motion hardly more than a tremble, but it didn't matter, he was gonna do what Chris told him to, because that's what big brothers were for. "Maybe I can hold out long enough to save Nick's ass. And if I croak, you guys gotta keep an eye on him." He shot a glance toward the angels, catching a glimpse of Eli's drawn face and Arioch's colorlessness. "Don't let him go sucking up any more demons."

"I don't suck demons," Nick whispered.

Chris cracked a startled laugh and pulled his brother into a hug. "There ya go. There's my smartass brother. C'mon, Nick," he said more quietly. "Let me help you, okay? It's what I'm good for."

"That's not true, Chris, you're good for everybody. You help people."

"Let me help you," Chris said again, and Nick finally agreed.

# CHAPTER 20

NICK DIDN'T DO IT ON *PURPOSE*. HE DIDN'T EVEN THINK HE could do it on purpose, because he didn't know what he was even doing, but what he didn't want was to kill his brother so he could live.

There was just too much power, that was the problem. He couldn't hold it all, and no matter what the angels said, Chris wasn't lousy with demon blood, not the way Nick was. Not in a way that meant he could control it, if what Nick did even *was* controlling it.

But even so he was human, and the demon magic wanted human souls to eat, so it surged toward Chris, trying to escape Nick's subjection. All by itself, it opened a channel, rushing to pour into Chris, to gain strength of its own so it could fight back against Nick.

*That*, though, that, Nick could control. He didn't even know how to open the channel, but the power did it for him, and once it was there, at least he could make sure Chris burned up with angel fire, not frickin' demon magic. That had to count for something, in the grand scheme of things.

Not nearly enough, but something.

The power didn't care. It wanted out, and whether it burned Nick or Chris up didn't matter. Both was fine, if that was what happened; all it wanted was to not be contained in a useless human vessel, if 'want' could even apply to angelic essence. The demon magic did what Nick told it to, or at least couldn't escape him. It flooded back through him where it had been compressed by the angel fire, and if Saboac was in there screaming anymore, Nick couldn't hear it anymore. Maybe it had burned all the way out itself, unable to take the influx of divinity. That would be a gift, too.

Chris's hug slackened, a sudden weakness that shot a spike of terror through Nick's gut. "No! Chris—?"

His brother's skin glowed from within, permeated with magic that human bodies weren't supposed to hold. The veins in his face were lit from behind, or from inside, standing out under his skin like phosphorescent rivers. He was breathing, but only just, shallow gasps that sounded like they hurt. Nick caught his weight as Chris slumped further, then lowered him to the floor, helpless tears spilling down his cheeks. "Chris? Chris, please don't die…"

"I'm sorry, Nick." Elemiah came to his side, regret in his voice.

Nick surged to his feet, facing the angel with hands clenched in fear and anger. "Aren't angels supposed to be able to heal? Didn't you help me? Didn't you just heal him?"

"You're Exalted." Eli sounded ancient, exhausted. "Your power, what you *are*, falls under my domain. I *can't* help your brother. He's dying, but he's not sick or broken. Broken, I can mitigate, but I can't draw the power from him. I'm made to constrain evil, and this is—"

"An act of grace." Arioch spoke softly, crouching at Chris's side. His wings were out again, open, trailing light. There were *eyes*, dozens, maybe hundreds, of eyes along the big bones of the wings, visible now that he wasn't in the midst of a fight. Many of them were open, though a few blinked slowly, their lashes like feathers, and all of them were clouded, whatever color they might claim rendered pale and indistinguishable. "Do you know what angels of the Thrones do, Exalted? We serve God directly, that we might speak Their will to the angels of the second and third Spheres, who are more closely bound to Man."

"You *see* God," Elemiah said with a strange hard note, and all of Arioch's eyes turned toward him, and his mouth turned bitter. Elemiah's gaze stayed hard, and after a moment, Arioch returned his attention to Chris, a hand spread over his chest now.

"We know grace, because we have bathed in it since the dawn of creation," Arioch said, less gently than before. Nick had the impulse to kick Elemiah, or throw something at him, because Arioch hadn't been pissy before, and the last thing Chris needed was a bitchy fallen angel towering over him. "This was grace," Arioch went on, "and grace is something even I may be able to channel."

"Arioch." The note in Elemiah's voice was warning, this time, but the fallen angel didn't so much as lift his gaze. He did curl his lip, and Nick echoed the expression, although he tried to smooth it off his own face, and Arioch made no such effort.

"Call it healing," Arioch said, and Elemiah shook his head.

"Thrones don't heal."

"And Powers don't give Exalted second chances, but yet here we are." Arioch's eyes closed, all of them, with a soft rush of sound that raised the hairs on Nick's arms. His wings curled inward, layers upon layers of light folded over itself, intangible but almost opaque, until his form, until Chris's body, were all but hidden in the mantle of light. Nick lifted a hand, blocking some of the brilliance, then scowled and tried to step inside the curve of wings.

The radiance stung his skin, deeper than his skin, sizzling through the power that had settled in him, but it let him pass. Arioch, inside the temple of his own wings, made a sound, maybe a hiss, but didn't cast Nick out again, only bent his head over Chris, who looked illuminated from within, not just absorbing the luminosity of Arioch's wings, but as if he was burning up from the inside. "Tell me," Arioch said, his voice low and unusually harsh. "Tell me how you draw the essence out. Is it a syringe, a flood, a wall?"

"A mist," Nick said without thinking about it. "It's like it's coming through a screen, like I can pull it through with my will and it's broken up so finely I can pull it all the way under my skin and it settles there."

"Pull it with your will," Arioch repeated. "As you might long for a toy as a child? As if you could lift it from its bedside shelf and bring it to your arms without your hands, if only you believed hard enough?"

"Yeah. Yeah, exactly, except I actually can." Nick hesitated, recognizing that this wasn't exactly the time to ask questions, and ending up saying, "I thought angels didn't *want* anything."

"We are not meant to," Arioch said, more harshly again. "And still, I've tasted of desire."

Nick, utterly unable to stop himself, looked toward Elemiah, and said, "And hold with those who favor fire?"

A hundred eyes opened and turned toward him with the weight of a clouded, filthy look, although Arioch's own gaze remained fixed on Chris. "Shut up, if you want me to save your brother's life."

"Sorry." Nick knelt in the circle of light, not knowing what he could do besides be there. Arioch's clouded eyes closed again with the same soft rush, like barnacles whispering shut on a beach rock, and Nick's breath sharpened as he felt a flex of power, very like calling his own grendel magic to life. External, though, and not, in the end, all that much like what he had felt when the bounty had used her art to corrupt his emotions.

*That*, he'd been able to follow, almost all the way back to its source. With a little effort, he could have unwound the bounty's mind, bent her and her magic to his own will. This—

—this was celestial, the music of the stars. It hissed and surged, burning too brightly to even come close to, much less conquer or comprehend. He could almost, almost, feel the strictures of his own explanation shaping the castaway angel's power, could almost sense how that power sought and desired and drew through a mesh like the one he had envisioned for himself. But the strength of the angel himself went back beyond the hot birth of the universe, much too powerful to follow.

And even so, it was constrained, uncoupled from the actual source of its glory. That was the fall, that was having been cast away, that was, and Arioch's own fury blazed here, that was the *choice made*, to turn his back on an unworthy god. That was a price paid, a price so vast, that cut so deep, that Nick flinched away from looking at it.

But the channels remained. Fallen was not desanctified, not cut off from the holy, only rejecting it. The price for that rejection was immense, yes, but Arioch could do what Saboac only longed for: he could carry that power again, would even be granted its grace by God if he were to repent of his sins. Clearly, he would prefer to bide in Hell itself than do that, but he *could*.

The fire lifted from Chris, though. Angel fire, stained with strains of demon desolation, neither meant for human bodies. Not even Nick's, despite the inhuman capacity he'd been born with Some of the burning inner light faded from Chris's skin, like his bones were no longer filled with searing embers, as particles of fire sank into Arioch's hands, his arms, his face, his wings.

His wings flared, violently bright, and for a heartbeat, a moment, the thousand eyes opened and were clear, brown and blue and gold and silver, green and grey and violet and red, all gazing beyond the walls that Nick could see.

Nearly all. A handful looked at him, a few others at Chris, and some at Elemiah, whose sigh could be heard even through the hiss of celestial song. Or maybe because it was part of that song, Nick thought, since nothing else seemed audible. Arioch's wings visibly solidified as the power coursed through them, even casting the outline of a fainter secondary, and fainter-still, tertiary set that Nick hadn't seen even during the battle.

"You are Seen," Arioch breathed. "Exalted, you are Seen, and so too is the Bonded, and that bond extends to grace, and that Grace, to—" A twist marred his mouth and the obvious ritual of the words, so he ended with, "To me," in a sardonic tone more like the one Nick had gotten used to in the time he'd known the fallen angel.

All forty minutes of it, or so. Maybe a little longer. Time had gone a little funny during the fight, but in the end, it wasn't long at all. He started, "What—" and Eli's hand closed on his shoulder, warning him to silence. Nick startled, not even having realized the other angel had come within the shelter of Arioch's wings, but he pressed his mouth shut and let the castaway finish his work.

'Grace' clearly meant something more to the angels than Nick fully understood, even beyond the vague understanding he had on the concept of divine grace and forgiveness. Grace was a kind of quantifiable strength or reality to them, something to draw on like Nick might draw a deep breath.

A rough laugh shook his shoulders. That tracked, because God knew—Nick suddenly wasn't sure he should throw that phrase around lightly, so he changed the track of his thought: *Nick* knew he'd drawn on Chris's strength about a million times in his life. If that was grace, then yeah, *hell* yeah, it was a real power, and if anybody could rely on it, he guessed angels in God's grace should be able to.

And even angels out of God's grace, it looked like, because that too-bright power that had burned inside Chris was settling in Arioch now. The strands of demon power ignited, though whether they were subsumed or eradicated, Nick couldn't tell. They didn't *seem* to sink into Arioch's bones the way the fire did, but everything was too bright to see clearly anyway, and his head hurt.

Chris, for the first time in what felt like forever, took a breath, and the rest of the fire smoldering inside him went out. Nick fell forward, grabbing Chris's shoulders and trying not to yell at him to wake up. Around him, above him, Arioch's wing-eyes closed with another soft buzz of sound. The brilliance of the light faded with the sound and Nick looked up to see his wings lurch, losing physicality toward the shadows of light again.

Arioch himself, though, nearly vibrated with substance, as if he'd taken on extra mass and could barely contain it within himself now. He stood and stepped back, one smooth motion, and his wings flickered away entirely, somehow adding to his own substantiality. His shirt was in tatters now, and maybe had been for a while. Nick couldn't remember.

Chris's voice rode a low, rough chuckle. "There's my baby brother."

"*Chris.*" Nick twisted back toward his brother, hauling him into a hug as Chris tried to sit up. Chris's arms closed around him, weaker than he should be, but still solid, still whole, still there. The world vanished into that frail embrace, with all the reasons they were even there disappearing. None of it was real anymore, how they'd gotten there, what the hell Nick even was, none of it mattered, as long as Chris wasn't dead. Everything else could be figured out, somehow.

"Aight," Chris finally muttered into his shoulder, loosening his grip without quite letting him go. "Aight, Nicky. 'm okay. We're good. Jesus," he said, audibly reconsidering that last part. "Did you get the number of that bus? What the hell."

"Quite the opposite," Elemiah murmured, and Arioch, a few steps farther away, gave a disdainful snort.

"Quite the quite. The divine reign in Hell too, you know, little Power."

"I told you to watch your epithets, Throne."

Arioch's voice went dangerously soft. "Do you really wish to test me now, Elemiah?"

"Will you two get a fucking room?" Nick snapped. "I'm trying to say hi to my brother who's back from the brink of death, if you don't fucking mind!"

"What do they mean, 'get a room?'" Elemiah asked, and Arioch at least laughed, breaking down the tension obviously building between them. He didn't answer, though, which was enough for Nick.

"What'd I miss?" Chris shifted far enough out of Nick's hug to rub the heel of his hand across his breastbone. "I feel like I got barbecued."

"Yeah, you almost did," Nick said roughly. "Don't do that again, man."

"How 'bout you don't go absorbing demons and angels and I won't do…whatever the hell I just did…and we'll call it even?"

"I think that'd be best." Nick tried to catch Elemiah's eye, and when that failed, found Arioch looking at him expectantly. "You kept saying they'd come after me. Demons. Because I'm a battery. Are they still gonna?"

"I'm less certain now," Arioch said slowly. "The grendel power is still a part of you, but the soul bond is stronger than before, and may offer some protection."

"The what now?" Chris sounded like he'd been swallowing fire, and not in the theatrical way.

Nick said, "There's water in the van," but Chris waved

him off, and he was willing to take that for an answer, at least for a minute.

"The soul bond," Elemiah said. "They're rare, and rarer still between siblings. And of course they even more rarely matter, in the larger sense."

Chris scrubbed his hands through his hair, then eyed Nick. "This guy making any sense to you?"

"Not yet."

"A soul bond is one of the rarest forms of—" Elemiah began portentously, and Arioch overrode him. "Your brother would do anything to keep you safe."

A snort of laughter jolted through Chris. "No shit. 's my job."

"It is, in fact, *not* your job," Eli said, less portentously. "It is your…calling. Your choice. Hence its power. Its strength. You shouldn't have been able to share that power. You absolutely couldn't hold it. But the selflessness—"

"The grace," Arioch said.

"—of the act, the willingness to sacrifice yourself," Elemiah went on, clearly trying to pretend he hadn't heard Arioch, "is a power unto itself—"

"Did he really just say 'unto?'" Chris muttered.

Nick elbowed him, trying not to laugh. "Quiet, he's pontificating."

"That's it, I'm going back to being dead, you can let me know when the pretentious *pontificating* stops." Chris fell over backward again, throwing a dramatic arm across his eyes.

Nick shoved him and he sat back up, a grin smearing over his face as Nick muttered, "'Pretentious,' huh?"

"I gotta learn something from my baby brother's oversized vocabulary, right?" Chris looked up at the angels and laughed through his nose, then ducked his head and rattled with more laughter. Nick glanced up, too, and made almost the same sound.

Not for the first time, both angels wore identical expressions of distaste, as if vaguely afraid human hysteria might somehow rub off on them. Elemiah had clearly given up on his lecture until they could receive it with sufficient dignity, and Arioch's impatience all but pulsated, although of the two of them, he appeared to find some faint humor in their inability to remain composed. "Mortality," he said after the brothers regained some semblance of dignity. "It makes you humans so overwrought, when avoided."

"Man, it has been an overwrought *week*." Chris rubbed his face again, then looped his arms around his knees, squinting up at the angels. "Can y—" He broke off with a yelp as his butt buzzed, loud in the comparative quiet of the church. He took his phone out of his back pocket, grunting to see the screen had broken, although he said, "Surprised it still works at all," before answering. "Yeah, Jakey. No, I'm not dead. Neither's Nick. Oh." He pulled the phone away from his ear, flicked to another screen, and winced as Nick saw a chat window with a *hundreds of messages missed* notification glowing in the middle.

Chris put the phone back to his ear. "Yeah, no, we're not dead. Where you at?" He tipped the phone up, said, "He's almost to Denver. How long was I out?"

"I don't know, man, you're the one with a clock in your hand."

"Oh. Right." Chris glanced at the time, then brought the phone back to his ear. "You can't be almost to Denver, it's only been like an hour since we talked. You're gonna get arrested. Look, tell the girls we're okay, all right? I'll call you back in a little bit, we got some shit to figure out here. Aight. Bye, Jakey." He hung up, flicked through the scroll in chat, and winced. "Yeah, yeah, okay, sorry, I didn't mean to get attacked by demons mid-conversation, whatever." He put the phone back in his pocket as Nick took his own phone out to discover he wasn't on that group chat.

"What, I don't get to be kept in the loop?"

"You were busy dying. Reading you in while I freaked out didn't seem helpful."

"I guess that's fair." Nick slumped, then glanced up to find the angels staring at them again. "What? Don't you guys have group chat? Maybe you should, maybe Raphael wouldn't have snuck up you if you did."

"I'll put a word in with the Spheres," Elemiah said dryly. "Are you...well?"

"We're not dead," Chris said. "I need somebody to tell me what this soul bond shit is without the flowery talk. Can you do that, or do I need an interpreter?"

Eli drew breath and Arioch held a hand up, clearly meaning to silence him. This time the smaller angel only curled a lip, and, with a visible effort, said, "Occasionally two people are sufficiently committed to one another's safety that they forge a bond that can withstand even celestial—"

"Or demonic," Arioch said.

"Or demonic," Elemiah echoed through his teeth, "forces. We call it a soul bond, which—"

"Sounds pretty fucking romantic," Chris said.

The angel exhaled so deeply he actually lost an inch of height, and spoke in a tone of infinite patience stretched to its very limit. "Yes. Most soul-bonded pairs *are* romantic, not fraternal. Or sororal."

Nick took a breath and Chris said, "If you're about to tell me that means 'sisterly' I will put my elbow through your teeth. I'm not stupid."

Nick weighed his options and decided, "I know you're not stupid," was by far the safest thing to say.

Elemiah stared at them until satisfied they were done before saying, "The bond allowed him to take on the excess power you carried. The fact that so much of that power was angelic allowed the castaway—"

"Who has a *name*," Arioch said.

"—to absorb it from Christopher. He couldn't have taken

it from you," Eli said to Nick. "No celestial creature could take power from an Exalted."

"But I'm a puny human so he could suck me dry?" Chris finished.

An expression of pain crossed Eli's face. "In effect, yes. That, and his own connection with the divine is severed. If I had tried such a thing..."

"You would have exploded." Arioch sounded pleased about the prospect. "Think of me as a dry river bed, Christopher. You set the waters flowing again for a little while."

"I tell you what, usually it's more fun to get somebody's waters flowing." Chris put his hand up and the fallen angel took it, pulling him to his feet.

An aura—a halo—of power burst when their hands touched, bright enough that Nick threw a hand in front of his eyes and even Elemiah flinched back. Chris jolted and pulled his hand free, shaking it. "Jesus, static electricity much, my dude?"

Arioch rubbed his own fingers together, pale eyebrows drawn in a knot above the bridge of his nose. "I think not, but neither am I sure what that was."

"A connection, man." Nick, getting to his feet without any help mostly to see if he could, put on the soppiest tone he could. "Like, a real deep meaningful connection. Like, *cosmic*, man."

"Oh my god, shut the hell up." Chris vaguely threatened Nick with a loose fist made from the hand he'd shaken, although he went back to shaking it almost immediately. "What'd I do, charge you all up?"

Arioch's mouth twitched and Chris said, "Oh, for god's sake, forget it," under laughter that started with Nick and spilled to the blonde fallen angel.

"I believe you did," Arioch said as his laughter faded to a sharp grin. "Perhaps significantly. Perhaps permanently."

"Well, great, remember me in your memoirs when you reign in Hell, then."

"Oh," Arioch purred, "I shall." He offered a hand to Chris again, who eyed it warily before ostentatiously stuffing his own hands in his pockets. Arioch grinned again, then copied the motion, sliding his hands into his own pockets as he turned on a heel to face Elemiah. "What now, Power? You've been called to this plane, but the boy is out of danger and you're no guardian angel. Will you stay?"

Nick, mildly insulted, said, "Hey," and Arioch slid a lazy, impatient glance his way.

"You haven't yet seen one and twenty years of age, Nicholas Cassidy. In this time and place, you're a boy, and as a thing that has existed an impossibly long time, anyone younger than Elemiah here is their infancy. Dinosaurs failed to reach adolescence, in the time scale of the universe, and they were *so* much more successful than your little species."

"Kind of arrogant, isn't he," Chris breathed, and Eli's eyebrows flicked upward.

"Thrones are not known for their humility."

"Nor would you be, if you looked upon the face and served the hand of God," Arioch said coolly.

"What do they look like?" Chris asked suddenly. "God, I mean. And if you say ineffable…"

The corner of Arioch's mouth twitched again. "And yet. God is most often seen in the eye of the beholder, I'm afraid. My description would mean nothing to you, and yours would mean little to me."

"I am no guardian angel," Elemiah said, as if the rest of the conversation hadn't taken place. "And for the moment, I believe my greater duty is to return and report with confidence that the Exalted has passed through the fire."

Nick, abruptly remembering that Elemiah had grabbed hold of him and gone all pillar-of-fire, said, "I *literally* did."

Elemiah flashed a grin as disarmingly bright as Arioch's.

"But Exalted rarely do, Nicholas, and the power remains within you. Not even the Spheres would expect you to deny or refuse its use, but if you do, it—" He hesitated, shooting a sharp look toward Arioch, whose jaw settled into a glacial thrust. "It clouds the future, so that not even the Thrones may see clearly. It's possible," he said thoughtfully, "that I would be remiss if I *didn't* stay."

"You see?" Arioch said. "You see how easy it is, to convince yourself that an exertion of free will is only tending to your assigned duties? Careful, Power. I know this path, and it's a dangerous one." He reached for the long coat he'd thrown over the altar what seemed like hours ago and shrugged it on over his tattered shirt. "My path between planes is no less fraught than yours, but certain responsibilities beckon me home again. Call on me as you wish, Christopher. I believe I'll hear even the most intimate of prayers."

"Oh my God." Chris passed his hand over his face. "Did you have to make it weird?"

Arioch cracked another grin. "I expect I did, yes. We're connected, you and I, and I rather think I'm going to enjoy it."

Nick swore that Chris would've tossed his hair, if it was longer. "Most people I connect with do."

Elemiah, not entirely sotto voce, said, "Is this where one says 'get a room?'" to Nick, who laughed sharply.

"Yeah. You're getting the hang of humanity."

"I'm not entirely certain that's wise." Eli didn't look displeased, though, and Nick grinned.

"Probably not. So you're heading…home?" He whirled a finger skyward.

"It seems necessary. Raphael should not be allowed to…"

"Control the narrative," Chris supplied, and Nick raised a startled eyebrow at him. "Yeah, yeah, I know, what's the dumb brother doing recognizing narrative arcs and shit. I watch movies, Nick. Look, I think we better go hang somewhere else before the cops get here." Chris gestured at the church, and Nick, for the first time, glanced around and grimaced.

It hadn't quite been reduced to rubble, but its structural integrity seemed in question. The roof sagged, rafters broken and holes punched through, a startling number of the pews were shattered, and a far wall had been half knocked out, cold air blowing relentlessly in. "Did I do that?"

"You could call it a joint effort," Arioch offered. "Given that you were inspired by my presence. The rest," he said with an easy gesture upward, "was largely courtesy of our archangelic visitor."

"What the hell was his beef, anyway?" Chris tilted his head toward the door, then began picking his way across wrecked pews in search of a clear path out.

"Humans have the audacity to praise others of their kind for miraculous interventions, and it offends his sensibilities. Raphael is committed to the premise that all thanks should go to God." Arioch followed him a few steps, then cut his own path across the church, only to pause in the broken wall he'd been thrown through earlier. "And if I were to call upon you, Christopher? Would you answer?"

Chris squinted across the dark church at the fallen angel. "Not if that means you're gonna pray my fine ass into Hell."

Arioch chuckled, stepping through the rift toward the night. "That seems unlikely, but perhaps it's worth exploring."

"Nope! No the hell it is not! N—augh, come back, where'd you go, you can't do that!" Chris glared futilely at the gap that Arioch had disappeared into, then turned nervously to Elemiah. "He can't do that, can he?"

The angel spread his hands uncertainly. "I'm not sure it's ever been tried. Angels rarely pray for mortal intervention."

Nick's eyebrows rose. "Do they *ever*?"

"I would have to consult the Books of Law."

"Well, you're going home anyway, right?" Chris demanded. "Get on that and get back to me, because I'd really like some reassurance here. I do not want to be prayed into Hell! *Do* I have to unpray you?"

"No," Elemiah said dryly. "Once my duties are tended to, I'm free to go as I see fit. Watch yourselves, Cassidys. Mortals who gain celestial attention rarely stray from it again. Your lives are so short, it's easy to watch you for a moment or two to see the path you take."

"Great, now *he's* made it weird," Chris mumbled. "Begone, angel, leave us, or something. There must be a quote for that."

"'Be gone, run to your houses, fall upon your knees,'" Nick offered, and got exactly the look he expected and probably deserved for that. "Julius Caesar. Shakespeare. Sorry."

Chris muttered, "Can't be both, man, they lived centuries apart," as he climbed over another broken pew, then looked up, looked around, and said, "Holy shit, but it worked."

"What did?" Nick, crawling over pews in his wake, followed his gaze, then swung around, searching for Elemiah. "He did the thing! Like in movies!"

Chris, sullenly, said, "I always wanted to do that. Poof, vanish mysteriously at the most dramatic possible moment. I mean, *rude*, but super cool. Even just the whole 'the bus drives by and they've vanished' thing, that's cool. Like, sexy cool."

"You could go stand beside Lucille and I could drive away," Nick offered. Chris gave him another dirty look as they left the church in the most ordinary, human way possible: through the kicked-in front door.

Nick somehow expected gawkers to be gathering, but the parking lot was deserted save for Lucille, sitting alone in a space closer to the street than the church. He couldn't think of an even vaguely plausible cover story, so it was just as well. Chris weaved a little on the walk to the van, like walking was something he'd learned how to do once but couldn't quite remember. Nick felt a lot like that, too, actually. Getting one foot in front of the other took a ridiculous amount of effort.

There was a bed in the van, though. If he could make it that far, maybe he could collapse and sleep for three weeks. Chris wobbled toward the driver's side, with Nick frowning vaguely at him until he could focus enough processing power to figure out why the idea bothered him. "You safe to drive?"

"I am extremely not." Chris got in the driver's seat anyway, so Nick got in the passenger side while Chris put both hands on the wheel and exhaled until his forehead touched the wheel, too. "We can't stay in the parking lot, though. We probably shouldn't stay within fifty miles of here."

Nick shook his head broadly. "You can't just drive off into the sunset. Jake's coming down here hell bent for leather."

"Ah, crap. Right. Text him, would you? Tell him we're going…"

"Out drinking, and to meet us at…" Nick scowled through the windshield, then cast a worried glance at the half-demolished church behind them. "Tell you what, start driving and we'll figure it out on the way."

"Good plan." Chris patted the dashboard, then pulled Lucille out onto the street, casting looks up and down it. "No traffic. Like, weirdly no traffic for suburbia."

"Nobody came to see why the church was on fire or what-ever, either. Maybe acts of gods come with special not-my-problem filters and people don't notice them."

"I really hope so, 'cause Lucille's registered under my real name."

Nick nodded, then scowled suspiciously at his brother. "I'm sorry, what? Do you have vehicles registered under not your real name?"

Chris, sanctimoniously, said, "That would be *illegal*, Nicky."

Nick snorted laughter, checked his phone, and said, "Turn left up there. Local events page says there's a good bar a few miles up the road."

"We've both spent half the day getting possessed or some-thing. You really think getting shitfaced is a good idea?"

"First, I didn't say shitfaced, and second, I think it's the *best* idea."

Chris cackled. "You might be right. Arright. Tell me where to turn, because if we're relying on me to read road-signs right now we're gonna be back in Sterling by midnight 'cause thinking is way too hard."

"So what else is new." Nick ducked his head over his phone, said, "Left again up ahead, then straight on till morn-ing, or at least, the bar," after a minute, then, not sure he wanted to be heard, mumbled, "Sorry about that, earlier."

Chris said, "Wasn't you," so quickly he clearly knew exactly what Nick meant. A knot tied and untied itself in Nick's gut, leaving him unsure of what to say, but Chris picked up the slack. "Not any decent part of you, anyway. The, uh. Grendel power? Is it still…?"

"There? Yeah. It's, um." Nick took a deep breath, trying to see if it pulled or stung at him the way it had before. "It doesn't feel as, I don't know, alive? Anymore. More like it's part of me, and not something of its own. It feels safer, I guess?"

"Good. That's good." Chris hesitated. "That means you could go back to school."

"Yeah. I guess so. I gotta…I gotta go take my midterms, and…med school in the fall."

Chris echoed, "Yeah. Yeah, that's good, Nicky. That's real good. After drinks, though, right?"

"It's Fri…Saturday? The weekend, anyway. Drinks first, for sure. Turn right up there. Maybe…I don't know, Chris. You want to drive out to the coast with me?" Nick shrugged awkwardly. "Or drive me out, I guess."

Chris shot him a look, then thumped his hand against the steering wheel and nodded. "Yeah. Yeah, I could prob-ably do that. See how the other half lives, huh? Maybe meet myself a co-ed. I gotta call Lauren and see if there's any jobs coming up, something normal and not grendel-y, but yeah, that sounds good. Didn't you say you got spring break soon?"

"Next week, so I guess getting back by Monday doesn't matter or anything."

"Maybe we could camp out for a couple days, if you wanted. Maybe, I dunno, catch up a little, without all this shit."

"That'd be great, that'd be…" Nick nodded roughly. "I mean the weather's gonna be shit."

"That's all right. We can go see Half Dome or something. I always wanted to do that."

"Old Faithful," Nick said eagerly.

Chris eyed him. "That's a whole different-ass park in a whole different-ass direction."

"It is?"

"Lookit that, I know some geography my big-brain baby brother doesn't. Yeah, Yellowstone's up north in the corner of Wyoming, man. Yosemite's in California. Dad was really shit about bringing us places like that when he was dragging our asses around everywhere, wasn't he." Chris thumped his thumb against the steering wheel again, then shrugged. "Don't see why we couldn't do both. It's a lot of driving, but that'll give you time to study, right?"

"I don't have any of my books, but yeah, maybe Steph—" Nick bit off the name and muttered, "The bar should be up here in just a minute."

Chris hesitated. "You gonna try to work that out?"

"I don't know. What I'm not gonna do is call and ask her to overnight the books to me. Maybe I can get copies online."

"Yeah, all right." Chris left it hanging a second, then said, "If the bar's good I'll text Jake and tell him to meet us."

"I don't care if it's good as long as they don't card me."

"Shit. Right." Chris shot him another look. "I guess the

good news is you're like nine feet tall and look like hell, so probably nobody's gonna think you're underage."

"Gee, thanks." The parking lot was busy, and the bar itself a loud cheerful-looking place with crowds around the big doors. "Go in and see if they're carding anybody."

"Yeah, all right." Chris hopped out of the van, went in, and texted a couple minutes later with *nobody at the door and they didn't ask my pretty face for ID so you're probably good. Got you some shots already though, just in case.*

Nick, aloud, said, "No tequila, right?" and followed Chris into a bar as loud and cheerful inside as it was on the exterior, with an array of colorful lights and wall decorations that ranged from pride colors to what was either a Cuban or Puerto Rican flag. A jukebox blared in the first room, and he could see a DJ, lit by black lights and painted with glowing streaks, at the back of the next room, beyond a wall of dancers in everything from jeans and cowboy boots to full-on party dresses.

Chris had found a table in the front room, backed up to a corner, and waved Nick down from there with a gesture at six shots sitting in front of him. Nick squeezed past through the growing crowd and took the other seat with its back to the wall. "Did I find the only gay bar in northern Denver?"

"If you were searching online for a good party bar, yeah, probably, because they usually are, but no, I don't think so. Either that or it's straight night, but those are usually Thursdays or Mondays, not Saturday."

"And you know this because?"

"Did I not just say they're good party bars?" Chris pushed three of the shots across the table at him, then lifted one of the drinks left in front of him. "To surviving the weirdest goddamn week I've ever had."

"To angels," Nick suggested.

"To grendels."

"To soul bonds," Nick said with an almost straight face.

A snerk of sound, like a laugh and a snort got tangled up in the top of his throat, erupted through Chris's nose. "To the fuckin' *Exalted*, man."

"To Cassidys," Nick offered.

Chris ducked his head, then knocked his shot glass against Nick's. "To our fucking awful father. I miss him, Nicky. I miss him so much it hurts."

"Yeah." Nick bonked his glass against Chris's, slammed the drink, and picked up the next. "To Dad."

Chris slammed his, too, picked up the next, echoed, "To Dad," before they both drank, then took the third, said, "To not getting involved in any more celestial bullshit," and Nick laughed.

"No way. Drinking to that seems like asking for trouble." He touched his glass against Chris's and said, "To family," instead.

"Yeah." Chris grinned sloppily, even if he was only two shots down, and raised the glass. "To family."

# ACKNOWLEDGMENTS

This is the book I wasn't writing, all the way up until it was the book I had written. I wrote it for the fun of it, and for my friend Kate, who spent uncounted hours world building and brainstorming with me. We had a wonderful time.

It's also a project I talked about extensively on my Patreon, as a demonstration for my readers as to how I develop a book. Hopefully they enjoyed that as much as I did!

All my thanks are due to early readers Rachel Gollub, K. Gavenman, and Mary Hargrove, who helped catch spelling and continuity errors that otherwise might have gone unnoticed.

All my love is due, of course, to my family.

# ABOUT THE AUTHOR

C. E. Murphy began writing around age six, although it took roughly another quarter century to be published. Murphy now has some fifty books in print.

Printed in the USA
CPSIA information can be obtained
at www.ICGtesting.com
LVHW051519221223
767218LV00071B/2303